For Pam
Always a smile and a laugh,
Life is too short

1994
A Friday Evening

"I hate you!"

The young woman screamed at the driver. He had been careening around the streets for the last fifteen minutes. Her fingers were ghost white as they clenched the hand-hold above her head in front of the door; her face was red with anger and fear mixed. She had been bouncing around inside the cab of the vehicle as the man slid around corners and through red lights. She prayed for the police to pull in behind them, to stop the rampage.

"I don't care!" The driver yelled back, his voice quavering on madness.

He spun the wheel with both hands as he carelessly negotiated another turn. The tires spit rubber out as they tried to grip the fog cooled road, blue smoke emanating from the surfaces. The woman reached for the seatbelt latch and fumbled with the button till the lock released the catch and the winder pulled the belt away on a straight stretch of road, after the g-forces stabilized.

"Stop now! Stop or I will jump out!" She pled as the horror continued.

The man reached across her chest and grabbed the handle to keep the door shut. It was just then the truck in front of them swerved. He couldn't see what kind of truck it was, definitely a tractor-trailer, but in the rage he felt he didn't recognize the make. It was in his lane.

With his one hand on the wheel he racked the wheel in the opposite direction of the truck but the car's speed kept the vehicle moving forward; at the last second the tires gripped and the driver's side of the car spun out from behind and gave the truck a full shot at the side of the smaller compact car. The woman screamed at the top of her lungs until she ran out of breath, she inhaled phlegm and a lock of her flowing hair as she braced for the impact.

The diesel struck the out of control car on the driver's side just behind the door and a deafening shriek of metal and collapsing steel punctuated the air. The windows exploded inwards from the impact sending razor sharp shards of tempered glass zapping around the interior looking for something to stop them. Hundreds of pieces slashed at both the passenger's faces and necks; the man could barely feel the stinging as his flesh was dotted with cuts, the woman felt the burning on her chest where her blue sundress exposed it to the clear blue projectiles.

The next sensation was spinning; like a ride at a county fair, the ones where you sit inside and spin a wheel as fast as you can to keep the small car rotating. The man was pushed against his seatbelt and the door as the momentum carried the vehicle across the four lane road, the woman grabbed at the dashboard to keep her in place, as the force pushed her in the same direction.

A violent clap of thunder sounded as the car instantaneously slammed into a light pole on the opposite side of the street, the thin metal caving into the driver's side, forcing the man to hit his head on the door post just behind him. Everything went black. Then it was white as time slowed to less than a crawl.

The impact launched the woman towards the left side of the car, her hands desperately looking for something to hold onto, her nails breaking and tearing as they dug into the plastic and vinyl. But the deluge was too great. The man opened his eyes the same instant she flew past him towards the now open window, he could see a flash of her blue dress as her writhing body ricocheted off the interior, he could smell her sweet perfume as she passed in front of him on her way out. Her small body flailing as it was thrown from the shattered window, striking the concrete of the sidewalk. Then the air went nearly silent.

A sound of rain, which actually was blood from a gaping head wound dripping into the man's ear, trickled into the now quiet. The concussion of the second impact into the pole had temporarily deafened the man; he could make out sounds of muffled screams of witnesses as they ran to the aid of the victims, the sound of the tractor-trailer screeching to a stop nearby.

His vision partially obscured by the blood and the banging his head took made the world around him spin. He could make out figures on their cell phones summoning emergency help; he could hear sirens in the distance. A crowd gathered where the body of the woman lay crumpled on the ground. Women had their hands to their mouths; the men had looks of desperation as they tried to pry the man out of the car.

In less than two minutes after the rampage met its obstacle, the scene calmed down.

The man heard the Jaws of Life prying the small car to pieces, the shouts of paramedics telling him to stay calm and keep his eyes closed as one held his neck in place with both hands. He felt pain cycling through his torso as they lifted him to a gurney, he felt dizzy as the doors to the ambulance were slammed shut and the Ford F-450 began forcing its way through traffic towards the closest hospital. He passed out from shock, but the last thing that crossed his mind was the yellow sheet draped over a human shaped lump on the curb ten feet from the halved car.

FIRST CHAPTER
Late January 2002

The hardest part of telling a story to someone, Josh thought, was remembering all the details. One could tell a story that involves love and sacrifice and leave those in the room wondering if you really sacrificed enough to love someone. Remembering the details always pulled the story together, sharp insight into the affair that someone conveys as a "life altering" event with another person. But this story could only be partially told, much of the truth would endanger lives, even to this day.

Before the dream, life was normal for Josh; after, his world spun on a needle point.

Only problem was, the images of his dream were vague, the face unclear. But when Josh woke from his night's sleep he could only think of the little sandy-haired blue eyed beauty from his past. The young girl he spent his long lonely summers with, well, previously lonely anyways. After Josh met Camela, his summer vacations were filled with youthful play, adolescent curiosity and eventually, young love.

Josh James Kennedy was sitting in his parked SUV about one hundred yards from where the beginning of the story took place so long ago, over twenty-six years ago, when Josh was first ten years old, a year older than Camela or Camy as she liked to be called. He glanced up into the rearview mirror, removed his sunglasses and looked into his own blue eyes. They've faded since then, thirty-six years old and the lines of age were showing. Along with the expansion of his middle, arthritis in his hands from too many broken fingers-broken while hauling in crab pots from his private charter business in San Francisco-and his greying goatee, age had been somewhat unkind to Josh. Not to mention, and rarely did he, his thinning and receding light brown hairline.

His usually tan and olive skin had been lacking the sun since his long vacation from the bay, the time he has spent indoors researching, recovering, so it was more flush egg shell white than his usual umber-brown. It had been a long painful month that finally brought him here, to the haunts of his childhood where he and Camy spent summer nights lying in her grandmother's front yard, on the cool freshly cut lawn, staring at the stars.

The smell of the lawn and Camy's cheap kid's perfume was almost as clear on Josh's palate as the odor of the asphalt under the afternoon sun outside his car right now. The Indian Summer in January had warmed the old neighborhood to nearly sixty degrees, Josh's buddy Jeremy would blame it on SUV's and global warming, but Josh knew this was the norm for his hometown of Sparks, Nevada, for this time of the year. Usually a week or two in January or February brought warm weather, mild to humid sixties, then dumped half a foot of snow a few days later.

Josh's 2001 Ford Excursion didn't really fit in here anymore, as if it would in his home of the last twelve years of San Francisco; but the 1960's era Probasco style homes in his young life now belonged to landlords who rent the two and three bedroom, single bath homes to low income and Section 8 housing. Junk sedans and older compact cars lined the streets now.

When Josh first pulled onto his street this morning, the street where he spent the first twenty-four years of his life, the residents probed his eyes and vehicle with suspicion. Cops drove new SUV's here, not tourists who remained close to the downtown core. After he parked in front of his old house; the one with the windows half boarded, the lawn dead and torn out in places, the six foot trailer-gate on the side of the house ripped from its hinges and the word *Norteños* spelled out in big black spray paint on the garage door he helped his father install when he was eleven, most of the suspicious residents figured he was a realtor and returned to their broken down domiciles and tattered porches.

He wiped a tear from his eye for the disrepair.

The house had been put up for sale several months earlier and had been vacant. Through the open bay window his father installed in 1980, he could see the bookshelves his late mother Alice had asked his father Robert to construct for her lovable *Ron Lee* figurines. Another tear came, as he thought about his mother, the times they shared laughter, cried at wakes there and were a real family with real neighbors-just like you see in old fifties television show.

~ ~ ~

In 1976, the summer air was filled with the smell of burning Kingsford Briquettes and lighter fluid. It reverberated with the sound of *"Skyrockets in flight..."* from the song *Afternoon Delight* by The Starland Vocal Band, and Wings' *Let 'Em In*. A three wheeled white and red motorcycle with a similarly striped umbrella over the top slowly made the rounds on the city streets playing *The Entertainer* on a loudspeaker with the white suited and capped elderly woman driver stopping to sell 50/50 bars and Push-Ups.

Children were safe to roam-day or night-without constant supervision, policemen stopped their patrol cars to throw a catch or toss a football with the kids playing in the streets. Life was idyllic as The Monkeys' *Pleasant Valley Sunday* described on the two pound, book sized transistor radios children owned and carried on a plastic strap.

Josh looked to his left-or across the street of his old home-and saw the house he played at most frequently.

There lived a girl named Carrie Ann Thomas, who was six years older than Josh, but loved to play the games and make believe that was so important to kids before video games atrophied their muscles in later ages. Her brother, Mark, the oldest in the family was a real honest to goodness Hippie, who drove a Volkswagen Bus painted with a pink peace sign on the back. He wore his hair long and spent evenings on the back porch playing sixties protest songs on his flat top with his free-love girlfriend from a few blocks away. Josh hated being over there when Mark and his girlfriend were together, they smelled like burned tea bags all the time.

　　　　Straight ahead and to his right a little, down the cross street was the house that Toni Stratford lived in. She was four years older than Josh, they were good friends until Toni hit puberty and started doing drugs, and then at sixteen she began living with her eighteen year old boyfriend. Her family was crushed; Josh was too, because she was the tomboy who protected him from the bullies in the neighborhood.

　　　　Josh hadn't seen her in years until they caught up with each other in a chance meeting when Josh was in town ten years ago. They spent the day reminiscing and had lunch, promised to stay in touch then went their separate ways. Toni was killed in a car crash two months later. Her mother sent Josh a letter with the obituary, Josh sent a sympathy card back and wept quietly to himself for days.

　　　　Josh opened the door to his Ford and stepped onto the cracked and broken sidewalk that was raised several inches from where it used to be by roots underneath. The same concrete that thirty some years before he wrote his name in with a ten penny nail. He walked to the corner, his home sat on the corner, and gazed at the old storm drain that he and his buddies from several blocks away would jam up with a three gallon ice cream bucket during cloud bursts to flood the street. Out would come the truck inner tubes and toboggans and summer thunderstorm fun was born.

At the corner, Josh looked hard to his right. The four foot cyclone fence was still in place in front of the Humbolt's home. The Humbolts had a red-head; red-freckled daughter who was actually named Ginger, Josh always wondered if it was a joke on her parent's part, or naiveté. Ginger and Josh used to walk the top of the seven foot redwood fences that ran around the entire community, going from one yard to another, one friend to another's via a two by four path.

Josh smiled when a thought passed through his mind, one night he heard a crash outside his window, peeked out and saw Ginger ramming her parent's 1962 Chevy Impala into the Peterson's truck, parked directly across the street from the Humbolt's home. Ginger was twelve at the time and the neighborhood was massed by cops, lookie loos and the Petersons, who rarely left their house. Few ever saw the strange family of four, even the kids kept to themselves at school. When Josh saw *Twilight*, he thought the Cullens were modeled after the Petersons.

That night was the exception, with all four of them out screaming obscenities at the Humbolt family. Ginger was in cuffs, her mother was crying and her father was looking at the steaming Impala, shaking his head. Josh didn't see much of Ginger after that, her folks moved away just a few months later. Josh thought they were a little over the top anyways, they were the first family in the neighborhood with an electric garage door opener and underground sprinklers that had to be turned on by hand; the Humbolts pretended they were rich.

Standing on the corner Josh finally looked to the reason he was here. Oxford Way made a lazy S curve from his house, a slight left then a slight right. Next door to the Stratford home, just a hair to Josh's left, was her house. 1917. The reason Josh drove 220 miles to this place, was

11

just to read the address off the home. Gone was the wooden plaque over the door that read NICHOLSON, as they had moved out in 1984. The finely trimmed lawn plus manicured evergreens that rose fifteen feet in the air and were so meticulously cared for by Camy's grandparents in the seventies, were gone and replaced with red lava rock, dormant roses and brown curled piles of meadowgolds. The house was in shambles, a FOR RENT BY NEW OWNER sign was wired to the chain link fence.

Well, Josh thought, at least a new owner meant new files to trace the past owners down, a new way to find her, if he could, he wrote the number down.

The address. For the life of him Josh couldn't remember the address. For a week he had tried calling the city's record office for an address, the county recorders and even the Exxon Station a few blocks away for it. No one could give him the information by name, there were just too many people living in the city anymore, and the Exxon Station-where Josh used to get his bike tires pumped up and an ice cold Coke for a quarter-was closed.

So after all that, he decided to drive here, just to get the number of the house. Perhaps with the physical address and the name both he would have more luck researching where the Nicholsons moved to. Not that it would do any good to find them now, they would be centenarians now and he knew at least her grandmother had passed away, but he could use the new information to dig even deeper. Dig deep enough to find out where she is. To find *her*.

CHAPTER TWO
November 2001

The dream was a pleasant one, not sensual or erotic. Just a few flashes of erased memories, a moment in frozen time replayed like in the dollar theater at an arcade. Most of the dream was black and white, and then she appeared. Camela. Camela what? Was it Nicholson? Josh didn't know for sure. It was her grandmother and grandfather's house across from his in Sparks. She was a visitor, then. She was a visitor last night.

He was thirteen again; his mind worked like it did when he was that age. He was free of the daily burden of surviving, not having to work, not having to provide for himself. The mental state caused by the dream was relaxing; he hadn't slept so well in years. He was back in his youth and the world around him was staged as it was then also, his tree fort high above the ground in the elms on the side of his family's yard, tinkle of the piano keys playing *The Entertainer Rag* as the ice cream woman made her rounds, the smell of barbeques, Mark the Hippie was listening to *Free Bird* by Skynyrd in his garage, the sound of children laughing and playing everywhere.

Josh was sitting in the yard, her yard-actually her grandparent's yard-the smell of the fresh cut grass, a sappy odor from the evergreens; the hot desert air carried the sweetness of honeysuckle and rose on it as it wafted from Camy's grandmother's back yard. A small table and chairs were set up, even though they had both outgrown the tea set years earlier, their rumps still fit in the little chairs. Lemonade freshly made by Grandma Tina was in the center of the table, two Dixie Cups with trivia questions on the sides sat next to the pitcher of canary yellow refreshment.

13

Her face hadn't changed, she still was twelve, she was wearing the same dress the first time he saw her, a shortened and less elaborate version of a princess dress. Camy was always wearing a dress, not once in his first early memories could Josh see her in anything but. He could visualize her in jeans and a tank top like Toni used to wear all the time, and that image of Camy made his heart flutter but in all reality she had never "dressed down", until later.

Her sandy blond-brown hair was curled to perfection, pulled back behind her ears with a white satin headband and tied into a bow on the top of her head. Her skin was pale, as it always was, she was milk-white at times, but that was never an imperfection. Her eyes glistened blue and that smile with the dimples just a little lower at the corners of her sharply curved lips made Josh smile outwardly in his sleep.

Excitement tickled at the dreaming man's insides as the review of his youth played out before him. Anticipation of her words-any words-made Josh shudder on his bed. He could hear her voice, her laughter in his head when he thought about her sometimes while awake, he wanted to hear those things now in his sleep, he wanted to see her laugh.

Camy spoke only once in the dream. "Where've you been?" was all she asked. Her face then moved closer to his, and Josh felt the warm sensation of her soft ruby lips brush against his, then as she closed her mouth tightly to his top lip, Josh awoke.

He jerked upright in his bed at home off of Geary Boulevard and near Point Lobos Avenue. His moist eyes searching the room for the visage that appeared in his mind. His heart rate had nearly doubled; he was feeling elated and energized. After a few seconds though, reality darkened his sight, certainty returned, and Josh was saddened. It was almost too real, it was electrifying, it was…

"Just a dream…" He told the nearly empty bedroom.

He shook his head. It was so real, like time had reversed and let him have the taste, smells, and the sights again. A pang of loneliness washed over Josh as he lay back and tried to restart the dream. He *was* there, she *was* there, they *were* together again, it had to be, it just had to be. But to no avail. As hard as he tried he could not conjure up the image of her youthful face, her little creaky laugh, or any else of the dream. It was gone. That notion left a hole in Josh's heart right then.

An hour and a half later, Josh was sitting at his favorite table at the Seal Rock Inn Restaurant. He used to love the view at Tony's from his table there, but the small place at the top of Ocean Beach on Point Lobos Avenue had closed for renovations and not reopened. He had moved to the Seal Rock when Tony's closed, met a young twentyish waitress who had a pleasant smile and disposition, and stayed.

The view wasn't of the Pacific Ocean, well not clearly anyways, you could get a glimpse through the eucalyptus trees and over the button shaped, golden-yellow flowers of dune tansy of the Sutro Heights Park. You could see the rocky outcropping of where the famous Sutro Bath House once stood before the fire in 1966 reduced the glass walled structure, which once accommodated nearly ten thousand people at one time, to rubble and foundation.

If Josh felt like it, and many times he did, he would simply step out the front doors of the Seal Rock Inn, walk about a hundred yards to his left, pass Tony's empty restaurant, pass the famous Cliff House and in just minutes be on Ocean Beach looking west into a storm or sunset, whatever fit his mood. One of the few reasons he had for moving here to north western San Francisco. If he summoned the energy, Josh could walk for just a few miles south and be at the main entrance to Golden Gate Park, next to the famous Dutch Windmill. He could walk the paths usually filled with joggers or bicyclists, mothers and their prams, or just the touristy folk that seemed to prefer the cool interior of the tree packed gardens.

Sometimes Josh would stop at the Japanese Tea Gardens and have a cup of hot tea and overlook the meditative waters of the garden's ponds. Another reason he moved from his childhood home when his father passed. San Francisco offered the bad side of morality to the dirty laundry side of the news often, with its political climate of do gooders and Hippie lifestyle reputation, but in reality- and you didn't really have to look hard for it-the City by the Bay was one of the most beautiful places on earth, and the people are one of the most friendliest.

Today Josh decided he was heading for the beach as he stared out the window at a woman jogger in a tight blue spandex running suit with a *49ers* sweatshirt tied around her waist. He still was attracted to pretty women of course, but since the dream last night he found himself looking only in curiosity instead of earnest.

"You look down today Mr. Kennedy."

Josh spun because his heart fluttered momentarily at the surprise of a woman's voice behind him.

"Oh…hi Leslie. I told you to call me Jimmy, everyone else does."

Josh had earned the primary use of his middle name in his post-teen years, there was another Josh in OUPV also known as Operators of Uninspected Passenger Vessels School, or as it was affectionately called "Six Pack" school. Six Pack refers to the number of paying passengers allowed on a charter boat after meeting the first level of class requirements and certifications, the next level-Master-Josh was still thinking about earning. Now everyone, including his uncle, who runs Josh's charter business during the summer for him, calls him Jimmy.

"Sorry Mr., I mean Jimmy. It's just that you're so..."

"Old?"

"It's out of respect, I promise..." Leslie had turned dark red, her pale olive skin revealed her embarrassment.

Josh laughed and held his coffee cup up. "Don't worry about it, Les. You'll always be my favorite waitress."

"You seem out of it today, everything okay?" She filled his cup.

Josh smiled and looked back out the window, a SYSCO truck was pulling up outside, making foodstuff deliveries to the restaurant. "Yes and no. I wish you were older, then I could talk to you like an adult..."

"Ha, ha, very funny. I'm twenty-nine."

Josh spun and widened his eyes in mock discovery. "Wow! You're over half my age..." He giggled a little and looked her in her brown almond shaped eyes. "Leslie, don't grow old too fast..." He turned towards the window and watched as the SYSCO driver wrestled a hand-truck full of sixty pound sacks of flour and five gallon butter buckets down the steep ramp from the back of the trailer. "Be young and full of life before it disappoints you."

"Are you disappointed in your life Mr., Jimmy?"

"No. Not up until this point. But I am sad that I didn't do more things earlier on in life."

Josh had drunk his coffee down and left the Seal Rock Inn. He was just passing Tony's and afforded a gaze inside the window of the empty place. Well, almost empty. The tables were all placed in the center of the building, the chairs stacked half-hazardly under, on and around the tables. The visi-coolers were all empty, the grill and other kitchen appliances were new and still covered in wrappings. There was a small sign on the window that read

OPEN APRIL. Josh moved his eyes to the old Sutro Bath House ruins.

As usual the shore birds were nesting in and on the old concrete pilings and footwalls of the pool areas, up higher in the rocks an old Chinese man and woman were dressed in Gis, he could hear a boom box playing Chinese traditional music, the couple was performing Tai Chi. Josh concentrated on the rest of the way down at his feet. The sidewalk was at a twenty degree angle from Tony's to the beach entrance and parking area. The area leveled out a little around the Cliff House and you had to be careful after a foggy night you didn't slip and tumble down to the beach level of The Great Highway.

Ocean Beach was hardly crowded this time of the year; November usually had the nicest weather around San Francisco if there wasn't a storm on the horizon. A light fog wafted around the shoreline, a thicker heavier bank was offshore about twenty miles or so, making the sea disappear into a wall of white. Very little pushing winds, just the normal breeze that came in with the tides and it roamed the sands, carrying with it the distinct pong that the Pacific Ocean had on the west coast. The smell of vegetable decay, mixed with brine and water vapor. To some it was offensive, to most it was incense. To Josh, it was grounded reality. Another reason he moved here.

He stepped down onto the sand and moved towards the north end of the beach where it ended at the base of the craggy rock, south of the Bath House foundations, and a lone pyramid of rock shooting up out of the water a few hundred yards off shore set the panorama. From there south it was all sandy beach and ocean. Crashing waves meant a storm was coming; they were tall and crested well out from the shore, only a handful of surfers were testing their mettle against them.

Josh stopped and inhaled as much air as his lungs could take, held it for just as long and exhaled slowly. His head swam a little, but the euphoria that lasted a millisecond made him feel better. Until the remnants of the dream came forefront again. He shuffled his feet towards the waterline and turned south. Maybe a half day adventure into Golden Gate Park would soothe the pain he was feeling.

It was pain wasn't it? A mixture of loneliness, sadness, loss, regret and anticipation panged his insides, from his chest to his hips. Everything seemed to tingle with remembrance and sting from loss. What happened? He couldn't remember quite how it all ended.

~ ~ ~

Each summer Camy's mother would drop her off at her maternal grandmother and grandfather's house across the street from Josh's. He could remember the awkward looking little girl, dressed in what Josh considered Easter clothes. Camy stepped from her mother's car that first fateful day, like they had just left church. He later found out that she dressed everyday like a young lady, never in a tomboy fashion like every other girl in the neighborhood did. It was something that her mother and grandparents insisted upon.

Josh was in his yard playing with his Tonka dump truck, he was ten at the time and the newer BMW was quite the sight in the old neighborhood. The mother got out, walked around and after some coaxing Camy slid out of her side of the car. *She had to be the mother*, Josh thought. They looked so much alike, hair eyes, clothing-she even was dressed in her Sunday go to meetings. While her mother went to retrieve the luggage, Camy just stood there, surveying the kids playing. She never engaged anyone's eyes, nor did she smile at the throngs of children that inhabited the streets of Sparks just a week out of school.

It was a time before video games and cable TV, so outdoors was the only place for a child. Usually after driving their mothers crazy in the house for the morning, they were escorted or simply tossed outside to fend for themselves during the day-lunches excluded of course-and clubs and clicks moved around the yards playing until one group tired of another, then moving on to play with another's toys. For three months, the ritual continued.

But the new girl, Camy, just stared at the homes and children at play and then turned her attention to her grandmother who slid open the ten foot long gate on wheels that completed the four foot cyclone fence encircling the Nicholson's home. The fence was more of protection against the dogs that roamed free in the area rather than for safety, but as Josh later found out, it was an added layer of policing for the Nicholson's granddaughter. Moving the gate was not only a strenuous task, but it made the highest pitched screeching noise when it was hefted open.

Mrs. Nicholson gave granddaughter Camy a big hug after a small embrace and peck on the cheek for her daughter, then took one of her suitcases and the trio ambled up the driveway and into the house, after Camy's mom yanked the gate shut with a squeal. Play in the neighborhood resumed.

Later that night or early morning Camy's mother disappeared with the BMW. When Josh's mom felt he had enough in-home time, his front door opened and out he went with the usual warning, *"Don't forget to check in..."* and *"...lunch is at noon..."* None of the kids had watches then, but the mothers were sure to ring the serving bell by stepping onto their porches and simply yelling, *"Lunch!"*

The first thing Josh did was to look at the house that held the newest kid on the block, or so he hoped, a new kid was like getting a new car now days. Fun to play with until you've used it up and then they become just a stop off when you tire of the antics of another. Josh was struck with a sad feeling when he saw the fancy car was gone. It stood out of course, the closest thing to new was the Holbrook's 1972 red Caddy rag top. A Beamer was like a gold coin in a sliver dish; even the windows were tinted to hide the passengers like the movie star cars on TV. Maybe the new girl's mom was a movie star! The California plates made the story seem more plausible.

A smile returned to Josh when he remembered the luggage, two suitcases. Not overnight bags, the full length ones like his dad used when he was gone for a week or more. The little girl had to be there still. So Josh plunked his behind down on the sidewalk and played with a red car he left there overnight in the gutter, until she came out.

"Lunchtime!" The maternal yelps echoed around the block. It was noon and the young new kid had not left the house at all. Josh had a sinking feeling that maybe she didn't stay after all. Maybe she cried and begged her mother to take her home.

Three days went by and not one sign of the little girl. Josh resumed his nomadic haunts, one house then another; when the kids became bored with each other, or a parent was tired of picking up after them, he moved on. Josh was walking the sidewalk along the S curve of Oxford Avenue towards his house when he glanced over his shoulder. The girl was outside!

She was dressed in a white and pink Easter looking dress (as usual) and was sitting down at a tea party table Josh had never seen in the yard before. The front of the Nicholson house was covered in six foot green shrubs around the bay windows and near the door, then the far side of the house, south from the Kennedy home where twenty foot evergreen trees surrounded the side. Camy was in between the two. She was eating a triangle of sandwich, without a crust and chatting to a doll that occupied the other kiddy chair. Her back was to Josh, and her head danced along with her hand gestures as she talked to the well-dressed figurine. Josh slipped across the street and onto the sidewalk that ran along the Nicholson's side.

"Hi." Josh's voice chirped.

The girl spun and stood, knocking the table over. The plastic tea pot and cups went tumbling, along with the doll on the other side. She said nothing; she just stared at him for a few moments. Then a faint smile crossed her face, her eyes sparkled bright blue. "Hi."

Her voice had the slightest crack in it, it was natural sounding. Small and angelic-even though at that time Josh didn't realize it.

"What's you name?"

"Camela."

"Huh?" Josh had never heard that one before.

"Camela!" this wasn't her voice this time, it was her grandmother's. "Camela you get inside now, okay?" The accent was pure Swedish and it was full of demand and a tinge of fear.

Josh had seen the elder Nicholson's around their house often, they kept to themselves mostly. Mark, the grandfather was around his fifties, mid or older. He worked outside often and every summer sported a great tan and he kept the yard immaculate. The lawn was mowed to precision twice weekly in the summer, the trees and bushes trimmed as neat and tidy as a tedious Bonsaist. He was always quick with a "Hello" or would walk to the gate every day to talk to the postman. Mark was a kindly looking short man with grey hair and rounded eyes that spoke of delight and content.

Tina, Camy's grandmother, was seen less often but was just as jovial and quick to say hi and even engage in conversation once in a while with a passing neighbor. She was a very short woman, with grey-blue hair and a chubby smile with mirthful eyes and glasses. Josh's dad would chat once in a while with Mark across the street one on each respective side of the fence. Tina would always wave at Josh when she saw him walking around or playing in the yard. Not today.

Today, Tina's eyes were full of suspicion and concern. After Camy passed her grandmother, Tina shot a look of warning Josh's way. He didn't understand it; he just wanted to talk to the new kid.

Three weeks had passed, Camy played out front in her kingdom surrounded by the wall of ten gauge wire fencing. Whenever another kid-girl or boy-ventured near, Tina was outside and marshaling Camy back inside. Josh decided to play his hand again, this time he walked straight across the street, then half-way up the block, over to the other side and then eventually behind the Nicholson's view, blocked by their evergreens. He approached stealthily and whispered.

"Hey, Camy. Don't look, but I just want to talk to you."

Camy raised her head in acknowledgement. "Hi." She whispered behind her. "What's you name?"

"Josh."

"Hi Josh."

Something in the way she said his name, with her crackly happy voice made Josh feel weird inside. As weird a feeling as a ten year old could get.

He thought of the primary thing a child of his age could to ask her, "How come you can never play?"

Camy just shook her head. "Cause…"

What Josh didn't account for came as a surprise to him and Camy both. Mark had been in the backyard and went out front using the side gate between the tall evergreens. He walked out of the back unsuspectingly right between the two.

"How you Josh?" Mark asked in his usual friendly and cheerful demeanor.

"Oh, hey Mr. Nicholson. Yard looks nice…" He mimicked what his dad said nearly every time when he bumped into Mark.

J Jay Ross

"Tanks, what you do today eh?" Mark's broken English was easy for a ten year old to understand.

"Just hangin' out, you know. Pool doesn't open for another two hours. Mom said she'd take me later, after her stories are over."

"Ah swimmin'. I miss dat when I was you ages, I swum all de time." He smiled a big toothy grin and walked towards the front of the house, just as Tina was coming out the front door to investigate the voices.

"Hey, you go home boy." Tina said sternly in Josh's direction.

"Awe motter, you leave him alone okay? He's good boy from across de street. Da quiet one. He's just talkin' to Cam." Mark raised a defense for Josh.

"Grandma!" Camy protested in her tiny squeaky voice, "He's just talking to me. I need a friend if I'm going to be here all summer!"

The words 'all summer' made Josh's inside tingle, like when he was on a roller coaster, he wondered for an instant if he was getting ill.

Tina was giving Josh the once over with her eyes and her mouth drew into a little smile.

"You eat yet boy?" She asked, nicely. Maybe there was some warmth towards Camy needing a friend.

"Uh, no."

"C'mon side. I'll fix up sandwiches."

Camy turned towards Josh and smiled, Josh returned the facial expression and put one hand on the fence and crouched for a leap over.

"Hut, hut! Use da gate, don't bend da top!" Mark warned.

Josh complied, he had never operated this gate before and it made him feel empowered to be allowed to do so. He followed Tina and Camy inside, he had also never been in this house before and his insides were full of new found glory and excitement, all in one day.

Inside the Nicholson home was a new world. The carpet was spectacularly clean, the upholstery on the two couches and two love seats in the living room were blue and gold Egyptian fabric. The walls were sparsely decorated, but enough to set them off; just one small painting and a few photo collages. An odor of cleanliness and order gained Josh's attention. Not bleachy or mediciny, more or less like the air was constantly being re-circulated with outside air, just clean.

Like most kids his age, going into a new home was a learning experience. New things to see, new smells to analyze. A person, even young kids, can acquire a new sense of surroundings in the first few minutes. Kids love going into another's home for the first time, it's new and almost like discovering a secret, unlike the same old boring house they come from every day. Josh's eyes were like an old typewriter's carriage. Moving back and forth, taking in the carpets, the kitchen as they passed, the small entryway into the family room.

The Nicholson home, as were all the homes in the neighborhood, was built in the early sixties on a style called Probasco, not at all depicting the Anglo-Norman visage that the name is famous for. It was a selling point to buyers who knew little about architecture. To hold true to the miniscule realty laws of the day, the project developer who bought the vast farmlands where the community was built was named Probasco-thus saving any trademark violations.

The home was basic, two or three bedrooms-the Nicholson's had three just like Josh's-one bath, carpeted concrete floors, eight foot ceilings, two car (barely) garage. The master bedroom was the front most part of the house, then the front door and living room were receded back and the garage was even with it. A simple plan, tract housing at its peak.

The Nicholson house had been remodeled, Josh noted. Just inside, if you turned left passed the wall, there would be the bedrooms and the one bath after a small hallway. And this was the case here he assumed, but when you turned right the living room opened up into the kitchen at his house separated by a wall and dining area. In the Nicholson home, the dining area had been enclosed; the wall that separated the kitchen from it removed, and a half-wall separated the dining/kitchen area from the living room. Someone had fixed it all up inside.

A small walkway led through the dining combo area. The Nicholson's had built a beautiful fountain about four foot high with a six foot long pond fed by a streambed, painted in blue and had eight goldfish swimming about in it. Josh had never in his life seen a fountain in a home before and his open mouth displayed his shock as he walked through to the family room.

"Close your mouth boy, you catch a fly." Mark laughed as he passed Josh heading into the screen room.

The family room was an addition, a screen room with all glass and white paneling. The room was built into the back yard patio, cutting down the yard size, but the beauty was worth it. It was almost another house inside, with a table for four, a television, patio furniture, and Astro-turf-a disturbing trend that came about in the seventies along with wood paneling and green and white shag carpeting. Though the room lacked the latter two it was tasteful in every aspect.

Camy led Josh to the backyard, where an identical tea party table was set up and she sat down. Josh followed, as he glanced around his surroundings some more. His focus changing as each new sight brought new feelings of familiarity.

Grandpa Mark was watching pro tennis on the TV in the screen room, Grandma Tina stopped in the kitchen to make some sandwiches. While she was preparing, she raised her voice just perfectly loud enough over the TV and to be heard in the yard outside the family room.

"Ju sure your motter say it's okay to eat here?"

"Yeah, um yes ma'am." Josh answered remembering his manners.

Even though he hadn't gotten his mother's permission, he would eat his lunch a little later. He just had to see inside this house, and spend some time with the mysterious new girl, Camy.

Tina brought peanut butter and honey sandwiches-adolescent staples. Josh and Camy ate in silence, every now and then Mark would exclaim over the TV, "Tina, dat Panatta has a mean serve eh?"

Then a thought hit Josh. He liked it here; he liked the new girl, Easter clothes and all.

They were encircled in the back yard by more ten to twelve foot evergreens, smaller shrubs and hundreds of roses. Carnations lined the walkway to the side gate and small daisies the path towards the other side of the house, towards Josh's home. Flowers of numerous kinds were everywhere.

Finally Camy broke the ice. She looked at Josh and began to talk freely.

Every summer, Camy explained, her mother would drop her off at relatives while she would go to different places around the world with her boyfriends. Her mother had lots of money and men were always around, wanting to marry her. Only problem was, most of the men didn't want a nine year old girl in the package. There was pain in her eyes when she told Josh this. Josh felt cold and sad hearing it.

Since her aunt and uncle were out of town most of this year, Camy was taken to her grandparents instead. She told Josh she didn't like it here much, she felt all alone. Until now.

"You like it better now huh hon?" Mark asked from the screen room, "Now you got da friend eh?"

Camy just blushed and looked down. "Yes." She whispered to Josh, "They hear everything…"

Weeks passed, a real friendship had bloomed between Camy and Josh. Tina would let Camy go over to Josh's house, "As long as you out the front…" A month later, they were allowed to walk to Burgess Park, several blocks away. One place they were forbidden was across the street from the Nicholson's and behind the Thomas' house, were vast empty fields of willow and cheat grass that ran for several acres until it met with Pyramid Way.

"No young lady should ever go to the fields…" Grandma Tina would tell her.

Later and later each passing day, Josh and Camy were allowed to play. Eventually, they wound up playing at Nancy's house. A girl a few years younger than Camy, she lived in an old broken down house behind the Nicholson's, in a big yard surrounded by thirty foot locust trees. Josh spent nearly every day with Camy.

Then summer came to an end, the BMW returned and the tall blond woman escorted Camy off, back to California.

But, nine months later, a new Mercedes pulled up out front of the Nicholson's and the young girl jumped out, ran straight across the street and hugged Josh, who was playing with a football in his front yard. A full summer ensued for both of them with each other, Grandma Tina even allowed Josh's mother to take them to Deer Park pool a few times. When August ended, the young girl once again returned home.

In June of 1979, Camy appeared again. This time it was late in the evening and she went to her room to go to bed. She didn't want to see Josh, who had been outside waiting for her all day for nearly a week. Josh was heartbroken.

Finally on day four of her return, Camy came outside. She wasn't wearing her Easter style dresses anymore. She wore blue jeans and a nice frilly halter top. Something inside of Josh snapped when Camy came to the gate in front of her grandparent's house.

"Uh, hi?" Josh felt weak.

"Hi Josh. Sorry, I haven't been out to see you, but I've...been sick."

"Are you okay? I mean now?"

"Yeah. It's a thing that happens to girls, you know, once in a while."

"Oh." Josh had no clue what she was talking about. "You wanna go to the park?"

"Okay."

They walked from the Nicholson's home towards the south, down Oxford Ave. A few blocks from the park, Camy did something that Josh will never forget his entire life. She quietly took his hand in hers and squeezed it a little. Josh could feel her hand was a little clammy, but the sensation in his arm made him feel tingly.

Then, he noticed things. For the next few blocks, things were different about her. She was wearing a perfume, faint, like a sweet orange or something. She walked slower, not like a child who was anticipating the park, but more of a stroll. A slow meander like on older couple did when they walked by Josh's house early evenings. Josh looked at Camy differently for a moment.

Her hair was not all prettied up like it used to be; she wore it a little longer and without the braids or fancy hair ribbons. Her face was a little more serious, sure she was still the same girl from summers ago, but she just looked-older. Her voice had lowered a little, but the creaky laugh and crack was still there.

Just different...

They reached the park and Josh broke Camy's grip and headed to the wooden play fort that the city had placed next to what was once a huge water display. There used to be a fountain with a blue concrete dolphin that shot water out of its nose high into the air. For as long as Josh could remember, he played in the spray of water with several other kids every summer. But, as with many other things in the seventies that politicians claimed Americans were running out of on the news each night, water was one. Water had to be conserved, so the fountain was shut down, the dolphin was eventually disfigured by teenage vandals and all that was left was the fifteen foot round concrete dish that held the whole thing. Skateboarders used it now.

Josh made it to the wooden drawbridge of the fort and ran across it. The squeaking and rattle shattered the silence of the day. Camy just walked by and headed for a swing. After a moment, Josh hopped down off the fort and walked to a second swing next to Camy.

"What's wrong?" He kicked at a pile of decomposed granite.

"Do you like me?" She quietly asked, looking at the ground.

"Sure. I mean, I..." Josh felt funny inside. "I couldn't wait to see you..."

Camy smiled and turned towards him. "I wished that school would end so I could be here. My mom wanted me to go to my aunts in Washington, but I wanted to come here."

"Cool."

Camy frowned a little and offered, "I wanted to be with you."

Josh kicked at the ground some more. "I waited all week for you to drive up."

The frown faded and a small smile crossed her face. "I like you Josh."

Weeks turned to a month, July was almost over and the heat was in the one hundreds, plus. Nights were the only time energy flowed from adults, who reluctantly took their kids to the pool every day, to keep the kids busy and to languish by water as the day melted everything. Parents would gather at night in various houses around the block to have barbeques and drink adult beverages and tell alcohol motivated stories; the kids were shuffled outside into the night to play.

Mark and Tina never participated in the block parties; they stayed home and watched TV mostly. Keeping an eye on Camy seemed like it was a full time job now, for some reason Josh couldn't figure out. He was still allowed to see her as much as they wanted to see each other, but her grandparent's eyes were more focused on them than before.

"It's 'cause I hit puberty…" Camy explained on night as she and Josh lay on the cool, freshly cut grass in her grandparent's front yard.

A meteor shower had been called for on the news, and every kid in the area camped out in the back yard and stared at the skies till they fell asleep, usually missing the stellar light show. Camy's grandfather set up a couple of blankets on the grass after he mowed it, then the little tea party table next to it to hold refreshments Tina was making in the kitchen. At nine-thirty, Camy and Josh met up out front and sat on the blankets eating pigs in a blanket and drank lemonade.

The sky was clear, except for the passing cloud of gnats every now and then; the air was humid close to the lawn. Crickets played concertos from every angle you could think of, a bat would whoosh by once in a while chasing after a bug. Except for the TV noise coming from the Nicholson living room through the screen door, it was calm and quiet as summer nights got with the parties going on. Every now and then someone at the party down the street would tell a joke and a burst of laughter could be heard.

Josh could hear only one thing, Camy's breathing. She was lying next to him-above the covers as warned by Mark-and she was gazing upward. Her little mouth was closed and it hinted at a smile. For some reason, Josh heard her breaths as they slowly made their way in and out. He glanced at her chest and saw it rising and falling, something else was different about her…

"Are you wearing a bra?" Josh asked quietly, as to not go above the sound of the TV elsewhere.

"Shhh! Are you trying to get yourself killed?"

"Sorry." Josh looked up towards the sky. "Wow."

"Josh. Do you think we'll be good friends forever?"

"Sure. Why not, we never fight over toys; we share everything like soda and snacks. And your grandparents like me."

Camy smiled and closed her eyes. She was in trouble inside. Her chest hurt from under her ribcage, where a pang made her think crazy things and see people differently than she did last year. Her body was changing, it hurt physically and mentally, but she could handle that. Josh hadn't noticed yet, or not as much as she had hoped he would, and she was growing impatient with his candor. She had this feeling, this prodding to do something…

"Josh, can I tell you a secret?" Camy quietly asked with her eyes closed.

"Sure…"

Camy rolled on to her side facing Josh. She scooted her body close to his, and after shooting a look towards the front door for prying eyes, kissed Josh on the lips.

"What the?!" Josh scooted backwards like a recoiling snake.

"Shhh!"

"Everting okays out there eh?" Mark called from the love seat in the living room.

"Shhh!" Camy warned Josh again.

Josh was breathing like he just ran the bases at the park in the summer heat.

"It's okay grandpa. The lawn is a little wet…"

"Okay honey." Mark called back.

Camy rolled closer to Josh. "See. That was my secret."

"Oh." Josh was still shivering, he noticed Camy was too. "I…I mean, I liked it. I just never had a girl, you know, kiss me before…"

Camy blushed bright red and was glad the darkness of night covered it up. "I've never kissed a guy before…"

"Wow." Josh licked his lips slowly. "Can we do it again?"

A huge smile crossed Camy's face. "If you're quiet about it, and I want to warn you, there is this little trick my friend told me about. It's how the French kiss…"

"Okay."

Over an hour and a half passed. Thousands of stars fell and the best friends never saw one. Josh was feeling like, well, he didn't know what he was feeling. His sides all tingled, inside and outside. His skin felt rigid and it melted at the slightest touch of Camy's. Whatever they were doing was scary at first, and then it felt as if it was meant to be done. His body responded, his mind was swimming with questions, his tongue? It was in a girl's mouth…

"I never want to be away from you Josh. Please promise me we will always be together…"

Josh didn't know what else to say. "Sure." He wanted more kissing.

The very next day, Josh picked Camy up early at her grandmothers and they walked off hand in hand towards Paradise Park. The walk was at least an hour long, but the park with its huge pond and maple trees offered a perfect place for teenagers to cuddle and kiss, or *neck*, as it was called then. Willows circled the shoreline of the massive duck and fish sanctuary, granite boulders and broken concrete conduits gave fishermen a place to sit in between breaks in the bushes and weeds.

Josh and Camy sat on a boulder in between two tall clumps of willow. They were still holding hands, it seemed perfect, and it felt right.

"Josh. Do you ever think about sailing away?" Camy asked as she kicked at a stump sticking out of the water.

"Huh?"

"You know, like one of those movies. Just getting on a boat and sailing off into the sunset."

"Sounds like one of those silly books my mom reads."

"Yeah." Camy figured she wasn't getting any ground with her line of thought, so she dropped the subject.

They spent the rest of the day walking around the lake, twice. Josh showed her his prowess of hunter gatherer by catching a crawdad hiding under the rocks by the shore, then they moved towards the small fenced pond in the back, the swan pond. The young couple stared at the swans swimming two by two as they passed. Camy placed her head on Josh's shoulder and he tilted his head to hers.

The rest of the summer was mostly like that first night and following day for Josh and Camy. They kissed everywhere they went, the park, the pool (out of sight of his mom), and the store. They held hands and when they laughed, it wasn't like a child's laugh in joy anymore and they looked into each other's eyes for long periods of time. Memorizing each other's features, watching each other enjoy one another. The daytime dollar movies had to be snuck into, because Tina and Mark would never approve of it, but they did and each movie was missed almost in its entirety, as the young lovers held each other and kissed.

They had never gone any farther than kissing. Josh didn't know what do to and every try he made to touch places he wasn't supposed to, his hands were swatted away. He liked the kissing more than anything else anyway he thought. And that's the way the summer ended.

Mid-August arrived and soon the Mercedes pulled up out front of the Nicholson's house one early morning. Josh woke up early and peeked out the window, as he had done every day for the last few days in anticipation of the impending departure of Camy. When he saw her mother's car, a tear filled his eye and a strange pain hurt his stomach and chest. He dressed quickly in hopes of getting in a few more hours with Camy before she had to go home for the school year.

He made it to the Nicholson's just as Camy came out of the house carrying her suitcase. Josh felt lower than anything right then, he saw her face. It was red and splotchy from crying, her hands shook as they held onto her luggage, she saw Josh and lowered her head.

"C'mon honey. We have to get home." Her mother said as she drug Camy's other suitcase to the car.

"Wait."

Camy dropped her case and ran for Josh. She collided with him and hugged him tighter than he thought was possible. He could smell her tears, he felt his own eyes watering, he could feel her heart beating hard in her chest, he could sense…foreboding…

"Promise me you'll be here when I get back next summer…" She sniffled in his ear.

"I promise. I'll always be here for you, if you ever need me…"

The two embraced and kissed-right there in front of God and everyone.

"Well, I'll be…" Mark said with a smile.

"Oh lord!" Exclaimed Tina with a gasp.

"Let's go Cam. Tell Josh you'll see him next year…" Her mother frowned.

Camy broke her hug and looked Josh in the eye. She didn't speak a word as her mother took her hand and led her to the car. Camy climbed in without breaking her gaze at him, she pulled her seatbelt around her without a blink. Camy's mother tossed the bags into the trunk of the car and as she walked around to the front she shook her head at Josh.

Josh raised his trembling hand to wave goodbye; Camy raised hers from the car and placed it on the window. The Mercedes roared to life and began to pull away from the curb, Camy's window rolled down and over the sound of the engine revving as it pulled away, Josh heard, "I love you!"

CHAPTER THREE
November 2001

Josh wiped the moisture from beneath his closed eyelids as he sat on the beach. The air was cool, but not cold enough for the chills and shivers running along his spine right now. He had dug a makeshift seat in the sand a hundred feet from where the waves lost their power on the shoreline of Ocean Beach. As the memories came rushing back, he just sat there and felt them with all of his body.

He smiled broadly at the happy thoughts, the smile on Camy's face. He felt the tremors in his body as she kissed him for the first time; smelled her perfume, her slightly sweaty skin, the fresh cut grass they were laying on. The tears formed as her remembered the last moments they had together.

Last moments, because that's the way the story ended. Camy never returned. After the whole month of June passed the next year, Josh went over to Tina's and Mark's. Mark invited him in and Tina had a plate of fresh Danishes on the kitchen table. She offered him a glass of milk and as the sound of the fountain in the little hallway gurgled, Tina and Mark stood in front of Josh, like two cops who were there to tell him a loved one had died.

"Little Camy," Mark began, "Won't be coming a back around here…" He finished, trying to hide his accent more than ever.

"Her motter got married, to guy over east coast ways," Tina continued, "Jersey I tink. We movin' there in year or so…" Tina placed her hand on Josh's hurting head. "We sorry, we know you a good boy and for liking our granddaughter. We miss you too."

The milk began to curdle in Josh's stomach. He got up and left the home that held the first girl he had ever kissed, the first he had ever felt strange inside for; he never stepped foot in the house or the yard since. Tina and Mark moved away later that year, to New Jersey from what Mark told him. A young couple with three kids moved in later that year, Josh not once visited that family, nor ventured near out of fear he would be invited inside.

~ ~ ~

Sitting crossed legged-or *Indian Style* as his mother called it-on the beach, Josh heard the waves crashing in the distance and that brought a small consolation to his hurting thoughts. Then another sound intensified behind him.

It was a sound many knew, the *fluff, fluff, fluff,* of paws on sand, coming at him from behind at high speed. In the distance he could hear the dog's owner yelling, "*Carter! No!*" Josh began to react, to turn and avoid the impending collision, but he moved too slowly. Just as his eyes opened he saw a young Chocolate Labrador flying at him and was within inches.

Poof! The sound of wind exited Josh's chest as the impact drove him onto his back, the white-pink slobbering tongue of "Carter" searching for open flesh to slime. Josh burst into laughter.

"Oh my God! I'm so sorry!" The woman yelled to Josh as she ran towards the heap of humanity and canine.

"No problem, I love dogs…" Josh managed to get out as Carter the lab was trying to get his new friend soaking wet. Josh kept rubbing the dog's side and half-wrestling with him.

"I took his leash off, there was no one around here, you know, just a few folks but I'm sorry…" she offered again. "Carter! Down!" She commanded the dog.

Josh grabbed the dog by the collar and looked at its mirthful eyes. He managed to get a glimpse at the tags.

"You're M. Desjardins?"

"Misty, everyone calls me Misty…"

Misty managed to get Carter under control enough to get his leash snapped onto the collar ring.

"Jimmy, everyone calls me Jimmy…" He said, trying to be a little coy with this very attractive brunette. After all, that's what everyone knew him here as anyways…

The woman shot him a look of confusion, and then smiled slowly, "Okay…"

Josh brushed the sand off of his behind and then his hands as he stood. He offered one to his new friend. "You live around here?"

"Just moved. From south, near L.A. You?"

She shook his hand, it felt warm and was slightly sweaty, this made Josh smile more. He hadn't touched another woman's hand like that since his wife died.

"Up around the bend there, past the hotel." He jerked his head in the direction.

"That explains your dress…" She nodded at his shorts

"What's wrong with the way I dress?"

"Shorts? It's November you know…"

"Yeah, and its sixty-five degrees out."

"Well, I guess I'm used to warmer climes…" She pulled Carter tighter to her as a seagull landed a few yards away, pecking at a clump of kelp.

Josh nodded at Carter. "He's a handful."

"Yeah, I got him for my son." Misty began, then stopped short when she noticed Josh's smile faded.

He glanced at Misty's ring finger that same instant. She caught his gaze and looked down to his. She smiled sheepishly, then started to back up, pulling Carter with her. "Well, gotta get this guy home and feed him. So he can get bigger and trash the rest of my house."

"Okay, well…" Josh debated for a moment on what to say next, and then opted for silence; he never had much luck with women anyways.

"See ya, huh?" Misty called over her shoulder as she turned towards the south end of the beach, cutting an angle upward towards the parking lot.

"Yeah." Josh whispered to himself.

The new woman was nice looking, not a model or a movie star type, but her face had a familiar curve to it. Her greenish-blue eyes accented her short brown hair that had a tinge of blonde around the edges in front. She was petit, probably five four or three and weighed no more than one hundred and ten. Her voice was relaxing and even flirty a little.

Josh watched as she jogged the dog back up the beach to the stairs leading to the parking lot. She was wearing a light blue Lycra running jacket and matching pants with old Converse basketball style shoes. Josh frowned at the fashion statement, but then again-he was wearing shorts in November, on a beach, on the coast.

The seagull had found a crab and was dragging it out of the kelp. It made a loud squeal like a laugh.

"Yeah, well I bet you aren't too hot with the ladies either, are you Mr. Garbage Breath?"

Josh walked back to his apartment off of Geary and glanced in his mail box. He saw the stack of bills he avoided yesterday and decided they could sit for one more day. He opened the gate to the staircase that led to his lofted home twenty feet above the street.

Closing the door, Josh tossed his keys on the table and locked the three locks that separated him from the slightly higher than usual crime rate for the city. He went to the fridge and pulled out a beer and snapped it open with a hiss. After taking along drag he set the can on the counter and walked to the bathroom, peeling clothes off as he went.

A long hot shower would be good; tomorrow he would be covered in fish guts and charter vomit at work.

Misty, on the south side of Golden Gate Park in a rental home had just placed a bowl of dog food on the floor in the kitchenette for Carter. She too had peeled the top layer of clothing off and was headed for the shower. She pursed her lips at the sound Carter was making as he devoured the dry food in his metal bowl.

As she passed the bedroom she caught a glimpse of herself in the full length mirror. She ran a hand over her belly down to her panty top, then back up to where her bra line began. It was child birth that gave her the little "extra", and she feared the running suit was too much for her new acquaintance. Not that it was accidental by any means, Misty had been trying to get "Jimmy's" attention for a few weeks now, this was the least subtle to date, but it worked. Guys love dopey dogs.

She slipped out of her panties while hopping on one foot towards the tub, then unfastened her bra and tossed it towards the hamper a few feet away. As her body shivered against the first few seconds of warming water she smiled, "See ya tomorrow…Jimmy…"

CHAPTER FOUR
Next Day

"Dammit Lester! I told you, no drinking before we go out. I can't have you swashbuckling again around the deck with six sea-sick charters, got it?"

Josh had just climbed down the ladder from the road above, Al Scoma Way, right behind *Lou's Pier 47 Restaurant*. Fisherman's Wharf was slow this time of year, tourist-wise and Josh needed a few dollars on the weekend charters to make the rent for the slip and the fuel costs. His uncle, Lester Kennedy the II, was his first mate, swabbie, and only real friend other than Jeremy, in San Francisco.

Josh's boat, the *Battered Sole*, was a 40' 1974 Grand Banks Classic with double John Deere 6404 diesels. Sometimes the joke of the harbor, she was prettier than *some* of the fishing boats that sailed from the wharf each morning, but in most respects she wasn't the pride of the charter fleets that staked out permanent slips. She could hold six charters with gear comfortably, after some minor remodeling Josh had made.

Below decks she had room to sleep four, after gear and stores were filled. Josh had tried to keep the place clean as possible inside, but he ended up just forbidding passengers from going beyond the head, he was just a pack rat and his uncle didn't help matters with his old sailor collectables and memorabilia or the fact Lester lived on the *Sole*.

Tarnished white and brown, barnacles clinging to her fiberglass hull like moss to a tree in Oregon, the *Sole* was Josh's pride, even though it wasn't his purchase. The boat had trawler lines, a three foot stainless steel and wooden rail ran alongside her side, right up to the three foot

pulpit extending from the bow. Traditionally the pulpit was only a foot or two at most, but Uncle
Lester had it lengthened after seeing the movie *Jaws*. He called it "Quint's Point". Lester fancied himself quite the sailor, and would spend most of the time on Quint's Point while underway when Josh was piloting. Josh had to smile when Lester did this, it added character to the *Sole* as she puttered in and out of the wharf, many times tourists would photograph old Lester on the pulpit from the points of the breakwater as the *Battered Sole* made for the bay and then open water.

Lester was the epitome of sailor. Thin and scraggly looking, he had the edges about him of a man that spent his life at sea. His thin hair was black and mostly white, sticking out here and there under his old navy cap like a neurotic bird's nest; his eyes were sunk way back into their sockets, and stuck out like cartoon bug eyes when he was excited or scared. He usually wore an old slicker on the boat and for hours afterwards, he liked the aura of it, the allure.

Little did he know that few folks liked the look or the smell.

Josh climbed to the bridge with Lester at his heel.

"No passengers today anyways nephew. They called this morning and left a cancellation message on the machine. Something about having trouble getting over Donner Summit."

"Hasn't been a storm in three weeks Les, what the hell are you talking about?" Josh yelled over his shoulder as he fired the engines up to warm.

"Don't harpoon the messenger, Jimmy. Just tellin' ya what the machine said…"

Josh leaned over the side of the bridge to look down at the greenish water of the harbor. He shook his head in disgust. They needed the fares today, and the ones tomorrow to pay for supplies and the bait bills. A seagull sitting on a bird poop stained piling squawked as if laughing at his dismay. A flash of yesterday's encounter with the woman and her dog crossed his mind and he smiled as the bubbling water spouted from one of the *Sole's* bilge drains.

"All right. Just you and I then. If you promise not to be too drunk to fish…"

"Can't ever be too drunk to fish, nephew." Lester called back as he was tossing the bow line off.

"Yeah? That last pole cost two hundred bucks to replace and another eighty to have Jeremy clean the lines from the prop shaft." Josh retorted as he slowly navigated the *Sole* into the waterway.

"Eighty gallons of diesel at three bucks a gallon…"

Josh was counting the loss of the day as he opened a beer and sat in the old rusty fighting chair on the deck.

"That leaves us four hundred dollars for the rest of the month. Not even enough to pay the harbor master for the slip or the Mexican for the squid. Why do folks always back out in the best month of the year?" He sipped his Bud and burped loudly.

"Cause folks don't have a clue about fishin', that's all." Lester replied, while trying to coax up his own burp. "Why don't we try some pot charters again?"

"Because we don't have enough money to get our pots out of the storage unit. It's all I can do to keep those folks from selling the damn things off for the back rent. Besides, if we can't get these landlubbers here at seven a.m. to go halibut fishing, how the hell do you think they'll feel about getting up at three a.m.?"

"Maybe we should think about doing bay tours or something like that…" Lester opened another beer and gave his pole a tug to check the tension.

"Can't compete with the *Red and White Fleet*, Les. They offer those tours for twenty bucks a person and have little radios with the tour broadcast over them. All I have is you and you can't even say Alcatraz by mid-after noon."

"Wow! What's gotten your sauce tainted this morning?" Lester swallowed his beer with one gulp.

Josh thought about it for a minute, he smiled, then started to reel in his line.

"I met a girl yesterday morning at Ocean Beach."

"Uh huh." Les's interest was only held by the fact he was moving secretly to get another beer from the ice chest. "Did you tell her about your dream, ya know, the one with *Camry*?"

"A Camry is a car, fishnet. *Camy* was the girl from so long ago."

"Yeah, so did you tell her about how you was going to hunt this girl from your past down and fall in love again?" Lester tried to stifle the hissing sound of the opening beer with his hand as he pried the tab up.

"No. I didn't. That's your last beer for an hour by the way." Josh said as he stood to grab the leader. "This girl was nice though, she had this smile...well, she made me feel different inside."

Lester took a small sip from his Bud, trying to conserve it. "Uh huh. Listen Romeo, it's been what? Seven years since Faith, right? I'd imagine you'd get scrambled innards from glancing at the sea lions at Pier 39..."

"Very funny. You just delayed your next beer by an hour. C'mon and get serious about catching something would you? We need something to sell at the market today."

"Yeah, yeah. Bet ya a twelver that I haul in a forty."

"If we haul in two thirty pounders, I'll even buy you dinner."

"One hundred and forty dollars." The man at the fish market counted out to Josh as he hosed the catch-cart off.

"Thanks."

Lester was proudly holding his twelve pack of Budweiser next to the two men and had a grin on his face wide and toothy as a shark's.

"How do you guys do it?"

The market man asked this as he motioned for one of his workers to come get the forty pound and the one seventy-eight pound halibuts that Les had caught. The limit is one per fisherman, but since Josh was skunked, the other bottom dweller counted as his. Add to the catch a couple of cod and a nice Albacore, and the money added up.

"I just tell the 'Ol Man of the Sea that he won't get any more beer." Josh said with a grin as he gave Les a shove towards the loading door.

The pair left the market and headed back towards the Embarcadero from Pier 45, the street-more of an alley really-was lined with fishermen who had bagged limits and was selling their wares for the day. Carts of iced fish and boxes of Dungeness crab were being hauled around the back side of the wharf, where some of the take would eventually end up on a dinner plate in less than a day or two at the fancy restaurants that lined the *Fisherman's Grotto # 9* and the other piers. Les loaded his beer booty in Josh's Ford that was parked in the private lot off of Pier 41 and climbed in. Josh stood by the door and shook his head.

"Nope. We're walking to the Grotto."

"But my leg…"

"Needs the exercise. C'mon it's just a few blocks. I'll buy you that dinner."

"I don't call a calamari basket with fries dinner. I was hoping for *Nick's*…"

Nick's Lighthouse has been a Wharf favorite for decades, the atmosphere of an old fishing port; they served meals for lunch and dinner with the flair and tradition of the old harbor itself.

"Not today, you smell like beer and fish guts. You'll scare off the tourists…"

Josh and Les crossed from the parking area of the *Boudin Sour Dough Bakery* to the Grotto when a woman's voice called out over a Rasta Band playing on the corner of the lot.

"Jimmy? Hey, Jimmy!"

Josh turned and saw Misty, the girl from the beach yesterday, walking straight across Jefferson Street towards them. A smile lit up his face.

"Misty?" Josh stopped and put his arm out to stop Les from going any further.

"You said you'd feed me!" Les protested.

Josh absently reached into his pocket and took out the roll of cash the market manager paid them earlier with. "Here…" he handed Les a twenty, "Say hi to Lisa for me at *Nick's…*"

Les opened his mouth to protest again, then looked at the twenty and knew it more than covered a meal; a few drinks would be affordable too. "Okay, Jimmy. See ya in the mornin'."

Misty and Josh met halfway across the entrance to the large parking lot, nearly under the famous sign depicting a Dungeness crab on a ship's wheel that read FISHERMAN'S WHARF OF SAN FRANCISCO. Josh could feel his insides tingle, excited that she picked him out of the crowd of tourists walking the streets.

"Hi, you hang out here too? Where's Carter?"

Misty smiled and stopped a few feet short in front of Josh. "Home."

"You, uh hang out here?" Josh forgetting that he asked her that already.

"Once in a while I get a craving for the shrimp basket."

They stood a few feet apart for a minute or two, and then Misty said matter of factly, "Shrimp baskets."

Josh was staring at her blue-green eyes when he realized they were standing in the middle of the driveway and Misty was indicating she was heading to the side of Taylor Street where the vendors lined the little alley with permanent booths, offering fresh seafood, calamari salads plus crab cooked and prepared in little boiling pots right there on the spot.

"Oh, yeah. Mind if I join you?"

"I hope I didn't scare your date off..." She nodded in Les's direction; he had made it halfway to *Nick's* with his pretend seaman's limp he had perfected for the tourists.

"No, as a matter of fact you just made his day."

"Really? Is he alright?" She nodded, indicating the limp.

Josh glanced toward Les. "Oh, that. He thinks it makes him look like a regular sea captain with his slicker and all. It's for show, really."

"Oh." Misty smiled at Josh and he saw her eyes sparkle in the afternoon sun. "I'm kinda new here, what do you recommend?"

Josh was entranced for a moment, then out of decency and the fact he might start acting like a schoolboy, looked away again in Les's line of walk, or shuffle as it were. Les had just made it to *Nick's* and limped into the bar, Josh shook his head. "Be late morning I bet..."

"Huh?"

"Nothing. Sorry..." Josh turned his attention back to Misty. "Food?"

"Yes."

"Well, there's *Tarantino's*, *Alioto's*, *The Franciscan* back over the Embarcadero, *Ghirardelli's* where you came from..."

"You decide. I'm just craving shrimp...maybe some place that doesn't mind how you're dressed..." She said with a chuckle at his work clothes.

"Oh, it's okay as long as you don't smell like spoiled tuna..."

CHAPTER FIVE
Same Afternoon

"No really, I'm captain of my own fishing vessel."
Josh and Misty had walked down Taylor Street to eat at a double decker sidewalk cafe. They had managed a seat upstairs overlooking dozens of fishing and charter boats in the marina below. Most of the fleet was in by this time and the marina was abuzz with activity from tourists and tired early risers heading home.

"Uh huh. The old guy you were with looked more like the captain."

"Les?" Josh chuckled. "Uncle Les couldn't navigate out of the breakwater if he had both hands tied to the wheel and auto pilot."

"Uncle?"

A waiter arrived and sat a plate of bread down in front of them; he gave a smirk at Misty and then pursed his lips at Josh and his sailor clothing.

"Can I get you anything to drink ma'am?" He smiled back at the nicer attired Misty.

"Vodka Collins and a twist please."

"Sir?" The frown again.

"*Admiral* Morgan, if you please."

"You mean, *Captain Morgan* sir?" The frown turned to a look of disapproval.

"Oh, did you know that actually Captain Morgan was promoted to Admiral as a privateer in the Caribbean? He fought the Spanish on the Main in 1667..." Josh looked at Misty with his eyes full of coyness. "It seems so belittling to call him captain when you don't actually know about him at all does it? Many have quite the wrong impression of him, the general consensus is he was a pirate first, however he actually rose to the ranks from bound laborer to Admiral, he didn't become a pirate until the British put a stop to all privateering.

"In reality he was not a son of aristocracy as most British captains were. He sued the authors of a book that listed him as an indentured servant and ended up in Jamaica in 1658 where he earned his credentials. Later, it is said that he used to 'dress up' in red satin and jewels to impress others buccaneers into joining him. Funny, how one who can look so gleaming on the outside can be conniving and ruthless on the inside. I could be a good client here, or friend of the owner, you never know…"

Josh glanced up at the waiter who was barely amused at the tale, until he caught the whiff of sarcasm and pointedness. Misty looked away out the window to hide a giggle. The waiter was now annoyed, but understood his place and backed away slowly from the table.

"An *Admiral* Morgan then sir. I'll be right back…" He turned and disappeared around the corner.

Josh turned back to Misty, who was stifling a laugh. "Sorry, if that twit only knew that the fish they served here came from my boat he'd have a stroke…" Josh picked up a piece of bread and broke it, placing half on Misty's plate. "Now, where were we?"

"Your uncle?"

"Oh yeah. He's harmless, really. He drinks a lot, but he is a good listener and friend and I don't know what I'd do without him. Maybe be a little richer, but…"

"He spends a lot of your money?"

"No, not really. He lives on the *Battered Sole*, that's the name of my boat. Our boat. When my dad, his brother died when I was twenty-four, Lester took me in. He had this old boat already, but owed dozens' of people for it, the bank, some loan sharks, some even shadier people. I took the money I got from dad's life insurance policy and paid them all off. Now we charter three days a week to pay the bills. Well, we'd like to, business has been slow lately."

"He 'took you in' when you were twenty-four? Stayed at home till a ripe old age huh?"

Josh looked away out over the fishing boats below. He drew a light breath and spoke softly, "My father had a stroke when I was eighteen, a year after my mother passed away. He'd lost use in the left side of his body, well, most of it anyway. He couldn't take care of himself, so I stayed with him to help him out. "

"Oh," Misty lowered her eyes and found a stich in the tablecloth to run her finger along, "I'm sorry. I didn't mean to…"

"It's alright. It does sound kinda funny the way I put it." Josh smiled reassuringly.

"Anyways, we take out fishing charters six or seven a.m. three days a week if we can, then I spend the afternoons cleaning up fish guts and messes from seasick landlubbers."

"Sounds, romantic…"

"Yeah, I can think of a lot nicer things to do with one hundred and forty thousand dollars now though."

Josh thought there was something else Misty was going to say, but she looked back out the window towards the marina and the boats that where lined up in the water.

"Is any of those yours?" She asked nodding.

"No. We're back behind all this. It's cheaper for the slip, but it's harder for the customers to find us."

Misty looked back at Josh and he caught a glint of familiarity about her. He cleared his throat.

"Do I know you, have we met somewhere before?"

"Not me, I mean not that I know of…" She looked away, then smiled and turned back at him. "Well, that's not exactly true. At Tony's, you always sit by the window and look out over the ocean. I've seen you there a few times before it closed. I didn't think you ever saw me, but maybe you did."

"Could be."

"Your uncle; is he the salt of the sea or did he just buy the boat for a job?"

"Les, no. He's a real navy man. Thirty plus years, three wars. He joined up in 1941 after Pearl Harbor. He has tons of stories to tell, most of them are true. He lives his life pretty hard, but then again he lived out his youth roughly too. He was a boxer in the navy, he worked in the bowels of an aircraft carrier for weeks without seeing the sun, he drank many under the table, and still does. After leaving flight school he spent twenty years overseas. He's ridden a hard road."

"Oh, I thought the sea aged him. He's a pilot?"

"No. But he thinks he was."

"So he's younger than he looks?"

"Nope. He's seventy-seven; they didn't care too much about how young you were then, when the war started, pretty good shape for an old man too. I've seen him tussle with some sixty year olds once at a bar..." Josh winked at Misty. "He was on an aircraft carrier, the Yorktown. He was nearly killed in the Battle of Coral Sea when the Yorktown was nearly sunk, then was again almost killed when it was finally sunk at Midway."

The waiter returned with their drinks and a nicer disposition, took the food order and walked away.

Josh continued as Misty looked at him with a smile and asked, "So..."

"So, after World War II he went back to school and became a flight engineer. He took part in the Berlin Airlift, then Korea, then Vietnam."

"Wow..."

"When he returned to America, he had nothing to do. So he made his way here and with his G.I. money, bought the *Sole* in 1976. Brand new. Been here ever since

"That's quite a tale. How about you though. Ever married?"

"And…"

"He passed away a while ago; his family has custody of our son, sort of. He has…had a good attorney. California courts see things differently sometimes."

"Oh. Were you high school sweethearts?"

"No. I never really wanted to marry him; I knew he was wanted the money my mother left me after she died. But he persisted, and then I got pregnant one night and the next thing you know, we're wearing rings and he's cheating with his first wife." She didn't mention why the family had custody, nor did she want to elaborate. Misty was happy Josh pursued the husband angle.

"Oh. Now I'm sorry."

"It's alright. Fair is fair. I only get to see my son once in a while, when he comes up, and that hurts more than anything."

"I can understand." Josh paused for a moment to let Misty wipe her eyes. "So I take it you're not from around here."

"No. I told you, L.A." Misty kept staring out the window.

"Oh yeah, I forgot."

"It's okay."

The couple finished eating and Josh paid the bill, even after protests from Misty. He left a large tip, just enough to say 'no hard feelings' to the waiter, and then they made their way to the door downstairs. Misty was quiet the whole time; she looked over Josh's way every once and a while, then back when he tried to catch her eye.

"I had a great time, thanks for inviting me." Josh said as they exited the café.

Misty appeared down. "Uh huh."

They walked a few blocks towards North Beach.

"Hey, you okay? Bad shrimp?"

"No. I just, well. I should be going."

"Can I...have your number?" Josh smiled sheepishly.

"Not right now, Jimmy. I'll get a hold of you, okay?"

Misty walked away with her head down; she crossed over Jefferson and headed up towards Ghirardelli Square. Josh was frozen for a moment, he couldn't believe what had just happened and was trying to figure out what went wrong.

"Hey! You want me to walk you?"

Misty turned and there was a slight smile on her face, she waved and shook her head then hollered back, "See you at the beach..." She then turned up Larkin Street and out of Josh's view.

"Well. Josh old boy...that was the strangest thing that has ever happened to you."

He turned and headed back to rescue *Nick's* from Uncle Lester. He looked back once over his shoulder when a cold chill hit his spine. He shook it off and returned his thoughts to the conversation at lunch with Misty.

"And you told her your sad story and everything...Usually chicks go for that kind of thing..." He said in a whisper to himself as he made his way back down Jefferson Street towards Taylor. "Maybe hers is sadder..."

"Maybe if you told her the whole truth." Lester said, rather indignantly. Annoyed because his night of rabble rousing had ended.

"You know how that ends up." Josh was walking Les back to the *Sole*.

"Truth never hurts."

"Well, you seem to be able spin a tale all the time."

"My days of woman huntin' are over. I don't care who or what folks think of me."

"Well, you've established a fine base then."

"Look Jimmy, if you like this young lady, then you have to be honest. Faith would want it that way."

"Yeah, I suppose she would."

CHAPTER SIX
November 23rd 2001

Josh was sitting by himself in his usual chair at the Seal Rock Inn Restaurant. He had gotten there just as Leslie unlocked the door and was not really in any hurry, about moving around today. Then he ordered his regular coffee and stared out the window, in the direction of Point Lobos Avenue. He was wondering to himself about his 'date' a few days ago with Misty, whether or not he had done anything wrong, or that maybe she was a little crazy. He figured both.

"Did you have a nice Thanksgiving Mr., uh Jimmy?" Leslie asked as she refilled his coffee.

"Just the usual night out on the town."

"Where'd you eat?"

"Buffet at the Tandoori."

Leslie made a sour face, "Eeww! Indian food?"

"Leslie? I thought you'd like Indo-Asian cuisine."

"Not for Thanksgiving. Now me and my old man had his folks over for dinner."

"How'd that work out?"

"The garbage disposal backed up, the bird was undercooked and his uncle got drunk and passed out in the living room watching football. It was perfect." She smiled and gave Josh a wink as she headed over to another table to serve new guests.

Josh wondered on his walk down to the restaurant this morning why he was so open to Misty right off, he thought maybe it was because she was so pretty, so outgoing, so…there. It had been a long time since he had female companionship, of the attractive kind, and decided that he just felt loosened up enough to discuss his late wife and child. He would tell her everything soon.

There was an air about Misty, the kind you get when you're in a room sitting by yourself; the room is full of strangers and you can feel all the eyes upon you, then someone who stands out walks by and smiles affectionately at you. You spend the rest of the time in the room glancing at that person, for another smile or maybe a nod, whether it comes or not. You think about that person for the rest of the day, for a week or more. Even if you never see that person again, you remember that moment for the rest of your life, every now and then the feeling returns.

He knew her too, maybe not from Tony's just a few hundred yards ahead of him, but somewhere. Recently? A while ago? Was she a friend of Faith's? No, couldn't be. She would have said something to that effect. Wouldn't she? Maybe she admired him from afar while he was married to Faith and out of respect waited this long to approach him. That *would* make her crazy, Josh thought. If she *were* a friend of Faith's, she certainly wouldn't be wanting to go out with him.

Josh sipped his coffee and was now wondering if he should walk down to the beach today; to see if Misty was there, or if he would be safer forgetting her all together and avoid his favorite spot in all of San Francisco. That wouldn't do anyone any good. He felt drawn to her; he had to talk to her just one more time.

"Penny for your thoughts?" Leslie came by with her coffee pot again.

"No thanks," He put his hand over the cup, indicating he didn't want anymore, "Les, tell me something. Do you think I would be a catch, would you wait nearly seven years to ask me out if you knew I was going to be available?"

"Is this a pass Mr. Kennedy? I would think that my old man would find you and thump you a good one..."

59

"Jimmy, please, Les. Well?"

"You're serious."

"Yes."

Leslie put the coffee pot down on the table and wiped her hands on her apron. Then she sat in the empty chair across from Josh, which startled him. She took his hand, which made the alarm rise even more, and squeezed it. Up close, her Chinese lineage was undeniable, though if you didn't look her in the almond shaped eyes, you could miss it. She was beautiful of course, and Josh felt his hand tremble a little.

"Mr., I mean Jimmy. If you were my age, I'd wait twenty years for you."

"Leslie, I'm only seven years older than you. I think you're just pulling my leg, trying to get a bigger tip. Besides, I'm usually the only one here this early in the morning anyways."

She stood up and pretended to dust herself off.

"Well, if you don't want me to wait for you…" She smiled and picked up her coffee pot. "Did you meet someone Mr., I mean Jimmy?"

Josh turned towards the window and looked out at the cars gathering in the Bathhouse's parking lot. "I hope so Leslie. I really do."

Josh made the walk to the beach slower than usual. He stopped every now and then to see if he could catch Misty near the surf, maybe walking her dog or just watching the waves roll in. No sign of her anywhere, yet. He continued his voyage to the sand stairs.

Just as Josh reached the stairs he saw a brunette sitting close to the water. She was on the sand with her legs crossed in front of her and her arms wrapped around them. She kind of rocked back and forth, then a little gust of wind came by she flicked her hair to the right. It was Misty. *Her beauty was insurmountable even from this distance*, Josh thought; he wondered how long he could last and not fall completely in love with her. He took a deep breath and made his way down to her, slowly, thinking of what to ask as he went.

"Hi."

The sound of the waves crashing off shore drowned out his approach and Misty jumped with a start.

"Oh! Jimmy! You scared the hell out of me!" She stood up and dusted her behind off.

"Sorry, I didn't mean to…I…"

"Where have you been? I've been here every day for the last two days."

"Really? I was working. We charter on the weekends, remember?"

Misty looked down and thought for a moment. "Oh yeah. Do any good?"

A happy thought crossed Josh's mind and he smiled, "You're good luck. We had a full boat all three days and came back limited out."

"Well, with the new moon on the 14th, both this month and December the fishing should be great." She smiled.

Josh cocked his head at her revelation. "You know about halibut fishing?"

"A little. I got bored when you didn't show at the beach here; I went home and looked it up."

Josh rolled his brow. "Oh." He kicked at the sand for a few seconds and looked down at his feet. "Listen, about the other day, did I say or do anything that upset you?"

Misty's face brightened and she smiled at him, her expression gave Josh a tingle.

"No, of course not. I was just thinking of Riley and how much I miss him."

"Riley? Your son?"

"Yes. He'll be here in a few days, so now I'm delighted. Can't you tell?"

Misty reached out and took Josh by the hand, which startled him a little. When she flexed her fingers he felt his hand was clammy and went to pull it back easily. But Misty squeezed a little tighter; he felt his hand warm up, along with the rest of his body.

Josh smiled at her and felt the urge to lean in and kiss her, but he resisted, it was too early to get slapped. Or, maybe kissing her gently on the cheek would get things rolling, but was he ready for that? Was he ready to be part of this woman's life, would she be willing to part of his was more like it, when he would tell her everything, and eventually he would, there are certain things that you can't hide if you establish a long term relationship. The truth being the number one thing you couldn't hide, not a truth like this anyways.

He cleared his throat and said, "How was your Thanksgiving?"

"Lonely." She responded by looking into his eyes.

"If I would have thought about it, I would have asked you to join Lester and I for an Indian dinner. East Indian, not the traditional feathers and war dance kind. I'm sorry; I thought someone like you would have lots of invitations."

"I had dinner with my neighbor, she was alone too."

"How sad. I feel terrible now."

Misty smiled. It was then Josh realized she was playing him a little.

"Would you take us for a cruise on your boat?"

"Anytime. On me." Josh smiled proudly, and inside he was burning, she wanted to see him again!

"No way. I have money, you need money, and we'll be a pain in the butt. I can assure you of that, you see, we both get seasick…"

"That'll be Les's problem." Josh laughed.

"Ahh, poor Les."

Misty gave Josh a tug on his hand, "Want to go for a walk? Along the beach?"

They walked south from the rocks just below the Cliff House, all along the beach. The breeze was cool and Josh offered Misty his jacket. He placed it over her shoulders and he lifted her shoulder-length hair as she slid her arms through the sleeves. Just as he was lowering her hair he caught a whiff of her shampoo or perfume, and it made him step back. He paused behind her and took a quick sniff of his hands. *Citrus. Lemon? Orange?* Josh felt lightheaded for moment trying to inhale the scent again as Misty turned. She was becoming more irresistible by the moment.

"I washed it this morning."

Josh turned bright red. "Sorry, I like the smell of your shampoo."

"Oh, I get it at Walgreen's on Geary as a matter of fact. Something cheap."

"I thought you said you had money."

"I do, and I intend to keep it that way. So I buy cheap, obviously it's good enough. You like it, right?"

"Yeah, sure."

For the rest of the walk-hand in hand-Josh and Misty stayed quiet. Misty was smiling and looking over at the surfers paddling out to the crests, Josh meanwhile was lost in thought. Was this happening too fast? Was he becoming smitten with this woman he has only known a few days. He scanned the side of her face and saw a small scar running from her ear to just above her eyebrow, not a distinct one, but one just the same. It was faded and barely white and would be hidden by a tan, but in November, tanning was scarce.

When they reached the end of the public beach area, Josh tugged her hand up towards the street. He felt like a walk in the park. They crossed The Great Highway, darting in between slow moving cars, Misty giggling all the way. Once the couple entered Golden Gate Park going up John F. Kennedy Drive, they walked towards the giant North Windmill. Josh sat down on the wet lawn and pulled Misty down also.

She looked up at the road sign and made the comment that Josh has heard more than a few hundred times, "You related?"

"Nope. But Les drinks like one though…"

They both shared a laugh at the Senator's expense for a moment, and then Misty slid close to Josh so quickly he didn't have time to react. He nervously put his arm around her shoulder and pulled her a little closer into the place between his arm and shoulder, as if it were natural. Her reaction was unnoticed, but if Josh had seen it, he wouldn't be disappointed.

"I love this city." She remarked after taking a deep breath. "The air is so fresh, the people are amusing and even enlightening at times, it's nothing at all like L.A."

Josh turned towards her, they were only a few inches apart from each other's lips, Josh felt someone had forgotten a woodpecker in his stomach, it was rattling from nerves so much. Sure he had kissed a few women since Faith passed away, but this was different, it was like he didn't have to work at it, it was too easy though. Misty pulled her head back slightly as if to convey that she read his mind, then turned her head, looking up to the windmill. They both had butterflies at this point.

"Why're you so mysterious?" Josh asked.

"Pardon?"

"You live close by here, right?"

"Yes, but we're not heading that way, if that's what you're asking."

"I'm not. But you seem distracted at times, I was just wondering if you were thinking about going home."

"I'm just…cautious, Josh. Can I call you Josh? I like Jimmy and all, but I think it's a pity using your middle name when your first name is so…so natural…"

"Sure, but how'd you know my first name was…"

Misty interrupted him, "I have to be cautious. I want to be sure that we, I mean that I… you know…" She shoved her open palm out in front of her. "I asked around a little. The pier and the restaurant, you know, Tony's."

"Oh. It's just the way you said my name, like you knew it all along."

"What do you prefer?"

"Well, most folks know me as Jimmy. Even my uncle calls me that, but Faith and her friends called me Josh."

"Jimmy it is then. I just want to be sure about you and I, we hardly know each other so far…"

A flash of fear shuddered through Misty's body, *careful Misty-don't scare him off*, she thought to herself.

"I understand. No big deal. Okay, what do you do for a living?"

Misty smiled big at him. "Nothing. I'm rich remember. Got several hundred thousand in the bank, that's why I have to be careful; guys are always after me for my money, I just want to be sure, that's all…"

Josh sat quietly for a second and looked straight ahead. "Okay, so buy me dinner."

Misty didn't laugh, Josh thought he had put his foot in his mouth and was now trying to find a way to get it out. Misty, on the other hand was waiting for this.

"I'm sorry. I should be offering to buy you dinner. It was a joke, I…"

"Do you like seafood?"

They both laughed and she pulled him tighter to her, her face was kept at a distance though, even though they both thought about a kiss they both were aware that many things seemed so out of place still. Josh knew that once he

65

told Misty everything about him, the chances of their remaining close, let alone friends was slim.

Misty was trying not to overstep her boundaries as the 'damsel in distress'; she wanted to spill her guts to Josh-or Jimmy-but she was afraid that he would be so confused about the truth of her past and the uncertainty of her future, that he would probably want to keep their friendship just that. She was afraid that maybe he would even run off and hide from her, afraid of what her past could do to them both. But she wanted to kiss him, so badly…

Josh wanted to kiss *her* so badly…

"I like you Jimmy. Or Josh, I mean, I really like you."

"I really like you too Misty, I'm so glad I met you…"

The dinner was that night at the restaurant McCormick & Kuleto's located in Ghirardelli Square, overlooking Aquatic Park. Josh had left Misty at the windmill and she was waving at him as he walked back towards Ocean Beach. He'd offered to pick her up, but she refused. Misty said she had her own transportation, though she rarely used it for one reason or another, and she was more than capable of getting around the city. Besides, Misty explained, she wanted him to see her walk into a place, she wanted him to experience her dressed up for the first time. She thought it would be great if he were just a little anxious to see her, to be surprised at how she 'cleaned up'.

Josh replied that would be interesting, and he thought it would be. This mysterious woman was adding to her aura every second. She seemed so interested in him, and Josh didn't really think he was all that charming. But still, he loved the game so far, it seemed he was winning.

The moon was just rising as the sun set on the other side of the peninsula. A bank of fog off the coast obscured

the sunset just enough to cause the skies over San Francisco to glow a reddish-pink hue, which also made the moon rising in the east over Oakland, red-cast.

Josh was waiting on Misty, who said she wanted to meet him here at six o'clock. It was now six-fifteen and he was thinking about a second beer at the bar. Fortunately a *San Jose Sharks* hockey game was on in there, he had something to take his mind off of the nervousness he felt grinding the bottom of his stomach. He knew she would show, but when?

Misty arrived at six-twenty two, according to Josh's watch. She sashayed into the bar area, up the steps and over to her waiting man. Josh's heart pounded with fury, Misty was wearing a blue and white shirred chiffon V-neck dress. Three thin strings held the dress in place over her shoulders on each side, the placement of the strings gave exposure to more skin, almost as much as a strapless gown; and Josh immediately thought Misty would have no problem holding up a strapless, anyway. He had never witnessed her in anything less than a hooded sweat-jacket and jeans. *This*, he thought, *was a dream...*

The accentuation of her chest and the clingy nature of the dress along with a six inch gap between the top of her knees and the bottom hem of the soft flowing material made heads turn from even the restaurant itself. Josh found his mouth drooping open, and instantly snapped it shut before Misty caught his glare. She smiled broadly with a confident grace and walked directly up to Josh and gave him a hug, which if it lasted any longer could have constituted a marriage ceremony. The bar patron's eyes filled with envy and amorous thoughts, their dates filled with jealousy and some of the women actually looked the other way when Misty passed them.

"Hi. I'm sorry I'm late." She winked. "You're a real hero for waiting for me."

"You know, I was going to say something about that, but I forgot. You look devastating…" Josh gushed.

Misty put her arms out to her side and looked herself over. "Thank you." She reached out and tugged at his light blue suit coat, which was over an open top light pink cotton shirt. "You look smart in that outfit." She finished off by brushing his shoulders with her hands.

Josh led Misty by the arm to the maître d's podium. They were taken up a soft carpeted staircase into the dining levels of the restaurant. The entrance to the restaurant and the walkway to the seats were decorated warmly with dark mahogany, long oval lighting fixtures and shined brass railings throughout and next to the main front window that overlooked Beach Street directly in front, the Maritime Museum just to the left and the Embarcadero far to the right.

Across the bay you could see the bright and shimmering lights of Oakland and Berkeley, Treasure and Angel Islands in the middle of the bay; the darkening sky above these floating lands was accentuated with the twinkling red and blinking white lights of cars on the Bay Bridge and above that the red moon was rising; to the center left, Alcatraz's lighthouse beacon cut a swath across the evening sky; far off to the north in the distance just to the left and lit like a Christmas tree was Marin with its sparkling dots of light.

The couple was seated and waiters sprang out from everywhere to meet the needs of the new arrivals. Crystal water glasses were filled, warm San Francisco sourdough was rushed right from the oven, fresh butter and olive oil/Balsamic vinegar cruets were readied for the bread right at the table. Josh just smiled over the furiously working hands of the servers as they prepared everything. After a nod, the attendants left, all but one waiter named Enrique. He gave a little bow, introduced himself and told Misty the special of the day. When he finished, Enrique turned towards Josh and gave him the same specifics.

Josh looked over the menu while he listened and when the waiter finished, just smiled up to him and said, "We'll have the Dungeness Crab Strozzapretti Pasta?" He asked both Enrique and Misty at the same time, she looked at Enrique and nodded with a satisfactory smile; then Josh added, "Smoked Beef Carpaccio as an appetizer, and…" He directed his eyes to Misty, "Do you like martinis?" She pulled her head back and smiled in surprise and nodded, so Josh finished with, "Two North Beach Tiramisus please."

"Excellent, you've dined here before?" Enrique asked with a bright smile as he took the menus from Josh.

"Not as much as I hope to in the future…" Josh responded while looking at Misty, who blushed a little.

"Very good, sir. Your drinks will be right out." The waiter gave a warm nod towards Misty, "Ma'am." And dashed off.

"In my opinion, this is the best place in town." Josh began.

"I can see why, it's so charming and not overly…snooty." Misty beamed.

"Did you know that in 1990 before this place opened, George Lucas, the *Star Wars* Guy who lives across the bay in Marin, wanted to put in a *Star Wars* museum and memorabilia shop? He was a friend of the owner of this place, Pat Kuleto, and well, this was the eventual result."

"I'm glad; I think Enrique our server is much more charming than *Darth Vader*."

Josh smiled, but a thought crossed his mind and the smile flip flopped for a moment. Misty caught the expression and her face went emotionless. "What's wrong?"

"I'm scared…"

"Why?"

"This place, you, tonight. It's just so perfect. I haven't had a night like this in over seven years, I…"

Misty smiled and reached for Josh's hand. "It's been a long time for me too, but I think the company makes it better. Let's forget our pasts just for tonight, huh? It's just you and me and the evening."

Josh grinned warmly and replied, "You know what. You're right. I do feel like a teenage boy on his first date though, just to let you know."

Misty reacted with a curious frown, and then smiled coyly as she responded, "Let's just see how dinner goes before we head up to lover's point in your dad's station wagon huh?"

Josh started to glow crimson. He knew he had crossed the line a little, but he didn't expect the results he had gotten. Misty seemed almost ready for a romantic evening and now he was even more anxious than before. He stared into Misty's eyes as she took a sip of her newly arrived martini. Her eyes bulged for a moment, and then he could see the warming effect it had on her. She drew her hand away from his and put it across her chest.

"Wow. Powerful stuff."

"One more of those, and I'll take you dancing."

"I don't need one more of these to go dancing with you."

"You don't, but I will." Josh laughed. "Folks are always telling me to 'sit down before I make it rain'."

After the appetizers, the dinner came and they ate, making small talk across the candlelit table. They kept looking out the window over the bay and Misty kept marveling at the beauty as she sipped her drink and often touched Josh's hand when telling a story or listening to him tell one of his. At eight o'clock, they had finished eating and then argued for ten minutes over who was going to pay the bill, Josh finally let Misty flip the tab and pay the tip, but only if Misty would allow him to give her and her son a tour of the bay and Golden Gate on his boat, when Riley arrived, free of charge.

Hand in hand the new couple emerged from the restaurant, then down the stairs into the brick walled and floored courtyard where seventies music was being broadcast. In the background The Jackson Five was singing *I'll Be There* over the small speakers mounted on the eaves of the brick buildings that surround the square, coupled with the acoustics of trickling water from the fountain with a mermaid holding a merbaby. The sounds merged with the music to a perfect rhythm. Josh stopped to listen to the music and Misty raised her leg to the brick lined step of the fountain and tied her high strapped sandal string. When she lowered her leg, she saw Josh was standing over her.

"What?" She asked with a smile.

"Dance?"

"Here? Now?"

"Best music in town, I love this song. It reminds me of when I was a kid."

"Really? I mean, you really remember this music that well?"

Josh closed his eyes and smiled, he thought of the songs that shaped his childhood.

"Those were some of the best days of my life."

"Mine too." Misty held out her hand for Josh.

Josh gave a bow and took her hand, and amongst a dozen people sitting around eating chocolate sundaes at little tables, they began to dance. They danced the rest of the song out. Next up was *I Like Dreamin'* by Kenny Nolan and Misty pulled Josh close to her, his hand slipped slightly to the top of her behind from her mid-back. He leaned the side of his head on hers and they shuffled to the soft music. He could smell her shampoo, a soft perfume on her neck and his insides were turning summersaults.

Misty could feel the familiarity of the man she was holding, the body next to hers trembled with excitement

71

and fear, anticipation and impatience. She could barely detect a hint of cologne, a whiff of sweat-just enough to tantalize. She pulled herself back slowly, enough to be within striking distance with Josh.

Their eyes focused on each other reflectively; each could see themselves in the other's eyes. Josh moved his head slowly forward; Misty tilted hers just a little to the right. Their lips touched, a shot of electricity shot through Josh's body as her lips closed on his. He felt…just right. This was perfect, but there was something here that seemed in place, she was…familiar. They stayed there, her lips, his, for minutes. He felt the rush of what he had missed for so long. He had felt the answer to his wonder of the perfect kiss at the perfect time, the perfect moment, the perfect woman.

Josh pulled back. He stepped back and Misty frowned at him.

"What's wrong?"

"This is familiar. I mean, like déjà vu. You know? Something isn't right. It just can't be this, this perfect…"

"Like you've done this before? Or like you'd expected more of me?" She asked cautiously.

"Like, I don't know. Like…" He held out his hands palms up. Then he smiled. "I think, I'm falling in love with you and I've only known you for a week…"

Misty stepped towards him. "How could that be familiar unless you've done that before?"

"No. I just…I…"

Misty moved slowly into his chest and used her lips to grab his lower lip. Then she placed her hand behind his head and pulled him to her. They kissed for a few more minutes, then walked towards the stairs, Misty leaning into Josh. They didn't hear the quiet little *ahhs* behind them from the sundae eating patrons sighing at the couple.

J Jay Ross

CHAPTER SEVEN
That Night

The door opened slowly to Josh's apartment. Josh reached
in and pushed the button for the lights. As with everything
else in his apartment, the light switch was the original dual
push button, and the not so original cool fluorescent
flickered then bathed the room in a soft glow that gave
shadows a softer shape, which made the room look larger
than it was.

"After you." Josh motioned his hand inwards for
Misty.

Misty stepped in, her high heeled sandals clacking
on the hardwood mahogany flooring after she crossed the
doorway. She closed her eyes and inhaled slightly, trying to
catch the ambience of the room, to feel with all of her
senses. Opening them she touched the tops of the couch
and table as she walked to the large Victorian angled bay
window. She had expected, and was not disappointed; the
view out from the half-octagon window was spectacular.
You couldn't see much outside; the fog had crept in while
they were driving here from the restaurant, but she was
feeling a tingle. She felt like talking away the moment, she
was not sure why, but she did.

"You know, when I drive by places like this, I look
into these windows. It seems everyone has the curtains
open for some reason, like they are allowing outsiders to
get a glimpse into their lives. I've always wanted to look
out one like this."

"The only way I was going to live here was one;
find a place by the ocean and two; the place had to have

one of these windows so I could look out and see the sea. Sorry for the view though. Would you like me to describe it for you?"

"Yes. Please do."

Josh set his keys on the table by the door after he closed it and locked it. He took off his sport coat and tossed it on the back of the couch as he walked to where Misty was standing in the bay window. He put his arm around her and pulled her to him, her warmth made his body heat up fast.

"Well, if you look off to your left here," he said, pointing, "you *would* see the tops of hundreds of eucalyptus trees."

"Fascinating." Misty whispered into his ear, teasingly.

"Then over here, you'll get a bird's eye view of the street we drove up on and parked my truck. Bird's eye of course if you were sitting on a ledge outside the window."

"Uh huh." Misty kissed Josh's cheek.

Josh was becoming aroused and his voice crackled a little, which made Misty giggle.

"And, if you look straight ahead, you'd see Ocean Beach. That is of course, in the eighteen hundreds. The trees and Sutro Heights Park block the view, and there was no way I could afford a place that overlooked the beach on a sailor's salary."

"Very romantic. Hey *sailor*, how 'bout a dance?"

Misty turned into Josh's arms and pressed her lips to his. The kiss was teasing and passionate, she pulled back a few inches from Josh and sighed with a smile looking up at his neatly trimmed goatee and blue eyes. Josh and Misty swayed to an imaginary band playing a favorite song, turned and sashayed, and Josh managed to get close enough to the stereo. Clicking on the radio, he was embarrassed to hear the station was tuned to the local weather-Josh listened to this every morning for boating information-so he quickly

75

gave the pre-tuned buttons a push until he found the seventies and eighties station. The Bee Gees filled the room with *Too Much Heaven*, and the dance slowed to a shuffle and rub.

Misty had her eyes closed and could feel her emotions melting into her desires, she whispered as she looked over the crook of Josh's arm, "The view is perfect anyways…"

"The view is remarkable, from here…" Josh remarked as he stole a glance down Misty's dress as she pulled back, albeit, for that reason.

"Of course it is."

She reached up and slid her left hand under the right string-straps from her dress, then repeated the action with her right hand on the left side. Her dress fell to the floor silently. Misty's hands tugged upwards on Josh's shirt and managed to get it out of his pants. Then she fumbled with his belt, when she let go a laugh.

"What is this?" She looked down and saw an oversize *49ers* belt buckle.

"Gotta root for the home team." Josh said with a shrug.

He placed his hands on both sides of her face and used his thumbs to brush her bangs out of the way. He kissed her on one side of her face, then the other. He could smell the citrus shampoo and the slightly sweet aroma of her perfume again. It made his head spin, he moved his lips back to hers, as he did he could smell her perspiration on her neck, mixed with pheromones and he slowly guided his mouth back down to her neckline, Misty moaned with pleasure.

Josh picked Misty up from the waist to her tippy toes and slowly walked to the bedroom, secretly in his mind he hoped he didn't leave his dirty clothes on the bed. After struggling with the doorknob and Misty again giggling at him, the heavy wooden door gave way and hit the wall with a bang, as Josh pushed Misty backwards towards the bed.

Misty could feel the soft feather pillow bed cover as she was lowered carefully upon it. She breathed in Josh's musk from the covers as she slid up towards the headboard while Josh undressed, clumsily, in front of her in the dark room. Her body tingled almost to the point of pain as she waited for him, waited for this day.

Josh crawled to Misty's face as he ran his hands along her thighs and calves, he placed kisses every now and again on her body, from her belly to between her breasts, to the nape of her neck. She was nearly writhing now, this moment had come. For both of them.

At two in the morning, they broke each other's embrace with a heavy sigh. Josh lay back against his propped up pillow and Misty did the same, pulling hers closer to his. Even though it was in the fifties outside, it was too hot to have the covers over them, so the soft cotton sheet was pulled down to the foot of the bed, the comforter on the floor and blanket was twisted around one of the support posts. Josh moved his head onto Misty's arm and she cradled his it, he could hear her heartbeat and her breath going in and out. It was the most relaxing thing he had ever heard, ever...

Josh started twisting a bead of sweat on Misty's tummy, chasing it around her naval and the fine little blond hairs just beneath; the moisture glistened in the moonlight coming in the bedroom window. He looked up to her eyes, which were following the impromptu game of tag on her abdomen and he asked, "So, what do you do all day if you don't work?"

A smile crossed her lips and she softly looked over to his eyes, which were playful at this point and replied, "Nothing. Absolutely nothing."

"Sounds great."

77

She raised her back a little causing his head to sink into her armpit and laughed a little, "Are you kidding me? I know now why housewives are drinking by noon."

"Seriously?"

"Seriously. I get up around eight; I have the house cleaned by ten. The soap operas are all the same after a while, the news at noon is devastatingly sad and my neighbor is usually stoned by then."

She drew her hand up to her face and wiped an itch near her eye, causing Josh's head to fall to his pillow. He let out a chuckle as he struggled to get his right arm free, it was behind her back and his hand was on her buttocks.

"So, I just sit around watching the flowers grow."

"Must be rough."

She smiled at him with a tiny crook on her lips as if there was a little pity on them and asked, "What do you do all day?"

"Get up before dawn. Before I finish my first cup of coffee I'm out the door and off to the pier to warm up the boat. I stop at the Mexican's place to buy bait and spend the rest of the day rigging and re-rigging snagged lines for the charters. Then I wash the vomit and fish guts from the deck just before I go home."

Misty let out a pout and said, "Ah yes, '*They that go down to the sea in ships, that do business in great waters, these see the works of the Lord and his wonders in the deep.*' "

"The Bible?" Josh sat up.

"Uh-huh. *Psalms 107:23-24.*"

"You read the Bible?"

"I told you, I have a lot of time on my hands. Besides, I love the sea. The open ocean, it's like an open book with no writing in it. You fill in the pages as you sail along, you write the story as you go…"

"Wow. You like Hemingway too?"

"That wasn't Hemingway. It was me. I write poetry sometimes, when I'm home alone."

"You are lonely all day huh? Maybe I should come around on my days off and cheer you up? Or maybe pop in on my way home from work in the afternoons."

"A...*nooner?*" Misty let out a belly laugh. "I've never had one."

"It starts like this..."

Josh rolled onto Misty's legs and slid up her stomach to her lips. He kissed them lightly and then added purpose, he was able to wrest his arm free from behind her to cradle her head.

Around four a.m., Misty got up to use the bathroom and turned on the light, which blinded Josh who lifted his head to watch her wiggle her little behind as she went.

"Ow!"

"Sorry." She responded with a smile and a wiggle of her butt as she closed the door.

Josh sat up and turned the nightstand light on next to the bed. He rubbed his eyes and then smiled at the closed bathroom door, finding a new relaxation in the comfort of his own bed, a resting mind he had not had in over seven years. And a beautiful energetic woman to share his night with was the icing on a long waited period of loveless encounters and bad dates.

Misty stepped out of the bathroom and shied behind the door. "Hey, that's not fair!"

"What?"

"The light!"

"You turned the bathroom light on!"

"Yeah, but that was my silhouette. Back-lighting, I don't think you're entitled to a full flooded scenic tour yet..."

"Oh. Nice necklace." Josh grinned, without moving to turn out the light.

Misty reached up and touched the golden jewel piece and ran her fingers sexily down the rope style chain to the locket. She undid the clasp behind her neck and balled the whole thing up in her hand as she made three long steps towards the bed, then jumped on it giggling as Josh was sent to the edge, almost tumbling off. She held the necklace out for him to see.

"It was my grandmother's. She wore it everyday, and night."

Misty handed it over to Josh and he inspected the locket, opening it and frowning at the picture inside of a small white dog, curly little hair and a poof tail.

"Who is this?" He asked confused.

"That's Marmot. He was my grandmother's dog."

"Oh."

Josh then looked at the cover on the other side of the gold heart shaped keepsake, he found an inscription, the words were half English, which he understood and another language he didn't.

"What does '*Bara en blick över my shoulder*' mean? Is it Irish?" Josh asked.

Misty took the locket from him and closed it with a small frown then hung it around her neck again. She spun the chain around her neck a few times while staring at Josh.

She said, "I promise, I'll tell you about it someday. It's a close thing to me; the time has to be right."

"Uh, sure." He paused for a moment, running her words around in his head and then looked up at her, "Okay. Is everything alright?"

She smiled and kissed him on the cheek, he did the same to her; she bit lightly at his neck and then playfully tugged at his ear with her teeth. After a few moments of giggling and wrestling, they were engaged in passion again.

Josh woke to the sound of Misty banging things around in *his* kitchen. Suddenly he realized that he had a huge mess in there from the day before. He leapt from the bed and pulled on a pair of sweatpants that was resting catty whompus on the chair by the window of the bedroom. Just as he made it to the hallway, he spotted her moving around and decided to spy on her a little. *Nothing freaky about that?* He thought.

Misty, oblivious to her secret admirer, was not out of her sorts at all about the cleanliness of the place. She was standing in the kitchen in one of his T shirts and her panties, had just found the coffeemaker, full of cold and moldy coffee. She promptly dumped the old science experiment out and then located the grounds; after getting the brewer going to make a fresh pot, she fumbled around for a pan to fry bacon. Then, realizing she had missed a step, opened the refrigerator and found six half empty containers of Chinese take-out, an unopened expired half-gallon of milk and a plate of semi-eaten fried chicken. She pursed her lips, closed the fridge door and looked around the place.

The kitchen stood center of the apartment, the front door to her left as she looked towards the living room and the tall bay window. Although scuffed a little, the hardwood floors were in a fairly good state of polish, the one small Persian rug under the coffee table in the living room matched in a contrasting way. The faded and earthquake cracked plaster white painted walls were adorned with hundreds of photographs of fishing and family. She made her way to one of the family collages and stared at the picture of Josh with his mother and father from the seventies. They were standing in front of their house in Sparks, the bright green lawn and blue sky provided the background for the white on white home. She nodded her head at it and smiled, closing her eyes.

Misty turned and looked at the two small end tables, one held a phone; another a picture of a young woman. She stepped over for a closer look. The very petit brown haired

81

and blue eyed woman was clothed in a summer dress, smiling as bright as she could. *This must be Faith*, Misty thought.

Moving her eyes from there, the rest of the furniture was out of place. Several bookcases lined the other walls, and were nearly filled with paperbacks. Several hardbounds books were on sailing, boating, boating safety and emergencies at sea, etc. All Coast Guard issue, one even had a stamp on the cover that read; *Property of the United States Coast Guard*. Misty shook her head and replaced it on the shelf. Another photo of Faith was sitting alone on a shelf with just a brass bell about the size of a toaster next to it. Misty picked the photo up. Faith's eyes were darker now, the room she was in was barely lit and Misty could make out the faint sign that read "Oncology".

"That was two weeks before she died." Josh's voice behind her startled Misty.

"I'm sorry, I was just…"

"Don't worry about it. We loved a lifetime." Josh walked over and took the frame from her.

"She was smiling all the time. Everyone commented on how friendly and giving she was."

"She sounds special."

Josh smiled at Misty and kissed her. The essence of last night's lovemaking was still on her skin in the form of a slight metallic and salt taste and aroma.

Josh returned his gaze to the photograph and frowned.

"You won't find any food here, by the way. Let's shower and I'll treat you to my usual."

"Sounds wonderful." Misty hugged him as tight as she could, and then dropped her underwear and his shirt she was wearing off on the way to the bathroom. "See ya there…"

Josh smiled at the naked woman crossing his floor to the bathroom, then looked down at the photo of Faith again. He wiped the glass of dust on his sweatpants and placed the frame back on the shelf next to the bell shaped urn that held her remains.

"You knew this would happen, right?" He whispered to the photo, then nodded with a smile and headed off to the bathroom himself, scratching his behind as he walked.

Josh and Misty were in the shower for over an hour. Jeremy, Josh's hippie friend, would have had a heart attack over the amount of hot water they used. After separately drying off, they dressed into the clothes from the night before.

"Why do you have to wear that again?" Misty asked, indicating his clothes.

"I figured since you were wearing your dress from last night, then I'd look like I was up all night too."

"Very funny. But it is nice that you feel my pain."

"If you want, I'll run you by your place and you can change."

An instant look of fear crossed Misty's face. It faded just as quickly, she turned towards Josh, who was brushing his shirt with his palm, trying to flatten out some of the wrinkles.

"No. This will do. If it's a place you frequent, then I can't imagine they would care..."

Josh stuck his tongue out at her in the mirror. "You insult my friends, and their Piggly Wiggly bags."

"Sorry. Do you want some coffee?"

"No thanks. We'll get some at the restaurant."

"But I made a fresh pot."

"You threw out my weeks' worth of coffee?"

"It was old."

"I still drink it."

"You're very weird."

J Jay Ross

Josh walked over and kissed her on her neck, even though the soap washed away the scent of their lovemaking, he still felt aroused just by tasting her skin.
"Of course, I live in San Francisco."

CHAPTER EIGHT
November 26th, 2001

Josh had walked Misty the two blocks from his apartment on 45th ^{and} they'd seated themselves at a table facing outside looking towards Sutro Heights Park. The sidewalk was still wet from the heavy fog last night and even though the fog had lightened a little, a dark cool haze hung over the area, obscuring the view of the Sutro Bath House remains. Josh had poured them both a cup of fresh coffee. Leslie was nowhere to be found.

"So, you just help yourself?"

"I know the owner fairly well, and the waitress," He looked around, "...usually is here by now."

Josh reached across the table and took Misty's hand. She squeezed and smiled at him. A flash of sadness crossed her face at that moment, and this time Josh had seen it.

"You alright?"

"Yes." She looked down at the table. "Just a little tired I guess."

"You should try to get some more sleep at night."

Misty smiled at him and shook her head. "I'll keep that in mind, next time. And you should too..."

Josh looked out the window at a woman jogger who crossed from one side of Point Lobos Avenue to the north side. She had a German shepherd running along wildly at her side; he looked at Misty, who was taking a sip of her coffee.

"Where's Carter?"

"Who?" Misty looked lost for a second, and then regained her composure. "Oh him. My neighbor watches him for me. She's a real animal person. There're a few animal persons here in this town."

"I know. I wish I had a dollar for every guy who wanted to bring his dog along on a charter. Come to think of it, I do. I charge twenty dollars extra."

"Ouch. I better leave him at home then."

"When?"

"You promised me a cruise when Riley gets here, remember?"

"Sorry, yeah. I was still wandering around my memories of last night." He smiled at Misty coyly.

A voice from behind them asked, "If by last night you mean the hours before you came in here and made yourself a pot of coffee?"

Leslie had stepped into the restaurant from the back; she was wearing her usual work clothes and was carrying a metal clipboard.

"Hi Les. Where've you been?"

"Ron's running late today. I had to check in the food order."

Ron was the chef and manager.

"Leslie, this is Misty." Josh introduced.

Each of the women gave a hard glance at the body features, and then their eyes narrowed at one other's.

"Hi."

"Hello."

"Are you eating today, Mr. K?" Leslie didn't break eye contact with Misty.

Josh pointed a finger at himself. "What happened to Jimmy?"

Leslie broke off the staring contest and looked at him. "I don't know, I figured it just sounds cooler, you know?"

"You've thought about this? I mean what to call me? I'm touched." Josh smiled. "How about two specials please, and juice?"

"Orange or apple?"

"Orange." Josh looked to Misty who nodded her approval. Leslie walked towards the far corner of the restaurant where the grill was.

Misty leaned into Josh. "She likes you."

"I'm old enough to be her dad."

"This is the two thousands; we've overcome the age gap."

"Hardly. She's just jealous. I've never been with anyone here before."

"I feel special then."

"You should. I've never been with anyone anywhere in nearly four years."

"Wow. No wonder you were so wound up last night!" Misty exclaimed a little too loud.

Leslie's head popped up above the grill area to see Misty holding her mouth as if she were caught talking in class. She shook her head and looked down as she prepared the meal, then lowered it back to where she could easily listen in and not be seen.

Misty said to Josh, "Well, to be honest, it's been nearly a year for me."

"And you hadn't forgotten anything…" He added; Misty just gave him a contempt look.

Leslie had appeared from behind the counter with the breakfast, as the couple was sharing another laugh over something Misty had said. Leslie set the plates down hard on the table and the water glasses rattled a little, Misty looked up with semi-apologetic eyes. She felt bad for this young girl, she was wearing a ring, but the little oriental girl had a crush on Josh, anyone could see it. It may be a playful flirting kind of relationship, but the waitress was looking out for him.

"Two specials. Anything else *sir*?" Leslie asked as she turned away.

Josh heard part sarcasm, part jealousy tone in her voice and decided he had better make nice. Leslie was after all, his only real friend beside Misty and Lester and he wanted to be sure she wasn't mad at him about something this simple. She was married after all...

"Hey, we're going for a trip out on the bay later. Would you like to bring uh, uh..." Josh forgot Leslie's husband's name, his eyes widened as he tried in earnest to recall it"...you know; your husband along?"

"Tim. And no thank you. Are you going out on your boat?" She asked, a little calmer.

"No. We were thinking about *Red and White* or maybe just a little charter. That way I don't have to drive and can have a libation or two. You're both more than welcome you know."

Apparently mentioning Leslie's husband had a cooling effect on her, she smiled broadly at Josh and poured him a little coffee, just enough to fill it to the rim. She took a deep breath and looked over to Misty and nodded at her cup. Misty smiled at her and nodded back, indicating she could use a warm-up also. Leslie smiled at her and repeated the pouring action, Misty flinched half expecting the hot brew to *accidentally* spill over.

Leslie took a moment and then said towards Misty's direction, "Thanks, both of you. But since I never see Mr. uh, *Josh* with anyone else here, I figure he could use the time with you, time alone. To get better acquainted."

Misty nodded and thanked her. Josh's mouth dropped open a little and it took a few moments for him to realize that he had solved the problem between the only two women currently in his life. One would burn his toast; the other could break his heart. *In times like these*, Josh thought, *it would be best to have both on my side...*

"Keep it in mind Les. If you or your husband ever wants to go out boating, let me know." He said, diplomatically.

"Thanks Mr. K. Tim gets seasick driving across the Bay Bridge, but I'll mention it to him. He loves fishing though too."

"We'll I usually have both occurrences on my boat anyways, so when he's in the mood, let me know."

Leslie smiled and walked away when two new customers walked in, probably hotel guests, and she immediately turned on the charm as she approached their table. Josh turned to Misty and rolled his eyes. Misty almost laughed out loud; she covered her mouth and looked out the window towards Point Lobos Avenue.

"Don't you have a charter or something today?" Misty asked after a bite of bacon.

"Nope. Its Thanksgiving weekend. Folks would rather spend it on the slopes near Tahoe or with their families than out on the bay. Even though the weather has been perfect so far, they just avoid spending money."

"Oh." Misty smiled and took another bite of her bacon, she hadn't had any this good in a long time; it was the maple. *Maple smoked, that's what it is*, she said to herself.

"That reminds me, I forgot to ask, how was your Thanksgiving?"

"Why did you forget?" Misty twirled her egg with her fork.

"Well, that dress you're wearing nearly made me forget who I was last night. I mean wow! When I saw you…"

Josh turned after realizing that he had raised his voice a little and Leslie was staring at him along with her new customers, who chuckled a little. Leslie just curled her lips up to her nose and walked back behind the counter to start breakfast for the new arrivals. Josh just turned a little red and lowered his voice.

"I was just glad to see you."

"It was so-so. I mean, how much fun can you have at a buffet downtown?"

"You had buffet too? Lester and I ended up at the Tandoori, how about you?"

"I forget the name, but it was Chinese…"

They ate breakfast, chatted and made eye contact constantly. Misty was a little shy about offering any more information about her dinner on Thursday, so Josh dropped the subject, and he was glad to; his wasn't a spectacular event either. They finished, had one more cup of coffee and Josh paid the check when Misty went to use the restroom. She wasn't very happy about it, but she let it slide since she knew Leslie would probably refuse to let her change 'Mr. K's' plans.

Josh helped Misty into his jacket, since in her haste to get out of her house last night to make her dinner engagement, she'd forgotten hers. He thought he wouldn't mind it too much, it probably had already warmed up to about fifty-five degrees outside and besides, he could hold her close to him as they walked, to wherever they were going.

Jacob McAllister was sitting in his office, his chair turned towards the window, his feet on the sill. He was tapping a pen to his temple; his rhythm mimicked the ticking of the grandfather clock in the corner of the office. The place was large, too large for the simple oak desk and flat screen monitor mounted on the wall just to the right of the frosted glass door; a few high dollar paintings garnished the walls, a few Remington sculptures were on pillars in the corners.

"Mr. McAllister, John Buckley on line one." His secretary's voice announced over the intercom.

"Thank you." He spoke to the phone bank. Then he lifted the receiver off the hook and pressed line one, without turning his chair.

"Buckley? I told you not to call unless you found them, so I take it, you found them?"

McAllister spun his chair around to face forward. He rested his elbows on his desk and set the pen down. Taking his right hand he massaged his temple where he had been whacking it with the ballpoint.

"Great. The boy too? Wonderful. Yes, payment will be made when I have verification of their whereabouts. Desjardins huh? Went back to her maiden name. Where? San Francisco? Jesus John, talk about hiding in plain sight. Misty, yeah. "

"How long before you can get all the information to me?" McAllister looked perplexed. "How long? Don't you have a fax? Oh. Okay, well, get that folder together and I'll make a payment so you can pay your sources. Now I'll have the whole thing in a week? Okay, you're sure she won't be gone by the time you get it to me? Good. Sounds as if she is expecting to stay a long time." *We'll see about that...*

McAllister rose and looked out the window behind him. "No. I'll take it from there John. This is something I have to do, she's going to pay for what she did, and the boy has to come home to his family. Just next-day me the details when you've collected it all, and when I see her myself, you'll get the rest of the fifty thousand. No, no cops. This is on me. If I find out you've been chatting with your old buddies from the PD, then the money will disappear and I'll make your life a living hell, got me? Good. Thanks again John. Bye."

Jacob hung up the phone with a satisfied smile on his face, like he had just won the lottery, not that it would matter. His company was built with his wife's money and he didn't have to share the benefits with her anymore. He didn't have to share a lot of things with anyone anymore as far as that was concerned. He had made plans, he had made choices, he had made an effort to remove his only competition-and that was a big one.

McAllister turned back to look out the window and survey the world below, the small world, full of small people. He would soon control a large amount of those people, their money, and their lives. Jacob smiled; when this is done and *Misty* gets what she deserves, there will be nothing to stop him, he'll have control over the family too.

He reached to the intercom button and punched it.

"Miss Taylor? I need an airplane ticket to SFO, a week after this Monday."

For the next week, Josh and Misty were nearly inseparable. After they left the Seal Rock Inn Restaurant Sunday morning, Josh invited Misty down to the beach for his usual walk on his days off; his regimen that kept him sane.

After shuffling along for several minutes quietly to take in the sound of the roaring surf, to smell the salty air and feel the mist of the light fog that covered the northern tip of the peninsula this nice morning they stopped and watched the waves roll in. Even though the fog made the skies look grey and foreboding, there was a relaxing feel to the atmosphere.

"Could you do me a little favor?" Misty asked with her eyes closed.

They had stopped just short of the surf as it approached the strand, the foamy white tail of seawater rolling a few feet from their shoes. Misty could feel the day becoming exhilarating, she knew that she should spend the day with her new beau, if he wanted to.

"Sure." Joshed looked at her and paused for a deep breath himself then said, "If you'll spend the day with me."

Misty smiled with her eyes still closed, she had her head tilted back to let the full effect of the beach surround her, slowly she lowered her head and looked at him.

"Well, that is just it."

"What is?" Now Josh had his eyes closed and his head tilted back, enjoying the fresh new day.

"I would like you to take me to Nordstrom's on Market. I need some clothes." She looked down at her dress.

Josh smiled and looked down to her, "I could just take you home and you can change there."

"No. I feel like some new clothes today, for a new chapter of my life." She leaned up and kissed him by his earlobe.

Misty's warm breath on the side of his face made his toes tingle; Josh felt a warming sensation trickle from the center of his chest to regions unaffected in recent years, a replay of the prior night flashed through his mind, causing a chill to run down his spine, he twitched his body to shake it off.

Misty stepped back and had a look of surprise on her face, she said, "Does that bother you?"

"No! I just had a shiver. Wow!" Josh blushed. "That'll never bother me."

"Good, I have so much saved up for you." She smiled and this time, they closed on each other.

Face to face, with the sound of the ocean in the background, the roar of the mighty water slamming into rocks offshore, the laughter of children building sand forts and a dog barking in the distance; passion rode high as Josh and Misty's body heat enclosed them. The grand kiss lasted minutes.

Instead of driving to Union Square, Josh drove Misty to Ghirardelli's Square and he miraculously found an open parking spot on the north side of the street a few hundred yards from Aquatic Park. From there the lovers made a slow walk up the street and waited to board the Powell-Hyde Line car, of the famous and fun Cable Cars of

J Jay Ross

San Francisco; at least that's how Josh described them as Misty gave him a concerned frown at the turntable.

Misty had been in the bay area for six months now, and had yet to ride one. She was hesitant because she didn't know the routes, and was afraid she'd get stranded somewhere.

"You don't have a car?" Josh asked. "You got all this money and no car?"

"I…have transportation. But I prefer to walk most places, it's good for you. If you recall, a reporter once asked Cary Grant how he stayed in such good shape, and Grant replied '*I take the stairs instead of the elevator*'."

Josh gave her an emotionless look, "Uh huh."

"No. Really. I walk just about everywhere, or cab it if I have to. But now, I have a man to chauffeur me around."

"Okay. Well, here's how it works…" Josh took Misty by her arms and slowly turned her to the crowd gathering at the boarding station. "Once the Cable Car comes down the hill there, the Gripman will slow the car down and stop here on this round table."

Josh paused to let Misty take it all in, then he said, "Quietly listen, to the street there…"

He pointed to the rails embedded in the asphalt and the center steel panel in particular. There was a low hum, almost a buzzing sound. Misty smiled back at him acknowledging she could hear the line running under their feet.

"I'll try not to be too technical, but this line runs up Hyde Street here, I think about fifteen thousand and seven hundred foot of hemp rope wrapped in steel wire or cable runs around nine and a half miles an hour. There are four cables left running in San Francisco; this one here on Hyde, then there's the Powell, the Mason and the California lines. We'll be on the Powell line when we turn inbound…"

"Inbound?" Misty asked.

"The route runs up to Powell and then the car turns around at Market and Powell. Then heads back downhill. Inbound is the most exciting, when we return, watch the Gripman. He puts on quite a show as we come up to California Street, because the two lines cross, the Gripman has to let go of the Powell Street cable or he'll cut the California cable in half."

Misty feigned a little excitement, it did sound fascinating though, "Wow."

A few tourists began to inch closer to Josh, they were pretending to take pictures, but in reality they wanted to hear more, he sounded educated; in fact he was. Josh loved the Cable Cars.

"But," Josh continued, "He has to let go at the precise moment, when the car is on the top of the hill or we'll lose momentum and roll back down Pine Street."

"I'm not sure this is the right time to be telling me about us rolling backwards down a hill." Misty said flatly.

"Well, after the Gripman drops the rope at the top and we cross the California cable, we coast down the hill for three and a half blocks without a cable. Just before that, you have to watch between the conductor and the Gripman as they work together. The conductor controls the speed of the car with the rear brake wheel in the back of the car."

"Okay. What's a Gripman?" Misty asked.

"The guy who stands in the inside front center of the car. He holds on to these two levers you see, one is the grip lever or the vise-like thing that surrounds the cable that is buried under the street. The other is the pad brakes, which instead of applying pressure to the wheels; it pushes a brake pad to that plate that surrounds the hole to the cable to slow the car." Josh pointed to the center plate in between the rails.

"That slows the car?"

"Well, the conductor has a brake at the back of the car, a little wheel he turns to apply brakes to the rear wheels, like I said, watch him when we go over the top of the hill. Then the Gripman has a foot brake in front of the levers that he can use to put pressure on the front wheels."

"It sounds kind of exciting." Misty said with a somewhat unsure smile.

"I haven't described it for anyone in so long; I guess it is kind of exciting. Now, we can get on here after they turn the car around, or we can board anywhere along the route, just by standing by one of these signs."

Josh pointed to a brown sign on a post. He continued, "You just wait till a car passes and hop on."

"While it's moving?"

"Of course."

The always original and tell-tale *CLANG! CLANG!* Of the car's bell could be heard.

Josh pointed to a Cable Car coming towards them, "See those white poles on the side of the car?"

Misty nodded.

"You don't have to ride inside or on the outside seats; you can hang on to the pole off the side there."

"What?"

"Just listen to the Gripman though; he'll holler instructions when it's time for you to lean into the car, like say, when you're passing another Cable Car or a bus or something."

Misty pursed her lips, "I'll be riding inside. Thank you."

The car stopped on the turntable, the riders got off, the conductor was then joined by the Gripman and the each took a side of the fancily decorated maroon and white car; just like you see in the *Rice-a-Roni* commercials, then the Gripman pulled a lever near his feet on the table, there was a loud clank under the platform, and the men pushed. The Cable Car rotated one hundred and eighty degrees, so the front of the car where the Gripman stood, was pointing up Hyde Street. The Gripman and conductor then moved to the back of the car and pushed it clear of the round turntable's tracks and onto the mains where the cable was humming underneath.

Misty smiled through the whole process; inside she was happy that Josh was enjoying himself too. She wondered how many times he stood somewhere in San Francisco along the route and watched this, with the same smile he had on his face right now. It was simplicity.

"Okay, board!" The conductor yelled to the ten or eleven people waiting to get on.

And they did so, in an orderly fashion. Naturally the tourists headed directly for the open part of the car, where the seats face towards the street. Josh took Misty's hand and led her to one of the inside benches and they sat down.

"I thought you wanted to ride on the outside?" She asked.

"Not really. You said you'd rather sit in here."

"Maybe I was just kidding."

"Okay, but watch…" Josh smiled and nodded with his head.

Just as he did, several late comers charged the car and pushed their way into the remaining few inches of space, crushing the tourists. Then a few others stood on the ledge, hanging onto the pole. It wouldn't have been so bad, but as the Gripman began his process of releasing the brake and gripping the steel cable that runs underneath the street, the car lurched a little and the hangers on were pushed in towards the seated folks.

"It can be kind of rough your first time, if you don't mind other people's butts in your face…"

"It's cozy enough in here." Misty ensured as she looked out the window.

As the car clattered up Hyde Street, Misty turned towards the driver or Gripman and watched him. He was dressed in a white long sleeved shirt, black pants and tough leather and worn work boots. He wore a grey vest and a dark coat, with several 'pieces of flair' pins on the lapels. He smiled widely at her and nodded, tipping his brown newsboy cap at her. She smiled back, and watched the show that Josh vividly described, and it was spectacular.

The Gripman was an artist at the controls, he danced the deck moving from one handle to the next, using the floor pedal to brake when needed and even taking the time to smile and nod at Misty or other riders who were entranced in his performance. He and the conductor signaled each other with the bell, and the clack-clack and groan of the steel wheels on the rails made for a real soundtrack surrounding the experience. She never knew what she was missing. The ride back was as exciting as Josh made it sound, she was in heaven.

After spending the afternoon at the malls around Market Street and eventually debarking the Cable Car back at Fisherman's Wharf, Misty stepped off the car dressed in her new purchases from Union Square, a pair of 505 Levis, a pale knit shirt with matching smart blue vest and new Adidas. Josh was still wearing what he had worn the night before.

"I don't see how it's particularly fair that you get to clean up."

"Hey," Misty defended herself, "I offered to buy you some clothes."

"I wasn't going to let you spend two hundred dollars on me."

"Why not? What did dinner cost last night? What's a tour of the bay on your boat going set you back in fuel?"

Josh considered this for a moment and just smiled, "That's not the point."

Misty appeared insulted, she shot back at him, "So what? You afraid of a woman having a little more cash than you?"

"No, I…"

"Are you afraid that I might tally up what I spend and then hold you accountable for it?"

"It's just that it isn't very gentlemanly to allow you to…"

"Gentlemanly? Hey, I let you get the doors for me today. I gave you my hand as we stepped up into the Cable Car. But I have money and you don't, so you think that you should have to pay for everything?"

"I have money…" Josh protested.

A smile finally came across Misty's face and at that moment Josh knew she was pulling his leg. She spoke softly and coyly, "I just like buying things for you."

Josh took a step into her and wrapped his arms around her neck and kissed her. He was a little turned on by her subtle stubbornness, the plastic bags with the clothes she wore last night and some new garments made a crackling sound as it was being crushed by the two. Minutes passed.

After Josh shuffled a few inches back from Misty, he took a deep breath and could smell her black cherry lip balm on his lips, which made his eyes sparkle at the thought of her sweet tasting kiss.

He tried to hide his lip smacking as he asked, "What now?"

"Well, I've seen the Wharf, the tourist traps, now I've just ridden in a Cable Car. We went to the gallerias, been to the beaches, what else is there to do?"

"Okay Jane Rockefeller, follow me." Josh said as he turned and headed for his truck.

When they reached Josh's Excursion, a yellow slip of paper was on the windshield between the wiper blades and the glass.

"A parking ticket!" Misty exclaimed a little loudly.

"Oops. Forgot about the parking hours." He slipped the ticket from its place and read the fine out loud, "$85.00"

Misty smiled mischievously, "Oops."

Josh put the ticket in his pocket and opened his Ford, "Oh well. Get in." He sighed.

He started the truck and made an illegal U-turn in the middle of Jefferson Boulevard just a little up the road from the Maritime Museum and headed back towards Pier 45. He turned on Taylor and made his way into the parking lot behind the Boudin Bakery and found a spot near the far southeast corner where he whipped into the space before anyone else could. Shutting off the engine, he felt a warm hand on his.

Misty had leaned over the center console and with her right hand drew Josh's face to the right; where her lips were waiting for his. Another long passionate kiss and some quick fondling nearly resulted in a backseat adventure, but they both realized after a few minutes of cars coming and going that it would be an embarrassing mistake, with parents and children traveling through the lot constantly. Misty pulled the sun-visor down and straightened her hair out; Josh did the same on his side of the car, to make sure he wasn't covered in lipstick or something.

They exited; both with huge smiles on their faces, and Josh led the way.

The afternoon sun had burned off the fog and the sounds of the streets and alleys had ramped up. Josh turned right and cut across the back of the lot by the pay center where people were supposed to slide their cash into a slot with the corresponding space number they were parked in. Josh had a pass in his truck; he paid one hundred a month for it.

Crossing Taylor the couple walked through the restaurant area and a covered area hall that led to the boats in a little marina. There were three lines of docks, one directly against Jefferson Street that most tourists could look down upon the fishing vessels; another in the center with a few older and more seasoned boats were tied; and the final row where sixteen were moored, some with a dingy laced alongside.

"Pretty." Misty said with a hint of sarcasm.

The area was enclosed with a square-like atmosphere, an opening on the northwest end was the access to the bay and open water.

"This is what I see every work day. Usually there aren't many boats here, but like I said, the holiday keeps most folks at home." He rebutted with mock seriousness.

"I'm sorry. It's charming, really." She smiled at his stern face, his frown melted. "Which one's yours?"

Josh looked to his right and along the last row of boats. Pointing to the far end he fingered the '74 Grand Banks. "There."

"Oh! Can we get closer? I've always wanted to be on an ocean boat."

Josh turned and took Misty by the hand and led her towards the gate that was marked with a rusty white sign that read in faded black letters,

RESTRICTED:
PASSENGERS AND CREW
ONLY BEYOND THIS POINT

"Scares a lot of folks away. I spend a half hour some mornings around here trying to find my charters. They don't realize they are the passengers." His head hung a little low as he pushed the gate open. "Sure would like to afford a slip by the wall over there some day."

Josh pointed to the wall that runs along Jefferson.

"How much are they?" Misty asked.

"I'm not telling." He answered.

"Why not?"

"Because you'll try to rent it for me and I can't have that on my conscience."

"Party pooper. If I was really serious I'd just ask the water master and get it for you anyways."

"Harbor Master." Josh corrected.

"Huh?"

"Harbor Master's Office. You said *water master*. That's the guy that reads the water meters on the streets."

"Oh." She pulled him close to her and wiggled. "Maybe you can teach me all this sea lingo one day."

Josh smiled as he held the gate open for her and followed her; she was stepping fast towards the boat he pointed out. They passed the bait shop and the older Mexican came out and greeted Josh.

"Buenos Dias Señor Kennedy."

"Good morning…" Josh was searching for the man's name. He always forgot this fellow's name.

"Chava…" The man answered with a smile.

""Good morning Chava!" Misty exclaimed as she passed him with a smile.

Chava smiled widely back at her and winked at Josh as he strode by. Josh shook his head and patted the man on the shoulder. The lovers walked down to the third from the last slip, to the older well used boat lifting and sinking slowly with the surge.

An otter was cruising in the water near the back of the vessels; he stopped to look at the newcomers and slipped under the surface as they approached. Misty slowed her pace and smiled at the sight of the mammal then her eyes turned towards Josh's fishing boat. She smiled at the boat and then at Josh.

"*Battered Sole*." She read the name on the wooden plaque on the bow as they approached the ladder rail with the chain across it. "It's very…"

"Homely?" Josh added.

"Oh no…I love it. It looks well used, but that's good on boats. Isn't it? I mean, what good is a boat that looks like it's never been out to sea?" Misty leaned over the rail. "Can we go aboard?"

"If you want. But no sailing today, the tide is coming in and the water's going to be pretty rough. Besides, I want to save it for the next Saturday." Josh fished his keys out his pants pocket and opened the rusty lock on the chain.

Josh climbed down first and then helped Misty the final three steps on the ladder. She immediately began walking around the deck, touching everything and admiring the finer points. She came to the gangway and the locked door. Josh stepped next to her and frowned.

"What?" Misty asked as she saw his expression.

"Lester. He was supposed to be here today. But if this is locked, then he didn't even come home last night to sleep."

"Where would he have gone?"

Josh pursed his lips and whispered, "I'm afraid to ask or find out…"

Misty giggled a little and tugged at the rusty lock on the hasp. "Can I see inside?"

Josh took a little breath and said, "No, I don't want you to see it this way. The cabin is probably a mess and the head-that's sailor talk for bathroom-would probably scare you away from here forever."

"Oh, it can't be that bad…"

"Trust me." Josh stepped back and offered his hand to Misty so they could go up to the bridge. "Another time."

"Awe, I wanted to have my first real *seaside excursion*." She winked at him as he hoisted her up.

"Oh god! Not in that bed…" Josh curled his lips in disgust, he didn't even want to think what Lester did in the bed, let alone lie in it himself.

Misty again toured the deck above where the wheel and controls for the *Sole* were; she rubbed her hand on the old fashioned rudder wheel and said, "You and I have to try *it* out somewhere on here, someday."

Josh smiled and nodded, "That…we will have to do…" Though he doubted it would be on this piece of garbage.

Misty slipped over the high railing and down to the mid-deck then sauntered to the pulpit, Quint's Point. She slowly ventured off to the end of it, her hands were white at the knuckles on the thin rails, but she pretended it didn't bother her much.

"Maybe in the summer," She said with a tone of uncertainty, sadness even, as she stared out over her right shoulder to the breakwater, "…when the sun is setting and the moon is rising. We could lie out on the deck there and sip wine, eat cheese and talk about our future. Then make love like it was our first time together."

Misty slowly exhaled and looked back over her shoulder at Josh, who was almost drooling at her spoken thoughts. He sighed lightly and replied simply, "Yes."

"Josh, this is very nice. I envy you."

"And I you. Shall we trade lives for a day? You can have Lester, the charters, the *Sole* and I'll stay at your place watching soaps and reading the Bible."

She smiled back at him, but her smile revealed a deeper sadness, deeper than the one in her voice moments ago. She knew he would never want to have her life, at least not with the baggage of a past she carried with her every day. "Maybe." He might not even want *her* living her life as it is…

The day on the boat ended as Josh helped Misty up the ladder to the street level. Once atop he wrapped his arm around her and asked coyly, "You, with all your money, have never had sex on cruise ship or anything like that?"

"A cruise ship is like a floating hotel. It's not the same."

Josh's heart slowed a beat and he felt a sudden dejection, "So that's a yes, huh?"

They had a lunch-dinner at *Tarantino's* then walked the street from there down Jefferson towards Aquatic Park, down the stairs to the beach just as the sun began to set behind them, in the summer months the sun set behind Marin a little more north and that would have been a romantic moment Josh thought. A man was swimming back and forth across the little bay, not noticing how cold the water was or afraid of the big sharks overplayed in the movies.

Misty stopped at the end of the beach looking up to the Maritime Museum above them.

"Josh, this has been the most…" She paused to find the right words as she looked at the ripples the swimmer was making off in the distance, "…unbelievable days of my life."

He rubbed her shoulders and pulled her tight.

"Well, we can do it all again all week. I don't have any work until Friday, so we can do more. Maybe go see the *Pampanito* an old World War Two submarine, or the *Jeremiah O'Brien* a troop ship from then too. Did you know that they filmed the engine room sequences from *Titanic* in it?"

Josh paused as he saw a look of disdain on Misty's face. She was semi-listening, her mind was obviously elsewhere. She responded to him though, "No, let's save those for when Riley gets here. He'd love that stuff more than I would."

"Okay, how about driving down the coast? We could stop off in San Jose and catch a hockey game, spend the night at the *Hotel De Anza* there. Or we could even go further down to Santa Cruz and hit the boardwalk. Maybe even to Monterey to see the aquarium."

She turned and sighed her biggest breath yet. Misty folded into Josh's arms and felt his chest expanding and contracting, his heart was pounding away, she noticed this whenever she got closer to him.

"Perhaps later. Let's finish today and then talk about tomorrow, tomorrow."

The week traveled by lightning fast for the couple. Josh and Misty spent hours mainly walking the beaches talking about all the stuff Josh suggested on Sunday, but instead found themselves in each other's arms by evening at his place. Misty only went home for one day, to 'catch a breather' and then finished Thursday with him. All was well, except the fact that both had a dark secret to tell the other and neither one of them could figure out how. They both secretly vowed to themselves they would tell the other, and that everything would work out fine and their lives would be perfect together. But things rarely work out in real life.

Misty spent the following weekend at her place, alone she said, and couldn't wait to see Josh and keep him to herself again Monday morning.

The plane from Los Angeles touched down on runway 28 Left and taxied to gate B 20 at eleven fifteen. The crowds were small, as usual for a Monday afternoon, only six or seven thousand folks meandered, wandered lost, or was rushing to catch a connecting flight. Their sweaty and wrinkled clothed bodies filled the airport spaces and harried aroma the air.

Jacob McAllister had only one bag, his carry-on. He headed straight out of the terminal and found a cab waiting; he climbed in and before the driver had a chance to ask said, "St. Francis." There were no pleasantries exchanged. The driver pulled off towards Powell Street, twelve miles away.

Misty had opted for a walk along the beach. It was Wednesday now and she was a little sad for some reason Josh couldn't grasp. They had eaten breakfast and Josh left an extra-large tip for Leslie, feeling somewhat guilty about cheating on her again. They had crossed Point Lobos Avenue from the Seal Rock Inn and were now headed south down the steep graded sidewalk past Tony's and were just a few yards from the front of the Cliff House.

Just as they passed the fine restaurant, Misty headed for the ramp off to the right which gives tourists a spectacular view of the ocean and the rock islands off the point directly in front of the ruins. Josh followed; he was carrying to-go cups of coffee for them both. Misty told him she had decided to walk to her apartments from there, since it was only two miles away.

"It is always so beautiful here. I can never get enough of this."

"Reason three I moved here," Josh smiled as he reached her, "chicks dig the scenery."

"Chicks? Wow, it's been a long time since I was called that."

The woman jogger with the German Shepherd was making her way up the sidewalk towards the top of the hill again, the dog had his tongue out so far Josh thought it would probably be dragging by the time they reached the cross street.

"I used to be in that good of shape." Misty commented after the woman flashed by.

"I haven't seen any difference."

Misty thought for a moment about what to say, then settled for; "Thank you."

The mist was burning off as the sun heated the fog from above; the air had a taste of brine, decaying veggies from the broken kelp on the shore, and tinges of automobile exhaust from the cars on Great Highway. Josh led Misty to the first break in the concrete wall that dropped to the beach. The tide was low, so the walk to the waterline was dozens of steps further, but after a few minutes of slogging in sandals and street shoes, the couple made it.

A black over red tanker was off in the distance, visible now as the fog pulled away miles from shore, the tanker was steaming towards the Middle East, most likely for a fill-up. A gentle wind blew the echo of the foghorn on the base of the Golden Gate across the opening of the bay, and it bounced off building, rock, tree and concrete as it settled over the nearly empty beach. Even though the day was still grey in color, blue was appearing fast to the east.

Josh had handed Misty her coffee as they stepped onto the sand from the stairs up by the highway, and they both silently sipped at the hot brew as they gazed out over the immense grey blue water in front of them. A couple with their children were heading down the surf line with a small dog on a leash, the dog yapping wildly at the white foam as it broached on the sand.

Josh looked to Misty; her eyes were slightly red around the cornea. Contacts, she wore contacts, he told himself. Misty finally felt his gaze burden her long enough and looked directly at him.

"What?"

"You need to wash out your contacts, your eyes are red."

Misty blushed, but hid her immediate shame over Josh's discovery. "I'm okay."

"If you say so. What do you want to do today?"

"I've got so much to do at home; I can't possibly spend any more time having fun…"

"Do you want some help?" Josh dumped out the rest of his coffee on the beach, he felt a twinge coming on, and he didn't want the jitters spoiling his kiss goodbye.

"No, thank you. Just some chores I've been neglecting since I met you."

Misty smiled slyly at Josh as he opened his mouth in protest. She reached up and touched her fingers to his face, which had a chill on it from the moist air. The sensation of his stubble on her fingertips made her tingle from her arm down to her toes, a feeling she had not felt in a long while.

"I'm pretty good with a vacuum, or dust rag, if that's what you've got planned." Josh broke her thoughts.

Misty pursed her lips and looked over to him.

"I'm sorry."

Josh asked, "For what?"

"I…I've…haven't had, well, it's been two years since I…I don't want you to think I'm cheap…" A tear formed in the corner of her eyes and she leveled them at the incoming waves.

"No! Not at all, I was a little over exhilarated by our…week."

"You see, that's what I…"

"I haven't been with another woman since Faith passed away." Josh added, interrupting her. "I was aggressive that night, I mean, wow. I had forgotten what it was like to have your body feel so much…"

"Pleasure?"

"Closeness. I've been so busy with the boat and the bills and keeping Lester out of bars, I didn't have much time to be so close to another woman. I'm glad we had *that* kind of evening."

"Me too."

Misty shifted her gaze back and forth from Josh to the ocean, the waves were roaring now hundreds of yards from shore, which meant a storm was coming in. She could feel the wind pick up as it trickled across her face, blowing a strand of her hair into the corner of her mouth. With a quick swipe of her finger, it was back, waving in the breeze. She felt the urge to say something she had been holding back on for a while, she tried to change the direction of the conversation away from sex, and she was becoming warm inside at the thought of spending another night with Josh Kennedy.

She said, "So, tell me. When I used to see you at Tony's, staring out the window, what were you thinking of, Faith?"

Josh smiled slightly and thought for a moment. Of course he did, most of the time. When you're alone and the one you love has gone forever, you can't help but think of her most of the time. But he wanted to get away from the subject of Faith. He was feeling intense inside about Misty, the tingles her glance brought him, the way her fingers felt so good on his chest, the little chirps of breath when she was excited.

"Sometimes. Mostly I just look out over the ocean and dream of sailing off and never coming back. And a lot of the time I just look at the Sutro Bath House and wonder, try to see how it was when it was still standing in all its glory. What it must have looked like inside, the laughter of its clientele, the splashing of the water from the kids jumping in, just the joy the place held."

"You mean like people wearing those funny bathing suits that covered all of their bodies?" Misty giggled as she rubbed her shoulders.

Josh laughed, "Yeah, that too." He stumbled over a piece of rotting kelp. "I just love it here, for those little things. So much…history, so much is gone, so much more for me to discover. That's one reason why I didn't leave when Faith died."

Josh accepted the fact that Faith would always be a part of his life, even after she had died, it was hard to stop thinking about her, even as this beautiful and strange woman stood in front of him, wriggling into his jacket he was putting on her shoulders.

"Thank you." Misty inhaled Josh's light cologne on the jacket as he adjusted it for her.

"Think nothing of it." Although the image of her in his coat would burn in his mind all day.

"Do I seem cold to you? I mean, not being as melancholy about my husband; or as you are about Faith's death?" Misty lowered her head like she was concentrating on the sand beneath her feet, but she didn't want to look in his eyes right now.

"No. I'm sure you have your reasons, right? You said he cheated on you, maybe you grieve in your own little way, I don't know."

"Maybe." *But if you knew the truth, you'd grab your jacket and run back to your house...* She didn't say. "So, here we are. An outcast and a widower."

"Lovers..."

"Yeah..."

The breeze turned to a small gust of cold sea air, Josh's jacket flapped up and the skirt Misty was wearing lifted nearly to her waist. She quickly took her hands from holding the coat closed to pushing down on the dress before the few gatherers at the beach got a peep show. She had purchased the underwear with Josh in mind, not all of Ocean Beach.

They walked in silence for a few more minutes; both had so much to say to one another, so many things were yet to be asked. But for right now, quiet seemed appropriate. When they had reached the halfway point of the beach, directly in across of Lincoln Way, the street that would lead up through Golden Gate Park to Misty's apartment, she slowed and stopped. They had sauntered four thousand feet from the time they entered the beach up near the Cliff House. Josh had not walked more than three quarters of a mile in years, his legs and feet ached.

"I've got to rest a sec..." He said, and plopped down into the sand, wiggling his butt to make a comfortable hole for it.

Misty giggled and kneeled beside him slowly, using the hem of her dress to keep the sand off her.

She said, "Want me to call you a cab?"

"No. Just give me a minute." He playfully panted. Josh took a few deep breaths and smiled at Misty, who was looking over the rolling water again. "Can I walk you home? All the way I mean."

Misty never broke her gaze on the crashing sea, white with fury on the top, deep green and blue in the curls below. "No, not today." She paused, hoping he would drop the subject, but added; "The place is a mess."

"So was mine, show me yours 'cause I showed you mine?" He slyly smiled.

Misty smiled out over the water a few yards in front of them, and then slowly looked into Josh's eyes. "Saturday night, come over for dinner and meet my son."

"If I can't follow you home today, how will I know where to go Saturday?"

Misty pursed her lips at him and sighed heavily through her nose.

"I don't believe you could make the walk through the park and up the hill to my complex, I'm behind on my First Aid training and might have to let you die from heart failure."

Josh blew a breath out between his lips, almost making a raspberry sound. Misty reached over to him and touched his face; he looked away playfully, then shot his gaze right into her eyes, as deep as he could penetrate. Her eyes still seemed a little red, she kept blinking.

"I could easily fall in love with you, just so you know..." He said.

Now it was Misty's turn to look away, but not with the same mirth as Josh had used, he noticed this.

He asked, "What? Is that wrong?"

"No, I guess not. I...I'm afraid."

She wanted to reveal her reason, but she did secretly want him to walk her up the hill to her complex-not to the apartment-but to the gate at least. If she told him what she was afraid of, he might just leave her here in the sand and head home.

"Of what?" Josh cocked his head like a dog trying to understand its favorite phrases.

"That I could do the same with you."

"Is that so bad?"

"No, not at all. But we've only known each other for a week, it's been years since I have had feelings like this and I don't want to ruin them, with a thought or two about a permanent relationship."

"You don't want permanency?"

"I can't have it right now."

"It's not like your job is taking you away, what's wrong with San Francisco? I mean other than the smelly sailors and their drunken uncles and the usual weirdoes?"

Misty let an easy smile flash at Josh. She had to think fast, or she just might belt out the truth, and then everything would be over. "I'm trying to find the best school for Riley."

"I thought your in-laws had custody?"

Misty didn't flinch, one thing she learned, was not to show weakness when caught in a lie.

"You never know, things might work out for the better." *You idiot! Try to keep your house in order...* She thought to herself.

Josh never registered anything other than concern. "Yeah, that would be great for you huh?"

"Yes. It would."

Josh looked away for a few moments and then back. "How about I walk you through half the Park, then let you finish on your own?"

Misty thought about this for a moment and replied, "Sure. Do I get to borrow your jacket?"

113

"If you'd like, but I figure by the time we reach Cross Over, the sun will be out and you'll be too warm."

"Then walk me to there, I'll give you your coat back, and I can get back to the cave and clean it up."

"Then you can have me over for dinner?"

"Not so fast, Saturday remember?"

"Sure, that's when your son is due?

"Around there," Misty hesitated, thinking fast again; "we can have a meet and greet."

Josh smiled, tickled inside he was going to get a glimpse into Misty's life finally.

"I'll even change my clothes after work."

"Or I can serve fish, then the place will smell as bad as your clothing…"

"Keep it up and I'll invite Lester to do the evening's entertainment."

Misty laughed out loud; the loudest Josh had heard her to date. "Now that's a sight I'll never get out of my head!"

They both shared a laugh about Lester at his expense as they trudged up the hill along Golden Gate Park, along Lincoln Way. After the giggles, Josh had to take a few deep breaths, Misty took him by the hand and squeezed. Josh looked down at her hand and smiled up at her.

He said, "Where is it you live up here?"

"Off of Carl, on Willard."

Josh's eyebrows went up. "You mean across from Kezar?" He stopped walking. "In a house?"

"Yes, why?"

"Because…" The accusation froze in his mouth. Things were going well with Misty; he didn't want to start nit-picking at her. He thought fast. "…I used to go to *49er* games there, at Kezar, when I was little." He looked down. Now he had a worry.

Misty sensed Josh's sudden concern. She said, "I'll go from here. I don't want you worn out for work."

Josh looked up to her, "I'm off until Friday. Yeah, I better get though; I have to find out what Lester has done to the *Sole*." He smiled and kissed her cheek.

"Jimmy, I think things are going to be alright between us, huh?"

"Of course, I mean, I'm excited for us. Who knows?"

Neither of them sounded sure.

Misty took off Josh's jacket and placed it over his shoulders; he slipped his arms through the sleeves and pulled the collar up. He could smell her shampoo on the inside of it. *Wow*, he thought to himself. Misty then took his hand and pulled Josh close to her, he responded by stepping into her and wrapping his arm around her waist. The kiss lasted more than two minutes, enough to bring an elderly woman out of her yard to the front to gaze at the lovers with envy.

Josh took a pen and a Walgreen's receipt out of the jacket pocket and scribbled something fast on the paper.

"Here, cell and home phone."

"I'll call."

"Please. Don't make me run up and down Willard Street yelling 'Misty!' Saturday night."

"That would be almost as entertaining as Lester coming over."

"Almost. See ya, huh?"

Misty just nodded at him and smiled. She turned and headed up Lincoln towards Frederick Street. Josh dropped back, walking slowly and glancing over his shoulder every now and again to see if Misty would do the same. Soon the hill obscured his view of her; he turned his head down towards the sidewalk and shuffled his way back towards Ocean Beach.

He could have walked through the park, taken Chain of Lakes Drive East, which would place him about four blocks from his street, but Josh decided he needed some alone time. A flash of concern rushed over him, his mystery woman was becoming a greater enigma with each coming day. He re-ran the conversation over in his head, *was she being intentionally deviant? Was she hiding something that might cause the relationship to implode? Was Misty just a little off?* Most folks with large sums of money Josh knew were half a bubble off center, so maybe she was just a little eccentric.

The thought of last night combined with the sun and cold wind made Josh shiver inside, and a little outside, as he walked along the sidewalk bordering Ocean Beach and the Great Highway.

Three days prior, Jacob had received his room key, tipped the bellman, and was now peering inside the mini-bar in his spacious Grand View Room on the twenty-third floor of the Tower Building. The St. Francis in Union Square was the epitome of elegance in the Bay Area. General Douglas MacArthur, President Ronald and Nancy Reagan had stayed in the Landmark Building, and famous jazz singer and one of the modern "Black Faces", Al Jolson, died while playing cards in his suite here, in 1950.

Luxury abound, Jacob had no intention of carrying out his self-appointed duty staying at a Best Western or a Comfort Inn. Sure, he had to pay extra for secure internet (Jacob used the newer technology called *Wi-Fi* in his office, but didn't trust it for what he had to do here), but most of all the view of the City and surrounding area was worth the price. He really wanted to have the Bridgeview Suite, which not only had the décor and atmosphere of traditional San Francisco, but an uninterrupted view of the Golden Gate, the Bay Bridge and Coit Tower-the phallic looking building which was designed and built to resemble a two hundred and ten foot fire hose nozzle on Telegraph Hill.

Jacob McAllister was perusing the semi-low brow alcohol and snacks that lined the shelves of the upper class refrigerator. There was six cans of Budweiser, four of Coors Light and Miller Genuine Draft. Two cans each of Coke and Pepsi, 7-Up and Dr. Pepper. Three pre-made sandwiches consisting of tuna, chicken salad and deviled egg graced the bottom shelf. Even though the packaging was better than the convenience store bought kind, the thought of eating something wrapped in plastic made his stomach bubble.

On the two shelves above the fridge was an assortment of one ounce liquor bottles, mostly high-end tequilas, low-end scotches, middle of the road vodkas and several different types of drink mixes such as ginger ale, tonic water and margarita sweet & sour in four flavors. A small bottle of Angostura aromatic bitters, Bloody Mary mix in an eight ounce can and a two once jar of pimento stuffed Spanish olives completed the ensemble.

On his third pass of the contents, Jacob decided to order from room service. He closed the cabinet and walked to the phone, dialed the proper number and told the woman on the other end to send up a bottle of the best Glenlivet Archive 21. A single malt that runs him about $1,200.00 a case down in L.A. He added a shrimp salad sandwich on a croissant and asked if he could get the scotch sent up first, then the food about two hours later. Confused slightly, but accustomed to peculiar orders, the woman agreed and told Jacob that the scotch was on its way.

Satisfied that he would have at least five minutes before the booze arrived, Jacob headed to the bed where he had set his bag down. He unzipped the carry-on, unfolded it three times, opened the inner zipper and carefully slid out a nice suit. He hung it up, then went back and retrieved another set of clothes-something more casual, denim khakis

117

and a light blue pullover Polo. On his return to the case, he lifted a laptop and a small box containing cords and a mouse.

It took a couple of minutes to hook up the internet and log on, making sure he used a non-descript account and an external hard drive. He wanted nothing of his future queries or storage on his workstation, just in case. He typed in his password under the *Buckley* file. A knock came to the door. Instinctively Jacob glanced at the clock in the corner of his computer; it read 8:45 AM. He rose and walked slowly to the door and the knock came again, this time followed by a young man's voice.

"Room service!"

Jacob signed for the two hundred dollar bottle of scotch, then added ten dollars for the tip. The young man seemed a little annoyed, but these youngsters expect so much for so little now a days.

The tray the Glenlivet came on was also set with two fine crystal rock glasses and a bottle of Evian spring water. Jacob sat the tray on the table by the window and poured the scotch neat, into a rock glass. He filled it to the brim, not wanting to have to get up again for a re-fill. He seated himself in the comfy chair and sipped, exhaling in delight as the warm liquor slightly burned on its way down his throat. He sniffed, and then returned his gaze to the laptop screen.

He opened another file he had on the separate drive, one titled "Rental Search". Jacob had often used this file at work, when he was tracking a new client or performing a background check for another party on a person. The file opened an online secure website and fitted the right password in, to a company that didn't exist, and several seconds later a prompt asked for a location, name, birthdate, Social Security number and the location he had waited so long for.

"San Francisco California, Misty Desjardins," He spoke out loud as he typed; an old habit; "May fourth nineteen…crap."

Jacob had to get up and find his notes; he had forgotten her birthdate and Social. After retrieving a legal pad and manila folder, he sat back down and typed in the information. Another ten or fifteen seconds and the screen showed three applications for rental units and one for a home that had been rented six months ago. A nice looking home according to the pictures, on Willard Drive near Golden Gate Park. He quickly scribbled the number down and then closed the application, always afraid someone might figure out who he was. Legal mind or not, Jacob was treading in seriously illegal territory here, a whisper in a Fed's ear could spark an investigation that would shred this whole operation apart.

He went to his bag and found a detailed map of San Francisco and ran his finger along the index till he came to Willard Street. Jacob folded the map to reveal just the area he was looking for; he undressed as he walked to the bathroom, and showered. He would head to the concierge desk after dressing in his casual clothes, rent a car and then find Willard Street and surprise Misty Desjardins. She had it coming, and, the boy had to be returned to his rightful family.

Misty had made it home and taken off her sandals as she leaned up against the counter in the kitchen. She went to the coffee pot and opened the top, peering in for grounds. She smirked at the used coffee fixings and removed the filter basket and dumped the brown stuff in the trash. After retrieving a can from the cabinet above the counter she refilled the basket with her traditional three scoops and replaced the basket above the pot. Next, instead of filling the pot with water, Misty pulled the kitchen faucet from its place and snaked it to the filling compartment on the back

J Jay Ross

of the coffee maker, filling it to the desired line. Lastly, she flipped on the switch and sat down at the breakfast nook.

After he showered and dressed, Jacob left the hotel in a rental car delivered by the rental company. He reconnoitered the city and some of its finer sites, the places his prey would surely visit if he had to follow her and just in case he lost her while he was tailing her.

On Thursday afternoon he began to follow the map from the hotel towards the place he had circled while waiting in the lobby for the car on Monday. He had studied the maps details and was nearly sure he could navigate the crowded streets of San Francisco towards his destination.

Misty had filled her cup and sat back down at the nook, reading the front page of yesterday's paper. She had forgotten to bring in todays as she passed the lower gate to her house, and was contemplating doing so. But some things were on her mind also, the fact she nearly let the cat out of the bag, she had recalled telling Jimmy about her son's arrival, the boy who was in custody of her late husband's parents, and then let it slip she was looking for a school for him. She half smiled and half frowned at Mark Twain's quote about lying; "*If you tell the truth, you don't have to remember anything...*" She took a sip from her mug then placed her chin on top of her closed fist on the table and closed her eyes.

Misty knew she had dozed, since she hadn't looked at the clock before she put her head down, she had no idea how long she was asleep. But a sound woke her. It was the rumble throughout the house when the gate downstairs closed, the gate was on a heavy spring and often banged against its frame when let go of. She rubbed her eyes and now looked at the clock, the hands making the telltale ninety degree angle to the left and up; twelve forty-five.

Then another sound, this one was quieter, more intentionally subdued. It was the rustling of clothing on the lower hallway wall. The narrow passage forced people once in a while to brush up against the wall. Then another familiar sound, the door handle being work back and forth. The hair on the back of Misty's head began to stiffen. A wave of panic surfaced and she trembled as she quietly rose from the chair at the nook. The two chairs had a tendency to make a scraping sound at the slightest movement across the wood floor. The sound at the door had stopped.

Misty looked quickly around for something to defend herself with, but nothing was within reach. She tiptoed to the door, looking for the bracing bar that slid into a notch in the floor and then into another notch on the door, making it impossible to open the door from the outside. It was leaning against the entryway coatrack.

She slid across the floor on her bare feet, trying not to create that squeaking noise made when flesh touches something making friction. She had her hands on the bar and then she could hear something being slipped into the deadbolt lock…a key. Each tumbler being pushed up by the notches on the key made a clicking sound and in the silence and terror of the moment, Misty could hear each click like a hammer dropping down on a steel table. She forced herself to grab the bar. She hefted the bar quietly as possible, but just as the security device cleared the floor, the deadbolt lock turned open and the door was being thrust into the room. Misty jumped back holding the heavy bar at her side like a baseball bat, ready to strike at the figure whose shadow was making its way into the room.

"Jesus Mom!"

"Oh God honey! What are you doing?" Misty lowered the bar to the ground.

Riley closed the door behind him and instinctively turned the lock closed.

"Half day, remember the note they sent home last week? Teacher's conference or something like that. Didn't you hear the bus outside?"

Misty slid her feet across the floor to her son and hugged him tight.

Josh was in a world all to himself right now. He had trudged the couple of miles back to his place, stopping a few times on the way up to Point Lobos, this was more than he walked since he was in high school. He closed his door behind him and slung his jacket, fresh with *scent of Misty* on it, over the chair in the living room. Not only was he feeling elated and light as air over last night, but every now and then a twinge of guilt would ride over him, and once in a while a pang of suspicion.

She had lied to him. Or she was just not being fully truthful. Josh had listened to her very closely, and twice Misty had made an error in what she said. Was it because she too was tickled inside? Or was there just plain dishonesty? But then again, Josh hadn't been totally truthful to her either. He had to tell her what he told everyone else, he had to stick to his story. Years ago he had made up his mind that he would tell people the twisted version of the truth, it wasn't much and no one could be hurt by it now, but he was feeling guilty about doing it. He made up his mind, if he and Misty got any closer, he would confess his sin to her, and hope she doesn't go running out of the room screaming in terror. Or maybe she would fess up her lie, or bent truths.

An accident on Geary and Divisadero right in front of Jacob stopped his pursuit of his prey. The street was sealed off as two cars, one from Divisadero and the other traveling west of Geary slammed into one another. He hadn't seen who had run the light, Jacob was barely keeping his eyes on the road as it was, he would wait for brake lights ahead of him to slow or stop. But now, as traffic backed up behind his Lexus rental car, he couldn't escape. He didn't want to talk to the police, let alone anyone other than his quarry here, and now he could see the red and blue flashing lights zigzagging their way through traffic towards him.

The investigation was still under way an hour later, the occupant of the car coming from Divisadero had to be rushed to the hospital and was in serious condition, the police had to have statements from everyone, even Jacob, who told the officer he was looking the other way and didn't see anything, but the officer told him to write that down.

"Okay, well, you just claim you didn't see anything, right Mr. uh Tate?" The officer read from the witness statement McAllister handed him.

"That's it. I was looking the other way. I looked after I heard the crash and that was it."

"Okay sir, we'll have these cars cleared up and out of the way in a few, and then you can be on your way. Here's your license back Mr. Tate, and oh yeah, try to keep your eyes focused on the road ahead, that could have been you up there…"

"Yes, of course officer. Thank you."

Jacob rolled his window up and leaned against the door. Patience was a virtue, and when you were using fake identification, you had to exercise it flagrantly. Even if it meant you were going to be delayed. After adjusting the radio to the news talk station, Jacob smiled at his ingenuity.

Randolph Tate. Born three years before Jacob McAllister, in Wyoming. He resided in San Diego, California and had died in a hang gliding accident four years ago. Randy was a client of Jacob's, and Jacob had assumed the man's identity on only one other occasion. The passport, driver's license and Social Security card were kept locked in a secure safe in Jacob's office, a safe with lots of other things the Feds would love to get their hands on, a safe with a built in tamper-proof system that flooded itself with indelible black and blue ink, enough to destroy any evidence.

His flight, room and rental car were all booked under this name. Only his secretary, Shirley Taylor, was the wiser and she wouldn't talk. She knew the consequences of betraying her boss of fifteen years, she had seen it displayed before. But the little blue folder in his "official" safe was his ticket, Jacob's secretary had forged the name of her prior boss to a huge check and was never caught, Jacob's private security service found the evidence, Jacob made Shirley aware of it being in his possession and a bond of mutual trust was established.

You can't go and do what Jacob was planning and have your real name all over the place. Jacob McAllister had boarded his private jet and was in the U.S. Virgin Isles for the week, a happy employee was "rewarded" with the free flight and resort, as long as he didn't sign his name to anything. When you own so much, so few can tamper with you.

So, with the happy employee pretending to be McAllister far and away, Jacob had the perfect alibi, if the Feds were watching, and he knew they were. With his secretary Shirley bound by blackmail, he was free to move about as Mr. Tate.

Jacob began his hunt again, heading up Geary to make his left turn towards the Park. Glancing in his rearview mirror, Jacob noticed a policeman from the scene of the accident was a few cars behind him. A thought trembled through his mind. When he was finished with his business here, would the cops remember Randolph Tate? Would this officer, who might be just on his way to coffee with his buddies, have a flashback of Tate being in the area after Misty Desjardins' body was discovered?

Jacob made the next left and eventually ended back on Geary, reversing his course. He had to change his plans for today; a more careful design had to be made now. After thinking as he stopped and started in the mid-afternoon traffic, he smiled to himself.

Since it was Thursday, it would take till Friday to get to his room, but he knew it would get here in time. Jacob lifted his cell phone and speed-dialed his office. When Shirley answered he rattled off the details of what he needed.

"So, you want the silver and black box from under your bar in your office, next-day shipped to the St. Francis?" Her voice seemed disinterested, which she was. It was just more work for her.

"Yes, and make sure it isn't opened. Matter of fact, place it in my old briefcase, the leather one, and mark it sensitive legal documents. And ship it from a remote location now, not from the office. Got the name, right?"

"Yes Mr. *Tate.*"

Jacob flipped his phone shut and drove back to the hotel. In the morning he would request a new rental car, an SUV with dark tinted windows and lots of room in the back.

"You scared the life out of me child." Misty was still panting.

"Sorry mom." Riley hugged his shaking mother and went into the kitchen area. "Do we have any *Cheerios*?"

Misty shook her head, barred the door and walked into the kitchen.

"Riley, I have a friend coming over to dinner this weekend."

"Uh huh. And you want me to play stupid, as usual." Riley shrugged. He didn't even turn from the cabinet he was looking in for the cereal.

"Not like last time. This man is special. He likes me and I want him to like you too, just don't offer anything to

him, you know, like if he asks you how you like living with
Grammy or Grampy in L.A."

"He thinks I live in L.A.?"

"Yes. I had to be sure I trust him fully before I tell
him the truth."

"Did you tell him about dad?"

"Sort of."

"You told him dad was dead, huh? You told him I
was living with Grammy and Grampy because you're
afraid huh?" Riley spun and looked his mother right into
her tearing eyes.

Misty looked away. Riley was twelve years old, but
he was as smart as a thirty year old man. He was book
smart, he was think-smart. He could solve difficult
problems in a heartbeat like an adult would. Misty saw to
this, she made him read when he was four years old. She
made him listen to classical music and took him to see
Broadway plays and opera. When Riley was ten he had
already learned to play the piano, guitar and saxophone-the
latter being the most trying, the sound of new sax player
was that of a sick calf in a small room-but she endured and
now the boy could play music, not just notes like anyone,
but he could make music. Make his instruments sound as if
he were at the Met, or even the Hollywood Bowl.

Then *it* happened. She and Riley had to make a run
for it. They had to get away, far away from L.A. as she
could, far from the reach of the police, from *him*. Riley had
been on the lam with his mother and he was smart enough
to know why, all she had to do was explain it to him, and
he was right behind her. Queuing off her lies as she told
them to people who asked, and played his part equally as
deceiving. He would cry on command, pout, be angry or
just disappear when Misty needed him too. And that
brought the guilt.

No child should have to endure the rigors she was
putting him through. It wasn't for his safety; he would be

well treated back in L.A. He would be coddled and spoiled and given power and money when he was old enough. Riley would be the head of a major company or president of some off-shore bank where the thieves kept their money. The thieves, her in-laws, the crooks would make a man out of Riley, a crooked man, a thief like his father. A killer maybe? Maybe make him part of the inner circle that took care of business the way the mob did in New York, but more discreetly, quietly. Or maybe he would make a mistake and end up in a Dumpster with his throat slit, the way many of his father's enemies and even some of his father's employees ended up.

No, this was all about Misty. She knew she was a dead woman walking. She knew she had a price on her head large enough to make any strung out drug dealer sell her location or name. So she hid in plain sight. She didn't change her name. She only went north a few hundred miles instead across the country, but she had to for a reason. She was looking for someone, someone who could eventually protect her and take her away. He was here, somewhere. He just had to show himself.

"Honey, when Mr. Kennedy's here, just act like you're a little afraid of him. You know, like you aren't sure if you like him or not. If he asks any serious questions, you know which ones, then it will be easier to shy away. Just like always."

"Mom?"

"Yeah honey?"

"Are we going to run again?"

Josh had been trying to think of a way to ask Misty about her inconsistencies, without putting himself in the spotlight. He knew she was almost perfect for him the way she was, but the little details bothered him, the little things that few people notice about another when they first start dating. A little lie here, a little enhancement there. Things that are

127

made up to make the person more appealing, not the rigorous honesty relationships should start out on.

But he was falling for the woman from the beach, her tan skin and luscious smelling hair. Her touch that was as soft as a child's, the way she smiled from ear to ear. Her laugh that tickled the stomach, her looks of sultry that boiled the middle. But they had yet to have a serious conversation, one that would end up revealing a little more about each other, the kind of conversations that new couples hate, the truth. *"What was your wife like?" "Did she suffer?" "How did you cope?"* Those Josh could deal with, but the scary questions were the ones he avoided. *"How did she die?"*

Josh ran the shower and undressed in his room. In two days he'd find out more about the mystery woman, and so she would learn about him too. Outright honesty, Josh thought, that's what he would do. Just tell her the truth and hope she would do the same. But what if her story is she's just a little mixed up? What if she's harboring no secrets, what if Josh bared his soul and Misty locked up, afraid of him, afraid of his past. He stepped into the shower feeling better about things, until he thought of this. Now he lowered his head under the water and felt miserable again. This past would haunt him for the rest of his life; he'd never get another woman to love him like Faith did, not when they found out the truth.

CHAPTER NINE
Two days later

The flowers were special ordered from a little flower shop in the Fillmore and delivered on time Friday. They were sitting in a vase full of water on the counter top in Misty's kitchen, the early Saturday morning sun lit up the light red flesh of the roses like a stained glass mural in a church. Little hints of the red color splattered over the countertop and Misty was standing there, half bent over leaning on the counter with one elbow and tracing her finger around the soft refraction of crimson. She had a look of contentment on her face, a smile of abandon, neither of which she felt deep inside, but the thought that Jimmy had thought of her, made her outside flush, and her lower quarters tingle.

Misty had been to the market already, the shrimp was fresh from the Grotto, the spices and herbs were from a little shop for organic foods on California Street. It had been a while since a home cooked meal like this one had been planned, prepared and cooked in the Desjardins household. Sure, Misty and Riley ate and ate well each night, but this meal was extravagant, if not for the night, but for the company.

Shrimp Pesto with parmesan and butter cream. Cracked crab fresh from the boiling pots that line Taylor Street at the Wharf. And the pièce de résistance; lobster bisque. It took nearly an hour to purée the veggies and the thickness was perfect. Misty wanted something different, other than seafood, but thought that Jimmy would avoid it most of the time, so he might be in the mood for something fresh caught and home cooked. It didn't matter to her; she was going to please Jimmy.

Her meager rental home was cleaned within an inch of its life, the dust was eliminated from every corner, every

129

thin groove in the railings and she even used a step ladder to pick at the dark areas of the crown molding around the ceiling. Misty had lit four Ocean Breeze light scented candles around various places, her bedroom, the bathroom, the kitchen (but the smell was drowned out by the cooking dinner so she moved it to the spare bedroom) and the foyer by the front door.

She lit another set of odorless candles and placed them on the tall accent table in the window, along with a satin red table cover that extended a few inches down each side, careful not to hide the hand-crafted wooden legs of the expensive piece. She had Riley help her arrange the leather love seat and couch to facing positions in the center of the room, the Basque cocktail table in the center on top of her fancy $4,600.00 Antolya Red Oriental rug. Two more long candles in hand-turned holders were spaced evenly with a newly purchased copy of *Building Kettenburgs* by Mark Allan, which set Misty back a measly $75.00 and a copy of *Follow the Southern Cross* by an little known author. She wanted contrast, and a little suggestion of romance.

Her bedroom was another problem. Misty had only the bed and a nightstand, a full length mirror and a hamper. Not one thing matched another, so she shoved the hamper into her bathroom and made the bed, turning down the right side exposing her golden satin sheets and placed a rose from Friday's delivery on top of her satin covered pillow. Just in case.

Riley was going to spend the night at Alexandra's, the woman who watched over Carter the lab. He would eat dinner with his mother and Jimmy, spend an hour or so chatting in the living room, then he would go. He hated this, and didn't know why adults liked to be alone so often, but he knew his mother needed a good friend and if Jimmy was any way like his mother described to him, then he would go to Alex's. Maybe they could play chess or watch

Animal Planet; Alex always watched that channel and would even talk for hours afterwards about the show in tedium. Riley despised Alex's snacks she made for him while he visited, since she was a staunch vegan everything was made from roots or sprouts or sap knots.

He once memorized a poem by Baxter Black called *The Vegetarian's Nightmare*, wherein a garden of vegetables are murdered, human emotions were used in describing the feelings the carrots and other veggies experienced as they were plucked from the ground to make a meal. Alex made a face like she had eaten a poisonous beefsteak when he told it to her. But she laughed nervously when he finished, out of courtesy Riley suspected.

Josh, on the other hand was nervous. He had taken a long shower, fussed for twenty minutes over what to wear, then decided to wear causal jeans and a nice golf shirt. He walked from the bedroom to the kitchen to make a pot of coffee, walked back into the bedroom and changed into a pair of khaki tan pants and a pull over long sleeve in blue. It wasn't everyday he met the nearly teenage son of a woman that tickled him so inside, and scared him at the same time.

Walter Mitty-like visions appeared in his head; he, Misty and Riley on the beach in the summer, the three of them at Six Flags riding stomach churning roller coasters, they would be out on a tour of the bay on the *Sole*, the trio eating at a nice restaurant on the Wharf. He could imagine them, even though he hadn't even met the young boy of the woman he was falling in love with let alone see his face, Josh knew he would look like his mother. Maybe it was because he was falling in love with Misty, but he had reservations about that too. He knew so little about her.

The mysterious way she appeared on the beach, the way she showed up at the Wharf, the sultry way she dressed at dinner and the fantastic night of love making. All told, Josh was ready for another one of those weeks, another few days of waiting until it hurt inside to finally see her when he could nearly stand it no longer to be without her. Then the rush of blood throughout his body when she presents herself. He might just faint when she opens the door to her place tonight. Josh looked in the mirror as he thought through of all this, went to his bureau and pulled out a pair of black Wranglers, a dress shirt and tie.

Jacob. Aka: Randolph Tate, had driven back to the St. Francis. He stopped at the concierge desk and ordered his new rental, the SUV with tinted rear windows. Since California has laws against having the driver's and passenger side windows tinted, he figured he could slip into the back of the vehicle and spy from there. He liked using the word spy, he was a secret agent on a search and destroy mission.

As he passed the front desk, the clerk called out.

"Mr. Tate?"

It took a second for Jacob to realize he was under cover. "Yes?"

"FedEx came in about an hour ago. Special Saturday delivery." The clerk reached behind him and pulled a box about the size of a large briefcase and hefted it to the counter top. "We signed for it, if that's okay with you sir."

A quick examination of the box showed it to be intact, the seals still in place. This made Jacob less nervous, but he still glanced quickly left and right, enough to make it look like he was cracking his neck. He let a smile cross his usually stern face and picked the box up.

"Thank you."

Jacob had the box under his arm as he rode the elevator to his floor, his fingers barely able to grasp the bottom. Once outside his room, he gave another glance over his shoulder, this time being more conspicuous about his intent. *Here*, he thought, *he could have a confrontation if need be.*

After securing the door with the obligatory deadbolt, swing hasp, push chain and key lock, he gave a little pitch and the package landed squarely on the second queen bed. Jacob stripped himself of his shirt and admired his features for a moment in the full length mirror in the vanity area as he entered the bathroom. His greying hair was neatly combed and gelled to perfection, a three day growth of salt and pepper stubble had broken the surface of his usual booth-bought tan. He smiled at the sprouting facial hair, it made him think he was rugged, Jacob felt almost indestructible at this point, for a moment he considered buying a Wahl clipper set and cutting the stubble to this length every day, he would be dashing, just sitting at his desk. A worldly businessman like Sir Richard Branson, head of Virgin Airlines.

He admired himself for a few more moments then, after using the bathroom, returned shirtless to the bed which he had tossed the FedEx box. A quick non-descript peek around the room out of habit, and he tore the strips that secured the box closed. Carefully Jacob pulled the box apart, not like a child on Christmas morning, but more like a rocket scientist assembling a fragile component for a satellite. After the final piece of cardboard was removed and folded into a disposable size, he carefully pulled the silver and black box out of the leather faux case.

The thin handle of the metal rimmed and reinforced container was secured to its base with four screws on each side, two four dial combination locks at the hasps on each end, a little monogram that read JAM in gold emblazoned near the handle and three curious little knobs that protruded underneath. The transport case cost him about eight hundred dollars to have made, he spotted a model of in one of those little spy-shops on Sunset Boulevard.

To correctly open it you had to twist the three knobs under the handle; the first is the left one if the case is resting on its bottom monogram face up. It has to be turned till it's tight clockwise. The next knob has to be turned in the opposite direction till it is tight, the third goes back to clockwise and *then* you can work the combination locks. According to the flyer on the pedestal the case was sitting on in the James Bond-like shop; the first knob releases a panel inside to keep the contents in a secret panel in case you have to open it in public and not want to reveal its fillings. The next knob silences a shrill siren, a burglar alarm; the third stops a bag of dye from exploding in the opener's face.

It was all mostly for entertainment, Jacob was no secret agent, nor had he any aspirations to become one, he just thought it was a cool gift for himself and bought it one time when he was in the shop purchasing a tiny surveillance camera.

He spun the knobs in the correct directions, then using his thumb on each of his hands masterfully dialed in the combination of 8 5 2 on the left lock and 9 6 8 on the right. A snapping could be heard as the tumblers unlatched, and the final process of twisting the handle a quarter turn to the right opened the safe-case. Lined with impact materials and special cut compartments in dark grey foam for his favorite tools, Jacob dug his finger in underneath the revolver first. He slid out a Smith and Wesson model 40 *"Lemon Squeezer"* .38 caliber pistol. Designed to fit in the palm of your hand for easy concealment, Jacob liked this gun. He had fired it many times at the family ranch and liked it for up close confrontations. It was loud, but kick was minimal and it did fatal damage point blank, as it was designed for. It held five rounds; Jacob kept a "Varmint Load" in the first chamber, a mini- shotgun round basically used for snake shot. Then the other four rounds were hollow point .38 special. Pure stopping power, the hollow point caused the bullet to expand at the tip when it struck an object, like flesh or bone, and spread wide open. This is called knock-down power, where the energy of the bullet is multiplied and is used to do maximum damage.

He flipped the cylinder open using the thumb switch unique to a Smith and Wesson, surveyed the loaded chambers, made sure that the bullets were ready to use, then closed it carefully-not like you see in the movies, where the handler snaps his wrist to the side causing the cylinder to slam shut-this damages the delicately machined parts. If you want your gun to operate effectively each time, you treat it with respect. Jacob slid it into a holster that was in another compartment in the foam lining.

Next he pulled out a garrote, a thin line of piano wire with two plastic handles on each end. Jacob never used this toy, but he thought it was cool carrying it with him, just in case. He coiled it up and laid it next to the holstered revolver.

Finally he ran his hand along the one thing this case was designed to hide, the weapon of his choice. He'd used this once before with spectacular results, and was going to be the tool for this job. It was up close and personal, it could be used with preciseness to kill instantly, to prolong the death sentence of its victim, or torture. Close enough to your prey that you could smell the fear emanating from the skin of your victim. Jacob wondered what Misty's fear would smell like; would it be like sour cream like his last subject, or would her perfume mask it, could the musky smell of her flesh make him tremble as he plunged it into her neck.

Jacob grinned and rubbed the instrument as he pulled it out, careful not to stab himself, and slid it carefully-while smiling satisfactorily-into its own custom made holster, which was designed to clip to his belt, and be discarded into a Dumpster or elsewhere if the need arose. It took a moment for the tingle inside to subside before he pulled out the last of the case's usual residents, a manila envelope containing emergency documents, just in case he had to flee the country. But he was confident this was going to be smooth, quick and painless-for him. In and out, get the boy, dispose of the woman who had made his and his family's life hell these last dozen years, fly home and return to his daily job of managing huge amounts of money for his clients and relatives.

Rising from the bed, Jacob went to the dresser and pulled out a pair of dark brown Dockers, a dark blue T shirt that read San Francisco on the front and a black sweatshirt. He changed out of his pants and pulled on the T shirt and folded the sweatshirt neatly and placed it on the table next to his wallet-Randolph Tate's wallet-and picked up his "toys". The *Lemon Squeezer* went into the small of his back, a metal clip on the holster securing it in place to his belt.

The coiled garrote was slid into his front pocket, and the 'pride and joy' had to be carefully clipped to the inside of his belt on Jacob's left side, the shaft of the case extending six inches inside his pants. He had to be careful sitting down, not wanting to plunge the thing into his thigh. Jacob then spun once in front of the mirror on his way out, he wanted to make sure there were no tell-tale signs he was carrying a small arsenal; satisfied he picked up the wallet and the room key and headed downstairs to pick up his rental SUV.

Josh had circled the block once in his company vehicle, the Ford Excursion, looking to make sure he had the right address. It took a moment to find a good parking spot, most folks in the Bay Area drove smaller gas saving, planet saving cars, it was sometimes hard to find a spot big enough for his "planet killer" as Jeremy the hippy liked to call it, even though he would ride in it once and a while when the VW bus was in for repairs.

Josh parked four doors down from the address Misty had given him. He sat for a moment and shook off the chills he was feeling. Not for being with Misty, those were lightning bolt-like sparks jumping through his skin, but more of a fear of meeting her son Riley, and the off chance that Riley wouldn't like him. Mothers often tend to respect their children's first instinct of another person, contrary to what you see in movies or on TV. A cold reception or rebuff from the kid and Josh could be back at home next week watching re-runs of *Full House* alone. Josh liked kids, but he wasn't sure how to handle himself in front of an older one, not one as bright as Misty described to him.

He steadied himself, and after a quick check in the review for any newcomer blemishes, stepped out onto Willard Drive and hopefully to his destiny with the mysterious woman he was falling in love with.

Misty had to pretend to herself she wasn't really watching secretly out the window for Josh to pull up, but she was; her stomach did summersaults when she saw him drive by the first time, then became anxious that he might have chickened out and drove off as he went around the block. Minutes later he reappeared as did the butterflies in her abdomen. She ducked back into the low lit room, behind the glare of the candles in the window, and watched as he sat there. He rubbed his face with his hand, he scratched at his ear, he rubbed his stubbly goatee, he was taking his time and it was killing her!

She took a deep breath, the sound of it echoed throughout the room and the sound made Riley come into the room and sit on the edge of the couch.

He asked, "You okay mom?"

"Sure, just waiting for Jimmy. He just pulled up." Misty tried hiding her impatience as she stared out the window at the Excursion. Finally the dome light came on inside the Ford and Josh stepped out into the darkening evening. Her insides tingled with anticipation now.

The front door opened just as Josh touched the second step with his foot. His body jolted out of surprise as the door opened, Josh hoped that his unpreparedness hadn't been noticed. A huge smile crossed Misty's face; Josh relaxed and took in the garment she was wearing.

Not as flashy or fancy as the dress she wore out last Sunday night, nor as revealing or sensual, the soft pillow collar sheath dress gave her a look of obvious femininity along with a conservative "We're with my son tonight" statement. It was purple, with a lighter color piping around the fringes, knee length with the traditional hem down the left side pulling the material into a wrinkled effect from several inches above the bottom to the breast, then an allowance of cleavage. She could have been wearing overalls, and made Josh's heart jump just as much. He spent more time concentrating on her eyes.

"Hi. I was a little lost, sorry I'm late." Josh spoke first as Misty held the door open for him and he removed his light jacket.

"Oh? I didn't notice you were late. C'mon in." Misty beamed.

"You look very nice tonight." Josh gave her a peck on the cheek as he walked by.

"So do you, all fancied up in tan corduroy pants and a Wisco shirt…"

"Ah, it's all I had clean."

Neither Josh nor Misty noticed the white mini-van across the street with tinted windows in the rear.

"Jimmy Kennedy, this is my son Riley"

Misty guided the boy from her side to the center stage in front of her.

"Good to meet you Riley, I've heard so much about you." Josh offered a hand and the boy took it, shook it firmly then looked him in the eyes.

Riley Desjardins was built like a typical twelve year old, if there were a model for one. Five four or five, a hair taller than his mom; brown hair with the usual fad tinges of blonde, like his mother; a good solid handshake, not like the fishy floppy ones many of his charters gave. An air of confidence about the way he led his head, his shoulders and his posture told Josh that this kid was strong mentally and physically for his age. Could be a good thing, or a bad thing, depending on how the night plays out.

Riley said, "Good to meet you sir."

"Jimmy or…"

"Riley is a good boy, he only addresses adults by their last names or sir." Misty proudly told Josh, while making a pointed look in her son's direction.

"Oh, well in that case Riley, call me Mr. K." Josh beamed back at the boy.

Riley looked at his mother and she nodded in agreement. "Okay, Mr. K"

"But I preferred if you'd call me Josh, which is my real…"

"Josh!" Riley exclaimed. He gave a quick glance to his mother who shook her head slightly enough for the boy to notice and not Josh. Riley cleared his throat, "That's okay Mr. K; it really is good to meet you though!" Riley went off towards his room with Josh's jacket.

Josh mistook the sudden excitement in the boy's voice as acceptance. He thought maybe the boy was so tensed up nervous about meeting him, and was relieved about being on a first name basis. Josh moved towards the tri-sided window in the front of the house. He admired the candles, then the thought of what originally was bothering him stung his side. He looked out the window to the street below; the darkening skies gave the large plum tree out front an eerie blood purple look.

"I thought you said you always dreamed of having a window like this, I didn't realize you had one." He kept his tone soft and light, without accusation.

The statement caught Misty off guard; she was coming out of the kitchen with a bottle of chardonnay. "Oh," A quick thought. "I think I said; I always wanted to look out one, like from your view."

She picked up her pace across the wood floor to be next to him for her excuse. She touched his shoulder and looked out the window with him, placing the wine on the table next to the candles.

"I meant; that your view is so much more dramatic than mine. With all the trees and houses, there's no horizon to marvel at."

Josh processed this for a second and fought off the suspicions for a moment. "Oh."

They both leaned back inside and Josh wrapped his arm around Misty and pulled her closer to him, he placed a gentle kiss on her neck, just enough pressure to cause her skin to tingle and quiver. The smell of her slightly sweaty skin and perfume made Josh a little aroused, so he stepped back and smiled. Her eyes were glowing tonight, he was lost in them and the tension left his thoughts and body.

"You're a very mysterious woman." He said, playfully.

"Yes, well today's world calls for a little caution."

"I agree. What's for dinner? It smells wonderful in here."

Misty picked up the wine and walked back towards the dining area, Josh following as she ran over the menu for him. When she reached the table she retrieved two wine glasses that had been set out on the polished red cherry finished top of the claw footed table. The finest china had been laid out, along with cloth napkins and two forks for each setting along with the large soup spoons for the bisque.

Fancy, Josh thought as he accepted his glass of wine from Misty. Misty stepped to the stereo by the front door and clicked it on; soft jazz began flowing from the speakers, intimate, but not overwhelming. Quiet and relaxing with just the right spark to keep the mood interesting.

"You do like crab, Pesto and shrimp right? And bisque?" She added a tone of concern for effect.

"Of course. I wouldn't live this close to the ocean if I didn't"

"Or have a boat."

"Who has a boat?" Riley asked as he rejoined them in the dining room.

Riley had smartly dressed in dark blue slacks and wore a button up shirt with a sweater vest and light tan loafers. He stopped to use the bathroom, and to give his mom a little time with Mr. K before dinner.

"Mr. Kennedy. A fishing boat, he keeps it at the Wharf."

"Cool!"

Josh gave a proud smile, "And we're going to go on a bay cruise pretty soon, the weather seems to be cooperating for the next few days." Josh took a sip of his wine and felt the tingle of the alcohol in his nostrils first. "If it's okay with your mother."

Josh knew he had permission already; he just wanted to make it look like Misty had the final say, a respect to her authority.

"Of course, you name the day."

"How about next Saturday?" Josh asked the both of them with his eyes as well as the words.

"Great! Yeah!" You could have said 'right now' and Riley would have been ready.

Misty frowned, "Don't you have charters?"

141

"Not this Saturday yet, and besides, you have priority."

"We feel special"

Josh lowered his voice and his head and looked directly into Misty's eyes. "You are."

There was a moment of uncomfortable silence in the room; Riley looked at his shoes then up at his mother. Misty looked from Riley to Josh, then back again. Josh seemed paralyzed for a moment; he didn't know what to say or whether or not he should move. He decided it was time to move towards the dining room table, maybe break the coolness that settled over the room. There was so much he wanted to say, to ask Misty, to find out about Riley, but right now he wanted the attention to swing away from him.

"Mind if I sit? I've been on my feet all day."

Misty shook a frozen look from her face and smiled, "Of course. I'm sorry; this is all a little overpowering."

Josh slid out a chair he figured would be Misty's and nodded at it. Misty gave a little curtsy but said, "Thank you kind sir, but I have to assemble the meal." Riley rolled his eyes at her.

Josh smiled and walked to the next chair, pulled it back and sat down softly.

"Yeah, I suppose so. I guess I'm not used to dating either, this is a little different."

Riley seemed surprised by this, "You don't date much?"

"No sir. I haven't been on a date in years." Josh smiled slyly, "How about you? A young strapping boy as yourself should have had a couple dates."

Riley looked from Josh, a little shock on his face, to his mother, who had a look of astonishment also. Riley saw the look on his mother's face and looked down at his plate as he scooted his chair in. A flash of embarrassment crossed his mug. "No, not me."

"So, your mother tells me you live with your grandparents in L.A."

Another look from Riley to his mother, this one was the cue they had practiced and used on many occasions. An established ritual, one that let Riley have control over the conversation, and his mother would fill in any missing details. They worked a basic story, a set of guidelines that could be followed to prevent crossing stories and getting caught in their little perjury. A defense mechanism designed to hide the truth, not from folks like Josh, but to protect those people who protect them. Bad people were after Misty and Riley, to include someone as innocent as Josh or another in their flight of safety might get those who care for them hurt, or worse.

Riley's brilliance with storytelling was that of an actor reading a script. Details were included, emotions telegraphed, facial expressions used to emphasize a point. He learned after the cue not to look back at his mother for authentication, she would add that if necessary, a glance in her direction might signal a conspiracy. Who can you trust more than a young boy of twelve telling a story and his mother nodding her head in agreement?

"Yeah. Most of the time. I'm tired of it though, they always take me places I've been to a hundred times, we do the same things over and over again. I don't have many friends because we live in a big house with a wall around it, so my friends from school have to call before they come over, and many of them just don't hassle with it."

"Sounds like you have some caring family though, to watch over you so close?"

"I guess, but you know. Like you said, maybe I want to meet a girl or something, I guess they're all intimidated about coming over. I just get so lonely."

Josh pulled his back from Riley a little and looked in Misty's direction. "Intimidated?" He took a draw of wine from his glass. "You sound like you have a better vocabulary than me."

Misty smiled at Josh and added, "I told you he was smart." She sighed and rubbed her son's arm. "He's growing up so fast, I feel so bad that things can't work out, sometimes."

"Work out?"

"His father's parents. We don't get along too well. But I want Riley to stay with me."

"And I want to stay with my mom." Riley added on cue.

"But, they have power and money."

"I thought you said you were rich?" Josh asked as he patted Misty's hand, the one that was resting on Riley's arm.

"No. You said I was rich, I said I have a big bank account. Besides, money isn't the problem. Power is. They have a lot of it, I have none."

"So, why let him come up here and stay with you, if they…" Josh searched for a word that wouldn't sting, "…don't agree with you?"

Misty seemed taken aback by this question, it took a second for her to regain her thoughts.

Riley quickly interjected, "Because I make life miserable for them if they don't."

Misty smiled at this, scooted her chair back and slowly pulled her hand from under Josh's and off of Riley's. She stood slowly and turned quickly for a moment and wiped a tear from her eye with a quick swipe of her hand, making it look like she was brushing a fly away. She looked back down at the table and up at Josh. Dinner is served."

Josh smiled, "Outstanding."

"More wine?"

"Please."

Misty walked from the table into the kitchen area and heard behind her, "So Riley, tell me about school. You sound so educated, very smart for you age."

She heard Riley tell his made up story, the one he liked the most. He didn't blow up his ego or make it sound as if he were a prodigy; he just kept the details simple and left very little room for question.

Misty lifted the lid off the pot containing the bisque and waved her other hand slightly over the top of the streaming soup to get a whiff of the thick sauce. Her mouth started to water. She replaced the lid then lifted the lid off of a smaller one and checked the pasta that had been simmering since she retrieved the bottle of chardonnay. She slipped a noodle out and popped in into her mouth, checking the tenderness. Any longer and it would have been paste. Quickly Misty pulled the saucepan off the burner and poured into a colander she had in the sink. The steam rose up and fluttered around the light above the prep area, Misty quickly ran some cool water over the pasta to keep the noodles from sticking together, then she shook the strainer free of any excess water and dumped the pasta back into the saucepan and added a dash of olive oil.

Next she retrieved a Tupperware container from the fridge containing the hand shelled and deveined shrimp, which had been marinating in a garlic and basil dressing. Her thoughts began to drift to the future, hoping this was a daily ritual. Hoping that this was going to be the first of hundreds of meals she prepared for Jimmy Kennedy, or Josh Kennedy.

She couldn't let on, not just yet. Things were too foggy still, about her future.

After bringing another saucepan to temperature with a couple of teaspoons of light olive oil in it, she shook the plastic bowl with the shrimp in lightly to make sure there was an even coating of the marinade and slowly poured the contents into the pan. Immediately it began to sizzle and send a plume of aroma up and around the kitchen; seconds later it reached the dining area where Josh and Riley were still talking about school. Riley had begun to tell tales of school he was attending here in San Francisco, but with the premise it was all happening in L.A.

"Wow! That smells incredible! Sorry Riley, go on…" Josh's eyes misted over at the redolence coming a half dozen yards away.

Riley let his voice rise a little, this was a part he wanted his mother to hear, "But there is this one girl in my class, her name is Beth and I like her a lot. I would sure like to spend more time with her…"

Misty, standing in the kitchen using a fork to stir the pesto sauce as the shrimp cooked, heard this and smiled. She knew he was getting to the age where you can't keep the inner feelings locked up. You had to let them run, the instinct, the urge to be with an attractive mate. Misty had had those same feelings when she was his age, when life was simpler-so to speak-if you call traveling around the country with your divorced mother all the time simple.

The sizzle had died now in the pan containing the shrimp, so Misty took it from the burner and poured the contents onto a platter, then using a wooden spoon; she shook off dabs of pesto over the freshly cooked shellfish. Next Misty pulled a large decorated porcelain soup server from the cabinet overhead and a ladle from the hanging utensil rack above her head. She spooned six full helpings into the server and shut the stove off under the pot. A pinch of parsley and a sprig of dill for effect and she slowly carried the platter with the shrimp to the table.

Returning immediately for the server of lobster bisque, Misty stopped to wipe her eyes again, this time the overwhelming need to cry made her set the large bowl on the sink and lower her head. She let it out.

A hush fell over the table where Josh was listening to Riley's exploits of his school days. Josh pushed his chair back and at the same time called out, "Misty? Is everything okay?" He started towards the kitchen. Riley lowered his head and teared up himself.

Riley knew about Jimmy. His mother had told him so much about the man she had met while walking Carter on the beach. He knew about the deep feelings she had for him and the way she felt safe around him. But he also knew a lot more about *Josh*, the man they came here to see.

A small glint of reflected light shone through the back left side of the tinted window of the mini-van. Jacob McAllister was trying to adjust his butt on the bench seat. He was pissed, as pissed as he could be without resorting to violence. The rental company had only a few SUV's to rent, since they were very unpopular in the Bay Area, and not one had tinted windows. The only vehicle they had that met the stealth requirements of Randolph Tate was a family Chevrolet Astro Mini-van with a child seat strapped in the back. But time was of essence, so he reluctantly took it and swore under his breath that someone would pay for this indiscretion when the event was over.

McAllister had managed to get a little comfortable in the last seat, the closest to the street and the house across from him. He was using an expensive pair of binoculars he had purchased earlier in the day at a camera shop on Embarcadero. After he had gotten the van he decided to use it to his advantage and follow Misty around as she did her errands, knowing and smiling to himself that he could have had her any time he wanted. She walked with very little care for a woman in hiding, darting in and out of shops, buying fresh herbs at one store, then later that day selecting fresh shrimp from the market on the Wharf.

Sure, Jacob was like a spy, he followed her around on foot, in the van, and even from a mere fifty feet from her doorstep. All day he spied. But he didn't see his prize, the boy. He couldn't take Misty Desjardins out without having the boy in his custody first, just in case Riley and his mother had made arrangements for him to disappear if she did. So Jacob had to wait. Then he saw the man.

Jacob knew that Misty would have a man, of course. She was beautiful, vibrant and an extrovert. Any man would be lucky to have her hot and slick sweaty body next to his, and Jacob had this fear in the back of his mind. But this changed the situation now, another body to dispose of more than likely, since Misty was bound to fill the man with the Excursion in on some of the details.

Another witness? Maybe not, but now Jacob had to find out more about the new pawn. Was he living with them? Probably not, since she let him in like they were on a date. Did he suspect she was being secretive as she was? Doubt it; he never glanced around for any suspicious cars or people hanging around on the corner. But how much did he know? Would he miss her and the boy immediately after they disappeared? Of course he would. The look on his face as she let him in, and the look on her face told it all. She had bedded this man, he was smitten, and they were a couple. They would die together then. As soon as Jacob could find the boy.

Jacob glanced in the street light that lit the interior of the van and then at his watch. 7:10 p.m. He pursed his lips and drew his cell phone from its holster and after a few seconds scrolling through numbers he found the one he wanted and hit *SEND*.

"Buckley." The voice on the other end answered, with a hint of annoyance.

"John. Listen, I have a plate I want ran."

"I'm in the middle of dinner with my family…"

Jacob inhaled sharply through his nose.

"*Write this down.*"

It came out as a serpentine hiss and the man on the other end of the phone knew it wasn't a request. Jacob then raised the binoculars to the back of Josh's Excursion and focused on the license plate, then read the number to John Buckley. "Got it?"

Buckley read the number back, twice to be sure. "What do you need?"

"Address, background, job, family history. Anything you can get, especially next of kin."

The silence on the other end meant that John Buckley knew where this was going. He mumbled something to whoever he was eating with and turned the phone closer to his mouth.

"This is going to be expensive."

A thought flowed through Jacob's mind at the same moment Buckley was making his demand. "I want you here; I need you to bring something. Five thousand, same as usual in the same place."

"But, San Francisco? I assume you mean tomorrow?"

"No, I mean tonight. I'll meet you at the airport; just call me on this number when you get what I want, and when you have reservations made. Also, the thing I need is very important, just a second…"

Jacob caught movement in the house across from him, Misty's house. The man got up from the table and was moving to the back of the room, where he couldn't see. Then he saw his prize; the boy. The boy Riley was sitting in a chair facing the back of the house. Bingo.

"I need a way in, a way the boy will trust me." Jacob was talking with his eyes to the binos, the phone cradled in the crook between his neck and shoulder.

"He doesn't trust his own flesh and blood?"

"Not your business Mr. Buckley. Just get me what I want." Jacob finished the call by describing in detail what he needed from his minion, then reminded the man of the importance of secrecy by simply saying, "…and you know what happens if this gets out."

He hung up before the dining man could answer. Jacob returned his attention to the second floor home. In the few seconds he looked away to clip his cell phone back on his belt, the room had cleared, even the boy.

"So, do you think we should eat?" Josh asked as he entered the kitchen, trying his best faux humor to relax what seemed to be a tense moment.

Misty smiled back at him over her shoulder and nodded. "I'm sorry; it's been a long day." She dabbed at her eyes with a dishcloth and picked up the server half full of lobster bisque she had set on the counter on her return.

Josh glanced over the fridge and stepped slowly to it. With a suave motion he opened it and spotted the plate of cracked crab covered in cellophane, he reached in and pulled the plate out and smacked his lips. At this point he didn't know what to say, should he ask why she was crying? Should he let it drop and pretend nothing was wrong and hope Misty stopped sniffling by the time she sat down for diner? He began to peel the plastic barrier off the plate and carefully arranged the crab appendages-more as a tactic of delay-then lifted to show Misty, who glanced at the plate then over it looking Josh in the eyes.

"Jimmy…" Misty began.

"Josh, please, just call me Josh."

Misty lowered her eyes and smiled. "Josh. I'm sorry, just a little emotional today. With Riley and all."

She shrugged her shoulders lightly, just a tender move that ignited a fire in Josh's heart. *She could move mountains with just a shrug*, he thought. He stepped closer to her, Riley had gone to the stove and retrieved the shrimp without a word and was heading towards the dining area with the freshly seared dish. He returned and pulled the warm loaf of fresh Boudin Sourdough Misty had purchased earlier in the day on the Wharf and returned to the dining room with it.

Just after Riley left the kitchen, Josh leaned in and gave Misty a sensuous kiss on the cheek, next to her ear and whispered, "This is all so wonderful, I don't know how you could have pulled it off and look so beautiful at the same time."

Misty blushed and slightly turned and picked up the server with the lobster bisque and winked at Josh as she shook her hips a little more profoundly towards the table. Josh smiled and followed behind with the crab plate and the three of them sat down at the same time. Riley forked some shrimp to his plate, and then passed it to Josh, who had used the tongs to give himself a claw, three legs and a lemon from the cooled crab plate. He passed this to his right to Misty, and she in turn passed the ladle for the bisque-which was centered on the table so no one had to move the heavy server each time. Riley took the big spoon and held his soup bowl at the edge of the server and gave himself three full ladles, and then swung the handle towards Josh. Misty poured Josh some more wine, and then added to her glass. Riley had a Sprite.

For the next several minutes little was said, there was slurping of soup; the snapping of crab exoskeleton, the telltale of sigh as a delicious helping of food crossed a palate. Misty ate a few bites of everything, but just a few. She would try not to look obvious as she would pick up her wine glass and glance up at Josh at the same time. Every time she did, he seemed preoccupied with removing a bit of pink-white flesh from a reddened shell and dipping it in the drawn butter that they had first forgotten, but Josh beat Misty to the kitchen in a lighthearted rush, found the sticks in the fridge and microwaved them in three finger bowls for thirty seconds before returning to the table.

A few more minutes of silence then Josh paused and looked around the room quickly.

"Where's Carter?"

A fork clattered to a plate. Before Josh could look up after asking the question a look flashed between Riley and Misty. Misty casually took a sip of wine to draw attention to her and not the boy.

"He's at the neighbor's." She said matter of factly. "I didn't want him crashing into everything out of excitement of seeing you."

"Oh. He doesn't bother me."

"I know, but tonight just wasn't the night to be under my feet. I was…nervous about you coming over and didn't want to have to lock him up in a room."

"No problem, it just hit me that's all. Guess I'm not very observant, I suppose I'm a little nervous too."

After twenty minutes the table was a mess. Broken crab shells filled a large plate next to the bisque server, which had dribbles over the side and left little pools of the creamy soup on the tablecloth. Misty had an empty wine glass and Josh was draining his as she watched him with a smile, running the tip of her index finger over the rim of hers. Riley was chewing the last of the sourdough bread that was left.

Dinner had passed, Riley had gone to his room and packed a backpack for the night at Alex's, he returned shook Josh's hand apologized for having to leave. Josh told him he could stay, but a sharp glance from his mother told him she wanted to be alone with the man for a while, so Riley politely said he had promised and couldn't back out of it. Josh accepted this and patted the boy on the back as he turned to leave through the back door. The contact with another man after this long caused fear and excitement for a fraction of a second in him. He spun back and gave Josh a huge smile of both affection and hope.

Josh saw the gleam, noting that he was being accepted by Riley, a primary reason for tonight, a path that he wanted to forge with both Riley and Misty.

Josh asked to use the bathroom and was directed down the hallway, second door to the right. The first, Josh noticed earlier when Riley was putting his jacket away, had to be Riley's room. He peeked inside as he walked by, a look of concern pooled on his face as he went to the restroom. After wards, Josh walked slowly back to the living room, where Misty was standing by the couch looking out the bay window. He settled in the center of it, knowing that if she wanted to sit close to him, she would have to sit on either side. Or, she could just sit in the loveseat across from the couch.

Riley had gone to Alex's five minutes ago, Josh and Misty said nothing. Misty had started a fire in the brick and plaster fireplace, and then sat back on the couch and sipped at her wine; Josh rubbed her leg which she had laid across his knees. They sat quietly and listened to the soft jazz on the radio and looked out the three sided bay window towards the street. Because of the two foot frame at the bottom of the window, the van with dark tinted windows that sat nearly directly across the street couldn't be seen. At least if you weren't looking for it.

"Can I ask you a personal question?" Josh asked, using his softest voice.

He didn't want to sound accusatory or suspicious, but he had to know, he was falling in love with Misty as fast as rain fell from the summer sky and he already felt as if he had Riley's blessings, but two things bothered him. He had to settle it now, even if it meant he would be kicked out. He could feel Misty's leg muscles stiffen slightly when he asked.

"Sure. If I get a return question."

"Okay." He took a deep breath, "Is everything alright?"

Misty sighed. Here was her chance to spill it all. Tell Josh everything from the day they first met to why she was crying a little while ago in the kitchen before dinner. But…

"Of course, why?"

"Well, it just seems a little strange around here. I don't know, like there is something floating around the room when you and Riley are together."

Misty let out a nervous sigh. "Like what?"

"Are you…I mean, like…hiding?"

A shudder rose from her leg on Josh's lap and he could feel the muscle constrict like Misty was about to leap from the couch. A second passed and her leg relaxed a little; Josh was trembling inside as it was, from building the nerve to ask, but he had to know.

"Josh, I…" She raised her hands to her face and tears flowed through the cracks in her fingers. "We…are."

The light in the house had dimmed, making it harder to see any movement. The man and Misty had moved from the dining room and the view Jacob had through the large front window, to the living area on the north side of the place. The best view was obstructed by the window frame and all he could see-even with binoculars-was the tops of the couple's heads. The boy had gone to the back of the house and hadn't been seen in several minutes. Jacob's phone rang.

"Yes." There was impatience and frustration in his voice.

"Okay, I'm coming in at ten o'clock, flight 2643 United."

"Which gate?"

"Don't know, but I'll have what you wanted also. You might have to make some alterations, but it'll fit in with your plan."

"My plan? Are you telling me you figured out what I'm doing?"

Jacob sat back hard on the van's seat, he felt a bead of sweat on his brow and with a quick swipe of his other hand he wiped it off and flicked it towards the seat in front of him.

"No sir, I just thought…"

"Nothing. You think, plan, or guess nothing. You are to do what I ask for money, you are my whore; understand?"

"Yes, I just thought…"

"There you go again, thinking." Jacob wiped his eyes and pinched the bridge of his nose with his forefinger and thumb. "Look, when do you leave?"

"Thirty minutes."

"See you in…" Jacob glanced at his watch, "…one and a half hours." And hung up.

Movement caught his eye upstairs in Misty's house. He trained the binoculars in the huge main window again, looking to see where the man and Misty went. Scanning left to right along the south wall was a long, tall bookcase full of its unreadable titles. Jacob estimated about two or three hundred books, and Misty would've had plenty of time since she disappeared to fill it.

Next, along the back wall-the east wall-from what he could see was a large 36 or 42 inch screen television on a platform that lifted it four or five feet off the ground, a small end table on each side holding a small lamp, and a grand painting about six foot long of a seascape done in watercolor, a terrible one at that, one that his mother or father would have to show their prowess over the art industry. Jacob took a long look at it, shook his head and began scanning with the binoculars again for the occupants.

The place was sparsely furnished, like someone on the run would have-except the books-easy to pack and get out in a hurry. Maybe the books belonged to the home owner she was renting from, maybe all of the furniture did too; that would make it even easier to flee, if the need arose.

Misty had made a move to get to her feet and was one step towards the kitchen when her answer hit Josh. A swelling of uneasiness came over him all of a sudden; he expected a "no" answer, not a "yes, we're hiding" response, not even a hint of the question was critical, nor was it point of fact he knew, he just was taking into consideration the fact that Riley seemed too comfortable for his first night home, and the room looked lived in, once again; not like he had just arrived. More like the boy had spent at least a few weeks, judging by the clothes on the floor and the books on the desk in the corner of the room. School books meant school, and Riley wasn't here during winter break, not this early in the month.

Misty had refilled her wine glass from the second bottle of chardonnay. She wanted to spill it all-the truth not the wine-tell Josh everything, the beginning to the end, but then…that would mean he would have to be the man she *thought* he was, and she still hadn't established his position. Now was the time to give him a sample-not all-if he knew it all he could end up dead, or worse.

"Is it your husband? Are you running from him?"

"Yes. And no. We're not running, I mean Riley…"

"Lives with you."

"Yes. His father and his grandparents are very stubborn people. I'm here, *we're* here living under my maiden name. I hoped this city was big enough to hide us, I hoped we would meet someone who could take care of us and put our past just where it belongs, in the past."

"Are you alright though? I mean, can I do anything for you or Riley?"

Misty sighed and set her empty glass in the sink. The warm wine buzz was twinkling in her toes, her thighs and calves felt a touch numb and there was a tingle at the back of her head. A warning tingle, something that ached to be let out. *Tell him everything! Tell him his life may be in danger if the family finds her…*

"Not right now, we're all alright now." *Liar.*

"Are you sure? I mean, you could stay at my place and we could…" Josh paused at this and thought, *you would find out my little secret…*

"No, look Josh; it's not that we are really hiding. Like I said, I'm using my maiden name; Riley is using that too. We just had a bad experience in L.A. and came here to get away from certain people."

"Like your husband." It was a matter of fact statement, even though Josh didn't fully understand.

Misty sighed, she wanted to tell the truth, but right then and there if she did, Josh would probably leave afraid for his life and never want to see her or Riley again. She said the only thing that made sense at the moment, even though she was sure she would regret it later. "In a way, yes."

Instead of returning to the comfort of the living room, Josh and Misty stayed in the kitchen, Josh leaning against the counter by the back window and Misty on the granite worktop by the stove and refrigerator.

It had been nearly thirty minutes since Jacob had seen the man or Misty in the front of the house. The rest was obscured by the height of the place, and the fact he couldn't park the van any further away to get a full inside view. He looked at his watch for the fourth time in those thirty minutes and decided he had better head for the airport, being it was a Saturday night and the place would be busy. He would park in short term parking with his rental van, careful not to draw any attention to its contents; after the events of two months ago on the eleventh, everything looked suspicious to airport police and even a simple passersby.

A mini-van with tinted windows and binoculars wasn't really a threat at an airport prior to then, but a rental van with the same characteristics was a red flag after the biggest attack on American soil and would jeopardize his whole mission here. Jacob was glad he left his "kit" back at the room in a hiding place. But he would use it later, and that thought made him warm inside. He pulled his toy from his belt and the pistol, stuffed them both under the farthest seat back as far as they would go and looked at the area from different angles, angles that someone would look into the van, and knew his hiding place was safe, unless the van was opened by airport security or the police.

One last look and Jacob crawled back over the seats to the driver's side, careful not to be seen by joggers or even a late evening dog walker. After a quick examination of the area and he was sure no one saw his movements, he started the van and drove off towards SFO.

As he drove, he formulated a plan. One that had to be foolproof, one that had the best chance of success and minimized losses. He calculated the losses, there would be two at least now, maybe three.

CHAPTER TEN
Later That Night

Josh was looking out the window now and saw the van that took the best parking space out front drive off. His head was swimming with confusion, so it didn't even register to him that he never saw the driver leave a house or apartment nearby, the van just drove off. He had stood in the living room deep in thought, after Misty told him her husband was abusive towards her, that all he wanted from her was money, the same money her mother left her when she died, around three million dollars, and he had successfully gained about two thirds of that.

She had nowhere to turn, no one to turn to, and no family left to hide her. Her story began like this:

She was living with her mother and stepfather back east and soon her stepfather, named Brice Martin; Brice with an *i* instead of a *y*, had to move to San Diego County where he had been conducting business for several years prior. The whole family had to uproot again and move across the country to a suburb of San Diego called Lemon Grove.

Brice was a profound structural engineer, and made quite a good living off of the practice of designing freeways, buildings and small dams to be earthquake resistant. After the Loma Prieta quake in 1989, Brice was called upon to design structures that would withstand another more serious temblor, one that was predicted in the very near future. Misty was twenty-two at the time, but still lived with her family while she finished her last year of school at Princeton where Brice graduated, and he was more than happy to see an alum in the family. But the job called and Misty decided she would finish up somewhere else if she had to.

159

The second month they were in San Diego Misty met J.W. McAllister. A rich businessman with family ties in Los Angeles and Southern Nevada. J.W. and Misty hit it off big, he was a good looking charmer with money of his own and after a night of partying at a local club and passionate lovemaking, Riley was conceived. One month after that, J.W. McAllister asked Misty to marry him and they shared vows at the prestigious Long Beach Pier.

The wedding cost a small fortune, but Misty's mother and Brice footed the bills, the McAllister family paid for the reception, which nearly equaled the wedding ceremony dollar for dollar at twenty-thousand. Misty and J.W. moved to Long Beach after that into a 5.5 million dollar home with six bedrooms and six bathrooms. Misty had first loved her in-laws, J.W.'s extensive family, but soon would learn the consequences of her love for them. They were crooks.

Not the kind you would find hiding in bushes and mugging couples at knifepoint, but the kind of criminal that extorted money from businesses through labor contracts, the kind of people that made sure if it was being built or planned, money was going to be channeled their way or certain politicians would change zoning laws or regulations. The kind of people that ran very vocal meetings behind closed doors, and even sometimes-or so the rumor mill chanted-folks would end up missing if they crossed the path of the McAllister family.

But, Misty swore, J.W. was not that kind of man, at least she didn't think so at first. He told her he had no input or received any of his money from his family. He was a self-made millionaire, his business dealings were from "honest" sources and he didn't indulge in the practice of bribery, blackmail or knee bashing. At first he seemed that way.

In 1992 Brice Graham Martin died of a heart attack in San Diego in his office chair. Misty's mother had moved to L.A. to live with Misty and J.W. on his property near Long Beach, Misty had cherished the idea, to have her mother near to watch over her grandson while Misty and J.W. would go out once in a while. But what Annette Desjardins-Martin found was more of a comic book twisted reality nightmare.

Her daughter was watched closely by the McAllisters, J.W. especially. Whenever Misty and Annette ventured out downtown or to the beach, a guard or tail would follow them. Whenever they went out to eat together, there would always be an extra car outside and an unknown person sitting across from them at another table, a person who ate very little but kept his eyes on the family members, and a hand near a fold of his jacket.

Time with Misty was brief, two months after her arrival Annette had a seizure while swimming one afternoon in the estate pool; and no one was around so she simply floated face down until she drowned. A gardener found her and called 911, but it was too late, Annette Kara Desjardins-Martin was dead, declared an "accidental" drowning by the coroner. She was buried in a small but elaborate cemetery owned by the McAllister family, paid for by the same.

Misty was distraught for weeks, she hardly ate. At one point her husband had to call for a doctor to care for her, she had become anemic and passed out. Finally after grieving made her deathly ill, she pulled herself together for one reason, Riley. He needed her, she was feeling uncomfortable herself around the McAllisters now, they were quieter and more secretive around her; J.W. asked her questions like; *"Do you have a will?"* Or *"Shouldn't you invest that money?"* Misty was becoming more and more suspicious about her welfare. And Riley's.

Misty was now rich. $3.8 million was deposited into her banking account after the legal hassles were over, another $1.3 million into a trust fund for Riley David

McAllister, the full benefit of the Martin estate, and Annette's life insurance policies. Riley's money was secure, no one but the young man at eighteen could withdraw it, but Misty's account was accessible in the event of her death. On one occasion J.W. told her she had to share with him at least half, "just in case" and there was no jovial pretense about it. That's the same time J.W. became more and more abusive, he had struck her more than once.

Misty made the transfer of $1.9 million into her and J.W.'s joint account under his watchful eye, but what he didn't see later that day, Misty had carefully redirected her remaining inheritance into a savings account bearing her maiden name, Desjardins, and kept the interest installments that ranged between 5.4% in the early nineties to an ending payment of 4.9% or $93,100.00 for example in the year 2001, hidden from her husband and family. A jaunt to the bank secretly disguised as a shopping trip to a nearby clothier once a year secured the cash for her in one hundred dollar bills. She had successfully amassed $820,000 in cash by May of 2001, which she kept hidden in her son's room. Eight thousand and two hundred one hundred dollar bills were not the easiest things to hide, but she found a niche near the door to the room, a small void that was probably used for a statue, that had been plastered over by the previous owners of the mansion.

Then all hell broke loose in June of that year. And that's where the real story ended as told by Misty to Josh, where she filled in the truth with falsehood and speculation, to protect him more than to deceive him.

"I ran off one late night in June." Misty began to finish her story, "Riley and I slipped out of the *compound* after midnight. I took a wheeled suitcase and filled it with the cash, when everyone was asleep Riley and I snuck out of the house. We boarded a bus to San Francisco and voila, here we are."

Josh remained quiet throughout the story. When he assumed Misty was finished, he rubbed his forehead with his sweaty palm and then rubbed his eyes, he wasn't sure how much of the watering in them was caused by tears or just tiredness.

"You and a twelve year old boy rode a Greyhound all the way to San Francisco with eight hundred thousand dollars in cash in a suitcase?"

"Yes. I suppose any one of those drunks on the bus would have a heart attack now if they knew what was sitting right at their feet."

Josh exhaled loudly. He turned his gaze out the window again.

"How did you convince Riley to go along with it?"

"Didn't take much. He loved his grandma Ann, and when she died he was despondent as any five year-old would be. But he saw his father strike me on more than one occasion; he knew in his little heart that hitting mommy wasn't right. When I said one day when we were alone, 'Mommy wants to leave here and leave daddy', Riley smiled and disappeared. A minute later he had his toys packed into a backpack and was ready to go." Misty looked at the floor and wiped her moist eyes. "It broke my heart that he was so eager to leave, but we always had this bond between us."

"It's very powerful." Josh noted matter of factly as he turned towards Misty. "I've noticed it too."

"So did his father." Misty sucked in a quick breath, then pursed her lips.

"What?"

"Nothing, I just…" Misty looked away.

Josh let it slide; he was more interested in hidden details.

He asked, "And all this time, no one has come looking for you? Not even using your maiden name?"

"They would be looking for Riley McAllister or Martin, not Desjardins. And they were led to believe I was headed back to the east coast, where the Martin family money is. No one knew about my secret savings account and my 'cash stash'. The family thought I was dead broke when I left, it would take months to figure out I had hidden the rest of my inheritance from them, and where."

"So if they found it intact?"

"Yes, it would all be there, all nice and pretty. All of the nearly two million dollars." Misty patted the couch next to her thigh, her bare tan skin exposed by her dress. The invitation was hard to pass up. "They would think that I took off without the money."

"But the interest?"

Misty swallowed hard; she couldn't reveal the details of why no one would miss the interest. Josh sat down next to her, he let his leg touch hers, even though he was wearing pants, he could feel the smoothness of her skin, and he could breathe in her perfume; sweet, citrus and the light musk from her sweating in the kitchen over dinner.

Misty said, "Only J.W. and his folks knew about the banking thing, he didn't know about the interest. As far as anyone knows, the money is in a locked interest account, unavailable to withdraw for five years."

"Oh." Josh looked away from her; he found a spot on the floor and concentrated on it. He swallowed and spoke, "So, what happens in five years when they look and find the account empty?"

Misty exhaled through her nose in a sad sigh. "They're going to be pissed."

"More pissed than when you took his son and ran away?"

A deep inhale from Misty told Josh that she was thinking, not for the better. She glanced off to her left and back to her knees, which she covered with her hands.

"It's…complicated."

"How so? I mean, you took this guy's kid…"

"My son!" Misty's voice rose, an argument was coming, the one she expected.

"*Your* son; ran off here with you. You said these people are ruthless, I would expect them to come looking for you as soon as possible."

Misty started crying again, she lifted her hands from her knees to her face and turned away from Josh, who pushed himself back a little. "I came here, looking for someone, for one person who I thought would understand what I did, and I hoped to find security with him. So I could stop running."

"Me?"

"I don't know now. I can tell you're upset, but I don't know why."

"I just see this as a huge mess; that people…you or Riley, might get hurt."

"Or yourself…" Her point was cold, sharp. "Don't worry; my husband won't be looking for us. I can guarantee that."

Josh rose to his feet. He slowly walked to the kitchen to get some wine, finding the half empty bottle on the counter, he poured himself a glass. A tear formed at the corner of his eye as he drank a large sip.

'*Why can't he just find a normal relationship? Why does there always have to be complications?*' He took a deep breath after swallowing another large measure of wine.

He said aloud to clear the kitchen, "I…don't think I'm the man you're looking for, then."

All he could hear in response was a muffled crying, Misty was sobbing into her hands. Josh poured the last of the wine down his throat; he could feel the warming tingle from his toes up his thighs to his waist. The warmth spread fast, faster than scotch or beer, his chest felt constricted.

He was fighting a war in his head, to tell Misty the truth about himself as she had just done, but his conscience was losing. He felt he needed to get out of here, get away. He slowly shuffled back into the living room, he found Misty still on the couch; she had pulled her knees under her and was leaning over on the leather arm of the sofa, breathing slowly, looking towards the window.

Josh had his doubts about the future with this beautiful woman at this point. She had a heavy past. Filled with bad guys who don't forgive and forget, his was only a past of deceit and death, and he paid his debt for that. But this arrangement could get him killed. He knew this was a cowardly way to handle things, but in his life he never had to rush to the rescue of anyone before and he wasn't sure if he could sacrifice his life or freedom for a woman with a sketchy past or a sketchy murderer husband and family.

"I guess maybe you're right." She whispered. It was the sound of defeat.

A bong sounded from the mantle clock, indicating it was ten-fifteen.

Josh opened his mouth to say he should leave when a clacking noise came from the kitchen, a rustling of some kind, like someone was trying to open the back door. The hair on the back of his neck stood, the momentary buzz from the alcohol he was feeling disappeared, he looked in Misty's direction, she was at full on terror. Another scratching sound like someone was trying to slide something in between the door and the jamb. Josh's hands began a little shiver and he quickly looked around the room for a weapon. He walked slowly, quietly towards the fireplace and hefted a poker from the utensil stand; the brush and tongs clanged and broke the dead silence in the room. The sound made Misty's heart stop.

Josh held the poker out like a sword; he was steadying himself for a confrontation, while Misty pulled herself tighter to the contour of the sofa, trying to hide. She whispered, "Oh God."

Josh then slid his body to the door frame into the kitchen area, he could see the door handle working side to side, a shadow was on the stoop outside but the lace curtains combined with the darkness out back obscured the figure's true outline. Whoever it was, they weren't trying to peek in the window; they were steadily working at the lock. Josh could see the dead-bolt was not in place through the small slit between the door and the jamb, his heart stopped also.

Everything happened like a flash of lightning after that. The room was filled with the sound of a click-click, the noise made when a lock disengages. Josh held the poker above his head with both hands, if Misty wasn't ready to throw up from anxiety, she would have giggled at him; he looked like a drunken Ninja; his sword held high, his eyes bulging from fear.

The door burst open and slammed against the kitchen counter making a banging noise that echoed around the room and into the living area. A figure dashed across the floor, close to the ground like he was looking for cover, he darted to the small table in the corner of the room and then Josh could sense the aggressor was headed into the living room, he cocked his arms back as far as they would go for a death blow downward.

Josh saw a shadow dart in his direction and steeled himself for attack. The figure then smacked Josh right in the crotch, the sensation was not that of a fateful blow, but more of a sensitive nudge. Josh let swing with the poker and it crashed to the floor, the pointed curve making a thuck! Noise as it stuck into the wood floor. The assailant then lunged onto its hind legs and smothered Josh with a soaking wet pink tongue.

"Carter! No!" Riley yelled from the landing outside the kitchen door.

"Riley! What the Hell?!" Misty yelled from behind the couch.

"Good Lord!" Josh exhaled as the chocolate lab lunged up and up trying to get his kisses higher on Josh's face.

"Sorry mom. I forgot my DVD's." Riley explained as he headed towards the hall.

"Are you kidding? You could have been hurt; you scared the daylights out of Mr. Kennedy."

"Sorry, sir." Riley spoke as he passed Josh and the attacking dog.

Misty rose from the sofa and walked past Josh and Carter into the kitchen. She took the door by the handle and was going to close it, but instead opened it a little more and stepped out into the cool foggy night air.

Josh managed to get Carter under control; the dog wagged his butt as he sped towards Riley's bedroom. Josh took a deep breath and looked at the poker lying on the floor. He had taken a chunk of flooring out about the size of a large caterpillar, he bent over and picked the poker up, returning it to the utility rack on the hearth. He looked out through the kitchen to the back window; he could see Misty standing on the landing. He exhaled sharply, mostly to relive the pressure that had built up inside of him, and then stepped out towards her.

"I'm sorry Jimmy."

"Josh, please."

Misty was staring out over the small high-fenced yards that surrounded the home. Each house had the same amount of fencing; the same "good neighbor" gate on the south side of the fence, each home had a two tiered staircase and a landing at the back door, just like the one Misty and Josh were standing on. Few lights were on, the one on the back of the house next to them was, and the gate next door was open.

Josh nodded towards the house just to the south of Misty's and said matter of factly, "Alexandra's."

"Yes." Misty's response was an exhale of relief in itself. "He's supposed to knock."

Riley had retrieved what he was looking for and he and Carter were headed back out the door.

"You're supposed to knock..." Misty said again as Riley passed them on the landing.

"Sorry, I thought that maybe, that you and, well..."

"Riley!" Misty's blood ran warm, not from anger, but from the thought of what her son was implying. She crossed her arms in front of her.

"Sorry, I'll be going." He said with a little sarcastic smile as he and Carter trotted down the stairs into the short-cut lawn and through the gate, closing it behind him. He reached the landing on the other side and a tall blonde hippy came out to meet and waved at Josh and Misty, they waved back with quavering smiles.

After the door next door was closed, the light went out and the shaken couple stood outside in the dark for several moments. The fog was heavy tonight and had already covered most of the Bay Area; including the few miles inland from Ocean Beach past Golden Gate Park and Kezar Stadium and Misty's home on Willard, a scent of brine and the mixture of the cool December air left a slight taste of changing weather on wind.

"I'm sorry." Misty offered.

"No need." Josh glanced over his shoulder towards the fireplace. "I guess I could've done a better job of protecting you though."

"Well, you did *spring* into action, but if you were more accurate, poor Carter..."

"Yes, sorry about that."

Misty wrapped her arms around him and gave him a deep kiss, Josh felt his tongue being pushed aside hard and forcefully, Misty was excited. He slowly backed into the kitchen and closed the door behind them, spinning to reach the door and kissing as he went. They never made it to the bedroom, the large leather sofa was the landing area of the entwined bodies, the groaning sound of the leather and sweaty skin was nearly drowned out by the moaning of the love makers.

CHAPTER ELEVEN
Much Later that Night

After leaving SFO International, Jacob had taken John Buckley to *Mel's Diner* on Mission Street a ways from the St. Francis. They ate big cheese dripping burgers and slurped hand-made chocolate shakes as fifties era rock and roll blared out of the speakers around the restaurant. Each table and booth had a little jukebox selection machine and the entire place was decorated in pure 1950's memorabilia. From huge posters of Elvis doing his slouch shouldered, leg sprawling, finger snapping, closed eye singing into a vintage microphone; to pictures from the film *American Graffiti.*

Even though the waitress was wearing something more likened to the nineties and had some piercings that resembled the seventies, she was friendly enough and the service was fast. It was now eleven-thirty, and the place was mostly empty.

The talk at the table wasn't 50's era either. It was in the now, the current situation that Jacob had found himself in as Randolph Tate, the man who was hunting a woman and his own flesh and blood. Buckley had brought with him a portfolio of sorts, a manila folder with a stack of papers a quarter of an inch thick, a dossier of the license plate and the owner's name and information Buckley gathered before his flight, with the help of his buddies on the police force, his former *partners*. The information Jacob had requested from a covert van parked across the street from Misty's house earlier in the evening; Jacob was perusing the photos and papers of the man associated with the Ford Excursion's plates.

"Humph. 'Joshua James Kennedy' huh?" Jacob read aloud. "Owns *Battered Sole Fishing Charters* out of the Wharf, since his father died in the eighties…"

"I think you'll like what you find here…" John Buckley said as he stuck his finger in between the pages in Jacob's hand. This drew a look of disgust from Jacob.

Jacob took his glaring eyes off of Buckley and glanced over the page. He started to chuckle, then the chuckle turned to a half-hearted laugh, the laugh then made his eyes go misty.

"Oh my God, this couldn't be any better." He flipped through a few more pages and chortled some more. "This guy, this is perfect." Jacob surveyed the restaurant for prying ears, when he saw none, he turned back to Buckley. "I knew he had to go, but this will make it so much easier, she'll never know what hit her…"

"Or him." Buckley added, like he was in on the joke, Jacob just snapped a look of superiority at him.

Josh awoke around one a.m. Misty was breathing deeply and softly, her nude chest rose and fell like small swells on the open sea; perfectly timed, in rhythm with her breaths. He carefully moved her leg off of his to the back of the couch they were sleeping on, both too exhausted from love making to get up and even turn the lights off. A musky air of ardor and lust hung in the room and Josh smiled as he thought of the passion that made up the night, and early morning as he and Misty wrestled out their frustrations of the day-yesterday-and finally dozed off in each other's arms.

Josh pulled the comforter Misty had retrieved from her bedroom, during a break in the action, over her exposed body and tucked it softly around her. She made little sharp exhales of excitement as he did. When Misty continued to sleep, Josh walked over and stoked the orange coals in the fireplace with the evening's earlier weapon and tossed in another log of oak. He located his pants on the floor near the door to the kitchen and pulled them on; the early morning temperature was chilly inside the house. He walked quietly across the floor back to the living area and sat back on the loveseat opposite Misty on the sofa, the cold leather on his bare back made Josh's eyes bulge out and he held back a shocked breath of air as he shivered the chill off. Then he watched her. He loved her.

Aside from her passion, Misty was tender and caressing. She listened and spoke without suspicion, she laughed at inappropriate times and cried unexpectedly-like in the kitchen earlier. She took a soft breath and the comforter rose with it, then it settled back down. Josh smiled; he knew he would fall in love with her, even with the revelation that she had been hiding some truths from him, that she had been *hiding* period. He was afraid for her, he was even afraid for himself a little, after the scary incident in the middle of Misty's chilling story about her ties to crime riddled family, when Riley came back for his DVDs.

He wanted to run away, the instant she revealed her mixed up tale of bad guys and escaping in the middle of the night. The sordid in-laws that seemed to do things to please themselves at the cost of others. The simple fact that her ex might be out there looking for her gave Josh the feeling he should bolt out the front door and drive home and nearly hide under his covers. But, the back door incident changed his mind. The second he thought she might be in danger, he looked for a weapon and moved in to face the peril-to hell with his own safety.

This thought bothered him a little, that he would forget instinct of run and cover for stand up and fight for this beautiful woman in front of him. He knew that deep inside, his action to protect her was a sign he would die for her, if need be. And that was love. The feeling he got when he looked at her sleeping, the tingle he got inside when she would make the tiniest movement under the cover over her while she slept, how she held him and told him she felt safe with him.

'Randolph Tate' and guest arrived at the St. Francis at one-fifteen a.m., the rental van was parked by the late night valet and Randolph led John Buckley to his room. Few notice a man and a man in the wee hours of the morning heading to a hotel room, this was San Francisco after all, and alternative lifestyles were part of the open pride the city boasted.

Jacob opened the room and nodded at Buckley to enter. Once in, the door was bolted and the table lamp was turned on, Jacob pulled a chair out from the stationary table and indicated he wanted his accomplice to sit on the guest bed.

"Cameras?" Buckley opened.

"Two, one at the elevator entrance and another at the end of this hall."

"Elevator?"

"Yes, but as we walked in I had my back to the lens the whole time and my body obscured your profile."

"Pretty good, boss."

"I'm not an amateur; I cased this place out two hours before I checked in. Knew where I wanted to stay and where to avoid the cameras, where the security stations are, who the security guards are and where they hang out during breaks. I know the time the maids make up each room and also know the schedule of the guests of both sides of my room."

"Good working with you."

"Yeah. Now, the items I requested."

"In my case, the big one. What's next?"

"I think I'm going to watch carefully for a few more days. Follow the woman to get a semblance of a schedule, find out the boy's habits. Then follow Mr. Kennedy for a few days, see what pops up, who he talks to, who he does business with. Makes it easier when he *disappears* with Miss Desjardins."

Jacob pulled the papers that Buckley had given him earlier from the envelope again and laid them out on the table in front of him and studied them. He said nothing more. Buckley turned on the TV and lay back on the bed, falling asleep in several minutes, snoring. Jacob looked at the chubby man and shook his head in disgust.

Buckley looked like a cop; overweight, tired and droopy dark circles under his eyes, nosey and spent too much time thinking about plans. He was about six foot two and two fifty, brown hair and balding at the top with dark brown eyes. It was the man's eyes that bothered Jacob McAllister the most, they were dark, deep, unrevealing. Jacob hated men whose eyes he couldn't read. They were dangerous and unpredictable in what they would do in certain situations; Jacob hated people who were unpredictable, like Misty Desjardins. She would pay for her crime, as well as the fat snoring man on the bed across the room; he might have to go to missing also. He was getting too expensive and knew way too much, even though that was McAllister's fault, John Buckley would pay for it.

Jacob smiled; a plan formed. This was a break, Buckley being here, the fall guy was ready for his close up.

Josh had quietly as possible made a pot of coffee, then found the towels and stepped into a chilly shower at four a.m., he had to be at the *Sole* by six-thirty, to help Lester get her ready for a seven in the morning charter. Since he had never used what he believed to be Riley's shower, Josh had troubles with turning the knobs in the right direction to get the water temperature just right. First he had it too hot and nearly scalded the skin off of his back as be adjusted the cold handle up; then as he stepped in the iron clawed-foot tub, the warm water he thought he had locked in turned ice cold and he nearly slipped and fell onto his butt when he scrambled to get the hot back up to warm the stream of water coming from the shower head. After two or three attempts shocking his body in different extremes, he had it just like he wanted; cold. Well, almost like he wanted, but he was tired of fiddling with the knobs and decided he could stand the chilly water more than he could a hot soothing steamy sleep inducing stream.

Quietly humming to himself he was using his hands to squeegee the excess water off of his legs when the curtain opened suddenly, sending Josh's heart into palpitations and he heard the fateful squeaking noise of his bare feet trying to keep balance on the wet porcelain.

"Coffee?" Misty asked.

"Jesus Marie!" Josh answered.

Misty smiled broadly; she had slipped on a nearly see-through sheer robe and was holding a cup of hot coffee in front of her. "Sleep well?"

Josh took several breaths as he gained his composure, all the while staring at his attacker with wide eyes. "I won't need the coffee to wake me up, thank you."

"Sorry, but I love that song you were humming. What was it?"

"*A Pirates Life for Me* from the Disney ride."

"Oh! The 'Yo Ho' one?"

Josh exhaled his last deep breath, "Yeah. I don't know why, but sometimes before I go to work I hear that song in my head and I can't get it out."

"That's so cute! Maybe because of your uncle? I think he looks like a pirate."

Misty had moved to the edge of the sink and was leaning her behind on the tile surface, still holding Josh's cup of coffee. Her hair was a little messy, turned off to one side with a dozen or so strands sticking here and there; the little makeup she wore was slightly smudged, but it was the negligee that kept Josh staring at her midsection rather than her eyes.

"Do me a favor though, don't tell him that? He already thinks he's the salt of the sea."

"Is your neck sore?"

Josh craned his neck side to side. "No, why?"

"'Cause you keep staring at my chest instead of looking in my eyes." She answered playfully.

Josh inhaled slowly and looked her in her sparkling blue-green eyes and said, "You're more beauty than I have seen in a while...I mean your body is..."

"Careful Mr. Kennedy, you'll end up being late for work..."

Lester had been pacing the bridge of the *Sole* for twenty minutes, waiting for Josh, who was late-even according to Lester's standards. Finally he saw his nephew climbing down the railed ladder to the deck of the boat.

"What in the Sam Hill? You and that woman going to get road rash if you keep it up!" He hollered down as the smiling captain stowed the bait bag in a locker.

"Did the charter cancel?" Josh asked without looking up.

"Nope. They're coming down the walk now..." Lester returned as he put his hand to his eyes, even though the sun wasn't high enough yet to get in his eyes, he just thought it made him look more sailorish.

The family of four was the epitome of "landlubbers". They were all dressed in Phoenix, Arizona clothing, from the feet to the hats. Josh had told the father on the phone when he called to make reservations that they should dress warmly, for cold weather and water spray. Although they each carried a sweatshirt, Josh hoped they had longer pants or sweats in the bags the mother of about thirty-five, father of about forty, and the two children ages twelve and probably about fourteen, were carrying. The

177

oldest child, a girl, was wearing a *Cardinals* jersey, the boy was dressed out in *Teenage Mutant Ninja Turtles* attire.

They stopped at the top of the slip and called down to Lester, apparently they thought he was in charge, most greenies did.

"Ahoy!" The father yelled, like every other tourist who came down to the docks.

"Hi!" Josh called back up, "Hope you brought some warmer clothes!"

"Sure did." The man started down, then looked up to his wife who looked as if she was going to refuse to climb down the over-painted rail and rung ladder. "C'mon honey, it'll be fun!"

'*Oh boy.*' Josh murmured to himself. This was the typical midseason tourist venture. The father had 'always wanted to venture out to sea', so while he was on vacation in San Francisco he would drag his family onto a fishing boat and think he was Ernest Hemingway, living out his fantasy. But as usual, the wife and kids were none too pleased with the excursion; the wife will be seasick most of the time, the kids will hook everything on the boat except a fish and Lester or Josh will spend more time administering first aid for puncture wounds than baiting hooks.

The wife started down the ladder and as usual, the fog made the rungs a little slippery, so her foot nearly slid off of the first one. After a screech that startled a gull on a nearby piling, she continued down the relic ladder and made footing on the *Sole*. The teenage girl was next and as per the rules of teenagers, she tried to climb down with all the dignity of a person who had no interest of being here, let alone being anywhere near her folks. She made it down without incident, and of course the boy had to try out something he saw in the movies once: grabbing hold of the handrails and sliding down without using his feet. This only works in the movies with men who have good strength in their forearms, Lester had not even tried it more than once, and the kid landed with a thud on the deck after falling about five feet.

"Oh! Honey are you okay?" his mother shouted.

"Yeah! That was fun! I want to try it again!"

'No the hell you don't kid, your dad is probably a lawyer and I don't need another suit!' Josh thought to himself. "Okay, everybody ready to shove off?"

The father emphatically nodded his head as he surveyed the *Sole,* the mother shot him a look of tendered murder and the kids ran for the bow, as all kids did.

"Stay off that thing in front!" The mother yelled, referring to Quint's Point.

Josh nodded to Lester, who fired up the diesel, then Josh went to casting the lines off and pulling in the fenders as Lester maneuvered the boat out of the slip and into the marina towards the breakwater and the bay. Immediately the woman was looking green and sat down nearest the stern of the boat, the kids were jumping up and down yelling "I'm the king of the world!" as the wind blew over their faces. Josh just shook his head and cursed that movie for the millionth time.

Not long after they cleared the breakwater, the family all gathered together on the deck and began pulling out sweat clothes from the bags they were carrying. The tops were embroidered with San Francisco and a little cable car on the front; the pants were matching with San Francisco running down the length of the legs in white screen transfer.

Lester looked to Josh, who smiled back with a tear in his eye. He nodded and went to work setting up the poles and rigging for bait. Typical, typical. Tourists were always coming here during December because they heard it was *warmer* here in the winter months. It was really warmer in some ways than any other month of the year, but it wasn't the tropics. So, here come the families, stepping off the plane at SFO or getting out of their car at the Golden Gate

Bridge Observation Park and feeling that first blast of cool sea air. The very next thing they do when they go to visit the Wharf is hit one of the dozens of over-priced tourist stores and buy the warm sweat clothes, each with its own unique version of *San Francisco* embroidered across the front.

'If I had a dollar for every one of those sweats brought on this boat...' Josh thought to himself.

All in all, the cruise wasn't bad; the weather held and the sun shined. The kids had each caught a fish, the boy reeled in (with the help of his father) a nice forty pound halibut and the girl brought in a 24" lingcod. The father caught a thirty pound halibut and the mother even fought a large fish of some kind up to the stern, but the animal unhooked itself and swam off. Lester swore to her it was a five foot Soupfin shark, and she was more excited than she had ever been in her life.

As with most of the charters, Josh took them on a little side tour of San Francisco Bay. He knew it was a waste of fuel and few other boats did it, but it was his chance to stay on the water till after one in the afternoon, and it gave the tourists something to talk about when they got home. Maybe they would mention it to a friend who was going to visit and Josh would have another customer.

Today's fishing took them close to Marin, so Josh puttered the *Sole* near the marina there, a very nice and expensive set of docks with nicer and more expensive boats and yachts, but mostly sailboats occupied the slips.

He then cut across the bay and coasted within a few hundred feet of Alcatraz, even though the father of the family mentioned he was taking his brood there later this afternoon. Josh told him to pick out the places they would like to walk to as they passed, since the prison island tour is self-guided. It would save them time when they arrived at the dock there.

After completely circling the island twice, Josh pointed the *Sole* back towards Sausalito and the docks where troop ships called *Liberty Ships* like the Jeremiah O'Brien were built, even though the O'Brien-which is just a quick trip from the harbor where the *Sole* is moored-wasn't actually built there. Josh informed his photo snapping patrons that some ships were built in less than thirty-five days to keep up with the demand from the war department.

Another turn away from the north end of the bay and a lateral across the widest portion put the *Sole* near Treasure Island, Yerba Buena Island then across to Pier 39, then past the old Ferry Terminal at Pier 41 and the Red & White Fleet headquarters at Pier 43 1/2, finally back to between Pier 45 and the Fisherman's Wharf Harbor and the home of the *Battered Sole*.

Even the teenaged girl had a good time helping Lester clean the fish and prep them in the Mylar insulated bags for taking the meat home, the boy was enthralled with Lester's war stories and the wife had a few chardonnays and 7-Ups, so she was in a very good mood and smiling the rest of the chilly trip back to port.

The man paid his $265.00 for the charter, bait and three lost riggings gladly and tossed in $35.00 as a tip. He claimed it was the most fun they had ever had as a family together.

Lester was hosing the deck off of the fish guts, Josh was securing the *Sole* for the night and the family scrambled up the ladder and took pictures for five minutes before disappearing towards the Wharf with their freezer bags of fish.

Minutes after the tourists left, a flock of gulls started harassing Lester as usual, for tidbits as the bloody fish remains were washed overboard. And, as usual, Lester tried to hit one of the gulls with a blast of water from the hose. But this time, he stepped wrong and one leg slipped forward as the other was locked in place; Lester had done an impromptu gymnastic split, which was difficult at best for a nearly eighty year old man.

After the laughter had settled, Josh helped his uncle to his feet and set him across the stern board.

"It's broke!" Lester cried out for the fiftieth time.

"What's broke Les?"

"I dunno...something is broke though!" He grimaced.

Josh would have burst into laughter again, if he hadn't realized he was going to have to haul his uncle up the ladder and to the Excursion, almost a mile away. It took nearly an hour.

"Battered Sole." Jacob's voice echoed off the wooden walls of the harbor. "What kind of idiot thinks he's so funny?"

He and John Buckley were standing at the top of the rung ladder, which had a chain and a padlock across it. Next to the ladder was a sign with a publicity picture of the *Sole* on the high seas and the selling points of a charter with the crew and boat, along with copies of flyers in a little box for those interested.

"Three hour venture. Sixty dollars per person, two dollars per rig, lunch included." Jacob looked to the other slips. "One of the cheapest here; must be desperate."

Jacob pulled his jacket close to him and slid the pamphlet back into the slot of the acrylic box. He took a deep breath and looked out over the charter boats all lined up along the docks and said, "God I hate the ocean, how could anyone stand to be on the water for three hours?"

"Looks like we missed them." Buckley said while nursing a crab salad tray from the Grotto.

"That's alright; we have some things to pick up and other things to take care of today. We'll meet up with Mr. Kennedy soon enough and I'll have an arsenal of information to do battle with him, thanks to you John."

"Nothing broken, but he'll be laid up for a while." Josh said from behind her, in the bathtub.

She had made the suggestion to Josh and he nearly fell over from the surprise of the question. She led him to the master bath, in the somewhat large bathroom and the largest tub Josh had yet to see here in San Francisco, which was situated in the middle of the room. Old style claw feet and iron, the thing must have weighed at least five hundred pounds empty.

Misty started the hot water and pulled a little box holding five, six ounce bottles of Aroma-Oil from under the sink and looked at each one by pulling it out and reading the flavors off to Josh, who was struggling with his shirt buttons.

"Eucalyptus, orange, lemon, mulberry or lavender?" She asked as each bottle was presented.

Josh shrugged his shoulders as he was pulling his shirt off over his head; he had given up on the buttons, "Any one you want."

Misty selected mulberry oil and dropped six drops into the water as the steam began to build over the mirrors. Josh was working on his pants' fly and watched with eagerness as Misty had dropped her sweatpants to the floor and unzipped her running jacket. She smiled slyly when she caught his gaze then spun around to take the jacket off. Then coyly slipping her T shirt up and over her head easily, and then she slid her sports bra off of her torso and gave it a flip towards the hamper in the corner-missing it-then slid out of her panties and the show was over.

She cupped her hands to her breasts and turned around, and with two hops was in the hot water. The ensuing wave splashed water over the sides, but she didn't seem to care much. Josh simply finished pulling his pants off then his underwear and slid in behind her. The oil made the porcelain slippery and he nearly fell on top of her as he did.

Josh had never bathed with a woman before, he was slightly nervous. Being naked was a thing of beauty, poets had written about it over the ages; but to Josh a naked man was the ugliest thing in the universe. He looked the other way at statues, art or frescos that depicted a man in the buff, it just didn't appeal to him and he wondered in the back of his mind what women saw in the misshapen form of the nude male. However, the female body was a true work of art, and he worshipped it with great respect; he treated women as the masterpiece they were and only what they are on the inside he had ever argued with.

Fact is; he and Faith had several minor disagreements but only one major argument-and that ended...badly.

Misty never let on she was just as uneasy; it was her first time too-that any man was interested in sitting in a tub of water with her made her anxious-maybe it was the subconscious fear that bathing was an act of cleanliness and not sensuality, it was more of a moment of weakness as your whole body is exposed not for pleasure but for washing; even though the way Josh worked the loofa was very stimulating, it was still a little nerve racking. Misty decided to suck it up and hope that he didn't find her body too offish. But he seemed to respond quite well during lovemaking. Misty was falling hard for this man, he was what she had hoped for so far and knew when she got inside his head more, she would be satisfied with what was there too, she hoped...

"That's lucky." Misty responded as she lay back to Josh's front in the steaming water filled claw-foot iron tub in her bathroom.

"Not really, he's staying at my place, which means pay-per-views and beer guzzling. He'll have quite a vacation."

Josh was using the loofa to softly scrub Misty's silken light brown skin on her back, carefully-like scrubbing tissue paper with sandpaper-her skin seemed so fragile and he was afraid to scratch it or even cause a red mark. He was admiring how the water enhanced the color of her skin, obviously a product of a tanning booth, but very well even and not overly dark. She had her hair pulled up into a knot and he took into inventory each of the little moles on her skin, the little freckles, the way her neck glistened closer to her ears from either the steam or sweat.

"I really have to sit down and talk to him one of these days, he sounds fascinating."

"Fascinating?" Josh stopped scrubbing and looked to the side of Misty's face. "That's the first time I've heard anyone say that about him."

"I get this feeling though, no matter how bad you trash talk him, you still love him."

Josh began running the sponge over her back again, over the areas he thought he hadn't covered yet. He smiled, "He's the best friend I have, and the only family I have left."

"Only?"

"We have distant relatives, but I barely know any of their names and don't think I know where they live at all. Our family scattered a hundred years ago, one branch went one way, the others faded into obscurity."

"Oh. I guess after my mother and grandparents died, Riley is all I really have left." Misty half turned and leaned back into Josh. Her breast brushed his knee as she kissed him, then she spun around to her knees and pulled herself from the slightly oily sweet smelling water. "Does this mean we're off for Saturday?"

"Oh no. I can operate the *Sole* by myself, and usually do even with the old man of the sea; I would never disappoint Riley like that."

"Weatherman says it's going to be nasty this week."

185

"Yeah, but nice on the weekend. Perfect time to be on the water, after a storm it's like the wind and the waves freshen the smell and look a bit. It's truly amazing."

Josh watched as Misty stepped from the tub after squeegeeing the moisturizing oiled water from her abdomen and legs. She grabbed a towel from the heated rack on the wall and dried herself off with her back to Josh; feet first, then her calves and thighs. She worked the towel across her belly and chest, then slung it over her back and using it like a polishing rag by a shoeshine boy, dried her back off. She finished with her neck and lightly patted her face dry when she smiled over her shoulder back to the tub.

"Not getting out?"

"I think I'll wait till the water gets a little colder." He said with a nervous smile.

Uncle Lester had Josh's apartment to himself for the week, except having to get up once in a while to take a phone call from prospective clients. The weatherman was right, a small but wet storm blew in on Tuesday, and a lot of rain to the Bay Area was the most it could muster. But what the storm does to the mountainous passes from Nevada to here is what affects the charter trade.

Nevada is where much of the winter business comes from, travelers must endure snow and ice and even road closures at times when there is heavy snowfall on the main artery of highway between Northern California and Nevada; Interstate 80. Four to six hundred inches of snow fall in the highest elevations throughout the months of October to March some years and the road over *80*, as it is affectionately called on both sides, tops out at 7,056 feet.

Donner Pass was named after the ill-fated famous pioneers heading from the east in November 1846 to a new life in California. They were stranded on the eastern slope during a harsh winter when the pass became-impassible-due to snow. The emigrants, reportedly numbering at eighty-one souls, became marooned in the ice and snow and only forty-five survived to eventually reach the other side into California. Reports of cannibalism amongst the survivors made national news and some scary bedtime stories back in the eighteen hundreds.

The travelers head over the pass to enjoy things that their counterparts in California head the other way to get away from. Tired of snow and cold the tourists will drop down into the Bay Area for walks along Pier 39 (the busiest of the tourist areas along the Wharf), eat at fancy four and five star restaurants, stay in a nice five star hotel, see a professional hockey game in San Jose, catch a *49er* or *Raiders* football game, or sometimes charter a fishing boat to put some quality seafood in the freezer.

Charters run the entire coastline of California, the most popular being the squid excursions from Bodega Bay north of San Francisco, where an amateur fisherman can haul in a decent hundred pound Cephalopod; the whale watching fleets that can get a person or family within a few hundred feet of a breeching California Grey whale or a large pod of Orcas; the halibut fishing fleets of nearly every port, and the tour rides on the San Francisco Bay including tours of the prison island of Alcatraz.

Some chance having to "sling iron" or chaining up their cars to go over the pass to take a tour of the famous wine country Napa-Sonoma, where adults can enjoy tours of wineries and sample the products of the vineyards.

Josh's phone only rang three times during the week, each time it appeared that Lester had gone mad with pain the way he dragged himself from the comfortable couch in front of the TV to answer the phone, not once did he think to bring the cordless receiver over to the coffee table that was cluttered with a Tupperware tub holding half popped popcorn and empty beer cans. The first two calls asked about the weather and inquired about the weekend prices. The third was a business man up from Santa Barbara who was interested in going out on Friday-alone-and would compensate for any other missed passengers. He would pay cash, double the going rate. The businessman said he was tired of sitting in his hotel's bar watching basketball and needed to get out, and he was willing to pay extra for it, as long as he got a receipt for an expense account.

Lester took the man's name and phone number, and then read him the standard *we are not responsible policies and rules* including the empty-bag return policy, which basically states the *Battered Sole Charter Company* is not responsible if they don't catch any fish that day.

The man said just getting out on the bay would be enough and hung up. Lester called Josh on his cell phone to book the day, then returned the phone to its cradle near the kitchen and hobbled back to the couch to watch 'Hawaiian Hotties' on pay-per-view.

Josh clipped the phone back to his belt and looked over to Misty, who was walking Carter the Lab and Riley along the hundreds of finely manicured palm trees near the de Young Museum in Golden Gate Park. The rain had subsided a little and even the tourists had come outside to take photos of the amphitheater or catch a lungful of fresh air outside of Steinhart's Aquarium, and the hundreds of school kids running around inside.

Riley's high school was out for Tuesday through Wednesday for proficiency testing, so he was able to spend time with his mother and Josh, something he was looking forward to, some semblance of a family get together. He was happy his mother was happy with Josh, they had spent a long time looking for the one who could. When she was contented, the world was a better place.

"Does Lester need a back rub?" Misty teased as she walked up to Josh, who was stowing the notes he had taken on a small pad in his pocket. Josh just smiled condescendingly.

"Nope. But I got a trip booked for Friday. Looks like the guy is desperate, so I'll have enough cash for a first class tour on *your* day." He nodded in the direction of Riley and Carter. "Maybe even a little stop and a bite in Marin."

"Oooh! The Yacht Club? We are royalty." She smirked back.

Josh sat back on a bench after wiping it down with his handkerchief. He wiped a spot for Misty too; Riley and the dog seemed content to keep running around playing chase. Misty scooted closer to Josh and pecked his cheek. She let out a small sigh and wiggled into his arms.

"Do you think we're moving too fast?" Josh asked, not very seriously, but with a touch of concern.

"Maybe." Came the response. "We seemed to have learned a lot about each other in the last few days though. Is there more I should know about you?"

Josh pondered this for a moment. *Yes*, would have been the appropriate answer, but he needed more time to figure out how to tell the woman he was falling in love with about his darkest days, the secret that kept most women away from him-at least the ones that knew the story.

Misty stiffened a little and looked to Josh's eyes, "You should answer quicker than that."

"I was just thinking, "Josh began, "What to do about Christmas. I noticed you don't have a tree yet, and I rarely put one up."

"Really?" Misty sat up.

"It's just me and Lester, at least for the last few years, so we eat out. We give each other a gift or two and that's about it. Once in a while I'll invite him over to watch a movie, but that's rare. I think we should get you a tree"

"Christmas is a time for families." Misty began, and then her voice became slightly incredulous, "You don't even put up a tree?"

"No. Maybe once or twice."

"Wow."

Josh was priming himself to expose a bit of his nightmare, but just as he opened his mouth Riley came running up and Carter threw half his wet body onto Josh's lap.

"Carter! Get down!" Misty commanded.

Josh just laughed and rubbed behind the dog's ears. He had dodged a bullet, but sooner or later, Misty would have to be told of his secret and that would probably put a strain on their relationship. No one who endured what Misty and Riley had been through would want to be subjected to more.

Josh knew he was falling deeper everyday they spent together, he would think of her and her face was the last thing he would see in his mind before he drifted off to sleep at night, even if they were together-which they were most nights-and would still feel anxious in the mornings when she would leave or he would have to run errands, until they were together again. But that wasn't the half of it.

For some reason inside, Josh felt he knew her. He knew her mannerisms and her laugh was like an echo he heard many times over, but he couldn't quite put his finger on it. He knew that he had never dated her before, they were from opposite sides of the country, but they shared a lot in common, even if Misty hadn't realized it yet. And Misty, on the other hand, acted if she was anticipating every moment of closeness they had together. Like she had planned in her mind what her life would have been like with Josh, even before they met. The feeling seemed outrageous to Josh, so he never mentioned it, but he still felt the pang once in a while.

Misty looked at the muddy paw prints on Josh's tan Dockers and realized this man was more than she bargained for. He was patient, kind; he loved the stupid dog that constantly kept mugging him for attention. There was a sense of serenity about him most of the time, even when he badgered about his poor uncle Lester, he seemed to have a spirit of kindness and acceptance. His sense of humor kept him usually smiling, his abilities in intimate moments made them seem to last a lifetime, his touch burned her skin with Eros; his kiss was passionate and purposeful, not just for the drive of foreplay, but for the sense he wanted to be part of her mind; as close as possible to her eyes and face as he could. Part of her world.

She was in love with him. There was no doubt, and Riley had taken a liking to him, hopefully in the near future Riley would love him like a father. Misty prayed for that.

"Can we go to the Tea Gardens?" Riley asked his mother.

She glanced at Josh who smiled back at her, his mind was on something else but he hid it well, she could tell. "Sure."

The rain kept Misty, Josh, Riley and Carter inside Wednesday. The first stop was at Josh's place to drop off Carter. Josh walked him around the little partition of grass that borders the front of his house, until Carter did his business. Using a plastic grocery bag, Josh scooped up the mess and threw it in his trash can as they bound up the stairs to his front door.

Of course, the only unhappy participant in the whole visit was Uncle Lester.

"Ain't no way I'm babysittin' that animal." He protested.

"Ah look, you're out of beer Les." Josh called from the kitchen. "And I was going to pick some up on the way back today. I'm sure you'll be able to hobble down to Walgreen's and get some huh?"

Lester's eyes bulged for a moment then he turned to Misty and Riley. "Does he pull this damn blackmail stuff on you at all?"

Misty turned to hide a smile.

191

Josh walked back into the living room where Lester had his *bum* leg up on the coffee table. There were four empty beer cans on the end table next to the couch and a pizza box with two slices left and Carter was hovering around the box, sniffing in the air around it as he kept his brown eyes focused on Lester. Josh walked over and in a simple act of diversion, introduced Misty and Riley to him.

"Les, this is Riley, and you remember Misty right?"

As soon as Lester looked in the direction of the presentation, Josh slipped a slice of pepperoni to Carter. The dog pretended he had nothing to eat in months, or so it seemed as he nearly swallowed the piece whole. Immediately the dog sat directly in front of the table, turning his head towards Lester, then back to the box repeatedly.

Misty cupped her hand over her mouth to hide the laughter she was on the verge of, and offered her other. "Good to see you again. How's your leg?"

"I hope they find they don't have to take it off." Was the grim reply.

Next was Riley, he stepped in and shook the old man's hand vigorously adding, "I hear you were in the war, did you really fight on an aircraft carrier?"

"Yep!" The leading question primed Lester's need to expound. "I was on the *Yorktown*, that was Admiral Fletcher's flagship. I was his personal assistant you know, he needed anything-I got it for him. Nearly lost our ship during the Battle of Coral Sea. Your teachers tell you about that one? But then, a month later we took bombs and torpedoes at Midway and lost our 'Island', you know what that is boy? That's the big thing that sticks out of the top of the deck. Anyways the old Japs thought they had sunk us at Coral Sea and when them 'Vals' came in to bomb us at Midway you could see their eyes wide with fright, knowing that Ol' Yorktown was there to do battle with them. A bomb blew up below decks and I helped carry most of the injured, lost sixty-six men that day…"

Riley sat down on the floor in front of Lester and the old man leaned forward, putting pressure on his bum leg, but he continued with his story. Misty had joined Josh in the kitchen again, where he was picking up empty beer cans and take-out boxes. Josh had a smile on his face and was shaking his head as he stuffed his trash can full.

"Wow. Looks like your uncle has an audience."

"Remind Riley later that most of what he hears is not exactly true."

"Really?"

"Well, the parts about the battle are true, and some of the details are a little inaccurate, but anything that he says he did besides work in the engine room, well, that's where the truth ends and his fantasy begins."

"He didn't save any lives?"

"Just his own. Rumor has it he was one of the first to be evacuated. Hungry?"

"Sure. How about *Tarantino's*? My treat."

"Sounds great. Then how about spending the day in the traps along the Wharf?"

"Like *Ripley's*? I bet Riley would love that. Or maybe we could just go to the mall."

"I could use some more Tylenol." Lester called from the living room, then he returned to his story he was telling Riley. "So after the destroyer goes down, we get the call to pick up survivors and I grab my lifebelt and head overboard…"

"Wow!" Riley gasped.

Josh was shaking his head, "We'd better get out of here before Lester gets to the part where he carried the A Bomb on his back into the Enola Gay."

Misty covered her mouth and giggled. "Maybe we should leave them together."

Josh shook his head, "No. I don't want your son to go to school with stories like this."

Riley was hard to pry away from Lester and Carter had made himself at home on the couch at Lester's feet. His big eyes looked at Misty as she patted him on the head on her way out.

"Hey!" Riley flashed a look at Josh, "Can we see your boat?"

"Saturday." Josh said with a smile.

"You might have to walk him every three or four hours." Misty directed Lester over her shoulder as she went out the door.

"If my leg don't give out on me…" Lester creaked as he rubbed his leg.

"There's an extra six pack in it." Josh added.

"Okay, okay. Now get before I change my mind."

An hour and a half later, the trio was dodging raindrops by going in and out of the trinket shops and tourist traps along Jefferson Street. They had lunch at *Tarantino's*. Misty wanted to see the shops at Pier 39, so by keeping close to each other they walked towards the end of Jefferson, stopping in at *The Wax Museum at Fisherman's Wharf, Ripley's Believe it or Not!* and *King's Fine Arts and Antiques*. During a lull in the storm, Misty, Josh and Riley made a break for the Embarcadero and got to the busiest part of the Wharf before a downpour began.

At Pier 39 they watched soggy street performers do acrobatic acts at the central stage, spent an hour in the Aquarium of the Bay. By early afternoon, the rain had subsided and was now just a little drizzle here and there; walking was again easy for the tourists and they abandoned the shops and the streets of San Francisco started to fill with folks enjoying the break in the weather.

As they neared Pier 33, Riley's eyes got big as they passed the Alcatraz Tours Ferry and grabbed his mother by her hand.

"Mom?" He asked in his tender *I want something* voice.

Misty looked to Josh, who had anticipated this venture and pulled out his Wharf Passes and led the boy and his mother to the ticket booth. By two in the afternoon, they were on a ferry to the prison island and then spent the next two and half hours wandering the island, taking the offered tours, enjoying the self-guided tours and just spending time chatting about topical things about the famous penitentiary before meeting the return ferry at the dock.

It was six in the evening when the tired trio reached the *Boudin Bakery* for dinner. Seated in the *Baker's Hall Café* Josh and Misty were side by side at the table, Riley was off using the restroom.

"This…" Misty sighed, "…was an incredible day."

"I hope Riley enjoyed everything." Josh said, looking over the top of the menu.

"Well, he did get a little fidgety at the wax museum, but I mean who his age knows all those people."

"Yeah. I thought I was going to have a heart attack trying to keep up with him at Alcatraz." Josh looked at the menu for a few more seconds, nodded and put it down. "How about clam chowder and a shrimp salad sandwich?"

"You can skip the sandwich for Riley, but he'll love the chowder. It does come with those little funny shaped crackers, right?"

"Oyster crackers. Yep. Wouldn't be authentic San Francisco chowder without them."

Josh paused for a moment as he looked out the big window towards the street. Cars were leaving in droves, mostly tourists who had been drenched while on vacation and were headed back to their rooms for a splash in the indoor pools and Jacuzzis.

"Do you think he would like to go to Hawaii?"

"You're kidding." Misty's expression was flat.

195

"Oh, been there before huh?" Josh frowned.

Before Misty could answer, Riley came back to the table and asked, "Been where?"

And, before Misty could stop him, Josh said, "Hawaii."

"Oh wow! No. We've never been there, I mean my dad…" With that he glanced at his mother and she looked at the tabletop. "I mean, we were going to, but…"

"It's okay Riley, your mother told me."

Riley cast a curious glance at his mother. "You did?"

Without looking up she nodded.

Josh said, "I'm sorry, I didn't mean to drag up any bad memories."

"You didn't, it was just that we had always talked of going on a big trip, like to Hawaii or Cabo. But we never did." She responded, still staring at the table but this time she was running her pink painted fingernail along the seam of the tablecloth. Riley dropped his gaze too.

The restaurant was slightly crowded and the din was at tolerable levels, but the table that held the man, woman, and near teenager was silent for almost three minutes. A waiter walked up, took their order and walked off, another few minutes of silence. Josh was feeling bad about mentioning it, but he knew he had to break this stillness.

"Faith and I had talked of it too."

Misty's mouth dropped open a little and Riley looked up from the table.

Josh continued, "She was a real island fanatic. She'd been there a few times, once after high school graduation, another after her parents divorced."

Riley looked up at him and asked, "Was that your ex-uh I mean, you know?" He turned white.

"Passed away. Late, whichever you prefer. Yeah, she loved the islands." Josh continued, but then his voice dropped off when he realized he may have crossed the line. But it was his line to cross.

Misty just glared at him, not sure what to say. Riley's color seemed to return when Josh didn't take offense to his question, and his mother didn't nudge him under the table.

"I've never been, but Lester's gone three times to Pearl Harbor. Says it was to memorialize his fallen comrades and bring back the time he enlisted just days after the attack there by the Japanese. I think you would like it Riley, you seemed so interested in his, uh, tales. He says even though he wasn't there, he could hear the attack happen in his mind, he could feel the bombs exploding and he even claims he's seen a ghost or two of sailors wandering around Ford Island."

Silence still wafted around the seats they were in, so Josh added, "Yep. Let's plan that trip, say next November? Take Riley out of school and we can…"

"Yeah!" Riley piped up.

Misty's eyes began to water and she smiled so hard she thought her tear ducts were going to burst wide open and flood the butter plate in front of her. She had found the man she was going to love the rest of her life. Josh tried so hard to be helpful, he worked at keeping them satisfied and even anticipated the tour Riley wanted to take to Alcatraz and bought presale tickets. He was even trying to kill a somber moment, not by backing down and being afraid of the subject he raised, but by being forceful and defiant of his late wife's memory and the situation that brought Misty and her son to San Francisco in the first place. A sort of, *To Hell with ourselves!* attitude, and *let's not make our past a problem for our future* position. She had, just now, fallen in love with Josh James Kennedy.

"Are you alright mom?" Riley's face popped into her tear clouded vision.

"Of course, it's just that I haven't heard you so happy in so long…"

"Well, we haven't had a reason to be in so long."

The waiter returned with their drinks, Misty opened and poured a packet of sweetener in her ice tea, Riley set out to harpoon the cherry in his Roy Rogers, Josh just sipped at his tea. He sat his glass softly down on the table linen and looked up to Misty.

"Can I ask you a question?"

"Sure, I think you still owe me one from the other night, but go ahead."

"What did you do since you came up from L.A.? You seemed to have missed all the sites around here, or you're just pretending that I'm a good tour guide."

"We had a lot of things going on; finding a place to live, a school for Riley, spent time looking at animal shelters for Carter and smaller things like just playing board games at home, just the two of us." Misty rubbed Riley's hand on the table and he pulled it away.

"Mom!" Came the urgent whisper, "Not here…" His red color returned.

Misty smiled, a pained one, but she knew her son was hitting the age when open affection was a no-no. "We didn't really venture out at first."

Josh thought about the next question that popped into his head, wondering whether or not it was wise to ask it in front of Riley, but he was sure that he and his mother were on the same frequency, Riley was very knowledgeable about his surroundings and Josh was sure that the kid knew more than he let on to. The waiter walked to the table with a tray of three bowls of chowder with crackers and two shrimp salad sandwiches.

"Were you afraid of being found? I mean, using your maiden name is kind of tell-tale isn't it?" Josh picked his sandwich up and took a bite.

"I figured my in-laws would be looking for my married name, they would assume that I would use my married name, since that was the one I used to open the bank account. They would figure I couldn't drag out any money unless I withdrew it under McAllister, but little did they know." Misty shook her packet of Oyster crackers into the chowder.

Josh watched Riley out of the corner of his eye, wondering how the boy would react to the story. He didn't, he kept ladling the thick soup into his mouth like he hadn't eaten all day and didn't even seem fazed by the query.

Josh had to know, so he asked, "You said you could guarantee your husband won't be looking for you. Why?"

Misty looked to Riley and took a deep breath; he nodded and took another spoonful of chowder to his mouth. Misty looked to Josh and took his hand on the table, Josh didn't pull his back like Riley had done, and he cocked his head and waited for the answer.

"Because he just won't."

Jacob McAllister was sitting in front of Misty's house on Willard for the last three hours. He hated it when he made an error in calculation, or 'miscued' as he called it. He knew the woman would have to return home, at the least he thought she would still be here with her man. Not even the boy had shown himself. Buckley was sitting in the seat in front of Jacob, eating a hot dog they bought hours earlier.

"Gave us the slip." Buckley said, a little too arrogant for Jacob's liking.

"No. I didn't plan for this. Obviously Misty is more of an outgoing person than she was at home in L.A." Jacob slipped over the seats to the driver's side and started the engine.

"Where are we going?"

"Back to the hotel. I have to make some plans, good plans that won't fail."

"Oh."

As the white van with dark windows drove off out front, Alex had the phone in her hands ready to dial 9-1-1 about the suspicious activity she saw out her front window. She thought better for it, after realizing that the cops might want to talk to her about the call she made and ask to come in. That would be bad; she didn't have enough time to hide her little garden on the back porch. Cops get all pushed out of shape when they see the kind of garden she grew; her parents were arrested twice for growing the things. But it was for her own use; she never sold it and never left the house when she smoked it.

Alex looked to the calendar on the desk by the window, Thursday. She had seen the van twice now in three days. At first she thought it might be a little paranoia, she had been hitting the chronic a little hard in the last few months-never when Misty's boy was around-but still, she was wondering if maybe she was getting to the point she should back off a little, even though it was for her back pain, she was afraid that a simple van out front would be the Feds, but they drove black SUV's, planet killers, and this van was too small for all the electronics needed for surveillance, at least from what she'd seen on television.

Alex placed the phone back in its cradle and stared out the window for several more minutes, hoping that maybe the van would drive by again and she could get a better look at the driver, or its other occupant. The new guy. This was the first time she noticed the other man in the van, yeah. Maybe the Feds were watching her. The Man was always out to get the innocent offspring of sixties Haight-Ashbury followers and children of the HANC (Haight-Ashbury Neighborhood Council) which her parents were still proud members of. The HANC fought The Man when he wanted to build a freeway though the Panhandle in the 50's and her parent's thought-as does Alexandra to this day-that he's trying to get his revenge.

Or maybe she was just smoking too much.

She didn't have a rough childhood, Alexandra Safflower Deterich was born in San Francisco in 1963 to Amanda (aka: Sky Shine) Dunbar and Robert (aka: White Surf) Deterich. Sky Shine and White Surf were the epitome of the Haight-Ashbury Day flower children, they believed in free love, smoked happy weed and dropped acid to experience life as Abbie Hoffman had offered *"a life free of all responsibilities"*. The offspring of well-adjusted socialites of the Bay Area, Sky Shine and White Surf broke from the money and royalty their families offered and decided that they were going to live away from the monarchy of American society and be their own rulers.

Of course, after Alex was born, money was needed for food and shelter, Sky Shine returned to being Amanda and married Robert, who reverted from White Surf. Amanda got a job as a waitress at a small restaurant on Castro Street; Robert took his father up on a job to run an offshoot of the Deterich family business. Although the couple was forced to reintegrate into mainstream willing slavery, they refused to leave their beloved Haight-Ashbury and eventually earned enough money to buy a home there.

Alex had the best life afforded to her; she was well educated and roundly so by her mother and father who taught her the ways of fighting the establishment from within as opposed to openly and destructively as they did in the sixties. She grew up knowing that she would have to be a functioning member of society in order to subvert the fascist pigs that ran the country, and she was well liked at her job as operations manager at the animal shelter.

It was there she met Misty and Riley, the wayward lost mother and son, who not only were looking for a guard dog for protection, but a place to stay. The two were living in a hotel paying weekly, and seemed out of style for this woman and her boy. The home next to Alex's had gone up for rent recently, furnished and clean, so she recommended

J Jay Ross

it to the young mother. Misty at first seemed the perfect type to rescue; her story was that of struggle and survival, and eventually freedom from man's control. Men. They were responsible for the way things fell apart and for most of the problems in the world.

Misty had cash, Alex had the connections and in just a day after they met; Misty, Riley and Alex were neighbors. The next thing she knew, Alex became the dog-sitter for Carter (she helped name the animal after her favorite President) and babysitter for Riley. She liked Riley though; he was young, intelligent and would not back down if they were having a discussion over issues they disagreed on. She respected him for that; he allowed the same for her. They had a close friendship that few ever had, Riley entrusted her with some facts about he and his mother's flight from L.A., and the chance they might be safer if they found a man to live with them, not just any man, but one his mother had been looking for-for months.

Alex was still not going to be challenged by any man; she knew he was the evil face of paganism, capitalism and the punishing power of politics. But she liked Josh, the man who had been brought over and introduced this afternoon by Misty as they gathered some board games to play at his house, and so Alex could again watch over Carter and Riley when he got out of school.

And, as if on cue, Riley knocked on the door.

"Hey Alex." He said as he came in and shook off his soggy raincoat on the tile foyer.

"Wow. That sounds like a sad voice, would you like a snack?" She asked, taking his over-clothes and hanging them up.

"Nah."

Carter came in from the kitchen and stood up to be scratched and hugged by his owner, then after several attempts to re-drench Riley's face, he settled down with a whump! On the floor by the fireplace.

"Why so glum honey?"

"I was hoping to go along with mom and Mr. Kennedy today. He's taking her to the *Jeremiah O'Brien* and the *Pampanito* today. I wanted to go."

"The who?"

"You know...the ships from World War Two at Pier 45..."

"Oh honey, I don't like warships, you know that. They're just extensions of man's anatomies used to kill human beings in the plight of playing the deadliest game of King of the Mountain."

Riley rolled his eyes out of Alex's view.

"Yeah, but did you know they filmed the engine room scenes from that *Titanic* movie on the O'Brien? I so much wanted to see the engine room. That's where Mr. Kennedy's uncle Lester worked on a carrier in the war."

"Enough war talk honey, you know it makes me twitchy. I'll make us some herbal tea, how's that sound?"

"Okay."

"Stop taking hundred dollar bills out of the bank with your toes!"

"I'm not!"

Misty was sitting cross legged and barefoot on the floor in front of the *Monopoly* board. She was the banker and Josh on more than one occasion had seen her use her finely pedicured toes to snatch a bill from the little tray to her side. The game had been one disagreement after another; do you get cash from *Free Parking*? Do you have to auction off property if someone lands on it and the person who does refuses to buy it? The arguments over 'loosely guarded rules over the years and tradition' lasted only a few minutes each, and ended with a kiss that made Lester protest. He was sitting on the couch, bent over rolling the dice.

"Hah! Doubles again!"

"Three doubles in a row means you have to go to jail." Misty chided.

"Does not!" Lester fought back.

"Uh huh Les." Josh defended Misty.

"Okay, I've had it! All you two want to do is neck after making up fake rules and I've had it. I'm goin' to take a hot bath and soak my busted leg."

"It's not busted Les, just a strain." Josh smilingly spoke as the old man rose from the couch and struggled to the hallway.

"What's the difference? Can't use it."

Lester stopped in the hallway as if he had forgotten something, turned and shuffled to the kitchen where he retrieved a beer from the fridge and then resumed course towards the guest bathroom.

"You two keep it vertical…" He half-heartedly warned as he shut the door.

Josh responded by leaning across the board game on the floor and kissing Misty passionately. They stayed locked to one another's lips for several seconds till Misty pulled back and sighed.

"Careful! My dad's in the other room." She whispered playfully.

"We could go to my room." Josh responded coyly, like a teenage boy would in his day.

"What about the tour of the boats?"

"Ship and submarine. It's raining too hard; besides, Riley would really want to go. I think we should take him when we do."

Misty smiled and sat back on her heels. "You're so thoughtful of him. He likes you, you know."

"He's a great kid. Bright, quick witted and he even likes Lester. That's a rarity in these parts."

"I like Lester myself."

"It seems he's building himself an entourage."

Glance Over My Shoulder

The bath water stopped running, so Josh and Misty had to whisper, both knowing that sometimes old men with hurt legs had nothing better to do than listen in.

CHAPTER TWELVE
Thursday Night

Jacob McAllister was not a happy man. Not only did he lose sight of his targets, he also lost his drive for the evening. He needed rest but his roommate John Buckley, the man he flew all the way up from L.A. to help him, wanted to go out to dinner. Jacob didn't want to be seen with Buckley as much as possible, just in case things went south or his final plan failed. He was working the final plan in his head now, for any chances of that failure.

While Buckley was in the shower singing some god awful tune, Jacob had opened his special briefcase and was tinkering with the handle lock, the one that had to be twisted a certain way to open, so any one could open it with no problem. He had selected some items from the lower tray, under the weapons partition, placed them on the upper section and made some final adjustments to the safety system, the one that fired a face-full of dye into an unsuspecting set of prying eyes. After he closed the case he turned the knobs under the main handle.

Setting the case on Buckley's bed, Jacob went to the mini-bar and pulled out a shot of the cheap scotch and poured it in a cup of ice he filled from the ever-full ice bucket. He stared at the glass for a moment and shook his head, "So it comes down to second class booze and help…" He poured the booze down his throat before the ice had a chance to leave the bottom of the glass.

"You say something?"

Buckley had left the shower running for some reason and had stepped out of the bathroom in a towel wrapped around his bulky body. The spare tire hung over the towel in such a way that Jacob's stomach almost reversed the alcohol flow back into his mouth. He coughed.

"Do you always leave the shower running?" Jacob hissed as the scotch burned his throat, cheap scotch did that.

"Nope, had to pee and I wanted to make sure it all washed down."

The simple thought and vision of what his fat accomplice had done in the shower made Jacob sit back down and place his head into his hands. The room was silent for a few moments as Buckley watched his boss shake his head. He shrugged his shoulders and started to walk back into the bathroom.

Jacob raised his head and said in a crackly voice, "When you shut that shower off come back in here."

"Okay." The water died to a trickle sound as it drained from the pan. Buckley returned to the room and began digging in his suitcase for a change of clothes while holding the loosening towel with his free hand. "What's up?"

Appalled and shocked by what he was witnessing, Jacob stood and looked out the window to the square below. He cleared his throat, "Hmmm. I want you to do something. This is very important, and you had better listen well."

Buckley had dropped the towel and was pulling on his whitey-tighties. Jacob had glanced over and then right back out the window, shaking his head in shame and revulsion.

Buckley said, "Okay."

"See that other case on your bed, my case?"

"Yeah."

"That case has sensitive information about me, you and this whole…" Jacob was trying not to say *debacle*, "…enterprise."

"Sure."

"I'm leaving on Sunday, going home when my plan is put into action. You need to stay until Monday afternoon, the room is paid for. Got it?"

"Sure, I have nothing better to do anyway." Buckley was pulling on his pants.

"Listen, this is important. I need you to take this case to the authorities if something should happen to me."

Buckley stopped short of pulling his shirt all the way down. "What?"

"I said…"

"I know what you said, but this whole thing is against the law. If I take that to the cops, they'll lock me up and throw away the key."

"Look here." Jacob opened the case with the combination and secret knobs, turned the handle and opened the case. "Come here."

Buckley pulled his shirt down and started tucking it inside his pants waist as he moved towards Jacob. As he arrived over his boss' shoulder he spotted a manila envelope and several packs of cash taped together with bank seals. Jacob hefted one of the cash bundles.

"There's thirty thousand dollars in cash here. You'll take that out, then this envelope," Jacob lifted the manila folder out and opened it, and then he closed it quickly. "Goes to the cops." He placed the cash back into its spot and then set the envelope back on top and closed the case, setting the locks again.

"The cash is for me, but what about the case? Do I have to open it for them there?"

Jacob rubbed his chin for a second in thought and then shook his head. "Just open it here and take the cash out, you can do with it what you please. But take the manila envelope to the cops; make quite sure it's more than an hour after I'm scheduled to return. Better yet, make it two hours. Now watch as I show how to work the combination."

Jacob placed the case out on the bed so they both could see the locks and special knobs. After several attempts by Buckley to open the case with complete failure, Jacob wrote the instructions down on a sheet of hotel stationary and stuck it under the handle of the case.

"Look dummy, here's the instructions. If you do it wrong the case will be locked forever and only I can open it. So, no cash, no absolution of you for the crimes I'm about to commit. Get it?"

"Can I try it again with the instructions?"

"No. No time, we have to get something to eat then I want you to watch the house again while I get some sleep."

"How long?"

"All night."

"Jesus!"

"What? You don't think I'm paying you enough?" There was sarcasm floating in the air from Jacob's reply.

"It's not that. I just didn't get a lot of sleep last night and now you say I have to stay up and watch the house."

"Just until after noon. The boyfriend should be back there by then."

"What are you going to do?"

"I have to see a man about a murder."

Misty stood from the floor to stretch her legs. As she moved towards the window, she stopped at the picture of Faith in front of the Oncology sign.

"Can I ask you a serious question?" She asked in a somber voice, careful not to sound prying or too loud. She suspected Lester was still listening in.

"Sure. I owe you a few." Josh had slipped four hundred dollars from the bank as she had her back turned and figured she caught him.

"Faith. You said she died of cancer?"

It was time. Time to let himself off the hook, all he had to do was tell the truth to Misty right here and now. He took in a deep breath and stood.

"No."

Misty spun in surprise. "What? I know you said she had died of…"

Josh interrupted, "I know what I told you. But that wasn't the truth, I owe you the truth. At least what I can tell."

Misty placed her hands on her hips waiting, then she slowly lowered them, realizing that she looked judgmental. She let her left arm dangle straight down and grabbed her elbow with her right hand. This was to hide the sudden trembling.

Misty knew deep in her heart that something was unsaid between her and Josh on the subject of Faith. He was too quick to pan off the cancer story, this was going to be good, and probably very bad at the same time. But-she had her own story that was full of holes and a secret still hidden from him. It was his turn, then maybe hers.

Josh moved slowly to her side and picked the photograph off the shelf and gazed at it, sluggishly. He scanned the beautiful face that he'd fallen in love with so long ago. Then he touched the brass bell shaped urn and ran two fingers along it. He lifted his fingers to his eyes as if he were inspecting them for dust.

"She was killed in a car accident."

"But you said…"

"She and I were arguing one night. Typical sad movie story byline huh?" Josh turned towards Misty; his eyes were filled with tears. "We fought over the dumbest thing possible, the name of our child. She *was* pregnant, a little boy."

"I'm sorry, but why? Why tell me this story about cancer?" Misty unintentionally took a step backwards, into the bookcase.

"It'd been so long since I held another woman, since I even talked to a woman. Sure a few times since the accident I went out with what friends I had left. Most of them were our friends and they blamed me for the wreck and her death, but a couple of them felt sort of sorry for me so we went out.

"It was three years later of course, but the first woman I was hooked up with asked me about Faith and I told her the truth. That was the last I heard of her. She went to the bathroom and never came back."

"But you could have trusted..."

Josh interrupted again, continuing, "Another one I told part of the story to, that Faith had died in an accident, but this woman figured out later what'd happened and never called again. She left a message on my machine telling me *'If I didn't have the guts to tell her the whole story, she didn't want to be with me'*."

"Maybe you should have told her the truth."

"She was right. I didn't have the chutzpah to do it. Not without telling the whole truth, and that ended badly already."

"So, you started telling everyone that she died of cancer?" Misty crossed her arms.

"No. Just you." Josh lowered his head in shame.

"Oh, that's just great. So what? Accidents happen, right? So you blame yourself? Get over it!"

"I'm sorry; I've been trying to tell you."

"Really? I pour my heart out to you and you hold this one little bit of information back? My God Josh, this is one huge lie. Not a *'your butt looks great in those jeans'* lie. This is an *'I don't trust your reaction'* lie."

Misty spun on a heel and looked out the window to the tops of the eucalyptus trees across the street. She felt a tear coming on. She was angry. *Why? She had held back information from Josh, was this his way of getting even?* Pride took over.

"I…I can't be with you right now." She said through tears.

"Maybe after tomorrow when I'm done with the charter I'll come and pick you up, then we can talk." Josh's voice was crackling.

"No. I'll call you when I'm ready."

"What about Saturday? The boat trip? Are you going to deny Riley…?"

Misty's face turned red with anger, "I deny my son nothing! How can you try to get sympathy from me by using my son!?".

"I wasn't. I just didn't want him to feel like he was caught in the middle of our argument."

Lester walked out of the bathroom in a towel wrapped around his waist. His thin bony chest and shoulders were dripping wet; soap was sliding off of his long frail hairy legs. He had placed his hands on his hips as he entered the room and was dangerously close to losing his towel.

"What the Hell is going on in here?" Lester's voice was almost shrieking.

This silenced the duo for a few moments. Josh looked out the window with the picture of Faith in his hands, Misty looked at the floor. Lester looked at Misty for a moment then over to Josh; finally he saw the framed photograph in Josh's hand. He drew in a long sad breath.

"Told her the truth huh?" He exhaled towards the floor and turned back towards the bathroom. "Tell her everything then…" Lester's voice trailed off as he slammed the door behind him causing the glasses to rattle in the kitchen cabinets.

Josh opened his mouth to tell Misty everything, when she cut him off, "No. I don't want to hear any more." She turned and headed for the door.

"I'll take you home."

"No. I'll walk, it's not that far." Her voice was unemotional, dry. She kept her eyes from Josh.

"No."

Misty lowered her head and nodded. "It's raining much too hard."

"Yes."

"You sure like these hamburgers huh?"

Buckley was talking with his mouth full of food, which made Jacob sick to his stomach.

"Why?" Jacob set his cheeseburger back down onto his plate, his hunger had lessened.

"Because this is the third time this week we've eaten at a *Mel's*."

Jacob had indeed found another *Mel's Diner* on Geary at Van Ness; this one was closer to North Beach and was usually busy. It was near afternoon and Jacob had been feeling the pangs of hunger before his meal arrived, but watching John Buckley eat was like watching an autopsy on a week old corpse.

"Close to where we need to be. Be sure you call and leave me a message if she or the boy gets home before I get back."

"How long you gonna be gone?" Buckley swallowed the large cud of food.

Jacob let out a sigh of displeasure and answered, "Just a day or two."

"Okay, why won't you have your phone on?"

"I don't wish to be interrupted, by you or anyone else."

Buckley lifted his giant burger and was about to take another bite when Jacob stopped him.

"If you have any more questions, ask them now before you tear another piece of meat off."

Too late.

"Humph?"

213

"Never mind. Let's get this straight, okay? I'll be back tomorrow afternoon, and then you can come back to the hotel."

"Right." It sounded like '*rife*'.

"Hmm. Then I leave again on Saturday; this time if I'm not back by six o'clock then you open the case, take the money and give the rest of the contents to the cops."

Buckley swallowed big again. "Why can't I go with you? Two heads are better than one."

"It would be counterproductive. Besides, I need someone covering my back in case things go south." '*Because you'll get me killed you gargoyle*' is what Jacob didn't say. "Finish up and get to the house. I want you there in case the kid gets there first. I need to know exactly what time he arrives."

"You got it." Buckley slurped his strawberry milkshake loudly. "Aren't you gonna eat?"

"Maybe later." '*After I can get you out of my sight*'. "I'll get a doggy-bag."

Buckley snorted a laugh and a small trickle of snot lowered to his moustache, "Doggy-bag, hahaha."

The rain had been pouring buckets for an hour now, Josh's Expedition slushed through the streets no problem, but once in a while he had to brake for a small energy efficient car that had stalled at a corner where rainwater had gathered a couple of feet deep. The whole ride to this point had been silent, except the swish-swash of the wipers and the whoosh of water hitting the underside of the SUV's floor.

Josh was scared to say anything more, to try and finish what he had to tell Misty. He was afraid that he'd screwed up again, this time in reverse. Usually when he tells someone about how Faith died, the person practically runs out the door screaming for her life. But Misty was the opposite. He told her the truth, after a while of course, but it was the truth-most of all of it, anyways. There was more to tell, but right now didn't seem to be the time, she wouldn't hear it. He'd already ambushed her with this morsel and it stuck hard, how could he reveal more knowing it would make things worse, the truth always hurt.

Misty was looking in between the raindrops on the passenger window wondering how all of this unraveled so fast. She was falling in love with Josh Kennedy, but he had held something back when they met. Not that she was angry about that, she was angrier with herself. She figured it was payback for what she was to tell him, eventually. But now, the whole story and the need to tell it seemed useless. He had a secret, as did she; he has more to tell, ditto. She played it in her mind how she was going to tell him now; maybe she could just ask him the rest of his story and she would interrupt and tell him what was eating her alive inside.

Josh turned up Jefferson Street towards Kezar. More silence as he turned on Willard and then just as he pulled his Ford in front of Misty's house she turned to him.

"I'm sorry." She opened the door.

"Me too." He touched her arm as she leaned to get out.

Without looking back at him she said, "Call me after your charter tomorrow, we'll talk."

"I will."

Josh watched as Misty tried to dart between the raindrops like a dancer towards the steps of her house. The gate on the front was locked from the inside, so she ran to Alexandra's front door and opened it without knocking. She glanced once back towards Josh and waved, then turned and closed the door behind her.

John Buckley pulled up twenty minutes after Josh drove away.

J Jay Ross

When it rains in San Francisco, it depends on where you are to what the atmosphere is like. At Josh's home around five-thirty a.m., it smelled like Old Spice and Budweiser in the living room; Josh wrinkled his nose after he left his bedroom. He had just showed and the air of the day had not oozed into his clothing yet, so any new smell, he could detect. He tried to think of something else as he passed the empty coffee pot.

"Would you mind cleaning this place up a bit today? It reeks."

Lester stirred from the couch and lifted his scraggly head with the three day old growth of salt and pepper beard above the arm. He yawned, "Sure. Soon as I get stretched out and loose."

"How much longer do you plan to stay, anyways?"

"'Bout three or four more days. That's when the doc says I can put pressure on my leg."

"When did he say that? I was there with you the whole time when you were getting x-rays; I don't remember him saying anything about two weeks off."

"It's what they always say, doesn't matter what this one or that one says; I can't work this leg for a couple more days."

Josh shook his head as he dumped the third spoonful of grounds in the basket. "Nice." He whispered to himself.

"What's that?" Lester had dropped his head back to the pillow on the couch and quickly popped his head back above the armrest again.

"I said; try putting some ice on it. I need you on the boat for Sunday."

"What about your little friend? Aren't you taking her out this weekend?"

"Little friend?" Josh filled the tank of the coffeemaker to the top and flipped the switch on. "What am I? Four years old?"

"You know what I mean." Lester dropped his head below the arm and closed his eyes, pursing his lips. "Kids." Now it was Lester's turn to whisper.

Josh heard Lester's remark and just smiled, knowing he had gotten to the old man. Every now and then you have to prod the old fellow to get life out of him. The coffeemaker had brewed about half a cup in a minute, Josh took the pot out from underneath the basket and held a cup underneath the drip spout. The auto-stop mechanism had died a long time ago, so if you took the pot out before the coffee had finished soaking through the grounds in the maker, the brown water would run out over the counter.

He practiced this little maneuver of getting his mug under the drip spout to fill his cup before the pot was done. With gracious speed, he lifted the pot off the burner and switched places between the decanter and his mug. Satisfied there was enough in the pot to make a full mug, he switched places again between the two, holding the pot off the burner as he grabbed a dishrag.

Then, with precise and practiced moves he swung the pot over his mug he had set on the counter and filled it the rest of the way, made a quick swipe with the dishrag across the burner, then returned the pot to the maker. A few drops spilled and hissed as they touched the hot plate.

"Why don't you replace that 'Ol thing?" Lester himself hissed, from the couch.

"I haven't replaced you yet." Josh shot back as he closed the front door behind him and turned his key in the lock. He knew Lester would spend the next half hour of so trying to figure out a good comeback.

Outside, the redolence was much more akin to what Josh needed to make him smile a little. The moisture from the last few days of nearly endless rain had soaked the grounds around Sutro Heights Park and the smattering of decaying vegetation wafted towards the inner peninsula, mixed with fresh flowers and ground bark from around the trees plus the briny air and pong of the kelp on the beach, the smell made Josh stop and inhale. He loved this smell, this taste of the north coast and freshness. Only rain brought this cleanliness perfume, and after the last few days of the wet deluge, the air was brisk and clear.

Josh hopped into his truck and fired it up, sipping his coffee and tuning his radio back to KGO, so he could hear the early morning news. It had been on a contemporary-eighties station; Misty had tuned it there a few days ago. Misty.

The good feeling Josh was having tingle around his fingers and toes disappeared. His stomach clenched into a knot and a slight tang of bile touched the back of his tongue. His thoughts immediately traveled to Misty and the fight they had. Was it a fight? Maybe it was more of an argument. He had revealed a secret; that Faith had died in a car accident, not from disease like he led her to believe and she was madder than a wet hen at him. But why?

It wasn't like she hadn't hid a few details from him, the fact that Riley was living with her, the fact she lived in a home much like his and led him to believe she hadn't-that was no big deal anyways-but the whole façade of living alone and not hiding from her ex, or worse, made Josh antsy too.

'*I'll call you when* I'm *ready...*' She said at first, but then told him, '*Call me when your back from your charter.*'

Josh thought he should have told her the rest of what he needed to right then and there, but she would not hear of it. Enough damage done for one day. Josh closed his eyes and tuned his thoughts out for a moment, he focused on the radio and the talk-show host was bashing the Bush Administration for the handling of 9-11, and was vehemently against going to war with Afghanistan. Josh thought about what he was doing just those three months ago when the world changed, when people who had a different view of how life should be, how they came in and killed nearly three thousand innocent people. Just because they have a different God.

He took a few minutes to think about the families of those who were killed and the pain of Misty was subsided, a little. *A horrible way to distract yourself*, he thought, but he needed relief.

Josh arrived at his parking spot at six-ten a.m. He took a sad deep breath and prepared himself for the day ahead, for the charter and the time he will spend baiting this guy's hook and hosing his vomit from the deck afterwards. He opened his door and stepped out into the familiar air.

Aside from the smells around his home, this was the second place he could breathe and be relaxed all day. The odor of fishing, diesel fuel, rotting wooden hulls, wet hemp, seagull and seal poop, mixed with the metallic bouquet of rain and Josh felt the tension from yesterday's disagreement with Misty melt away. Okay, he was ready.

Josh fumbled with his key FOB and beeped the alarm on his Excursion then walked the few paces to the bait store, which was just a doorway in the alley with a sign above it that read BAIT. He bought his usual three pounds and paid the old Mexican salesman and walked towards his dock.

He approached the top of the slip that led by staircase down to his boat and saw a sophisticated looking man sitting on the chain that ran between the two posts at the top of the ladder. He was smoking a cigarette and looking out towards the breakwater, perhaps watching as other nicer charters were making their way out towards the bay. The man turned towards Josh as he walked towards him and he stood, tossed his butt to the asphalt and ground it in with his cowboy booted foot. The charter was about six foot three and nearly two hundred pounds, blond hair and clean shaven. His eyes twinkled a little blue and there were some signs of European or maybe Lithuanian lineage,

219

his jaw was hard lined and he was in very good shape. He wore a brown and blue suede looking short down-style jacket, blue jeans and a dark blue knit cap. He smiled at Josh as he approached.

'*Cowboy boots…Great.*' Josh thought to himself. Josh supposed it was a good thing he kept spare rubbers for charters like this. Folks tend to forget that fishing is dirty and usually bloody and always wet. But the rest of the man's dress indicated he knew it would be cold.

"Mornin'" Josh said and smiled.

"Good morning. You *Battered Sole Charters*?" The man's voice was pleasant and eager.

"Yep. Let me get that gate and then come on down."

Josh set the bag of bait on the ground and retrieved his keys from his pocket and tangled with the rusty old lock a little before dropping the chain. He picked up the bag and smiled at the charter and dropped the bait bag to the deck and clambered down to the *Sole,* picked up the bag again and dumped the fish into the bait tank locker. Just as he turned around, the man was nearly beside him; this made him jump.

"Sorry." The man said as he walked around as if surveying the vessel like a maritime inspector. "Nice boat."

"Captain Kennedy, but you can call me Jimmy." Josh offered his hand.

"Derrick Doyle." He took Josh's hand and shook it firmly.

Josh nodded at the man and walked to the door that separated the outside from the lower and inner decks, and the head. Another rusty padlock was opened and Josh turned on the light.

"Welcome aboard the *Sole*. The head is through here, second door to your right. Be mindful of the mess please." Josh made it sound like a joke.

"No problem, neatness is a sign of a messy mind." Derrick offered.

Josh climbed up to the bridge and fired the John Deere's to life, then pulled out the generator switch. The gauge pegged at the CHARGE mark, meaning the refrigerator had nearly drained the batteries.

Josh hollered down to Derrick, "Be just a few minutes while I warm up these old engines. Get the oil flowing. Speaking of which, I'll have the coffee pot on in a few minutes, or there's iced coffee in the cooler directly across from the head door."

The man nodded and walked into the cabin, Josh resumed monitoring the dials that would tell him if he was seaworthy; fuel levels, electrical power, oil pressure, engine temperatures, and of course, bilge pump operating light. Everything was in good shape, so Josh jumped to the main deck and unlocked the thin steel cable that kept the expensive sea poles lashed to the holder on the back of the bridge. Then he traveled to each locker along the sides and unlocked them.

He dropped to the main deck and retrieved an old fashioned validator for credit cards and pulled a receipt from a locker.

"Credit card?" Josh asked.

The man was looking over the side of the boat into the water and turned towards him, he smiled a little and reached into his jacket pocket, then said, "Cash okay?"

The man pulled out a small roll of bills and peeled off three twenties, and four tens.

"Just in case I lose a few rigs." The man said as he handed the cash to Josh.

Josh heard a familiar sound as he was heading for the bow cleat to untie the *Sole*, a drink can being opened. Josh looked up quickly to see the man had opened a beer, first thing! He shook his head and unwrapped the line and coiled it on the deck.

"Don't get seasick too easily huh?" Josh asked as he finished his job on the bow.

"Nope. Just need a kicker to clear my head from yesterday. I'll pay for it."

"No need. Beer or soft drinks are on the package."

Josh felt the craving for a cold beer himself, but that was a big no-no piloting a charter. He resigned to going below and making a pot of coffee. He took a packaged sandwich out of the fridge and stepped back up to the deck.

"Got sandwiches here too."

"Saw 'em. I'll have one later." The man took a small sip of the beer, his eyes not even leaving Josh. "We ready?"

"Yep. Let me toss the stern lines and we'll be off." He stuffed half of the sandwich in his mouth and set the other half in the package next to the seat on the bridge.

Josh did what he said he was going to do and perched at the wheel to navigate the *Sole* out of the breakwater and the bay. Just as he was ready to make his first turn in the harbor he looked down at the charter and asked, "First fishing trip?"

"No. I've been out on many charters, usually down in Cabo San Lucas. I love fishing San Pedro Bay for marlin."

Josh laughed, "Well, a sixty pound halibut won't fight as hard as a pissed off marlin, but get them close to the bottom and it's like trying to peel apart a grilled cheese sandwich."

"How deep we going?"

"Between sixty and one hundred-eighty. That's the max for this time of year."

"So, we aren't really leaving the bay?"

"Not if we don't have to, there's some shallow water outside the bridge, and we can even putt around the lower end of Tiburon or Marin. There should be some good fishing today."

Derrick sipped his beer as the *Sole* made for some water clear of boats to lower a line or two, Josh usually dropped some bait himself when he had small charters. An extra few pounds of halibut put a few more dollars into his pocket, or at least paid for bait.

As he idled to a unique spot he usually was successful with halibut, Josh had his mind in other places, mostly up on Willard Drive where Misty lived. He was glad that the charter didn't feel like talking much, usually they ask a million questions like; *how deep is it here?* every ten feet, or the classic: *do you have enough gas to be going out this far?* Charters were a pain in the butt sometimes.

But not this guy; and Josh was thankful that Derrick concentrated on the sights, he seemed interested in watching how Josh navigated the tight spots and passed the freighters or tankers heading in and out of the bay.

Soon enough as there was room at Josh's favorite spot to drift the Sole and fish, he slowed the boat to near nothing and hopped off the bridge to start the rigging process for his charter's line. The man watched as Josh took a pole down from the rack and began to set the leader on the line. During the process, Josh dropped a pyramid shaped sinker made of lead to the deck and Derrick bent over to pick it up with his back to Josh. That's when he saw the gun on the man's belt.

Josh's hand started to shake a little from the sight of the big barrel pointing out of the back of the guy's jacket right at him; he went to step a little back and banged his head on the support beam for the bridge. The rod slipped out of his hand and fell to the deck, Derrick turned to his side to look at Josh without standing up straight and Josh saw a smile on the man's face. It was a mischievous smile, like a child that had been caught sneaking a cookie. He saw that Derrick had seen where he was looking, and immediately moved his eyes back from the man's hip to his face.

"Oops." The man said casually, with the smile.

"No, biggie. I mean I don't see many folks out here with guns." Josh nearly stuttered, wondering what he was in for.

Derrick stood up straight and put his hand out for Josh. It took a moment to look down at it and in his hand was the sinker. Josh took it from him. Then the man slowly opened his jacket all the way and pulled the right side back behind him. Josh was waiting for the quick draw that never came, he was always a little afraid of other people carrying guns. The man just tipped his head down at his beltline. Josh looked.

The badge was the standard police issue shield, not the star that most cops carried up north here and in the west. It was easy enough to read Los Angeles Police on the front.

"Detective Derrick Doyle. L.A. Police." The man said in a serious tone.

"Whew. I had a moment of thought that you wanted to hijack my boat. Been a lot of rumors since 9-11." Josh responded with a smile, a nervous one.

"Nope. Not me." The man reached for his beer on the fighting chair.

"I thought you said you were on a business trip?"

"I am, more or less. Mostly more." The man took a big swig and crushed the can in his hand. "Looking for someone."

"Me?" Josh forgot about the pole on the deck and pointed a finger at himself.

"No. But you know her…it seems."

"Her?"

"Camela Nicholson."

Josh heart stopped cold. *Camy?*

CHAPTER THIRTEEN
Friday December 2001

Misty was vacuuming the carpet in Riley's room. The noise was a distraction from the voices in her head, which until she started cleaning house had whispered to her heart bad things about Josh, things she would never think about on her own. One was telling her that she should bounce out of town right now, just pack up Riley's things and go. Another told her she could be opening herself up for hurt, that maybe the man she was looking for was a bad person. The last one, the one that made the most sense, told her she was dumb for not asking more about what had happened.

Did Josh kill her on accident? Well, that was obvious right? If he killed her intentionally he would be in prison right now. But what could possess a man to think he killed her? She was afraid to hear the truth, that's why she cut him off and demanded to be taken home.

Sometimes you just don't want to know the whole truth, like when you're a child and you find out Santa or the Easter Bunny isn't real. It devastates you inside, even though you try to pretend the reality of the seasonal spirits doesn't affect you, it does.

She was afraid also, deep inside, that she would have to reveal her true reason for coming here to San Francisco, and Misty didn't think Josh was ready for that kind of pressure right now. Or was he? He would need to know, before he discovered it on his own, he could go to the library and use the computers there to look her up since he didn't have one of his own.

She thought back to yesterday, just before deciding to play Monopoly, she had asked him; "*You don't own a computer?*"

He replied, *"Naw. They cost a good deal of money, and every week they come out with a new version that is ten times better. Maybe someday. But what could I use it for anyways, other than Lester using it to look for porn, and I don't need that on my mind!"*

"But you could use it for business; you could look up things you wanted to find out more about..."

"Like you, for instance?"

Misty about folded in two right then and there. It was 2001 after all, what was on the internet that could lead Josh to her past? What could lead others to her and Riley? Her own thoughts about computers seemed to make her ill inside after that.

She was lucky to play it off and change the subject. She was glad then he was in love with her, he trusted her. Love is trust, and she trusted him-right up to the point he confessed he lied about his wife's fate.

God, she hated being in love. And that's what it was. Love. *Right?*

"Excuse me?" Josh cleared his throat, he had forgotten totally about the gun and badge; he even forgot he was on his own boat. "Did you say Camela Nicholson?"

"Yes. But you might know her by her alias, Camela Misty Desjardins."

Josh swallowed hard. Derrick headed down to the galley and opened the fridge.

"Beer now?" He called up the gangway.

Josh nodded, still staring out over the side of the boat, the pyramid shaped lead sinker in one hand and the other still pretending to hold the rod, he had forgotten he had dropped it. It took a few seconds to realize Derrick couldn't see him nod, so he cleared his throat again and said, "Yes." *To hell with the Coast Guard.*

"She goes by her maiden name, Desjardins. Her mother's maiden name was Nicholson, but she married a man named Desjardins and then after their divorce, married another guy named Martin. Camela kept her name Desjardins, the man adopted her after all, and then when she married this man McAllister in Los Angeles, used Nichols." Derrick handed the beer to Josh, already open.

"Huh?" Josh took the beer and guzzled half in one breath.

Derrick smiled, "Confusing huh. Let's just say this woman uses a lot of aliases and now I think I got her nailed down to this place," The detective motioned his hand towards the city in the background, "and she pulls an Earhart on me."

"Why are you looking for her?" Josh remembered the money.

"Well, for starters, she killed her husband."

Misty started to clean the bathtub and remembered when she and Josh took a bath together, how tender and caring he was; how it felt so right to be with him so close. The proximity of his warm body next to hers in the warm slightly scented water made her close her eyes and squeeze the tears back.

J.W. never took a bath with her, he did little with her as a matter of fact, tender things and moments like a bath or a quiet night walking along the beach was not done. For one reason or another J.W. did very little that would be considered romantic, one justification for staying close to home, especially in the latter months before Misty disappeared he was a marked man by most of the more clear headed drug dealers. They were beaten, bullied, murdered, and their families were even clipped sometimes in the name of fair trade. In the McAllister family, J.W. handled the narcotics side, and along with that came the enforcement of the rules the family had for dealing drugs. The best stuff came over the border-or under it actually, in secret tunnels-then it was stepped on a few times by employees of the family, then bagged and distributed.

Stepping on coke or crank meant cutting it with a various array of inert ingredients like baking powder, talcum powder, flour, sugar, small amounts of battery acid or powdered drain cleaners, etc. Oregano or even tea was added to pot to spread the total amount out for more baggies, and more profits.

J.W. was marked for death by the organized dealers, mainly because he was the enforcer, and because he did a lot of enforcing himself. He had been known to show up at an *unauthorized* crack house with a shotgun or shot-pistol such as a Taurus Judge .410 filled with 000 buckshot.

But, Misty sadly smiled in the mirror as she cleaned it, being home was more dangerous than he thought. That's where he died. Murdered, more like it.

"I don't believe it." Josh said as he took the last swallow of beer and walked to the galley for another.

"Doesn't matter what you believe Mr. Kennedy." Derrick shouted a little to keep the conversation going, "I know she's here and I know she's been seeing you."

Josh's hand froze just before he grabbed the handle of the fridge. *Great*, he thought.

"Did a background check on you too," Derrick continued, "I found some interesting stuff."

"Yeah?" Josh grabbed two beers and closed the door. He walked back up to the deck and handed a beer to Derrick.

"Yep. See, you've been seen with her. So I had to run you too. She know you did time?"

Josh took a deep draw of beer and slowly swallowed it, looking directly into Derrick's eyes. "Nope."

"Good thing not to tell her I guess." The cop rubbed his right eye with his finger. "Could really muck up a relationship."

Josh drained the beer he just got. He burped the carbon dioxide back out and threw the can towards the trash bin but it bounced off of the rail behind it and clattered to the deck. "What do you want Detective Doyle?"

Misty finished the spare bathroom and headed towards her room. She spied the phone on her nightstand and without thinking walked over and picked the receiver up. She stopped for a second to consider the consequences of interrupting Josh on his boat, and thought better for it. She returned the phone to its cradle, sat on the edge of her bed and cried. She would tell him tonight. She would call him over and tell him the truth about her and her husband and what brought her here to San Francisco. That would probably end it all right there.

Or, maybe just maybe, he would understand. He could take them away.

"So, if you cooperate, I'll see to it you aren't charged with anything."

"But I didn't know anything about this, how can I be charged with a crime?"

"You know now. So, if you still see her and refuse to set up a place to turn her over, you'll be harboring a fugitive from justice." Derrick finished his beer and tossed the can towards the bin and it went directly in.

"Great." Josh felt like he was beaten with a spiked bat.

"After her husband was found dead, by some kind of poison by the way-so watch what she feeds you-she disappeared. His family are looking for the boy, Riley, and want him returned safe. They have a substantial reward for him, about twenty thousand dollars last I heard."

Josh felt like Anna Sage; the woman in red. The woman who led John Dillinger to his death by tipping off the FBI. Now he knew what it felt like to betray someone. Did he have a choice?

"What do you want me to do?" Josh asked; his voice hoarse with emotion.

Josh idled the *Sole* backward into its slip and shut the engine down. The detective from L.A. shook Josh's hand and nodded towards the surface streets above.

"Remember, if you spill anything she'll bolt again and I'll be pissed. Harboring is a serious crime."

"I'll keep that in mind."

"Please do." Doyle nodded.

Derrick Doyle scrambled up the ladder and stopped at the top, then turned.

"If this works out, things will go better for you. The reward money will be yours; I'll get Mrs. McAllister back to L.A. for interrogation and the boy to his grandparents. The law will be served and you'll probably get things straightened out in your life. You'll have her there?"

Josh felt a panic attack of some kind coming on. His whole body shuddered as he spoke.

"Yes, I will."

Misty picked up the phone in the kitchen. He would be back to his dock by now, or at least close to it. The clock on the stove read one p.m. and Josh said he had his charters back on time every trip. She dialed his cell phone number.

"Hello?" The voice on the other end sounded clouded, sick.

"I'm…sorry."

Silence.

"Josh?"

"Yeah?"

"I said…"

"I heard you. I need to talk to you as soon as possible. Can we meet somewhere?"

"Did you have a place in mind?"

"Uh, yeah." A moment of silence. "Let's meet at Sara's Crab Salad."

"Okay. We'll talk then. Alright?"

"Yeah. I'm sorry…too."

There was a click on the other end.

Misty hung up the phone and cried into her hands.

Josh was sitting at a table he requested at Sara's, looking out over Taylor Street, towards the darkening skies and the usual street performers making their way to spots on the sidewalk for the evening's entertainment of tourists.

He saw the "Bush Man" walking along the square, carrying his tree limbs and a smile came to Josh's face. Just a few days ago he had led Misty into the Bush Man's trap. The large black man, probably in his forties and dressed in layers of clothing and an old green army topcoat, would sit between parked cars or next to trash cans lining the street and hold his tree limb up to hide himself. Then, when an unsuspecting tourist would walk by, he would shake the branch and make an "oooooo!" sound, or judder the limb at the passer-by and simply shout "boo!" or "Ha!"

Misty or Camy, whatever-about had kittens that day; she smacked Josh on the shoulder and laughed out tears. Josh rewarded the Bush Man with a few dollars in quarters, as many other surprised and laughing victims did. But now, Josh was required to do the ambushing himself, and there would be no tears of joy or laughter.

He looked around the restaurant as inconspicuously as he could, trying to see if he could spot Detective Doyle's partners, the ones who had been spying on him. Doyle never came right out and said that he was having Josh or Misty-Camy followed, Josh just supposed. Doyle had said he knew Josh had been seeing Misty-or Camy, so he assumed that meant he was being trailed. As he turned his eyes back towards the street, he saw the cab pull up and Misty getting out.

The next few moments passed through Josh's head so fast he barely had time to think about them. Camy. Camela was the girl of mystery here. Here she was in San Francisco, looking for someone she said. Was she looking for Josh? Could the girl from so long ago be looking for him just a few days after he had a dream about her? Josh doubted it, he didn't believe in things like that, like fate or destiny.

All those years behind them. The nights on the moist grass out in front of her grandparent's home in Sparks. It had to be just a little fate, right? Sure, she made no qualms that she was looking for the right *someone*, but was she really looking for him after all these years? Could it be that it was just happenstance that they crossed paths or has she been stalking him, waiting for a moment to approach him? He felt somehow violated, that he could be watched, not only by the cops, but by a beautiful woman that he'd thought of, trying to find him. Did he see her somewhere in her natural blond hair and blue eyes, and then have the dream out of recognition?

But, here she was. In the Bay Area, and Josh had run into her whether or not it was fate, it was still more than likely that Misty was looking for him, and now he had to turn her in to the cops or face jail, again. He had thought about this for the four hours since returning from the charter, since he told Doyle he would call him for an arranged setup and Doyle could sweep in and make an arrest. Betray Misty. Betray Camy, the first girl he fell in love with so, so, so long ago.

The cab stopped just outside the window of the Crab Salad. Josh's heart felt as if it would beat out of his chest, he picked up his glass of water and took a sip as he watched the pretty young woman slowly get out of the taxi. She was wearing a long casual dress, blue and white, with comfortable white shoes. Her hair was at its usual shoulder length, but the blond bangs were a dead giveaway, now that Josh knew the truth. It was her.

It was Camy. His heart sang and sank at the same time. So long he had been looking for her, inside, and now here she was. And to stay out of jail he had to turn her in to the cops. For murder.

The details of the dream were the last thing that circulated through his mind before Camela sat down at the table across from him.

"Hi." She said solemnly.

"Misty?" His voice cracked.

"I want to say…"

"Contacts."

"Pardon?"

"I noticed you're wearing contacts a while ago."

"Yes, what's that got…"

"Your eyes…are blue."

Misty sighed and looked down at the table. "Yes."

Josh took a deep nervous breath and folded his hands in front of him. "Your hair is naturally blonde." He put a finger under her chin and lifted it.

Misty looked up and was going to say, *How'd you know?* But instead reached up with her index finger and pulled the right contact out. Then the left. Her eyes shown bright blue. She pulled a case out of her purse and put them away. Next she pulled her hair back into a ponytail exposing her blond bangs prominently, giving her hair a full on blond look.

Josh's heart fluttered. She was here. It was Camela, she was here. He could see it in her eyes, in the way her hair no longer made her look tough, sophisticated. She was here.

"Yes. It's me." Camy said.

"Why?"

"I told you; I was looking for someone."

"Me?"

"Yes."

Josh felt a tingle in his midsection, one that started to extend out beyond, to his arms and hands, legs and toes. He wanted to cry; he wanted to leap across the table and hold her and tell her everything would be alright. But it won't; at least not yet. He cleared his throat.

"We were fighting. Like most married couples, we argued a lot. Stupid things, things that meant absolutely nothing to our relationship. Sometimes I think we just fought because we ran out of nice things to say to one another. Or maybe we should have just said stuff we'd needed to get out into the open, habits we disliked. I don't know."

"Josh, you don't have to explain…" Camy reached for his hand, but he didn't take it.

"It was a nice night; we had planned to take a cruise down 101. Lester had called, a charter for the weekend had cancelled and I was irritable. Faith was excited a little about our trip, it wasn't often we had gone out, with her work on the weekdays and mine on the weekends…"

Josh reached into his back pocket and withdrew his wallet. After sorting through a few pictures in the little plastic folders he found the one he was looking for and slowly pulled it out, never taking his eyes off of it. He stared at the photograph for a few moments then set it in the table in front of Camela. She leaned over and looked at, picked it up carefully, studying Josh's eyes to make sure it was okay, then looked at the picture of Faith closely. It was the same one she had seen in his house, the one with her in front of the oncology sign.

"She wasn't a cancer patient?"

Josh took a deep breath and half smiled, half frowned. "No. She was an oncologist's assistant at the hospital. The picture helped me make up the cancer story.

She looks pale here because she was seven months pregnant."

"Seven!" Camela's eyes drew large.

"James. I wanted the young baby to be called James. She wanted Marshall."

"You argued over the name?"

"She died over the name."

A tear dropped from Josh's eye and rolled down his left cheek. He continued, "We were both angry, I know it's hard to tell from that picture, she was always loving and sweet and hardly ever raised her voice. She was quiet most of the time and rarely started any of the arguments. But this one she wanted to win so badly, she wanted the baby named after her father, Marshall."

Camela took Josh's hand this time, he had left it sitting on the table and she'd managed to grab it before he moved it back to his lap. His hand was shaking, cold and clammy; he was reliving the day.

"We still both got into the car, a small piece of junk compact. I'll never buy another one. We were arguing about the name, then we started to pick things apart about each other we didn't like, you know, like; the way she hated me chewing ice near her, the way I hated how she never put gas in the car, the time we got stranded at an airport in Wyoming, because she was late."

"Everyone argues about the little things…"

Josh interrupted, "Yes. The little things, the stupidest, smallest reason to fight. But this was just a day with nothing but anger and even borderline hatred. I was driving, fast and crazy. I was swerving in and out of traffic, the louder and angrier she got at me for driving like a madman, the wilder and more careless my driving became."

Now both eyes had filled with tears and Josh had to wipe them to continue, Camela had to do the same.

Josh's voice cracked as he spoke, "I was on the verge of some kind of breakdown I was so angry, so full of rage, so explosive. I saw a truck coming, a big tractor-trailer, and I don't know why…"

"Josh, please…" Camela begged, her eyes were burning.

"I…turned the wheel…and…"

Camela squeezed Josh's hand so hard he had to pull it back.

"I wanted both of us to die. I forgot about my child, my baby, my future. I was so angry at Faith that I wanted to show her I was in control."

By now a few couples at the tables surrounding them had quieted down and was listening in. Josh looked around and saw the curious faces and smiled. He let go a half laugh and lowered his voice as he smiled at Camela.

"The truck driver at the last second swerved to his left, he struck the passenger side of the car, we spun several times and hit a pole; that threw Faith across the seats, right in front of my face! Her body flew out the window and onto the street. She broke her neck on impact. She died instantly."

The rumble of the other diners began again as they could no longer hear the story.

Camela felt sick to her stomach. She asked, "The baby?"

"The ambulance rushed Faith to the hospital, tried to deliver the baby by C section. He died too. I was treated for minor cuts, a broken arm, a slight concussion and then arrested for vehicular homicide, two counts."

"My God."

"I pled guilty to second degree manslaughter and spent the next two years in San Quentin. This is why I have a hard time getting friends or dates, many of her friends thought I should have done life without parole."

"But, why didn't you leave? Get away from here?"

"I'm also on five years probation. This is my last three months; I have to check in weekly with my parole officer. I can't be caught do anything illegal. I'm not supposed to drink, but my P.O. says he'll look the other way. We've become good friends, but I still have to follow many of the rules, and number one is; I can't leave the city and I had to take six months of anger management classes, I lost my *faith*, both my wife and my trust in God," He paused and took a breath, "I'm slowly developing a relationship with *Him* again."

"I'm so sorry Josh; I don't know what to say…"

"There's more."

Josh looked around the dining area, they had to get out of here, but where could they go where they would be out of the prying eyes of the public or the cops who might be following them?

He continued, "But not here."

Josh pulled a ten out of his wallet and returned the billfold to his back pocket. Setting the note on the table he stood and reached out for Camela's hand.

Camela hung up her cell phone and put it back into her clutch-bag. She had to keep stopping to keep the signal; some areas down along the water had intermittent service.

"Riley's going to stay the night at Alex's."

"Are you sure that's safe?"

"Why?"

Josh and Camela had left Sara's and were walking along the beach at Aquatic Park. It was the only place Josh could watch out for anyone following them or spying on them. The fog had drifted in and had settled for the most part. It gave the area a sinister look, each street light around the docks and street above had a white cone of light beaming down from the top of the pole and very little else could be seen. The wind was still and it was chilly, Josh had lent Camela his jacket again, he was too fired up and nervous to feel the fifty degree air. He walked with his head down while she talked on the phone; he was trying to find the words he needed to ask her.

Camela coughed a little and looked to Josh.

"How'd you know?" She asked, with a hint of suspicion.

"How did your husband die?" He asked without looking up.

"What?" She acted incredulous.

"Did you know the police are looking for you?" Josh stopped walking and looked to her face for a reaction.

Camela stopped as few feet in front of Josh and stared towards his eyes. The fog was tight, but she could make out their color.

She said, "No." Emotionless.

"Did you kill your husband and then run off to San Francisco?"

"No."

"Did you take Riley from his family after killing your husband?"

"What has gotten into you? Who have you been talking to?" Her voice was rising slowly.

"Today's charter, he's a cop from L.A. He's here looking for you and he knew we were seeing each other. I'm supposed to be handing you over to him right now."

"What!? A cop? What the Hell are you talking about? We ran away from my husband's family in the middle of the night like I told you."

"I'm supposed to call him and tell him were we are meeting later. I told him earlier that you were too busy to see me right now, you were cleaning house or something and we would meet later on, around nine or ten."

Josh looked out over the water; he could see a man swimming because the fog bank was passing through. It had to be someone from the Aquatic Park Swimming Club across from where they were standing on the beach. The water was cold, but every now and again he would see someone swimming at night here. He shivered at the thought of the water, and wished he had his jacket back, plus he was a little unhappy with Camela right now. Both for the lie of who she was, then the lie of why she was here and whether or not she's lying about killing her husband.

"Look." Camela started, "My husband was a drug dealer. He worked for his crooked family and was an enforcer. He was killed by one of his enemies or friends."

"Some friends."

"In his business, you keep your friends close..."

"Yeah, yeah. And your enemies..."

"*Dead*." Camela interrupted. "You take your competition out by force; you carve them up or put their head on a street sign as a warning to others."

Josh didn't realize his mouth was drooping wide open and his eyes would dry out if he didn't blink soon.

He said, "How could you marry someone like that?"

Camela looked to the sand at her feet. "I didn't know till it was too late."

The sound of small waves crashing slowly on the sandy beach at the couple's feet. There was an air of separation, lovers would be arm in arm or shoulder to shoulder, but Josh and Camela felt a wall of ice forming between them.

Camy reached to her neck and found the locket. She took the necklace off and handed it to Josh.

"You asked me once about this..." She said as he took it.

"Your grandmother's. Grandma Tina?" He asked, remembering.

"Yes." Camy helped him open it, the closeness made them both feel uncomfortable right now. She said, "It says, '*Bara en blick över my shoulder*'. It's Swedish, it means '*Just a glance over my...*'"

"*Shoulder*. Yeah I figured out that part."

239

"When my grandmother was very young in Sweden, she bumped into this young man who was just in town from his family's farm. She had seen him play hockey once in a while, but never considered herself to be part of his world. You see, she was part of the poorer families, the ones who worked and toiled all day to provide for their families. She was fifteen.

"Her father died in an accident years after she was born so she had to work when she was eleven to help put food on the table and clothes on her back. But one day, this man comes into the little market where she worked and he smiles at her then walks past her towards the back of the street, but just as he turns the corner, he looks back over his shoulder and sees my grandmother staring at him.

"He said, after that day he knew he was in love by just the way they had made eye contact. He said just by glancing over his shoulder, his whole world and life changed forever. 'Just a glance over my shoulder', he told her, 'and I was yours for the rest of eternity.'"

Camy took the necklace off and handed it to Josh.

"You have changed my life. I looked over my shoulder all those years ago to this young boy who simply said '*Hi*' to me in my grandparent's yard. You changed my life. You deserve this."

Josh put the locket and chain back into Camy's hand and curled her fingers around it.

"No. This is yours, and I haven't earned it. I do love you, but not until we get this whole thing straightened out, not until I know we can spend the rest of our lives together as a family, will I ever accept this."

"You mean…"

"I love you, we can get through this. *If* we get through this, I know we can make it through anything…"

The doorbell rang again. This was the fourth time someone was pushing the button, the fourth time Alexandra squinted her eyes at the sound.

"Are you going to get that?" Riley asked.

Alex was staring out the window. The van wasn't there, but she didn't trust the fact that someone was ringing her doorbell. No one ever rings her doorbell, not this time of night, not at any time of day, not at all. The Census People didn't even come by in 2000. This was not right. She put her finger to her lips and shook her head at him.

Another ring.

"Damn it." Alex cussed just a little above a whisper and tiptoed to the door.

Peeking out the peephole, she saw some man wearing a suit, a nice tie and he was pretty good sized, maybe six foot two or three and a couple hundred pounds. His jacket was open and she couldn't see his belt line, but was very suspicious of him. His blond hair was cut short-cop short-no moustache, but he had *the look*. Cop.

"Who is it?" Alex tried her best grouchy old woman voice through the door.

"I'm looking for uh, Misty Desjardins." The voice said back.

"I didn't ask who you were looking for, young man, I asked who *you* were." She raised her voice a little to show her annoyance with the man.

The man didn't look up to the peephole; he just raised his hand up with a badge in it. The gold shield read Los Angeles Police Detective, and he held it in place for several seconds.

"I didn't call the police." She hoped to piss this guy off so he would leave her alone.

"I'm not here officially ma'am. I'm here to find Misty Desjardins. She might be going by the name Camela Nicholson. Do you know her? She lives next door to you, has a young son named Riley."

241

Riley's eyes widened at the sound of his name. He turned towards the door and mouthed, '*Cops?*'

Alex nodded and returned to the door. The man knocked this time.

"My name is Doyle, Detective Doyle." Now his voice sounded annoyed.

At the sound of the knock, Carter ran out from the kitchen where he had been eating and he stood about three feet from the door. His noise twitched rapidly, and then he looked up and down at the door, then right and left. The hair on the back of his neck from near his ears to mid-center stood straight up, the dog's nose curled up and for the first time Riley had ever noticed this about Carter, was he could look deadly fierce. It scared Riley just to see it.

A deep, deep throated growl rose from the belly of the dog and gurgled across and out the dog's mouth. He kept swiping his tongue back and forth around his teeth and chops. Carter never broke his stare at the unopened door like it was a beef broth smothered steak. Riley stepped back towards the kitchen door.

Alex motioned Riley to go all the way back into the kitchen and close the door behind him. It was difficult at first to understand the maniacal motions she was making with her hands and arms.

"So this guy gets aboard your boat, tells you he's a cop from L.A., then says he's looking for me because I killed my husband?" Camela was almost stuttering; both fear and the chill had crawled down her back.

"That's about it." Josh was shaking a little too.

Camela stared straight out over the bay; the beam of light cutting across the sky like a knife swinging right to left, was coming from the Alcatraz lighthouse. The fog bank had lifted a little more, making the night seem less intimidating.

"Josh. I didn't kill my husband; something is very wrong here. Let me call Riley." She reached for her cell phone just as it rang. She almost dropped it. Flipping it open she nearly whispered, "Hello?"

Josh looked at the woman beside him as Camela's eyes went wide then her skin went so pale she almost lit up like a glow in the dark poster. She hung up the phone and looked to Josh; she was on the verge of panic.

"I need to get home."

"Is everything okay?" Josh's voice was quavering on fear, he knew things seemed out of place too, but he didn't know what to expect next.

"I called my mom." Riley whispered from the kitchen, "She says to get my bags ready."

"Okay, I'll take care of Johnny Law here."

Riley nodded and slipped out the back door to his house, he called quietly for Carter, but the dog refused to budge from the front door of Alex the neighbor's.

Alex unlocked the door and opened it as far as the chain would let it go. The detective leaned to his right to see in the small crack and smiled at Alex. He held the badge up again for her to see more clearly.

"Yeah, yeah. I saw it. What do you want?" Alex asked again, with a bit more impatience.

"Ma'am, I've received a tip tonight that Misty Desjardins is in great danger from someone she trusts, someone close to her. Have you seen anyone around her lately?"

"Well, not really…" Alex was pondering about Josh. Misty had told her the last night when she picked up Riley that she and Josh had a fight and he was not the man she thought she knew, a moment of panic struck Alex. "She in trouble?"

The man smiled again, "No ma'am. I'm here to find her and bring her home safely. It seems someone close to her is trying to kill her…"

Alex thought long and hard. "She'll be home in an hour."

The detective smiled wider, "Great. Look, I'm going back to SFPD to sign some papers. I'll return in an hour and a half, let her know she's in great danger, and tell her to keep close to her son."

"I will, I will." Alex hesitated for a moment before closing the door; the man was nice, not like a cop at all.

Josh and Camela had walked quickly back to Boudin's parking lot to pick up his truck. They had not said a word since the beach. Josh was hurrying, just as Camy had asked him to.

"When were you going to tell me?" He asked, looking straight out the windshield into the foggy night.

Camela shook her head, "I don't know."

"Why?"

She took a deep breath, "Do you remember the night we sat out under the stars and watched the meteor shower?"

Josh smiled slightly, "Of course."

"You said you would always be there for me."

"But I wasn't."

"My mother and I moved back east to Jersey that very winter. I had no friends, no one was brave enough to walk up to me like you were, and no one was brave enough to hold my hand."

Josh sighed at the thought of being a kid again, "I'm sure things worked out. You were so beautiful…"

"Were?"

"Of course. Now you are more than before, but then, when you're young-beauty is angelic. It's innocent, the world hasn't weighed down your smile, the pain of having to work or be an adult hasn't yet marked you. Beauty of youth is always the purest form."

Camela was smiling as he spoke, at his words. When Josh finished she looked out the window, not being able to see much because of the thick fog bank and sighed herself, "Sure, there was a guy months after we moved. But I always remembered you."

Josh shook his head, "I just don't know how to feel right now…"

"I wish you could feel the way I did when I first saw you at Tony's. I almost knocked over a table walking by. You were staring out the window towards the sea, your face locked into an emotionless abyss. I wanted to walk up and tell you who I was and how much I missed you."

Josh cocked his head towards her, "Why didn't you?"

"I went to the restroom and threw up." Camela lowered her gaze to the door handle of the truck, "I…just couldn't think of what to say."

"What about, hello?"

She folded her hands in her lap and looked at them, "Okay. Hi, my name is Camela. Do you remember me? I was the little girl that spent her summers across from your house in Sparks, and I want you to protect me from my gangster husband's corrupt family; oh yeah, by the way, this is my son and the son of the drug kingpin of L.A."

Josh just shook his head. "I guess that would've been difficult. But I think I would've understood, after the shock of seeing you, that is. I can't tell you how much better this whole thing would have been without our secrets."

He put his hand on her thigh and rubbed it reassuringly.

Riley was stuffing the last of his belongings into an old fashioned duffel bag. He knew that he had little time

245

before his mother would be home to scoop him up and a grab a few of her mementos, maybe something that she grew attached to here. They had discussed it before, if there was a warning sign or alarms went up, they talked about what to pack, what they would leave and maybe, if their luck held out, they could come back and retrieve what they left behind.

Most of his shirts, pants, sweaters, undergarments and other clothes would fit nicely into three duffel bags, his mementoes and toys, models and collectibles would fit into one large suitcase with wheels. He had already packed that one.

When his mother got home, she would rush to pack her four bags and two suitcases with her clothing and items she had collected while they were here in the bay. Many other things were kept in a storage unit that was along the way out of town. One suitcase keeps keepsakes that Misty aka: Camela had already filled. His schoolwork. The dishes, paintings, books and other things that could be replaced; would be eventually. The television would remain, along with other valuables, and if they returned or could ask Alex to watch over them until they did; would be retrieved at a later date. Carter was going to be brought along of course.

Riley was sad for leaving, not because of having to run again, but because he didn't want to leave Josh. He liked Josh a lot; the man was always laughing and joking with him, something Riley's father never did. Josh was going to take them on a cruise of the bay tomorrow in his boat and Riley felt that hurt the most. He really wanted to go out on the bay on Josh's boat. It seemed selfish, but Riley realized he had few things fulfilled that he wanted, mainly because they were always on the run, it seemed.

He would miss Josh's Uncle Lester, who was a war hero and had great stories about chivalry and righteousness, he had been telling Riley stories about how he had fought the Japanese, North Koreans, the Viet Cong and the Reds most of his life. He he wanted to fight for America because that was the best place in the world to live. Riley hoped someday he could make a difference like Lester did.

Would he ever get a chance to find a girlfriend? He met a nice girl at school here, Dawn was her name, and he was starting to feel comfortable about staying in San Francisco. Riley bet he and Dawn would have been good friends, then maybe they could have gone out on a date or something, maybe to a show like the actors did in the movies. He would pretend to yawn and wrap his arm around her, share popcorn, and hold her in a scary scene. But not any longer. Another town and another-hopefully-girl was in the making. Riley was tired of running.

Alex had come over a few minutes ago to tell him that the cop was leaving and going to be back in an hour. It was then that Riley explained the best he could what was happening to Alex, he tried to make it sound plausible, that his father's family was trying to get him to live with them and that he didn't want to. He explained that he wanted to live with his mother, because his father was a bad man who beat her and he knew that the cops would surely take him away from her and force him to live with his father and grandparents. Alexandra nodded through the whole story, she touched the young boy's chin when he finished.

"I understand." She said. "I'm going to miss your company. I'll go get Carter ready."

Alex sighed and left; Riley went to his mother's room to get the phone and tell her that they had a few extra minutes.

Then he heard Carter starting to bark loudly, angrily. He thought Alex had forgotten to close the back door all the way. A chill tingled his stomach for a few seconds; he slowly sat the bag down on his mother's bed and walked towards the back door. Suddenly, Carter stopped barking.

Just as Riley made it to the kitchen, he saw the door swinging slowly closed. He turned to run to the front door, a glance over his shoulder told him he wouldn't make it.

"Tell me what you're thinking." Josh asked.

Josh was making the turn from the top of Point Lobos onto the Great Highway and down the hill. He had to drive agonizingly slow, the fog was thickest here and he couldn't even see Ocean Beach or The Cliff House. He hadn't spent much time driving around the backstreets, so he took the only route he knew the best, especially in the fog-he didn't want to get lost driving the woman he had fallen in love with twice, to her escape.

"That I worked so hard to find you; that things almost worked out. I'm trying to think of how to get out of here."

"Do you need my truck?"

"Josh; I've caused you so much harm in the past few days…"

"I didn't say I forgave you, I just wanted to know how I can help. Maybe things will work out between us, somehow…damn!"

"What?"

"I missed Lincoln, I've got to try and make a U-turn."

Camela was going to make a joke about getting to her place safely, but thought the wiser of it.

"You! What the hell are you doing here?" Riley asked, his voice cracking from panic.

The man was standing between him and the front door.

"What? You don't miss your own family?" The man asked. He had drawn a handgun and was pointing it at Riley. "It's time for you to come home."

"No. Not without my mother…"

"Your mother is dead. And her boyfriend." The man snarled.

Riley's eyes filled with tears and he was about to fall to his knees when he saw a movement behind his assailant. Alex was charging from the back door out of the kitchen, she was holding a knife high like a killer in a slasher film does, aiming. When she entered the lit part of the room, Riley could see her hair was matted red and her left eye was closed and bruised, she started to scream a tenth of a second too early as she brought the blade down and the man ducked to his right. When he did, he swung his left shoulder up and his right fist, with the gun in it, up and towards Alex's face. The connection made a terrible cracking sound and Alex fell to the floor face first, the knife tumbled five feet in front of her and came to a rest near the sofa as her hand and head struck the wood flooring.

"Damn you!" The man yelled to the woman's body as he landed on his right knee.

Riley made a break for the back door as the man's attention was turned, but he was able to stand quicker than Riley had anticipated, the man lunged for him and Riley used all of his strength swinging for the man's face. He caught him in the right cheek and the boy could feel something pop. The gun dropped to the floor.

The man swayed a little but was able to grab Riley by the arm before he could build up another strike; he squeezed so hard Riley felt like his arm was being torn off. He tossed the boy up against the wall and he slid down to the floor from the impact, dazed for a moment.

"This is how you respect your family? That whore of a woman taught you this didn't she?" The man was screaming and Riley saw blood trickling out of the corner of his mouth.

The assailant used his right hand to wipe the blood from his lips and cheek where it had dripped, all the while reaching for the pistol with his left. When his hand touched it, he grabbed it up and instead pointing it towards Riley, he pocketed it.

Lunging, the man grabbed Riley again.

"Let me go!" Riley responded by kicking his attacker in the groin, the man winced.

"We're going to do this the hard way then…This isn't what I had in mind!"

As he spoke, he reached for his beltline and drew his favorite weapon from its lavish holster. Riley struggled when he saw the flash of steel heading for his neck, but he couldn't break free. He let out a scream as he felt the metal pierce his skin near his ear.

"I'll drive you, wherever you want to go."

Josh was making the last turn onto Willard from Parnassus Avenue.

"You can't. You'll break the conditions of you probation…"

"I don't care, I love you. I'm not going to lose you again."

It was panic and adrenalin speaking from Josh's heart now. He was afraid he would never see Camy again, just like when he was a kid and she went away that day, never to return. He had feared that this was going to happen again, that she would have to hide so deep that no one would ever find her, Mexico or Canada maybe.

He pulled to a stop in front of Camela's house. He shut the engine off and reached over and put his hand on Camela's leg again before she could open the door. "Please…"

Camela sighed, "You can give us a ride to where I keep our…" She paused as she looked to Alex's front window. The lights were off, but Camela's were on. "Strange."

Josh looked up and saw the same thing, but he didn't know what was going on. He took a deep breath and opened his door, rushed to Camela's side and met her as she exited the Excursion. He wrapped his arms around her and squeezed as tightly as he thought she could stand. He could smell her citrus shampoo, the cheap stuff; he could also barely smell a metallic sweaty scent: fear.

"I'm sorry about everything. Let's start over, please. I don't want to lose you again. I don't want you to have to find a new place for Riley. Maybe we can make this whole thing work out with the detective."

Camela shrugged into Josh's arms. She felt home here. He felt so safe and relaxing, maybe, he was right. Maybe they could find a safe place to hole up and then negotiate with the cops in L.A., tell them the truth. But what about her husband J.W.? What if they still believed she killed J.W.?

"Let's go get packed, we'll talk about this while we're doing that, okay?" She kissed him by the ear and whispered, "I love you, I'm sorry too."

They turned and walked towards Camela's house hand in hand. Suddenly she stopped in the street.

"That van."

"Yes?"

"No one's moved in in the last few weeks, but that van just started showing up a week or so ago. Alex noticed it too."

Josh looked closely at the white van with blackened out windows and he remembered seeing it pull away from Camy's house the night he came over for dinner.

"Let's go this way." Camela led Josh by the hand towards Alex's place.

At the door, Camela knocked once quietly then reached above the frame for the pass key Alex kept there for Riley. They could hear Carter barking somewhere in the house, as the door opened, and Josh stepped in front of

Camy on the way in. When he turned to lock the door behind them Camy called out.

"Riley?"

The barking stopped for a few seconds, and then Carter started to whine. The sound was coming from the kitchen, so Camy and Josh started that way. The whining got louder and Josh's stomach knotted up inside so tight he thought it would drive him to his knees. He squeezed Camy's hand tighter when the approached the closed kitchen door.

Josh pushed slowly on the door, just a crack at first, then all the way. They both stared at the red stain on the floor by the back door. Carter was scratching at the pantry door to get out so Josh slowly led Camy that way, both of them still staring at the liquid crimson on the polished wooden floor.

Josh could feel Camy's hand shaking as he turned the knob to the pantry door, Carter burst out towards the center of the kitchen then he stopped to sniff at the puddle of what looked to be blood. His hair stood up all along his back and he charged the back door, and outside into the small yard that separated the houses. Josh pulled back at Camy as she tried to follow.

"Wait!"

"My son! I've got to get to Riley!"

Josh yanked on her arm and nodded to her face. He put his index finger to his lips and shushed her, then he reached into his pocket and pulled out his cell phone and hit redial. The only number he had called in the last few hours was Detective Doyle, to lead him on a wild goose chase so Josh could talk to Camela. The phone rang twice and picked up.

"Doyle."

"This is Josh Kennedy."

"Mr. Kennedy, you are playing games with me, you didn't show up."

"I know...I'm sorry. Something has come up and I need help, you're the only cop I know and I'll help you if you help us."

"Us? Is Misty with you?"

"Yes. We want to make a deal."

"We'll talk then; where are you really?"

"At her place, something is wrong, there's blood all over the floor of her neighbor's kitchen..."

"The woman that lives next door?"

"Yes."

"I was just there about a half hour ago. Stay put, I'm on my way."

"Alright."

Josh tugged at Camy's hand. "He said stay put."

"Not until I know my son is safe." She pulled free of his grip and dashed off towards the gate in the fence. Josh wanted to yell after her, but instead he followed.

CHAPTER FOURTEEN
Moments Later

The back door to Camela's was open a crack. The duo tip-toed up the creaky stairs and peered in; nothing was moving. Carter was sniffing at the frame around the door and Josh put up his hand to signal Camy to wait. He grabbed the dog by the collar and had to drag him down the steps outside to the yard, where he found the leash he had seen last weekend and clipped it to the whining dog's collar.

"Stay." Josh commanded quietly.

Carter sat on his haunches and lapped at Josh's face with his tongue. He whined a couple more times then sat quietly as Josh joined Camy back on the top step at the door. The dog cocked his head as he watched the two step inside the kitchen.

The lights were on in the living room and Camela quietly walked towards the open kitchen/living room door. She felt her stomach gurgling, bile rose to the top of her throat as she peeked into the living room. The TV was on and she could see the back of Riley's head, he was staring at the television.

"Riley?" Camy whispered.

No response. Josh walked up behind Camy and motioned for her to wait, then he glanced over his shoulder to the back door and stepped out into the living room. He took two strides towards Riley on the couch when he caught a glimpse of the shadow sitting in the easy chair in the corner by the door. He felt as if he was going to faint, the blood rushed so fast around his body and his heart began pumping a two hundred times a minute.

The light snapped on and the room lit up.

"Detective Doyle!" Josh yelled at the man sitting in the chair.

"No." Camela said as she stepped into the room, and added with a sinister sneer, "*Jacob McAllister.*"

Jacob was sitting in the La Z Boy he had turned towards the center of the room. He was dressed in a heavy winter jacket with a tall collar, jeans and boots.

Camela glanced over to her son's place on the couch and ran to him. His body slid on to its side to the cushions as she touched him, Camela screamed.

Josh made a move towards Jacob and the man raised his hand with the Smith & Wesson in it.

"You die now and she goes painfully next!"

Josh stopped short, he was breathing heavily. He was feeling rage and wanted to grab the man that had deceived him on the *Sole*, the man who Camela feared for so long. His words trembled with anger, "You! Her husband?"

The man laughed as he stood and pointed the gun between Josh and Camela, who was holding her son in her arms. "No. Her husband was cheating the family and was going to sell out. He won't have the chance."

"You killed him!" Camela shouted.

"Your husband? My brother? Yes."

"No you bastard! My son!"

"No. He's drugged." McAllister slowly reached to his beltline and retrieved a stainless steel syringe, like they used in the early 1900's. "Acepromazine, he'll be completely out for at least twelve hours." Jacob hefted the syringe up like a prized knife at Josh. "Used it all too, on him and her…"

Jacob nodded to the corner of the room by the window; both Josh and Camela moved their eyes towards the body that was sat up there, posed like a sicko serial killer would do. Her head was on her chest, her arms at her side, her legs splayed out with her skirt neatly folded along the crease to give her a more dignified look instead of the half-hazard way she tumbled to the floor when the *Ace* went into her bloodstream. Her feet were pointed askew with one shoe missing.

Josh gasped; Camy broke down and cried even harder, holding her son's motionless body against her bosom. Josh looked back to Jacob.

"God! Why?"

"She was an unexpected casualty. I hoped to lure my nephew here by himself, but she was resilient." Jacob switched hands between the gun and the shiny steel syringe.

"Why Jacob, why? Why all of this?" Camela asked from the couch, still holding her son.

"Because you had to run just when I was going to get things going for the family. I had it all planned out, you would get blamed for J.W.'s death, mom and dad would get Riley and I would end up running the busiest side of the family store. But then, you would have ended up committing suicide after you were released on bail. Poor widow just couldn't live with herself for killing her son's father."

"You're sick. What did you do to J.W.?" She asked, sobbing.

"He died of a drug overdose. I told mom he was doing too much."

"You liar, he didn't do a bit!"

"I know that, but no one else did. He was found in your room, you were supposed to find him…"

"But Evelyn did." Camela finished his sentence morosely.

"Yes." Jacob wiped a small tear from his eye, "Mom found him. I had no choice but to tell her he was doing drugs, since you were gone I couldn't pin it all on you."

"I knew you killed him." Camy said with hatred and anger.

"Ah, but you *did* find him, didn't you?"

Camy looked to Josh then back Jacob. "Yes. When I found him, I knew we were going to get blamed for his death."

"We?"

"Okay, me." She spoke quickly defiantly.

"And you were afraid that…"

"I knew that you and your sick family would blame me, that I would be fingered for his murder. So I grabbed Riley and ran."

"And the money? Where did you get the money to run and hide in such lavish conditions?" Jacob looked around the room and nodded at various articles.

"None of your business…"

"Of course not."

"You planned this all so perfectly, but now what?"

Jacob waved the syringe in the air a little bit, and then threw it at Josh's feet like a knife. The large gauge needle stuck in the hardwood floor in front of the couch, just as Josh stepped back enough so that the hypo didn't stick him in the foot.

"Now, once again, I'm having to change my plans. I'm out of the Acepromazine that I had for you three, it seems little Miss Woodstock there was almost immune from drugs, huh, go figure." He raised the gun at Josh. "Sit on the couch next to your lover-girl."

Josh slowly complied; he raised his hands to chest level and sidestepped towards Camela, who was rocking Riley back and forth now. When he brushed her leg as he walked by, she jumped and looked at him. Josh had never seen such terror and anger mixed in a person's eyes before. Camela turned from Josh to her brother in law.

"I'm going to kill you."

Jacob laughed as he looked around for his chair, "Hardly. Acepromazine is fatal in the right dose, unless you're a hippy hop head, but you and Captain Nemo here are going to drown just the same." He sat down and rested the gun hand on his knee as he fumbled behind his back for the handcuffs he had brought with him; then said, "I was going to inject you two then send you on a nice sail into oblivion, but now it looks like things are going to get messy. Here…" He tossed the cuffs to Josh, who caught them. "Give the cuffs to her, and you Miss Desjardins, will cuff your lover-boy."

"I refuse you sick bastard. I'll kill you first."

Jacob's face flushed a light red and he said, "I don't want to fire this thing in here. It makes a lot of noise and the other neighbors I haven't killed yet might hear it and call the cops. I want him cuffed because I know you won't try anything."

"Good guess you ass…"

"Because," Jacob interrupted, "the first round goes into your kid. I want to bring him home to help mom with the loss of her son; but if he dies I'll pin that on you too. I'll tell her you and old lover-boy here went off sailing the seven seas alone, you didn't want any extra baggage so you killed the boy and left him here."

"My God, you're a sick man." Josh said as he placed his hands behind his back.

"Yes. Stand up Mr. Kennedy, I want to watch her clip those cuffs on."

Josh stood and Camela clicked the steel handcuffs on to the second catch, but Jacob leaned forward and turned the gun towards Riley's head.

He said, "They don't need to be comfortable."

Camela clicked the cuffs four more times till steel met flesh all the way around.

Jacob scooted back into the chair. "Great." Josh sat back down.

Camela shot Jacob a look pure tendered murder and asked, "Now what?"

"We wait till the fog lifts enough for sailor-boy to get out of the dock safely. I want you to go into your room and change into some warm clothes, just like you were going fishing."

"Why?"

"Because, just in case they find your body, I want you look like you belonged on the boat, not at a whore's cocktail party. Go now!" He leveled the gun at Riley's head again. "And remember, I know you would do anything to keep your son alive. If you do, he lives. If you try and muck this up, he dies first."

Camela defiantly wiped the tears from her eyes and stared at her former family member for a moment. "You're going to pay for this."

"A little honey, but in the end, I'll be running J.W.'s side of the business and mine. And then I'll be in control. Soon, when dad dies, I'll have the city at my beck and call. Go on."

Camela narrowed her eyes at Jacob and slowly turned, just as she did Jacob said, "Tell lover-boy anything goes wrong and the same bad thing happens. He slips up or you, the boy dies."

Camy stopped and didn't even turn around. She lowered her head as she headed down the hall again and whispered in a broken voice, "Josh…"

"I promise." He said.

"Just wait here while she changes." Jacob said, his voice a little louder so they both could hear him, "We're going for a ride in a few hours. Sit back down."

Josh complied.

"But the fog…"

"I'm doing the driving. You need to be silent." Jacob talked and used the gun for gestures. "We go for a cruise, if anything happens to me, my partner outside in the van is instructed to come in and finish the boy off. I return in…" Jacob looked at his watch, "…eight hours, and the boy goes home to Grammy and Grampy and lives out the rest of his life a rich powerful man."

Camy had changed into 501s and a simple white T shirt. She figured she wouldn't freeze to death, Jacob would probably let them put on their jackets before they leave, like he said, he wanted everything to look normal. She moved to leave the room when she quietly side-stepped to her nightstand and slid the drawer open. She pursed her lips and wondered if it was worth the chance.

Jacob tightened his lips and looked to the bedroom door down the hall. He stood quietly and put his finger to his lips and smiled at Josh, who could not muster a more deadly look back at his kidnapper than he was giving him right now. Jacob made his way silently down the hall and stopped short of the bedroom door. He pressed his shoulders against the wall and looked back to see if he still had Josh in sight, then raised the gun at eye level at his handcuffed prey and waited as the bedroom door opened.

Moments later, Camy emerged from the bedroom and turned to find her brother in law smiling in her face, he spun the gun from Josh to her breast. She jumped out of fright and let out a small chirp as when she felt the barrel of the *Lemon Squeezer* on her body.

"You know Mr. Kennedy?" Jacob said in an accusing voice loud enough for Josh to hear in the living room, "Mrs. McAllister is a smart animal. She's been hiding out here in this city for months now and I bet my Smith here that she had a gun hidden in her room. I'll even bet that she knew it was illegal to have a gun in the city limits, but she didn't care because she wanted to protect herself and her boy from bad guys."

"You are the bad guys you ass…" Camy began but stopped short when the barrel of the gun was pushed harder into her.

Josh just shook his head and looked at the floor. He was trying to find a plan in his head.

"I'll even wager your freedom, Mr. Kennedy, that she has concealed that same handgun on her person right now…"

Camy opened her mouth to protest, but was cut off.

"Yep. I'll have to search her. What do you think Mr. Kennedy? Should I have her strip for us down to her skivvies or should I just do an impromptu cavity search?"

Jacob's condescending tone and sheer thrill over his recent thoughts infuriated Josh. He felt a fire race in his blood like the night he and Faith fought, the night he killed his wife because he was enraged. He felt the pounding of the blood in his ears, the surge of adrenaline in his veins, the near hyper-heartbeat. He quickly assessed whether or not he could get free, or close enough to this man to apply his anger on him. It took a few seconds, but realized it was futile. *Later*, he told himself, *later you son of a bitch…*

"Not enough time. Shame. Camela, take your shirt up."

Camy hesitated, but when Jacob reached for the hem of her T shirt, she pushed his hand away and lifted it above her breasts. Jacob made sure nothing was hidden in the bra.

"Okay. Now, drop the drawers." He spoke like a child, using slang. He was highly entertained.

Camy unbuttoned her 501s and slid them down her thighs. Jacob searched her panties in a very crude and heartless way, then stepped back and shook his head.

"Tsk, tsk. You would be walking out of here Mr. Kennedy. I guess I would've lost."

"I would never abandon her…jackass." Josh had lips as tight as they would go and still allow sound to escape.

Camy started walking back to the living room while buttoning her pants back up when she felt the gun against her head.

"Let's have the pant legs up honey."

"Do it yourself you bastard!" Camy stopped and put her left leg out.

"What? And let you kick me in the face? I think not. Lift the legs or I just shoot the kid and get this crap over." He moved the pistol in the direction of the couch.

Tears began streaming down Camy's face as she lifted the right pants leg to reveal an ankle holster and a pistol in it.

"Oops. Guess you get shot first Mr. Kennedy. She gets to watch you die."

Jacob stepped forward, balled his fist and sent it with half his might into Camy's stomach. She doubled over and screamed, fell to the floor and retched on the wood.

"Better yet, I'm going to let him watch you die first. It'll make for good theater. Now get up and sit by your lover-boy." Jacob gave her a kick in the side for good measure after he retrieved the Saturday Night Special from her holster and deposited it in his inside jacket pocket.

Camy's hands, feet, legs and arms were shaking as she pushed herself up from the floor. Josh's eyes were flooded with tears of empathy and rage. A combination he thought he could never feel. She struggled to her feet and walked to the couch, sitting next to Josh.

"Okay. Try to grab some shut eye, huh? We leave in…" Jacob looked at his watch, "…four hours."

Jacob sat down and pulled his cell phone from its holster on the other side of his belt, opposite the syringe holster. He flipped it open with his mouth then pushed a couple of numbers with his thumb and put it to his ear and waited.

"Yeah. Stay where you are, remember our agreement? Good. If everything goes well, I'll see ya around noon. That's right." He looked over Josh and Camy. Then he smiled at Riley's sleeping body, "And don't forget what you do if I don't show. Bye."

Four hours drifted slowly, agonizingly dragging. Jacob got up once to make some coffee in the kitchen, always pointing the gun into the living room. Josh's hands were cold from circulation being cut off by the hand cuffs, Camy was trying to doze. She knew she had a fighting chance if she was alert and awake. She nestled against Riley, who would stir once in a while and then his breaths would slow again. Camy hugged him tight and kept whispering how sorry she was into his ear.

Josh had just drifted off into the world between sleep and dream for what seemed seconds when he was awakened by Jacob opening and closing the chamber to the *Lemon Squeezer*. He had been looking out the window and when lights lit up the fog outside, he spoke.

"Alright. Everyone up." Jacob was pulling on his jacket, gun in hand.

Camy stirred and tried to shake her son awake, but with no luck.

"Leave him alone. I promise you as your brother in law, that he will be okay as long as we get along."

"Some in law," Josh croaked as he stirred his tired muscles. "Killing his own brother."

"And don't forget his brother's wife." Jacob returned with a smile as he pointed the gun in Camy's direction. "And her stupid weak boyfriend."

"Let me loose and put that gun down and I'll show you weak…"

"You've already shown me weak by not charging me, even with your hands cuffed. Even though you would have been killed, you could've demonstrated how much of a man you were by trying to get me."

"Josh. Leave him alone, he's got a violent temper and really isn't worth it." Camy interjected as she was standing to stretch.

"Yep. Got a mean temper. That's why J.W. was so sweet on you. He wanted to be tough for someone, since he couldn't be tough on me." He turned to Camy, "He beat you a lot huh?"

"None of your business." She replied.

Jacob turned to Josh, "Black and blue. She was a real mess sometimes." Then he looked out the window one more time and said, "Now let's go. Here are the rules."

Josh straightened after Camy helped him to his feet. He tried to stretch but the cuffs limited his movement. Camy rubbed his shoulders and hands.

"One: we leave here nice and quiet. Two: we get into your Excursion," Jacob pointed to Josh with the gun, "Three: we drive off nice and easy all the way to the harbor."

A knock came to the door. Jacob smiled at Camy and then gave Josh a *friendly* bump as he walked by to the door; when he reached the viewport he looked out and then smiled back at the room while turning the locks open. John Buckley started to walk in, but was stopped just inside the entryway by Jacob, who put the barrel of the gun into his chest.

"Outside. In the van." Jacob said, impatiently.

"Okay." Buckley answered. His voice was rough like he had just awakened also.

"Wait till we're gone then you follow your instructions."

"Got it."

Buckley turned and headed down the steps to the sidewalk; Jacob picked a jacket off the coat rack by the door and hung it over his arm with the gun, hiding the

Smith & Wesson with the shoulder of the coat. He then reached into the pocket of the jacket he was wearing and removed his badge; Jacob blew across the brass top of the shield as if it were dusty and then clipped it to his front shirt pocket. He turned and waved Camy and Josh towards the door with his camouflaged weapon. "Just in case the neighbors get suspicious. They'll see the badge and think you've all been arrested."

He motioned to Camy with the gun arm, "Keep your hands in front of you or lover-boy gets one in the head. Now you lead. And don't forget your jackets."

Camy took one step towards the door and stopped. She leaned over and kissed Riley on his forehead and pushed his hair away from his closed eyes. "I'm so sorry. I love you."

She then knelt by Josh's knees and rubbed his legs. "Is that cramp gone?"

She then helped Josh sling a jacket over his shoulders. He gave her a strange look.

"Touching." Jacob said as he gave Josh a push with the gun. "She drives, you sit in the passenger seat and I'll sit behind you. Now one wrong turn, one mile an hour over the speed limit, one little mistake and you'll lose your mind." He chuckled to himself. "Did you hear me Missy?"

Camy nodded and walked towards the door, grabbing her own coat off the rack. She nearly hissed at Jacob as she passed him, feeling like just grabbing a hold of his face and using her teeth to rip his flesh apart. But she knew, he would get at least one shot off, maybe two. One would go into Josh and if Jacob had a second to recuperate, one would go towards the couch where her son lies. It was nearly impossible, but she managed to keep her anger at bay as she led them out the door.

Josh was being silent for a reason. He didn't want to provoke his captor for fear of him shooting Camy or worse, Riley. He didn't care at this point if he was shot, he would gladly take a bullet for both of them, but only if he were guaranteed that Jacob couldn't harm the woman he fell in love with so long ago, or her child. He smiled a little as Camy passed him, hoping that she understood why and she nodded at him slowly.

She smiled a little back too. An *I'm sorry for this* smile. As she reached into Josh's pocket of the jacket she had placed over him and retrieved his car keys.

The cool early morning air hit them in the face as soon as they cleared the little hallway from Camy's front door to the ground level. The fog had settled a little and was still sparkling in the streetlamps, giving off that eerie shaped cone of suspended mist. Traffic was non-existent as it always was this time of night, this part of town like most of the other residential areas was asleep. No one peeked out their windows as three people crossed the street to Josh's Ford.

John Buckley was leaning against the grill of the minivan, his arms crossed and a half smirk, half look of concern on his face. He just nodded and climbed in the van after Jacob and his prisoners passed by. He sat there inside staring at them as they got into the Excursion.

Jacob *helped* Josh in by shoving his shoulders towards the interior of the elevated vehicle; Camy climbed in and put her seatbelt on. After Josh was able to scoot his butt enough to get his body tight to the seat, she leaned over and buckled him in too. Cops were always looking for things to do this early and in California, not wearing a seat belt meant getting pulled over, and that would mean a gun fight and the death of some if not all involved.

"A nice easy drive to the boat please, Miss Desjardins, or should I call you Misty?" Jacob chuckled to himself.

"Whatever." Camy replied.

She started the engine, turned on the lights and pulled out onto the abandoned streets of San Francisco. It didn't take long for Jacob to get bored, so he did what he always does; he began to let people know about his power over them.

"Missed you Cam. Sure could have used you magic touch around the place a few weeks ago."

"Screw you Jacob. How could you kill your own brother?" She responded, not taking her eyes off the dark, foggy streets.

"It actually was an accident..." There was a slight hint of sadness in his voice as he looked out the side window. "He was supposed to be unconscious for a few hours so I could take his place at a huge confab. But as I put the needle to his arm, he grabbed me by the neck and out of reflex I injected a lethal dose."

Camy wiped a tear. The story was hurting her; she did love J.W. at one time. "Oh, poor you..."

Jacob's voice went somber, "Yeah. Poor mom and dad too. Boy they hate you now." His voice perked up as he nodded at her. "They blame you, because I told them you did it."

"I'm sure Evelyn will understand when I tell her it was you."

"Hmm. From the grave Cam? Dead women tell no tales, to borrow a phrase from Disneyland."

"I'm not dead yet."

"Neither is Riley. Yet."

Camy gripped the wheel hard and the friction made a rumbling sound as she made her way along Geary. She would take the only route she knew to the Wharf, down Geary to Divisadero, then left and straight to Marina Boulevard. Right on Marina and follow the coast road until she was near Ghirardelli Square, then she'd have to ask Josh for directions from there. She was forming another plan in her head, hoping this won't get her or her son killed, and certainly she didn't want to see Josh harmed either. It was all her fault he was sitting next to her with cuffs clamped to his bruising wrists.

She should've told him right off, then they could've made plans for something like this. She should have confided in him and described Jacob and his family members in great detail so he could've avoided them. Or maybe they should've run.

Right off, she could have told him that she was on the run from her murderous in-laws and they needed to go. But where? Josh probably wouldn't have left his boat or business, or even San Francisco for that matter. Nope. She was all alone one way or the other. The whole idea of coming here to find Josh and rekindle the flame they had for each other when they were kids was ridiculous, she knew it now.

The *plan*. It had to be foolproof and not put Josh in jeopardy. He was in the firing line, he would be the first fatality. And if she failed, then she would be dead. But then again, that was the whole plan anyway. Jacob couldn't die; he had to tell his fat accomplice that everything was okay and that he'd be there to pick the boy up. Jacob said if he dies, Riley dies, and Camy knew Jacob didn't play games. At least not that she knew of.

"Okay," Jacob whispered as if there was someone who could hear him outside the moving vehicle, "…here's the procedure: We get to the parking lot, I undo the cuffs. We get out and calmly walk to the boat. We board and lover-boy takes it out into the bay, then I drive. Anyone asks, we're charters, me and the Missus." Jacob gave Camy a tap on the shoulder. She flinched and knotted her upper lip in disgust.

"And then you kill me for cooperating." Josh said evenly. His hands were numb.

Jacob took a deep breath and looked back out the passenger window.

He said, "Pity. I kind of like you Mr. Kennedy. Since you're a con and all. Maybe you could go to work for me, huh? All you'd have to do is pull the trigger on your girlfriend."

Josh just shook his head and looked to Camy, who looked back at him. She smiled, the thought of Josh killing her was kind of funny, she didn't know why. Poetic justice and life's circle.

"After all Mr. Kennedy, you clipped your last love, right?" Jacob was fishing.

"And I've paid for that with a lifetime of pain and suffering. You'd be doing me a favor by killing me." Josh's voice was cold and graven.

He lowered his head in disgust. Misty glanced over with a look of concern.

Josh just kept his gaze focused straight ahead.

"So, here's the story huh? Camy and you hit it off, she has a secret past that is going to kill you; you had a past that you'd killed someone. Kinda like fate in a way. Karma, huh?"

Jacob began rubbing one eye with his finger. He continued, "So she is rich and doesn't want the power my family wields, she just falls in love. My brother falls for her, only after she gets pregnant mind you, and he starts to collect her money. They have the kid and then things go bad. She wants to avoid my family; she wants her son to avoid their influence, so she's always making excuses not to come over. J.W. had to start forcing her you see. Threating her. But she doesn't threaten easy; she's a strong willed woman. So he threatens her with the only thing she really cares about, her son. She gives her money to J.W. without question; she visits mom and dad more often."

"Yeah. Good luck finding that money." Camy said with an evil smile, still looking forward.

"Why? What did you do?"

"I hid it. Every dime. It's gone and only I know where it is. One person meddles with the account and the lawyers get it all, including my diaries."

"Pig snot." Jacob leaned forward to her ear, "If there were any diaries, the cops would have had them by now. You're bluffing." He sat back, confident.

"Insurance. Only in the event of my death."

"Well, the only folks who'll know you are dead will be you and me and your boyfriend. And well, only one of us is going to walk away. You're going to disappear, if I wanted to just kill you, you'd been dead already. I need you unavailable for questioning by police."

"You're still framing me?"

"Of course. It's already in motion, you weren't listening earlier. I told them you were responsible, you helped him overdose and then boogied with your kid, against his legal guardian's wishes."

"They aren't his legal guardians!" Camy was starting to swerve a little as she tried to catch Jacob's eyes. She wanted him to see the fury in them.

"Already been applied for, just waiting on the judge to sign the papers."

"No judge in his right mind…"

Jacob interrupted, "Austin Taylor. Remember him? He's on our side."

"He has no right!"

"Of course he does, he's a judge and he owes us. Evelyn has already had a room made up for Riley."

Camy just shook her head. The tears were flowing from her eyes, dribbling down her cheeks and dropping to her jeans; leaving a dark blue stain. Josh looked over to her and he felt his heart melt. He felt so bad for her. He had to figure something out.

Jacob put the icing on the cake, "And I'm heading back to run the money side of the business."

"With your fat friend." Camy hissed over her shoulder.

"Oh," Jacob laughed to himself, "He's going to go bye, bye too. He just doesn't know it yet."

Buckley waited the allotted time. He checked his watch again for the third time in ten minutes to make sure he didn't botch up the bosses plans. He started the van up, put it in drive and headed back to the hotel.

It was simple; the instructions were laid out days before. McAllister was going to make contact with the woman and her boyfriend, then John was to drive the van to the address on Willard Drive, in the middle of the night. He was to park outside the place and leave the interior lights on until he saw Jacob in the window. Then he was to turn the lights off and wait.

But, he had slammed back two cups of coffee when he got up and had to pee, so he headed up to the front door and was rudely directed back to the van. So he just took a leak on the sidewalk with the driver's door open when he got back.

At three a.m. McAllister came outside with the woman and the man-John wondered where the kid was-and walked to the Excursion parked in front of the van. John got out and Jacob repeated what he had said on the phone, so Buckley guessed he meant wait thirty minutes for him to get to the harbor, and then go back to the hotel. His instructions.

Back at the hotel Buckley would pack everything of his and have it sent down to the lobby then he would open the fancy locked briefcase with the folder inside and get it to the police station. The other envelope with the cash would go in his pocket, he would go down to the lobby, get his belongings and return the van to the rental place. Then he was on his own. Fly back, bus back; buy a new Cadillac,

271

whatever. He was free of the bonds of employment. Until the McAllisters needed something else.

CHAPTER FIFTEEN
Four Forty-five a.m.

Jacob made them wait in the Ford until he got a chance to look around and watch the goings on. It was a little early for the charter fishermen, and way early for the line fishermen. The crabbers were already in their boats, a few were still straggling around the docks, but they didn't matter. They probably wouldn't know Josh, the different levels of boat owners were like socialites in L.A. The crabbers were the highest paid, the regular fishermen the middle class and the charters were the ones who lived paycheck to paycheck.

Camy had shut the truck off and leaned her head back. She had closed her eyes for a few minutes, still trying to form a plan, but the vision of her son at the head of the McAllister table for Christmas- forced her eyes open.

Josh was silent also. He had kept looking around to see if he knew anyone, the only face that was familiar was that of Jose, or was is Juan? The guy that ran the bait shop had just opened his door and walked out for a smoke. The shop was several hundred feet in front of them, but Josh knew the guy on site. Carlos? Josh couldn't remember. If he could somehow get a message to the guy, maybe then the bait shop proprietor could call the Coast Guard. But what would that bring?

If the Coast Guard came flying in on a chopper, they'd make all kinds of racket and the element of surprise was gone. If they sent a cutter, Jacob would see it coming for miles and have a chance to kill them before being intercepted. He could just say he stole the boat, or even flash his fake badge and tell them he's on an investigation. Josh was confusing himself now; he didn't know what would work or what the perfect solution was. He would try to alert the bait shop guy somehow.

They waited another thirty minutes, making an hour till sunrise, and Jacob nudged Josh in the back of the head with the cold gun barrel.

"Listen closely. Gun's on her. Let the seat back slowly, very slowly understand?"

"Why?"

"I'm going to take the cuffs off. Let the seat back and lean forward so I can get the key in them. Nice and slow or Missy here gets a lead infection."

"Idiot." Camy whispered.

"Don't like my witticisms? Sorry." Jacob let out a chuckle.

Josh did what he was told; he pitched his right shoulder up and the left one down, then let his nearly numb fingers find the recliner lever. He pulled and the seat slammed into Jacob's lap.

"What the hell is your problem jerk? You want to kill her?"

Josh pursed his lips and murmured, "Sorry."

He then leaned forward as far as he could go, the pain shooting up his forearms and into his back. He told himself that relief would come when the metal bracelets were released, and it did. Jacob keyed the locks and let them slide off Josh's wrists, then reached down and picked them up. Stuffing them in his coat pocket he scooted back into the seat and said, "Okay, let the seat back up. Slowly!"

Josh complied with a certain satisfaction on his face. After a few moments the bait shop owner came back out and lit up again, this time closing the shop door and walking around the alley. When he headed in the direction of the Excursion he could hear Jacob tensing. Josh knew this guy was just as panicky as he was, but able to hide it better. The man stopped short of his door, and because of the darkness; was unable to see any occupants of the Ford, even under the sodium orange lamps that lit the parking lot. He took one final drag of his cigarette and flicked it towards the opposite building. The butt exploded into a shower of orange sparks and settled to the ground. Satisfied, the Mexican returned to the confines of his shop.

Jacob waited a few more breaths and then said, "Okay. Remember your place. Let's go, nice and easy to the boat."

Josh opened the door first and stepped out rubbing his wrists. The blood was flowing again and they ached slightly. He stood and looked around for someone, or anything that might help them escape, but as usual it was quiet. The crabbers were all on their boats heading out; the other fishermen were warming their boats up or hadn't even arrived yet. He had no real friends amongst these men anyway. He felt bad for a moment about that, he just figured he had more time to make friends.

Camy was next out after handing the keys to Jacob. He demanded them as she took the four keys and FOB out of the ignition switch, then he dropped them in his coat pocket, opposite the one with the cuffs. She stretched and felt a sharp pain in her side where Jacob had kicked her earlier. He would pay for that. If anything, if she does die out on the sea today, her former brother in law will feel the sting of her suffering, she promised herself that. She winced and rubbed the spot where his shoe connected.

McAllister was slow getting out. He kept looking left and right, then he searched the tall long buildings of the back of the Wharf for signs of peering eyes. Satisfied there was no one watching, he nodded towards the direction of the docks. He then pulled out a navy knit cap from his pocket and pulled it down tight over his head, close to his eyes. Next, he zipped his jacket up close to his chin and pulled the collar flaps near to his cheeks. All he had to do was lower his head and his face would be obscured, mostly.

"Let's go." He reached into his coat pocket and pushed the lock button on the FOB, and the horn sounded once. Jacob stopped again and gave another recon, he forgot about the alarm sound. He then crossed his arms with the gun in the crook of his left armpit, allowing the barrel of the *Lemon Squeezer* to be exposed just a hair.

"Move!" Jacob sternly whispered.

The trio headed down the alley, which was beginning to lighten from the rising sun, and the fog was lifting above roof level in some places. Josh passed the bait shop and the Dutch door bottom was closed, but the top was open half way and as he walked by he heard the shop owner call out to him with a happy smile.

"Hey señor Jimmy! You want good bait today?"

Josh curled up his hands into fists and turned. He said, "My name is Josh! I wish you'd get that straight!" He turned and walked away.

"Lo *siento…*" The man sounded dejected, but as Camy and Jacob walked by he said to Josh, "See you this afternoon, *si*?" Josh just nodded. Then the man said quietly, "Algo es no bueno aqui…"

Josh just nodded again as Jacob picked up his pace. He leaned in towards Josh and jabbed him with the pistol. "You learn Spanish if you live in L.A. Just keep walking and pat me on the shoulder and laugh like this was a joke I told you."

Josh did his best acting job to date and Jacob laughed back at him like they were old chums. When they were far enough from the doorway that the old Mexican couldn't see, Jacob shoved Josh forward.

He said, "If *Sancho* calls the cops, several of these people out here are going to die because of you. I'll shoot innocent women and children on my way out if I have to, you ass."

Josh looked up and saw people waiting for charters. It was way too early, but for some reason the docks had at least a dozen people milling around. There were two teenage girls and one boy leaning over the rail watching the sea lions, which were lazily resting on a floating dock.

Josh shook his head nervously. "No. Please don't."
Jacob just nudged him with his gun arm.

They reached the *Battered Sole*'s ladder and Josh
looked over to Jacob. He said, "I need my keys to open the
lock."

The kidnapper scrunched his lips together tight and
though about it for a moment. He reached into his pocket,
careful not to expose the gun to the other folks on the pier
and tossed the keys to Josh. Josh missed the catch and bent
over to pick up the keys, when he noticed he had forgotten
to lock the chain yesterday. He was so distraught by what
Detective Doyle had told him he had completely skipped a
groove. Josh wondered what else he'd left open. He
pocketed the keys and pulled the chain off the top rungs of
the ladder. He slid down the rails and landed with a thud on
the deck of the Sole, followed by Camy, who used the
rungs and was very cautious about her descent.

McAllister tried to slide down the rails like Josh
did, but caught his foot on a rung and nearly toppled to the
deck face first. Josh and Camy's hearts stopped for a few
seconds, hoping he would. But at the last second Jacob
managed to get control of his fall and hopped the last three
feet to the deck. He took a quick look around and pointed
the gun at Josh. Jacob's back was close to the small
platform-about three feet wide-that separated the boat from
the pier and his body was out of view of the people above.

"Get this piece of crap ready to go." Jacob hissed.
His adrenaline was pumping after his near miss.

Josh pulled his keys out of his pocket and selected
the small round one, the key to the rusty locks on the
gangway door and the lockers along the sides of the boat.
He stepped to the door and noticed he had forgotten to lock
this one too. He just shook his head and looked around to
the lockers and the fishing pole rack. The lockers were
secured, the poles were tied down with the thin steel cable

and locked also; Josh shook his head at his absentmindedness.

Jacob re-hid the gun under his arm and stepped to Camy's side, the barrel of the Smith & Wesson at her breast level. He cleared his throat and said, "Let's get this show on the road, or water."

Josh looked back to them and knew that the gun was pointed at the woman he had fallen in love with. His heart sank, but he found the energy to climb up to the bridge and slipped the keys into the ignition. He pumped the handle back once out of habit, diesels didn't need choking, then turned the key on, allowing for the glow plugs to warm up. Seconds later and several groans of resistance from the John Deere's, the engines began to warm up. Josh scanned the gauges and found he had used very little fuel yesterday; they had enough to go beyond the Golden Gate by several miles and back. Not that he wanted to go that far.

And with hope he would be coming back, one male charter short.

Next he pulled the generator switch and the voltmeter. The needle pegged again meaning the fridge had been running all night. Josh just shook his head again and throttled up to increase the warming time. He stepped to his side and clambered down and forward to the bow line, uncoiled it from the cleat and moved to the stern to do the same. Ten minutes after Josh started the engines, they were on their way out of the docks and nearing the breakwater.

"Get us out to open water, beyond the bridge." Jacob said as he sat down on the seat by the railing. The wind chill was extremely breathtaking and he didn't want his companions seeing him shiver. He patted his left hand next to his thigh and said to Camy, "Come and sit down. I'll warm you up!"

She shot him a look of disgust. He brought the pistol out to full view and said, "Oh, I insist!"

Camy debated whether she could push him over the side without being pulled in with him, and decided to wait till a better chance arose. She sat down a foot away from Jacob and he smiled, then shook his head. Josh meanwhile, was searching the channels for Coast Guard boats or someone close.

They were about a mile from the Golden Gate when Jacob stood up and while holding the gun on Camy, started to survey the area around them. He inhaled the briny and cold air, smiled again and looked up to Josh.

"Keep us as far away from other boats as possible. I don't want witnesses." He turned to Camy and lowered the gun. "Do you know what an anchor is?"

Camy rolled her eyes in sarcasm and looked away.

"When I was on board this boat yesterday, I noticed a nice anchor and a lot of thick chain at the front." He raised his voice so Josh could hear and said, "I want you two to get the anchor and chain from up front and drag it back here."

Both Josh and Camy hesitated. Jacob looked around the immediate area and waited till after they had cleared the bridge. He went to the bridge and told Josh to stand below with Camy. He took the wheel and pointed the Sole directly west and gave the diesels full throttle. He turned and surveyed the area around the boat again and this time pointed the gun directly at Josh from above.

"I want you both to get the anchor and bring it to the deck back there, now!"

Josh crossed his arms and said, "If you're going to kill us, why should we help?"

Camy nodded upwards to her captor and smiled at him.

Jacob McAllister pursed his lips, looked around one more time and then looked back to the pair on the deck he was pointing the gun at. He smiled. "You're right."

He fired the pistol.

Camy's left shoulder popped sideways as the snake shot entered her chest just above her left breast and below her clavicle. Dozens of lead pellets went in just above and around her rib cage and tore through flesh, drilling through muscle and deflecting off the bottom of her scapula-her shoulder blade. She collapsed to the deck and screamed in pain.

"NO!" Josh screamed as he dropped to his knees next to her. He peeled her jacket back to reveal the entry wound and the blood gushed. He tore off his own jacket and pushed it tight to her wound. "Hold on Cam, hold on!"

Josh rose to his feet and headed for the gangway to get the first aid kit and was met face to face by Jacob, who shoved the gun under Josh's chin. He leaned into him and said, "Get the anchor!"

Josh stood defiant. "No. Kill me now. If I can't stop her from bleeding, then I'll just die here."

"It was snake shot. She's not going to bleed to death, not yet. I wanted to get your attention. I got it now right? Next one is a hollow point and it will tear her shoulder off."

"I help her, then I'll help you or I die here and now."

Jacob seemed to debate the choice a moment and stepped back. He lowered the gun and looked down at Camy writhing in pain and gritting her teeth to keep from screaming. He looked at the blood oozing out of her shoulder, staining her jacket, and nodded.

"Okay. It'll be less of a mess for me to clean up before I return to shore. I'll get the kit, you can help her. But then you'll drag that anchor out here or you'll feel twice the pain she is."

Josh nodded. He would do anything to give them a fighting chance. Jacob returned to the bridge and slowed the speed of the boat down till it came to a stop. He shut the engines off and climbed down to the deck and went in the cabin, with the gun pointed out the door at Josh as he knelt next to Camy, comforting her.

Once just inside the door he quickly turned and saw the white box with the Red Cross on it, the same place he had seen it the day before, mounted to the wall by the head. Checking to make sure Josh wasn't moving in on him, Jacob shuffled back past the mess inside the cabin and pulled the box from the mounts. He shook his head at the mess of blankets, which had seemed to have grown since yesterday.

"Messy…"

Before he headed out and up to the deck, Jacob again assessed that Josh was still next to Camy, which he was, then shuffled out to drop the box next to the couple. Jacob again scrambled to the bridge deck.

Josh opened the box and quickly pulled out a large gauze dressing and reached under Camy's jacket and shirt to her shoulder where the shot entered. She winced and groaned in pain as he did so, but still managed to keep from shouting or screaming. She didn't want to give Jacob the satisfaction. He felt his way to the larger holes and stuffed the already crimson soaked gauze into them. Then he took his jacket off, placed it under her head to be used as a makeshift pillow then used the tail of her jacket crumpled up to put pressure on the wound.

Jacob was looking around making sure no other boats were within binocular distance and then addressed the man with the bloody hands on the deck below. He cleared his throat and said, "Okay. Bleeding stopped. Now do your job."

Josh rose from his knees and looked forward to Quint's Point next to where the rusty anchor was locked to the deck, the even rustier chain running off of it to the deck below. He shook his head, looked up to the bridge and told Jacob, "I haven't used that thing in years."

"We're using it today." Was the cold reply.

Josh stepped to the railing and shuffled along the cabin to the bow and grunted as he lifted the sixty pound fluke to the deck from the holding bracket. Then he unwrapped the inch and a half chain from the windlass, which had been re-mounted to the left of the pulpit. Because of the remodeling of the bow to extend the pulpit, it was the only place for it. Directly below the back of the windlass is the deep steel box that runs down along the inside of the bow, which holds the two hundred feet of anchor chain.

After only being able to get about thirty feet out of the bow-box, he found the link connector and tried to undo the length he pulled out from the rusted ball stuck below deck. It wouldn't budge, but the rust was sparse on this part so he grabbed the chain with two hands and started banging the connector on the anchor fluke. After several seconds, Josh tried the nut again. This time it slipped free. Josh separated the chains and struggled to the deck with the heavy anchor in his hands.

It took ten more minutes to get all of the chain and the anchor to the center of the main deck, because of the weight and he stopped once to check on Camy, who had tried to get up. He managed to talk her into lying back down.

The anchor and its chain were piled in the center of the deck, Josh was tending to Camy, and Jacob was rubbing his chin in thought. He stood over them from the slightly higher bridge deck and curled his lip in thought.

"Now, it's time." Jacob reached into his pocket and found the handcuffs and tossed them to the deck. "Cuff her hand to the chain with one side and the other to yours."

"No." Josh stayed.

"No?" Jacob laughed. "Okay." He bent down to his knees, just at face level to Josh.

Jacob swung his arm back and with all the force he could bring out, struck Josh on the side of the head. Josh crumpled to the deck next to his love. All he could see was stars, bright and shiny, he could feel a metallic taste in his mouth and then his head was throbbing like it was in a vise.

All at once the rage came back, but it was different this time. He saw Camy's face as the bullets struck her; he saw the smile on Jacob's face as he shot her. He felt the heat of the snake shot as it passed him and hit her. Josh felt it boiling up inside, just like the day he killed his wife. He struggled to his feet with the cuffs.

Like a defiant child, he tossed the cuffs to the deck at Jacob's feet and spat a line of blood next to them. "No. If I'm going to die, it's because you killed me. I'm not going to help you."

Jacob was dumfounded for a second. He knew that they would resist, but he had inflicted enough pain on them to get what he wanted, but they both were not going along. He became angry himself. He dropped off the bridge to the deck next to insolent man and lunged at Josh striking him in the belly, knocking the wind out of him. Josh barely was able to deflect most of the blow, but Jacob was larger and stronger than he was.

Josh hit his knees. He pulled himself to Camy and laid his head on hers, then kissed the top of her head. She had stopped sobbing in pain and had managed to sit up, Josh moved with her. She started laughing.

After a few moments, Josh started to giggle and then laugh out loud too. This did not amuse Jacob. He didn't know what to do, other than shoot them. He became highly annoyed, a small little thought in his head told him he had lost control of the situation and he was determined to get it back.

"What's so damned funny?" He demanded, pointing the gun at Camy.

Camy just ignored him and turned to Josh and asked, "Did you think when we were growing up together that this would ever happen?"

Josh's laughing got louder and he kissed her cheek and responded, "When we were laying in the grass that summer night, all I could think about was you and me just being so close and I wished that night would happen again for four years after you disappeared."

Jacob lowered the gun. He was standing in front of them with his mouth wide open; he couldn't believe what he was hearing.

Camy said, "At least now, we're going to spend eternity together."

Josh replied through tears of pain and mirth, "I wouldn't have it any other way."

Jacob could hear no more, "You mean you two knew each other as kids?" He stepped closer to them. "This is incredible. I can't believe it!" He felt a little laugh out of the irony himself coming on.

Camy laughed harder until the pain in her body made her wince. She cried a little more then tried to laugh again.

"What's the matter honey? Pain too much for ya? If I had some stuff left in my syringe…" Jacob reached for his ancient toy in its holster, but it wasn't there. He had forgotten he had thrown it at Josh's feet back at Camy's place. "Son of a…"

Then all of Hell broke loose.

A slight creaking noise came from behind the gangway door. Josh looked in the direction of the door and Jacob followed his gaze just as the door exploded outward and a wild-eyed ghostly thin man burst out of the doorway with a gaff in his hands above his head.

Lester was screaming some kind of death threat, but it sounded as if a lion had been wounded and cornered. Jacob reacted slowly by this new development, he was slow to bring the gun to target and Uncle Les made the connection to his shoulder with the sharp curved tool with a sickening sucking sound as the barbed fish grabber went in.

Jacob screamed like a dog hit by a car, then sank to his knees in front of Camy and Josh. The gun went off.

Josh leapt to his feet and knocked the gun free from Jacob's hand, then sent a crashing blow to the man's face with his knotted fist. It hurt Josh's fist, but the damage was far more devastating to Jacob, who fell backwards over himself and grabbed his shoulder in pain.

Lester fell back against the side of the boat, a small red circle forming on his side.

"Lester!"

Josh ran over to apply pressure to the wound. Lester pushed his hand away and looked him dead in the eye and said, "Get us out of here!"

Josh nodded and ran towards the small steps to the bridge, when he saw Jacob's gun on the deck. He picked it up and with as much as he could get out of his aching body, threw it into the Pacific Ocean. He glanced over his shoulder at Camy, who was using what energy she had left to hold Jacob down; he was in extreme pain, mainly because Camy kept twisting the gaff.

"Damn you! Ow! Stop it, you're killing me!"

"No. You're going to live just long enough for me to get my son back, and then you'll die." Her voice was grave, heartless and consequential.

Lester began to float in and out of consciousness. He knew he had taken one to the liver and that was eventually going to be fatal, but he pretended it was a flesh wound, so Josh wouldn't panic. He managed to keep pressure on the bullet hole as longs as possible, his fingers were tingling as the body naturally pulled blood from the extremities to protect the central organs, in this case, causing him to bleed internally.

Josh, meanwhile, had re-started the *Sole* and had run the throttles up to full, heading towards the bay. He figured they were at least ten miles out, maybe more, but the fog was obscuring his reference points. If he missed the opening to the bay under the Golden Gate, they might crash into the rocks that are shallow in the low tide, or even into the little rock islands across from the Sutro Ruins. He didn't care too much about any of that right now; he had to get as close to shore as possible and get Camy and Les to a hospital.

Camy had dragged herself over to Les, who was now fading in and out of consciousness. She tried to keep him awake, but he would just smile at her and say, "Take care of him..." And drift back off.

Josh had his eyes trained on the compass and a fix on the shoreline hidden behind the fog; he could hear the foghorn on the Golden Gate. He didn't see what was coming.

Jacob had managed to pull the gaff from his shoulder in a rush of pain. He gritted his teeth so hard, he felt a molar crack and break, but he didn't want to scream out to alert his captives to his next move. Slowly with his right hand, he reached into the inner pocket of his coat and retrieved the Saturday Night Special that Camy had tried to smuggle out of her room. He pretended he was too injured to move as he inspected the chamber for shells. Five, full load.

Camy was feeling better, but moving still hurt like hell, so she just kept her eyes on Jacob, who had curled into a fetal position. She knew he was in pain and something bothered her about how he was keeping his back to them and not screaming out in rage. Something was up...

Josh saw a small break in the fog and knew immediately he was heading in the wrong direction. He was heading directly for the shores of Ocean Beach-where he and Misty first met-and the several areas of rocks that were just below the water line. He started to make a turn for the north, towards the opening of the bay...

Jacob wheeled around on his hip, found Josh in his sights and Camy screamed.

"Josh!"

It was too late. Jacob got off three rounds, one hit the console in front of Josh, the next one went into his arm above the left elbow and the third struck Josh in the back and went through and out the front of his chest, narrowly missing his heart by about an inch and a half. He shrieked in pain and dropped to the deck below.

Lester found a surge of adrenaline and jumped to his feet and grabbed the gaff, but Jacob managed to get off another round and the bullet's force drove Lester back over the railing and into the sea.

"No!" Camy shouted.

She rolled to Jacob who fired his last round at her, the bullet missed and stuck into the wooden lid of the bait locker. As he tried to defend himself from her she dropped in front of him and picked up the cuffs from the deck. Jacob swung at her face and she ducked the blow as she managed to get one cuff's arm into the anchor chain. The next swing Jacob made hit Camy directly in the side of her face and she felt blackness engulfing her. She shook off the new pain and kneed Jacob in the face and chest, found his foot and wrapped the chain around his ankle twice, then slipped the cuff arm into the opposite end of the loop and snapped the cuff shut, making a lock.

Jacob gathered what was left of his senses and grabbed Camy by her shirt and jammed his hand onto her gunshot wound. She howled in pain and nearly lost consciousness, then Camy felt the other side of the cuff being forced onto her wrist. It almost clicked the first notch when another barrage came at Jacob from behind.

Josh used all the energy of anger and hatred for the man who was trying to take the life of the woman he loves, he used the feelings he had the night he killed his wife, the frustration and the pain that built up for the three years in prison, the need to explode that rage on someone who deserves it. For the man who took his uncles life. He rose to his feet not feeling any pain.

Jacob was still struggling with Camy to get the cuff completely closed to the hilt when he saw movement near the side of his face. Josh had grabbed him, picked him up off of the deck and was nearly holding him over his head, anchor chain and all when Jacob grabbed at Josh's throat. Josh was now being choked.

This was her last chance. Camy fought pain and dizziness and reached to her right ankle, finding the holster she had strapped on at the house. In the holster was the steel syringe and large bore hypodermic needle that Jacob proudly carried. She jammed it into Jacob's cheek and the needle struck his jawbone just as the cuff lock clicked once onto Camy's wrist. He howled in pain.

"Now! Throw him now!" She demanded.

Josh had no idea about the death bond Camy shared with Jacob. He threw the killer with all his might, Camy, who was on her knees with the chain locked to her wrist and Jacob's leg, grabbed the anchor from the deck and jumped in after.

"No! Camy, no!"

Josh watched as his love, the woman he would fight to the death for splashed into the greenish water alongside the man who tried to kill them both. He watched in horror as her white T shirt disappeared into the abyss below. Josh had no more energy; he passed out from the loss of blood.

He could hear sounds in the distance; his boat's engines were running. He heard what he thought was a helicopter, he heard a deafening crash and grinding metal on rock and the crushing sound of fiberglass. He heard nothing else.

CHAPTER SIXTEEN
December 23rd, 2001
Two Weeks Later

"I'm sorry Faith. Faith? Oh no, Faith…"

Josh awoke to the sounds of a hospital-type machine beeping in his left ear. At least that's what he thought it was, because he tried to roll over and a sharp pain shot down through his shoulder to his finger tips on his left arm. Pain and bright white light, he was here before, seven years ago. Same kind of pain, same sounds of machines, same smell.

The door to the room opened and let in in more light, *if that was possible* Josh thought, and in stepped a nurse in blue scrubs. She was pretty, maybe in her late forties or early fifties, greying hair surrounding an original brunette color. There was an exotic stripe of white mane down the middle and parted off to one side. She walked over and reset the beeping machine.

"Awake I see. How are you Mr. Kennedy?"

"Hospital?" was all Josh could manage under a croak in his voice. He hadn't talked much in the last week or so.

"Yes. Do you know who I am?" She asked with a smile.

"Nurse?"

"Yes. Nurse Stacie Tolliver."

The name struck a nerve. Stacie Tolliver was a friend of Faith's; this could be a bad thing. To be placed in the care of a friend of the woman you killed, *that would be bad…*

"You knew Faith?" He managed.

"We were friends. Yes." The smile remained. *Curious…*

Josh was beginning to wonder how this woman could keep a smile on her face after what he put Faith through. He concentrated real hard for a moment and then some flashbacks occurred to him.

The nurse continued, "Do you remember anything about what happened two weeks ago?"

Josh shook his head no.

"You were kidnapped and nearly murdered, according to the FBI. They were here to see you hours after you were first brought in, along with about ten cops from SFPD. Apparently you were very heroic in trying to save the life of a woman and your uncle."

She took a deep breath and sighed, her face went a little south, "I'm sorry."

Josh was getting confused, he did remember someone shooting him, then he could focus on...on...*oh no. Camy. Lester. They were dead.* His eyes watered.

"Faith would have been proud of you."

Josh's eyes opened wide-but he thought he was still dreaming or at least hallucinating.

With that, Nurse Stacie spun on a heel and went to the window, opening the blinds to allow even more light into the room. Josh was blinded. After a few minutes of blinking, his eyes adjusted to the brilliance of the room and he saw something sitting on a table by the window. A tree, a green pointy tree, a Christmas tree, three foot high with ornaments and fake candy lights.

"Christmas tree?" He managed to say.

"Yes." Stacie stopped and admired it a little. "Came in a few hours after the cops left, it's fresh, can you smell the pine?"

Josh sniffed until his chest hurt, he winced.

"Oh god, I'm sorry. I forgot...you had a collapsed lung. Jeez..." She rushed over and rubbed his forehead. She was sincere; she didn't mean to hurt him.

Josh forced a smile and said, "Smells beautiful."

Stacie smiled again and gave him a peck on the forehead. "There's a present under it too."

Josh squinted into the light again and saw a box about four inches square, wrapped in pretty pearl-white paper and a gold ribbon. He nodded towards it. Nurse Stacie took the hint, walked over and picked it up, delivered it back to him. He clutched the box and started to look for some energy to open it when the door swung wide and in stepped three men.

Instead of looking at Josh, the tall man spoke to the nurse.

"Is he awake?" A young but determined voice asked. Josh put his arm down holding the present.

"See for yourself." She nodded at the man in the bed.

"Josh Kennedy? I'm Special Agent Michael Feller. This is Special Agent Na Ngyen. The other man is a police detective and he's not with us…" The agent nodded at the older, more interesting looking man. "We'd like to have a few more words with you, if it's okay?"

Nurse Stacie stepped to Josh's bedside, smiled and whispered, "You don't have to if you don't want to. You're not under arrest."

Josh cleared his throat a little and smiled back at her. "Thanks. I'll be alright."

She nodded and gave him another kiss on the forehead and walked out of the room. The detective turned slowly around and looked at the room, taking it all in. He studied Josh a moment and then sat down by the window and the Christmas tree. He pretended to be interested in it. The man ran his fingers over the needles and studied the ceramic bulbs and candy made to look like little lights.

He then rubbed a little of the sap on his fingers and smelled it, then said, "I love that smell." Then he looked back at the FBI agents and nodded. "Go ahead, I'll be alright here."

Agent Feller clicked his lips in disapproval, but he turned and leaned in towards Josh.

"Do you remember anything you told us nearly two weeks ago?"

Josh shook his head no.

"The doctor said you were awake on adrenaline and shock with a little Demerol and might not remember details, so you've forgotten since then?"

"Yes, I don't remember talking to you." Josh's voice sounded dry, dusty.

Agent Feller sighed like he was frustrated and began, "You said that you were taken from a Miss Camela Misty Desjardins home early Saturday morning by her estranged and deceased husband's brother, Jacob McAllister, apparently also now deceased."

"Desjardins? I thought she'd be called McAllister." The detective in the corner asked, much to the dismay of the agents.

Feller turned toward him with his body, but kept his eyes on Josh and said in an annoyed tone, "We'll call her Desjardins for now. It seems to confuse things with the matriarch of the family, Evelyn McAllister."

The detective raised his hands in the air, "Okay. Just asking…"

Feller moved his body slowly back to Josh.

"He took you to your boat near Pier 45 and you boarded so he could dump you and Miss Desjardins off in the ocean somewhere, and then he could take possession of her son and return to run as a drug kingpin of Los Angeles. Does this sound familiar?"

Josh nodded. *Camy, poor Camy…*

"Mr. McAllister struggled with you and your uncle, who was apparently hiding in the cabin of the boat, the *Battered Sole*, and you both were shot, your uncle fell overboard. His remains have been recovered." A sympathetic but rehearsed pause, "I'm very sorry."

293

Josh nodded with a frown and a tear forming in his eye.

"Apparently, he stayed out late drinking the night before and decided to sleep it off on the boat, he had a key?"

"Yes. He lived on the boat; he was only staying at my place while his leg healed. It…it was the way he would have wanted to go, at sea, fighting for our lives." Josh's voice was clearing a little now.

"Miss Desjardins fought with Mr. McAllister and during the struggle was pulled overboard also, both of whom were clipped to an anchor with handcuffs?"

Josh nodded. *Camy? What about Camy?*

"Neither Mr. McAllister's or Miss Desjardins body has been recovered as of yet. We're having a hard time pinpointing the exact location they went over, and since they were tied to an anchor, they won't surface for a while…"

Josh turned his head so the tears pooling under his eyes could drain off his cheeks.

"We know this much since we last saw you," The agent went on, "Your story was verified with Chava Dominguez, the bait shop owner who said you tried to send him a warning or something. He called the Harbor Master, who called the Coast Guard.

"A few other fishermen have acknowledged that you were indeed in your boat with a man and a woman. You also said that Miss Desjardins' son, Riley, was knocked out by a drug and left in the house?"

Josh nodded. It was all coming back now.

"We searched the house on Willard and found no one. The boy was gone; the place was cleaned out of all personal belongings except the furniture and books on the shelves. There were no notes or anything to indicate that the mother or her boy lived there. As for the neighbor, you claimed she was killed by Mr. McAllister and propped in the corner of the Desjardins house?"

"Yes. She was given an overdose of some kind of drug."

"Acepromazine." The agent continued, "Horse tranquilizer. Toxicology lab did a quickie and found it in her system, autopsy found her heart and lungs were paralyzed and she suffocated. But, she wasn't in the Desjardins home like you stated."

This made Josh try to sit up, "Oh?" His heart rate increased and the beeping picked up on the monitor by the bed.

"She was found in her house, in her bed, covered by a blanket. Did you or Miss Desjardins move her?"

"No, we didn't have time. Maybe it was the accomplice..."

Ngyen finally spoke, "Um, Mr. John Anderson Buckley; forty-eight years old. Former L.A.P.D. Detective with a bad rep."

This made the detective sitting by the Christmas tree sit up straight and look towards Josh.

"I didn't know him. McAllister said he was supposed to go inside and kill the boy if we didn't cooperate with him, that's all I know about him."

Ngyen continued, "Mr. Buckley never went inside. He was arrested just a few hours after the rescue of you occurred. He was trying to get a flight to Los Angeles, and set off airport security when the case he was carrying was found to have three pounds of C-4 inside of it."

Feller seemed a little irritated that Ngyen gave up this information and cut him off, "Now *we can't* give you all the details; but it seems according to a confession Mr. Buckley gave the airport police, Mr. McAllister told him to open the case at the hotel and give some files to the police to clear this whole thing up. Mr. Buckley seemed like a slightly less than intelligent man to me, so when he couldn't get the case open, he tried to fly home."

Ngyen played off his partner's sour side and said, "The case was rigged to explode when opened. Thus, giving the San Francisco Police and us the reason to believe Mr. McAllister and the aliases he used while here, was dead. A pretty good try, except his help was rather…slow."

Feller spoke fast again, this time to quiet his fellow agent down, "The rest we can't elaborate on right now, since after 9-11, carrying a bomb into an airport is a really bad thing…"

Ngyen nodded with a smile at Feller and then at Josh. "The guy is singing like a caged bird now, after he found out his employer was going to blow him up."

Josh cleared his throat completely and looked to Feller. His eyes began to water as he spoke, "What about Camy, did you find anything else out about her?"

"No. Apparently, if she did escape her death, she took her son and disappeared, if that's what you're asking."

Josh lowered his head. "It was."

Feller's demeanor turned serious as a heart attack, "Look Mr. Kennedy; if she did survive, she is a special witness for the FBI's case against the McAllister family. We want them on RICO, racketeering and narcotics charges; a Grand Jury has already convened in the matter. We need her testimony and her deposition. If by some miracle she did survive and contacts you, you are to call us right away, understand?"

"What if she doesn't feel safe enough to talk to you?"

"We'll offer her protection…"

"Worked great so far…" Josh added sarcastically.

Feller's face went south, he was not happy with Josh's observation and the cop near the tree smiled so wide he had to turn and pretend he was looking out the window. Nguyen just nodded affirmation.

Feller took a cleansing breath and said, "I can't give you the details, but we were ready to approach her when she disappeared with the boy. She is now wanted by us for questioning, so basically she *is* considered a fugitive."

Over by the window the detective turned his attention back to the tree. He scrunched his eyes at a slip of paper near the top and pulled it off the branch, causing an ornament to fall and shatter on the table top. The room's awareness suddenly turned to him. He studied the paper for a minute and sensed he was being watched, so he turned slowly towards the FBI agents and Josh.

"Sorry, just a label. Inspector 13..." He crumpled the paper up and cleaned up the broken thin colored glass without looking back.

"Do you have anything to add Mr. Kennedy?" Feller asked.

"Can you take the McAllister family down without her testimony?"

"Probably, but it'll take some time. She would make things better and the Buckley deposition will help." Feller sighed and it sounded almost like pity, "If the boy tries to contact you, or the mother Miss Desjardins, call us."

Feller set an FBI logoed business card on the small food tray next to the bed. He turned to the detective by the window and asked, "Do you have anything for us?"

The man just shook his head and went back to studying the tree. The agents thanked Josh and left, making one last look around the room, out of drama Josh thought. The room fell silent for a few minutes.

Finally the man rose from the chair and walked to Josh's bedside. His smile was of compassion and understanding.

"According to what I could put together, you were about two or three hundred yards from shore when she fell over. Do you think Mrs. McAllister or Desjardins-whatever, could have, with a gunshot to the shoulder and

probably other injuries, *could have* swum ashore?" The
quiet and secretive detective asked as he stopped at the foot
of Josh's bed. He placed his hands on both sides of the
frame and looked down at the buttons used for moving the
bed into contortionist positions.

Josh secretly thought she could, Camy had to be one
of the strongest people he ever met, but he wanted to keep
hope alive that she survived and the police would never
find her. He just shrugged his shoulders.

"Mr. Kennedy? My name is Detective David
Doyle…"

Josh's insides liquefied. He nearly threw up as he
spoke, "I…I've heard that one before…"

Doyle smiled again and stepped back out of Josh's
space. "I know. And I can't tell you how sorry I am that
someone used my name for such a heinous crime." The
man reached in his suit coat and found his wallet. He
opened it and set it on the food tray. "This is my real badge
and I.D. Did the man show you his I.D.?"

"No. I just assumed…" Josh's voice trailed off as he
realized how dumb it was to just see a piece of brass
without seeing a photo ID, but then again, he wasn't
expecting an armed man to show up for a charter either.

"It's alright. Lesson learned I suppose. McAllister's
buddy was a coworker of mine years ago; I guess he got the
name and badge from Buckley; probably had fake ID too,
so it wouldn't have done you any good to check it anyways.
These are ruthless people. Again, I'm sorry."

Josh nodded slowly, not taking his eyes off of the
I.D. on the tray.

Doyle continued, "Buckley was a bad cop, he was
fired for working both sides of the law. I've been with L.A.
for nearly twenty-five years and haven't met a more less
than average idiot in my life. Thank God he never had to
watch my back."

Josh pursed his lips and asked, "What can I do for you Detective Doyle?"

Even saying the name made Josh's insides tumble from the memory of the day on his boat.

"I bet we can work out a trade."

"A *trade*?" *This can't be good*, Josh thought.

"You and I both know that a boy like Riley is smart, but he's not cunning enough to have cleaned up after something like this and move Miss Deterich to her house and place her in her bed. Her house was cleaned pretty well too.

"What Flotsam and Jetsam didn't tell you is they also found a large amount of THC in Miss Dietrich's blood, meaning she consumed a lot of marijuana. But there were no plants around her house or any paraphernalia for smoking it. Someone looked out after her, after she was dead. Only a good friend would do something like that." He paused for dramatic effect, "Or a neighbor."

Josh looked down at the floor and then up to the detective's eyes.

"No…" Doyle continued, "I think someone helped Riley clean up and then disappeared. Another thing the Hardy Boys didn't say to you was that your place had been cleaned up too and a Christmas tree was placed in the living room. Nice one." He looked over towards the one by the window, "Just like this one. I know it wasn't there before, you said last time we spoke that you forgot it was Christmas and hadn't gotten a tree yet."

"I don't remember talking to you…" Josh began, but Doyle kept on going.

"Now, you were here, your uncle was killed at sea, and I am sorry about all of this. So who could have mastered the whole cleaning and tree thing? Funny, I found out that the FBI is opening surveillance in New Jersey; they feel she might have family ties back east.

"You see, coincidentally, the McAllister case was mine. I was on the verge of several arrests, including Jacob for the murder of his brother J.W., who had flipped on the family after an arrest for possession with intent to sell, when the Feds moved in. They took my case, my notes, my glory.

"No big deal really, even though I did put a lot of effort into this case, I'm sure the FBI will crack it and get good convictions. I believe the McAllister family will spend time in prison and they have me to thank for it. But the way the Feds moved in and took over without consulting me, well, it pissed me off…"

"Your point?" Josh was getting tired, but was awakening inside at the direction the detective was heading.

"I think the FBI is sure she's alive. I think she might not try to contact you again, but she wanted you to know she survived and wishes you well. A woman with that kind of money could get emergency surgery anywhere."

"Really? How do you know this?" Josh asked. He felt the present by his leg with his hands.

"Let me ask you this first, Mr. Kennedy." Doyle stepped closer. "I have a friend here at San Francisco PD. I ran into him last week when I first arrived, I happened to mention your name and he knew you. He was a traffic accident investigator seven years ago; he worked the scene of a fatal accident that took the life of your wife."

Josh turned his head towards the bathroom door, away from Detective Doyle. "So?" His voice cracked.

"So, he said something that bothers me. Do you know what it is?"

Josh shook his head and kept staring at the door. Looking away, he knew.

"He said; after the trial in which you pled guilty to manslaughter, it was discovered that the truck driver's blood alcohol level was so high that he could have never maintained a lane. My friend says that there was no way possible that you swerved into the path of the truck, that the truck swerved into your lane and you turned to keep the passenger side away from the oncoming crash. My friend says he thinks that you lost control when the truck struck your side of the car and spun you into the pole."

"That's not what happened. I swerved the passenger side towards the …"

"C'mon now Mr. Kennedy. I'm a cop, and a damned good one. My buddy's a damn good cop too. He swears by what he found. But here's the interesting part, rumor has it that you were told of this new evidence even before you were moved from the county jail to Quentin. Rumor has it that you told your defense council to forget about it, that you'd testify against any new evidence. All I want to know is why? Why did you go down for all those years, when you could have gotten off on a technicality?"

Josh's face fell. Tears dropped from his cheeks and he turned towards the detective.

"Did you ever have to shoot anyone?" Josh asked quietly.

Doyle pursed his lips, "Yes. Eight years ago. A fifteen year old boy on the East Side was running at me with an Uzi in his hand."

"Kill him?"

Doyle seemed more unnerved now. "Yes. Three shots to the center of mass. What has this got to do with…?"

"Faith died because I turned left instead of right that day. She died because I was mad and wanted to scare her and make her believe I was in control of our lives; not her. I was angry and raging. Whether or not that truck turned into us, I could not live with myself knowing I wasn't punished

301

for the way I felt. Not punished by being killed in that crash also."

"But her death, wouldn't that be punishment enough?"

Josh looked around his room, then he looked to the ceiling and said, "There are people just a few floors above us who think I should still be in prison, detective. They'll never forgive me for that crash, they'll never say '*Oh well the truck driver did it*' and come and shake my hand. The D.A.'s office made it clear I was at fault and that's all there was to it. I pled guilty, did my time and now I'm healing.

"Simplistic as it sounds, love is not just being with another person, giving them what they need, caring for them forever; love is knowing in your own heart that they simply can never be replaced.

"How about you? Do you feel that you should have been penalized for shooting that boy, even though it was justified? Do you for one minute every day not think about that kid and what you could've done different? Don't lie to me, I've been there."

Doyle seemed to consider this and half smiled. "Fair enough Mr. Kennedy."

"I will pay in my own mind for my anger and hate. I have paid the state for having to look at me and say, '*We're square now…*' In a month or two, I'm off probation and then I'm going away. Away from here and the memories. I have nothing left, the boat's destroyed, Lester's dead. I have no other life to hold me here."

Doyle walked closer to the bed and then looked quickly around the room. He pulled the piece of paper he took from the tree out of his pocket and set it on the food tray and then picked up his badge wallet, stuffed it in his jacket and winked.

"I think, you'll find, that once you forgive yourself, then the world will forgive you also. I knew someone who once gave his life for another and that was the greatest price ever paid. You gave your life for this woman and will do the same to protect her, if she lived. Officially, I'm going back home and close this case for now, as far as I'm concerned, Misty Desjardins, aka; Camy McAllister is dead. I just wanted you to know that, and that I think I owed you one, for the indiscretion of the ass McAllister using my name."

Doyle turned and walked out of the room without another word.

Josh sat confounded by what had just happened. A few minutes passed and he struggled through the pain to get to the food tray. He picked up the piece of paper that Doyle had set there and opened it up. It was a note, in Camy's handwriting.

Josh's eyes watered as he read the short cryptic letter;

Thank you for saving us. We owe you. Merry Christmas, I told you I'd get you a tree. I'm so sorry about your uncle, he was a great man. Won't see us again, but the gift is yours. You know how I would close this note, so say it to yourself for me. Heading east. Sometimes what we have inside are the only possessions we really need, but it takes nearly a lifetime to realize it... M

Josh rolled the paper back up into a ball and threw it in the trash can by the bed. The paper bounced off the wall and ended up in the center of the can. A smile crossed his face as he thought about how Camy managed to swim ashore, get medical help for her wound, get home and get Riley and her the hell out of the bay area. After cleaning up the mess in Alex's house, his house and now, Josh realized why Camy never showed anyone what she drove. She kept the vehicle hidden from everyone. She walked everywhere or took a cab. She knew that she might have to eventually

J Jay Ross

escape from her pursuers-now the FBI-and needed anonymity in her travel arrangements.

Josh opened the present and tears filled his eyes fully. "Yep." He said to no one.

He placed the gift wrap and paper next to him on the bed then looked at the tree and whispered to himself, "I love you, too."

LAST
Early January 2002

The realtor, Janice Davis, made her way around the old house. The new owner followed her past the corner of the broken-down place. They both made the rounds for the second time in a week, the new owner wanted to make sure that the place looked somewhat like it did years ago. After the second trip outside, they both went inside and did a once through.

"The rooms were re-painted. Seems the last owners let the renters do whatever they wanted. This room was painted red with gold piping...yuck!"

"Maroon and gold. It's the high school colors."

"Oh. It still looked gaudy."

"Might have been a kid who was proud of Sparks High..."

"Yes. Well, we did the bone-white and it took several coats of course..."

Janice led the way through the house, even though the buyer had been here dozens of times already. The inside had changed dramatically, the dining area had been used to work on motorcycles at one point and the door to the garage had been modified with what appeared to be an ax and sledgehammer to allow the larger girthed bikes inside.

"The framer is coming next week to do that door..." Janice noted.

They passed through the kitchen, what had been a powder blue in the seventies was now more of a gunpowder brown color. Grease from the stove had stained the wall behind it, the exhaust fan opening had a bird's nest in it, and the straw was sticking out into the room from the vent cover. A wooden counter top had been used to cover the Formica one that was original.

"Kitchen will be redone in a week also; the counter-top is on its way." Janice reassured.

The carpet throughout the house had been replaced, and it still reeked of animal urine, the white linoleum in the kitchen was worn brown and bore a two foot hole under the table area. Most of the areas of the house that had been immaculate at one time were now shambled. The once clean sterile air had been replaced with a musky oily smell. Not one room in the house went without one hole or more in a wall.

The pair rounded the corner of the kitchen down the little hall that led to the screen room; the first thing that was obviously missing was the fountain. The little streambed had been filled with rocks and what appeared to be plants at one time, but now the vegetation was ripped out, leaving little holes in the rock and dirt.

"This is where the cops found the marijuana plants…" Janice said pointing to the streambed.

The little pond that once held eight goldfish was now filled with motorcycle parts and grease. The new owner winced at the sight with a wispy eye.

The screen room was mostly intact, mostly, as the windows had been replaced at least once or twice with cardboard and then plywood, in varying stages it seemed. The Astro-turf was replaced with tattered throw rugs where the green plastic had worn out from who knows what kind of activity was going on in here.

The new owner walked to the screen-less window and peered out into the yard. The evergreens were gone, red and white lava rock filled the gardens that once beheld flowers of dozens of species. The grass area was now dirt and mud with several piles of petrified dog waste scattered around. Lumber and scrap wood lined the redwood fence, which had been repaired dozens of times with chicken wire and plywood.

The new owner sighed. "Guess you can't go back huh?"

"Pardon?" Janice was grimacing at the dog mines.

In the center of the screen-less room was a card table with various documents on it. Two chairs sat across from one another. Janice turned from the window and headed for one of the chairs.

"Everything is in proper order. The title company kept the previous four owner's files open like you requested. All we have to do is get these pages signed and we're finished." Janice paused and looked around the room. "Are you sure about this?"

"This place is a memory, a good one, no matter how bad it looks. I'm going to get it fixed up and rent it out. In a few years I might sell it, but it's going to serve a purpose until then."

"Okay, I'm not supposed to say anything like that, but you know…"

"It's okay. No matter how bad this place looks, it could never take away the memory of the beautiful things that happened here."

Just as they sat down a huge Chocolate Lab ran in through the open front door and made for the screen room. He hit the card table square, knocking papers all over like little kites dancing on the wind.

"Carter! Get Down!" The woman yelled.

"It's all right Miss Davenport; it'll take just a few seconds to get them arranged. He's such a beautiful dog…"

"Thank you, and call me Misty. Everyone does…"

END

<u>Author's Note</u>

As you read the first few chapters of this work, many of you who have read *Follow the Southern Cross* will notice a similarity in certain parts of the story. Many of those who read *Follow* and commented wanted the story the lead character told on the sailboat to be a larger piece and found it to be one of the more likeable themes.

In *Glance Over My Shoulder* I wanted to fulfill that story and finish it. Of course it would have been better to write it into a sequel of *Follow*, but I decided to write the theme into a whole new novel and since *Glance* is a thriller/suspense on top of a little romance I thought it would be best to let Josh tell a story from his past and let it fill itself in, in a dramatic way. Sort of a "whole new genre, whole new world" set of creative licensing ideal.

It test read well and so I kept the story in.

I hope you enjoy the story as much as I have writing it and the three pages that became two chapters here flow easily for you...

JJ.

Acknowledgments

First of and as always I want to thank everyone who read *Follow the Southern Cross* and *Circle the Moon*. My thanks for the input and advice. I wish this book could be in hard print right off the bat, but you never know about the future.

A very big thanks to Catherine Gray for help in editing and structure as many of you know I have a problem in those areas. But also let me say she worked very hard and if there are any errors found in the text or basic structure of the story-they are solely mine as I did the final review and the blame lies strictly with me.

Thank you to everyone at RFJ, you guys are the greatest and the best friends I've never met face to face. Jess, Briar, John and the list that never ends-Keep the faith!

As always to my father who lends his support financially as well as morally on so many things for us kids. We couldn't do it without you.

Thank you deeply to the City of San Francisco for easily being an inspiration, the characters that walk the streets and the sights that never end. My apologies to the Seal Rock Inn and Restaurant if I didn't paint your establishment in the most perfect of lights like I really wanted to-the only place I will stay in the bay is The Seal Rock Inn anymore, and you make my experience always the best.

To all the agents I queried in the last year with my fumbling attempts to convince you to take me on as a client, I know my Query Letters left a lot to be desired, but then again-If I could sell myself, I probably wouldn't need an agent...

Also Available from J Jay Ross

Circle the Moon

Follow the Southern Cross

**An Australian Adventure: Follow the
Southern Cross Screenplay
Darkness in the Shadow (NEW!)**

**You can find J Jay at
www.circlethemooon.net**

www.ingramcontent.com/pod-product-compliance
Lightning Source LLC
Chambersburg PA
CBHW071248170626
46809CB00001B/131